Portraits
of a
Marriage

Portraits
of a
Marriage

Sándor Márai

Translated from the Hungarian by George Szirtes

ALFRED A. KNOPF   NEW YORK   2011

This Is a Borzoi Book published by Alfred A. Knopf

Translation copyright © 2011 by Alfred A. Knopf,
a division of Random House, Inc.

Previous editions of this work were published in different forms;
in Hungary as *Az igazi* by Révai, Budapest, in 1941; in Germany
as *Wandlungen Einer Ehe* by J. P. Toth, Hamburg, in 1949; and
in Germany as *Judit . . . Es Az Utohang* by Uivary Griff, München,
in 1980. This edition was originally published in Hungary as *Az igazi.
Judit . . . és az utóhang* by Helikon Kiado, Budapest, in 2003.
Copyright © by Heirs of Sándor Márai, Csaba Gaal, Toronto.

Library of Congress Cataloging-in-Publication Data
Márai, Sándor, 1900–1989.
[Igazi. English]
Portraits of a marriage / by Sándor Márai ; translated from the
Hungarian by George Szirtes. — 1st American ed.
p. cm.
ISBN 978-1-4000-4501-3
1. Marriage—Fiction. 2. Married people—Fiction. 3. Spouses—
Fiction. 4. Mistresses—Fiction. 5. Triangles (Interpersonal
relations)—Fiction. I. Szirtes, George, 1948– II. Title.
PH3281.M351413 2011
894'.511334—dc22   2010034251

Jacket design by Peter Mendelsund

Manufactured in the United States of America
First American Edition

Part I

Look, see that man? Wait! turn your head away, look at me, keep talking. I wouldn't like it if he glanced this way and spotted me; I don't
want him to greet us. Now you can look again . . . The little squat one
there in the fur-collared coat? No, of course not. It's the tall, pale-faced
one in the black overcoat talking to that blond stick of a girl behind the
counter. He is just having some candied orange peel wrapped. Strange,
he never bought me candied orange peel.

What's that, dear? . . . Nothing. Wait, I have to blow my nose.

Has he gone? Tell me when he has gone.

He's paying now? . . . Can you see what his wallet looks like? Describe
it carefully; I don't want to look that way. Is it brown crocodile skin?
Yes? Oh, I'm so pleased.

Why am I pleased? Just because. Well, yes, of course, I gave him the
wallet, for his birthday. Ten years ago. Was I in love with him? . . .
That's a hard question, dear. Yes, I believe I did love him. Has he gone
yet?

Good, I'm glad he's gone. Wait, I must powder my nose. Does it
show that I have been crying? . . . It's stupid, I know, but see how stupid
people can be? My heart still beats faster when I see him. Can I tell you

who he is? I can tell you, darling, it's no secret. That man was my husband.

Come on, let's get some pistachio ice cream. I really can't understand why people say you can't eat ice cream in winter. I love this patisserie best in winter for the ice cream. There are times I almost believe that anything possible to be done should be done, not just because it's good or makes sense, simply because it's possible. For some years now in any case, ever since I've been alone, I've enjoyed coming here between five and seven in the winter. I like the crimson décor, the Victorian furnishings, the old waitresses, the big metropolitan square beyond the shopwindow, watching the customers arrive. There's a sort of warmth about it all, just a touch of fin-de-siècle. And there's no better tea anywhere, have you noticed? . . . I know the new generation of women don't go to patisseries. They prefer espressos, places where you have to rush, where there are no comfortable chairs, where it costs forty fillér for one black coffee, where they can eat salad for lunch, that's how it is now. But it's not my world. What I want is refined patisseries like this, with such furniture, with crimson carpets, with their ancient countesses and princesses, their mirrored cupboards. As you may imagine, I'm not here every day, but I do call in during the winter and feel comfortable here. My husband and I used to meet here pretty regularly, about six o'clock, at teatime, after he finished at the office.

Oh yes, he was on his way home from the office just now. It's twenty after seven, his home time. I am familiar with every part of his routine, even now, as if it were his life I was living. At five minutes before six he rings for the office boy who brushes him down and presents him with his hat and coat, and he leaves the office, sending the car ahead so he can walk behind it and get some air. He doesn't do much walking, that's why he is so pale. Or there may be some other reason, I don't know now. I don't know the reason because I never see him, don't talk to him, haven't talked to him for three years. I don't like those prissy little separations where the two parties walk arm-in-arm from the court, dine together at that famous restaurant in the park, are tender and solicitous toward each other as if nothing had happened and then, after divorce and dinner, go their own ways. I'm not that sort of woman: my morality, my blood pressure won't allow it. I don't believe that men and women can be good friends after divorce. Marriage is marriage; divorce, divorce. That's what I think.

But what do you think? True, you've never been married.

I don't think that relationships people have entered on and nurtured for decades, vows they have unthinkingly kept, are empty formalities, you see. I believe in the sanctity of marriage. I think divorce is a kind of sacrilege. That's how I was brought up. But I believe it anyway, not just because of my upbringing, but because my religion demands that I believe it. I believe it because I am a woman and a divorce is no mere formality for me any more than the ritual in the church before the registrar is a formality: either it binds people together, body and soul, for once and for all, or it divides them, absolutely, and sends them their utterly separate ways. Not for one minute did I console myself with the thought that my husband and I would remain "friends" after our divorce. He was courteous, of course, and remained concerned for me, and generous too, as custom dictates that he should be. Not me, though. I was neither polite nor generous. I even took the piano, yes, as was my right. I was furious for revenge, and would happily have taken the whole house, right down to the curtains—everything. The moment we divorced I became his enemy and I remain so, as I will till the day I die. I don't want a friendly invitation to dinner at the restaurant in the park from him; I don't want to play the little woman, to be delicate, to be someone who visits her ex-husband's home and looks after things when the servant steals his linen. I wouldn't care if they stole the lot, everything, nor would I rush over to him if I heard he was ill. Why? Because we are divorced, you understand? It's not something to which one can become resigned.

Wait, I withdraw what I just said about him being ill. I wouldn't want him to fall ill. If he did I would visit him in the sanatorium. What are you laughing at? Are you laughing at me? Do you think I'm hoping he'll fall ill so I can visit him? Well, of course I hope that. As long as I have hope, I will carry on hoping. But I wouldn't want him to be too ill. He was so very pale, did you notice? . . . He has been pale like that for some years now.

I'll tell you everything. Have you got the time? Sadly, I have all too much.

Look, here's the ice cream. After school, I found a job in an office. We were still writing to each other then, weren't we? You went straight off to America but we carried on writing for a while, for three or four years, I think. I remember, there was an unhealthy, foolish puppy love between us. I rather disapprove of that now. It seems we can't live without love. But then it was you I loved. In any case, your family was rich while we lived in three rooms and a kitchen opening onto a corridor— very much a middle-class kind of apartment opening onto a corridor. I looked up to you and that kind of admiration, I now realize, is already a sign of emotional attachment with young people. I too had a nanny but mine had to get her hot water secondhand, after I'd finished my bath. Such details are very important. There are frighteningly many shades of gentility between poverty and wealth. And from poverty down, how many shades of poverty do you think there are? You are wealthy, so you can't know the enormous difference between four hundred and six hundred a month. It's a bigger difference than between two thousand and ten thousand a month. I know a great deal about this now. Back home, our income was eight hundred. My husband earned six and a half thousand per month. One had to get used to this.

Everything was just a little different in their home compared with ours. We lived in a rented apartment; they in a rented villa. We had a balcony with geraniums; they had a little garden with two flower beds and an old walnut tree. We had an ordinary icebox that we filled with ice in summer, while my mother-in-law had a small electric refrigerator that could produce nice neat ice cubes too. We had a general handyman working for us; they had a married couple, a servant and a cook. We had three rooms; they had four, five in fact if you include the hall. But their hall was a proper hall with light chiffon covers on the doors, whereas ours was only an entrance hall with the icebox in it—a dark, urban Pest kind of entrance hall, together with a brush rack and old-fashioned coat stand. We had a three-valve radio set assembled by Papa from individually bought components, which received whatever station it felt like receiving; they had a radiogram, which was both a radio—on which you could even pick up Japan—and a gramophone, which worked by electricity and changed records automatically. I was brought up to earn my living; he was brought up, first and foremost, to live a refined, polite kind of life, one according to important social rules. Conformity was vital. There was an enormous social difference between us but I didn't know it then.

There was a conversation we had over breakfast once. "Those mauve covers in the dining room are a little tiring," he said. "They are quite crude and loud, like people who are always shouting at each other. Take a look round town, my dear, and find some different covers in time for fall."

Twelve chairs needed recovering in some less "tiring" color.

I looked at him in confusion. I thought he was joking. But it was no joke—he carried on reading the papers with a perfectly serious expression. I could see that he had clearly thought through what he had just said, that the mauve color—a little common, I must admit—really did irritate him. My mother had chosen it. It was brand-new. I cried when he left. I'm not completely stupid; I understood perfectly what he meant . . . What he wanted to say was something that could never be said directly, in plain, simple words: that there was a gulf in culture between us, that his world was not mine; that though I knew everything and had learned all there was to learn, that though I was middle-class, just as he was, my circumstances were—in tiny but vital details—different from those he had loved and had gotten used to. The middle classes are far more sensitive to such subtle distinctions than the aristocracy are. Those in the middle are forever having to secure and display their status. The upper class have no such need: their positions are assured from birth. Those in the middle are always aspiring to some position or protecting it. My husband was no longer of the aspiring generation: he had in fact surpassed even those who had something to protect. He talked about this once. He was reading a German book, saying how he had discovered the answer to the great questions of life in it, including questions of the self. I don't like such "great questions"—my view is that life consists of a million little questions and that it is always only the totality of those that really matters. So I asked, a little mockingly:

"Do you really think you have finally come to know yourself?"

"Of course," he answered. And he looked at me from under his glasses with such childlike seriousness and goodwill that I regretted asking the question. "I am an artist," he continued. "It is the only thing I have any gift for. It's not uncommon in my class. That's how families eventually come a cropper."

He never talked about it again.

I didn't understand it then. He never wrote, never painted, never played any musical instrument. He despised "art lovers." But he did read a lot, "systematically"—his favorite word—a little too systematically for my taste. I read passionately, according to mood. He read as though he were carrying out one of life's important duties. Once he had begun a book he wouldn't leave it until it was finished—not even when it annoyed or bored him. Reading was a religious obligation for him: he valued letters as highly as priests do relics. But he was like that with pictures too, and with museums, theaters, and concerts. Everything interested him, literally everything. But the only thing I was "interested in" was him.

It was just that he did not practice any art. He ran the factory, traveled a lot, employed artists, and made a point of paying them particularly well. But he was very careful that he should not impose his tastes, which were far different from those of the majority of his employees and advisers, on his colleagues. He never raised his voice. He spoke gently and courteously, as if he had constantly to be apologizing for something; as if he were at a loss in some matter and required help. At the same time he knew when to stick to his principles in important matters—and in business.

Do you know what my husband was? He was that rarest of all beings in creation. He was a man. He was manly.

I don't mean in the romantic, theatrical sense of the word. Not the way a champion boxer might be said to be manly. It was his spirit that was manly: inquiring, logical, restless, adventurous, and suspicious. That was another thing about him I didn't know at the time. Discovering such things is one of life's hardest lessons.

It's not what we learned at school, is it, you and I?

Perhaps I should begin at the point when he introduced me to one of his friends, the writer, Lázár. Do you know him? . . . Have you read his books? . . . I've read everything he has written now. I have burrowed my way through his books, thinking there must be some secret hidden in them, as if they might solve the enigma of my own life. But no. There are no answers to enigmas like that. It is life itself that provides the answers, sometimes quite surprising ones. I hadn't read a single line of his before. Yes, I knew him by name, but had no idea my husband knew him personally—that they were friends. I came home one evening in the third year of my marriage and found him with my husband. This was the beginning of my other education. It was the first time I realized I knew nothing about my husband. I'd been living with a man yet knew nothing about him. Sometimes now I think, or rather I know, indeed am all too aware of the fact, that I had no idea what he really liked, the kind of things he preferred, and was utterly ignorant of his desires. Do you know what the two of them were doing that evening, Lázár and my husband? . . .

They were playing.

It was a strange, unsettling kind of game.

It wasn't a game of rummy: nothing like it. In any case, my husband hated and despised all formal recreation, and that included cards. They were playing, but in a grotesque kind of way, a little frighteningly, so I simply couldn't understand it at first but was frightened and nervous as they talked, as if I had blundered into some lunatic conversation. I couldn't recognize the man engaged with that stranger as my husband. As I said, we had been married three years. The stranger leapt to his feet, glanced at my husband, and, very politely, said:

"Welcome, Ilonka. I hope you don't mind me bringing Peter home?"

And he pointed to my husband, who stood up awkwardly and gave me an apologetic look. I thought they'd gone mad. But they didn't really pay me much attention after that. The stranger slapped my husband on the back and said:

"We met on Arena utca. Imagine, he didn't want to stop, the idiot—he just said hello and went on. I wasn't going to let him do that, of course. I said, 'Peter, you old fool, you're not cross with me? . . .' Then I took his arm and brought him home. So, my dears," he said and spread his arms, "give each other a hug. I will even allow you a kiss."

You may imagine how I stood there. Gloves in hand, my handbag on my arm, still wearing my hat, I stood in the middle of the room like some donkey, wide-eyed and staring. My first thought was to run to the telephone and ring the doctor or the ambulance. Or the police. But my husband took my hand and kissed it, saying:

"Let's put this behind us, Ilonka. I am so pleased you are happy together."

Then we sat down to supper. The writer sat in Peter's place, took charge, and issued his instructions as if he were master of the house. He addressed me using the informal *te*. Naturally, the maid thought we had all gone mad and was so frightened she dropped the salad dish. They didn't explain the game to me that evening and that, in fact, was the point of the game. I should be told nothing. They had planned it, the pair of them, while waiting for me, and they acted it out perfectly, like professional actors. The game was based on the idea that I had divorced Peter some years ago and had moved in with the writer, my husband's friend. Peter was so upset by this—in the game, that is—that he had left everything to us: the house, the furniture, the lot. In other words the writer was now my husband. Peter, so went the game, had met the writer in the street and the writer had taken him by the arm—by "him" I mean my offended, divorced husband—and said: "Look, let's have no more of this. What's happened has happened, come and have supper with us." And Peter had accepted the invitation. And now we were together, all three of us, in the house where I had "previously" lived with Peter, having a friendly supper, the writer now "being" my husband, sleeping in Peter's bed, taking his place in my life . . . You understand? That was the mad game they were playing.

But the game had some subtle refinements.

Peter pretended he was on edge, tortured by his memories. The writer pretended that he was rather *too* free and easy, a little too relaxed about it, because, after all, the strange situation was not entirely without stress for him either, since he would have felt guilty with Peter there, and that, precisely, was why he was being so loud and jovial. I "pretended" . . . but no, I wasn't pretending, I just sat with them and stared, now at one, now at the other of these two grown, intelligent men who, for some reason I couldn't begin to guess, were playing the idiot. I did slowly begin to understand the more subtle "rules of the game." But I understood something else that evening too.

I understood that my husband, whom I had previously believed to be entirely mine—every last inch of him, as they say, right down to the recesses of his soul—was not at all mine but a stranger with secrets. It was like discovering something shocking about him: that he had served time in jail or that he had perverse passions, something that didn't fit the picture I had of him—I mean the picture I had been painting of him in my own soul. I understood that my husband was only tied to me in certain specific ways, but that in others he remained a mysterious, unfamiliar figure, someone just as strange as the writer who had stopped him in the street and "brought him here." I understood that what was going on was in some way against me but above my head; that, more than comrades, they were accomplices.

I understood that my husband inhabited worlds other than the one I knew. I understood that this other man, the writer, exercised a certain power over my husband's soul.

Tell me—what do you think power is? . . . Because there is so much written and said about it. What is political power, what's the cause of it, how does it happen that a man can exert his will over millions? And what does our power, women's power, consist of? Love, you say. Well, maybe it *is* love. Myself, I have occasional doubts about the word nowadays. I don't deny love, not by any means. It is the greatest earthly power. And yet sometimes I feel that men, when they love us, do so because they have no choice, and that they even look down on love—on us—a little. In every real man there is a kind of reserve, as if he had closed off some part of his soul, kept it away from women, and said, "You can come so far, darling, but no farther. Here is my seventh room. Here, I want to be alone." It drives the more stupid kind of woman quite mad. They lose their tempers. The wiser sort are first sad and curious, then resign themselves to it.

But what kind of power can one person have over another's soul? Why did this unhappy, restless, clever, frightening, and at the same time foolish, wounded person—this writer—exercise his power over my husband's soul?

Because power he had, as I was to find out: a dangerous, even fatal power. One time, much later, my husband said that the role of this man was to be "a witness" to his life. He tried very hard to explain this. The way he put it was that there existed a witness figure of some kind in everyone's life: someone we meet in youth, someone we recognize and consider stronger than we are, so that everything we do afterward is an attempt to hide whatever we are ashamed of from this witness-turned-merciless-judge. The witness-judge doesn't readily believe us. He knows something about us that no one else does. We might become important people—we might be ministers of state, we might be awarded the Nobel Prize—but the witness simply stands by and smiles as if to say, "Do you really take yourself so seriously?" . . .

And he went on to explain that everything we did was, to some extent, done for this witness: it was he who had to be convinced, it was to him we had to prove something. Our careers, the great struggles of our individual lives, were all, first and foremost, for the witness's bene-fit. You know that awkward moment when a young husband first intro-duces his wife to "the" friend, the great companion of his childhood, then stands by, anxiously watching to see if the friend approves his choice of partner and finds her attractive? . . . Naturally the friend is courteous and thoughtful, but secretly he is jealous, because, whatever he thinks of her, he is the figure the woman is replacing in a sentimental relationship. So, you see, that was the way they were both weighing me up that evening. The trouble was, they already knew a great deal, the two of them, much more than I could begin to guess.

Because another thing I understood from their conversation that evening was that these two accomplices, my husband and the writer, had their own thoughts about men and women and about human rela-tionships in general, thoughts my husband had never discussed with me. This hurt, because it suggested that I was not worth talking to about such things—about things in general.

When the stranger left some time after midnight, I confronted my husband and asked him directly:

"Tell me honestly, do you look down on me, just a little?"

He gazed at me through cigar smoke, tired, his eyes screwed up, as though he were suffering a hangover after an orgy, and considered my question carefully. To tell you the truth, by the time this evening was over, by the time my husband had finished playing this peculiar game with the writer he'd brought home, I felt worse than if he'd been at a real orgy. We were both exhausted. Strange, bitter feelings were stirring in me.

"No," he replied solemnly. "I don't look down on you, not at all.

Why should you think that? You are an intelligent woman with powerful instincts," he added.

It sounded convincing but I didn't quite trust him. I sat down opposite him at the cleared table—we had been sitting at the table the whole evening, not moving to the comfort of the parlor, because the guest preferred sitting and chatting among a heap of cigarette butts and empty bottles of wine.

"Yes, I am intelligent and have powerful instincts," I answered, then hesitated. "But what do you think of my character, my soul?"

I was aware the question sounded a little pathetic. My husband gave me his full attention, but did not answer me.

It was as if he were saying: "That must remain my secret. Let it be enough that I acknowledge your intelligence and the power of your instincts."

That might have been how it started. I remembered that evening for a long time.

The writer was not a frequent visitor. Nor did he meet my husband very often. But whenever they did meet, I felt like a woman who notices an unfamiliar scent on her husband, a scent that clings to his hands even though he has only shaken another woman's hand. Of course I was jealous of the writer and for a while nagged at my husband to invite him to supper again. It embarrassed him and he dismissed the idea.

"He doesn't lead much of a social life," he said without looking into my eyes. "He's a loner. A writer. He works all the time."

But I discovered that they did sometimes meet in secret. I spotted them in a café one day. I was just across the street. I felt I'd been stabbed with a sharp object, a knife or a needle: it was a wild, sick feeling. They couldn't have seen me. They were sitting in one of the booths, my husband speaking, both of them laughing. My husband's face looked so much like a stranger's: it was quite changed, nothing like his face at home, the face I knew. I quickly walked on and knew I had gone pale. The blood had drained from me.

You're mad, I thought. What do you want? . . . That man is his friend, a famous writer, a special, highly intelligent person. So what if they meet sometimes? It means nothing. What do you want from them? . . . Why is your heart beating so fast? . . . Are you afraid they will not include you in their games, in one of their peculiar, grotesque games? Are you afraid they don't think you clever or cultured enough? Are you jealous?

I had to laugh. But the pounding in my breast did not calm down. My heart was beating just the way it did the day I was to taken to the hospital to have the baby. But that second wild beating of the heart was a sweet and happy sensation.

I carried on down the street, walking as fast as I could, feeling cheated, left out of something. My husband didn't want me to meet with this extraordinary man he felt privileged to know from his youth. My husband was not much of a talker generally. I felt I was being cheated, even betrayed somehow. My heart was still pounding that evening when, at the usual time, my husband came home.

"Where have you been?" I asked as he kissed my hand.

"Where?" He looked blank. "Nowhere. I've come home."

"You're lying," I said.

He gave me a long look. He looked almost bored as he answered.

"You're right. I forgot. I bumped into Lázár. We had coffee together. You see, I had forgotten. Did you see me in the café?"

His voice was sincere, calm, and just a touch surprised. I felt ashamed of myself.

"Forgive me," I said. "I just feel unhappy knowing so little about that man. I don't think he is a true friend of yours. Nor of mine. Of either of us. Do please drop him. Try to avoid him," I begged.

My husband gave me a curious look.

"Oh," he said and wiped his glasses with great care, as always. "There's no need to avoid Lázár. He is never intrusive."

And that was the last time he mentioned him.

By now I wanted to know everything about Lázár. Having found some of his books—all dedicated, with special inscriptions—in my husband's library, I read as many as I could. What was peculiar about the inscriptions? They were . . . how to put it? . . . disrespectful . . . No, that's not the right word . . . they were strangely mocking. It was as if the author despised not only the dedicatee, but his own books, and himself for ever having written them. There was something a little self-deprecating, ironic, melancholy, in the tone of them. It was as if what he had really written under his name was: "All right, I've signed, but I am not quite the person this book implies I am."

Up to that point I'd regarded the writer's calling as a kind of secular priesthood. The book was the solemn pulpit from which such people addressed the world! I couldn't understand everything he wrote. It was as if he disdained people, even the reader, people such as me, and was determined not to reveal anything valuable about himself. Readers and critics had a great deal to say about that tendency of his. There were many who hated the writer, though, of course, some people hate anyone who is well known. He never spoke about his books or about literature when we met. He just wanted to know something about everything. One evening he called in and I had to explain to him in great detail how to prepare rabbit stew. Would you believe it? Yes, rabbit stew. He wanted it down to the last detail; he even asked the cook. Then he started talking about giraffes. It was all very interesting. He could talk about anything and he knew a great deal; it was only literature he never spoke about.

Was there a touch of madness in the two of them? I myself thought there might be at first. But then I dismissed the thought. It was simply—as so often in life—not what I expected. They were not mad, I thought, they were just peculiarly private people.

Then Lázár dropped out of our lives. We read his books and articles, but we didn't see him. Sometimes there was gossip about his connection with some politician or a well-known woman, but no one knew anything for sure. Politicians swore that our famous author-friend was a member of their party; some women boasted of having captured this elusive exotic beast and bound him head-to-foot. But time after time, the fugitive went to ground and disappeared. Years passed and we saw nothing of him. What was he doing in that time? I don't know. He lived. He read. He wrote. Maybe he performed conjuring tricks. And that reminds me . . .

It's five years later now. I'd been married to my husband for eight years. The baby was born in the third. Yes, it was a boy. I sent you his photograph. I know—he was gorgeous. Then I stopped writing to anyone, including you. The child was everything: he was all I lived for: everyone else, close or distant, disappeared. One shouldn't be allowed to love so intensely. Nor should anyone be the object of such love, not even our own children. Love is the fiercest kind of selfishness. So yes, when the child was born, our correspondence came to an end. You were my dearest friend, but I didn't need you—not even you—anymore, because the child had arrived. Those two years while the child was alive were as much happiness as the world could offer. I felt superhuman, calm and fearful at once. I knew the child wouldn't survive. How did I know? People just know such things. Some of us feel everything and are fully aware of our fates. I knew that such happiness, such beauty and goodness as was concentrated in that little child, was not to be. I knew he would die. No, don't argue, and don't look so horrified: I just know this better than you do. But those two years were years of happiness. He died of scarlet fever. It was winter, three weeks after his second birthday.

Why do innocent children die? Can you tell me that? Have you thought about it? I have thought deep and long. Not even God answers questions like that.

I don't have very much else to do, so this is what I think about. Yes, even now. And I will think about it as long as I live. One never recovers from such a loss. The death of a child is the one true form of torture. Everything else is merely a shadow of this one agony. You are not acquainted with it, I know. And you know what? I don't know what to say, whether I envy or pity you for not knowing it . . . I think I pity you.

Perhaps it would have been different if the child hadn't arrived that third year. And other things might have been different too, very different, if he had survived. They might. A child is, after all, the greatest of miracles, the one true meaning of life; and yet—we shouldn't deceive ourselves on this point—no child can resolve the problems between two people. A child cannot calm fits of anxiety or solve insoluble complexities. But there's no point in talking about that now. The fact is, the child was born on a particular day, lived two years, and then died. I spent two more years after that with my husband, and then we separated.

I'm quite sure now that we'd have separated in the third year of the marriage had it not been for the child. Why? . . . Because by that time I knew I could not live with my husband. There is no pain like the pain of knowing you love someone but cannot live with them.

"Why?" I asked him once, and he told me what he thought the problem was.

"You want me to give up my humanity," he said. "I can't do that. I'd sooner die."

I immediately understood and replied: "Then don't die. Live on and remain a stranger to me."

He always meant what he said: he was that kind of man. He didn't always do it straightaway—sometimes it took a few years for words to become deeds, but sooner or later deeds followed. Other people talk about hopes and plans after supper by way of conversation, then immediately forget what they've said; when my husband talked of such things, action followed. It was as if he were bound to his words in some visceral way: what he said once remained with him and would not let him go. If he said "I would sooner die," then I was to know he meant it, that he would not surrender himself to me but would rather die first. It was part of his character, his fate . . . Sometimes, in the course of a conversation, he would let fall a few words, criticizing somebody, or suddenly reveal a plan—then time would pass without further mention until, one day, I'd notice that the person he'd criticized had vanished from our lives; that the plan mentioned in passing had two years later turned into reality.

By the third year I knew our marriage was in deep trouble. My husband treated me with courtesy and tenderness. He loved me. He did not cheat on me. He was not involved with any other woman, only with me. And yet—please look away a moment, I think I am blushing—I felt that in the first three years of marriage, and especially in the last two of being together, that I was not so much his wife as . . .

He loved me, no question about it. But at the same time it was as if he were merely tolerating me in his house, in his very life. There was patience and tolerance in his manner, but it was as though he had no choice in that matter and he'd simply resigned himself to living with me, to sharing a home with me, sharing one room of his life. That's how it felt. He carried on talking to me as charming and affectionate as ever, taking off his glasses, listening, giving advice, sometimes even joking, and we'd go to the theater and lead a social life—and I'd watch him lean back, his arms folded, taking good-natured stock of the others, with just a hint of suspicion visible in his mocking, doubtful expression. Because he did not entirely yield himself to others, either. He listened to them seriously, fully sensible of his obligations to them, then answered them politely; but there was in his voice, I saw, a patronizing note, a certain pity, as if he did not quite believe them, as if he was aware that under even the most sincere human declarations there remained unarticulated layers of despair, fury, lies, and ignorance. It wasn't something he could actually tell people, of course, and that was why he listened through to them with that deprecating forbearance, with that serious skeptical expression, smiling occasionally and shaking his head, as if telling the other person: "Do carry on. I know what I know."

You were asking me earlier if I loved him. I suffered a great deal with him. But I know I loved him—and I even know why I loved him . . . I loved him because he was sad and solitary; because he was beyond anyone's help, even mine. But it took a long time, and a lot of suffering, before I realized and understood this. For years I thought he was looking down on me, that he had a low opinion of me . . . but it was something else.

At forty years of age that man was as isolated as a monk in the desert. We lived in a world capital, in fine style, with many acquaintances, part of a considerable society. It just so happened that we were alone.

Just once I saw him in a different light, just once and for a moment only. It was the moment the child was born, when that pale, sad, lonely figure was first allowed into the room. He entered awkwardly, as if he were taking part in a scene that was deeply embarrassing, overfamiliarly human, as if he were a little ashamed to be an actor in it. He stopped by the crib, leaned forward uncertainly, his hands clasped behind his back as usual, wary and reserved. I was exhausted at the time but I watched him very closely. He leaned over the crib and then, for a moment, that pale face of his lit up with some inner glow. But he didn't say anything. He gazed at the baby for a long time, for maybe twenty minutes in all, without moving. Then he came over, put his hand on my brow and stood silently by my bed. He didn't look at me but stared out of the window. It was dawn on a foggy October day. He stayed by my bed a while longer, stroking my brow. His palm was hot. The next moment he was talking to the doctor. It was as if he had abruptly finished one conversation and started another, with a different subject.

But now I know that in that moment, perhaps for the first and last time in his life, he was happy. He might even have considered revealing something of the secret he called his humanity. While the child was alive he talked to me differently, with a greater intimacy, but I still felt I was not entirely part of him. I know there are people who struggle desperately to overcome a kind of inner resistance, some blend of pride, fear, sensitivity, and uncertainty, that won't let them join the crowd like the others. But he would, up to a point at least, for a while, have made his peace with the world for the sake of the child. I could see him struggling with himself and was filled with a kind of crazy hope while the child was alive. He was trying to change his nature, to domicile it the way a circus trainer tames a lion. Silent and proud and sad as he was, he was doing his best to be humble and obedient. He'd bring me presents, for example. It was enough to make me weep the way this newly "humble" man—a man who'd always been ashamed to bring me little presents for Christmas or my birthday but insisted on something expensive like a pleasure cruise, a fur coat, a new car, or jewelry—now started bringing me what I had really been missing, touching little gifts hardly worth anything, such as a bag of hot chestnuts he'd bought on the way home, sweets, and so on. Up till that time I'd had the best of everything: the best doctors, the finest nursery, and this wonderful ring I am wearing now. Yes, it is valuable. But now he'd arrive home wearing a shy smile and clumsily unwrap a little package containing, say, a delicately crocheted baby's jacket and bonnet. He'd put it down on the nursery table, give a brief, apologetic smile, then quickly leave the room.

I tell you I could have wept at those times. Wept with joy and hope.

But there was another feeling too, an important part of the complex whole, and that was fear. It was the fear that he would not win the struggle, that he could not overcome himself, that neither of us could manage our lives, not even with the help of the baby. It was the fear that there was something not right about all this. But what could it be? . . . I'd go to church and pray. Help me, God! I pleaded. But God knows that the only help we can receive is that which we ourselves give.

But he certainly struggled with himself while the child lived.

I can see you're impatient. You ask me what the problem was between us. You want to know what kind of man my husband really was . . . It's a hard question, darling. I have been puzzling over it for eight years. Even after we parted I continued puzzling. Now and then I think I finally have the truth. But it's made up of entirely unreliable pieces of guesswork. I can't name the disease: I can only tell you the symptoms.

You asked me if he loved me? . . . Well, yes, he loved me. But I think he only truly loved his father and his son.

He cared for his father and was full of respect for him. He visited him every week. My mother-in-law dined with us each week. "Mother-in-law": there's something nasty about the word. But this woman, my husband's mother, was one of the most refined creatures I had ever met. When father-in-law died and when this wealthy, highly elegant woman was left alone in the big house, I feared she would get too used to us. People are so prejudiced. But she was all sensitivity, all consideration. She moved into a small apartment, was a burden on no one, and managed all the difficult, fiddly bits of her life by herself with considerable care and foresight. She asked for neither pity nor kindness. Of course she knew things about her son that I couldn't know. Only mothers know the truth. She knew her son was tender, respectful, and attentive; it was just that she didn't love him. Such a terrible thing! But we should consider it calmly, because that is what I got used to with my husband—it was something we both learned from Lázár: that the truth had a certain creative, cleansing power. There was never any argument or disagreement between those two, between mother and child. "Mother dear," said he, and "Yes, dear son," she answered. There was always that ritual of kissing hands, a certain formal courtesy, if you like. But there was never any intimacy. The two never spent any time alone in a room together; one was always standing up and finding something else to do elsewhere, or inviting someone in to join them. They feared being left alone together, as if there were some urgent matter that they'd immediately have to discuss and there would be trouble, real trouble, if their secret was revealed, some secret that they, mother and son, could never talk about. That's what I felt, anyway. Was it really like that? I sometimes wondered. But yes, that's how it was.

I would like to have made peace between them. But that could only be when they were not cross with each other! I tried to probe the nature of the relationship, proceeding very carefully, the way you'd probe a wound. But the first touch frightened them and they immediately started talking about something else. What could I have said? . . . Neither accusation nor complaint had any clearly visible, tangible object. Might I have suggested that mother and son had injured each other some time in the past? I couldn't, because both were, perfectly properly, "fulfilling their obligations." It was as if they had been constructing alibis their whole lives. Our name days, birthdays, Christmas, those lesser and greater tribal rituals common to all families, were properly conducted, down to the minutest detail. Mama received a present; Mama gave a present. My husband kissed her hand; she kissed his forehead. At dinner or supper Mama took her place at the head of the family table and everyone conducted respectful conversations with her, on the subjects of family and the world at large, never arguing, listening to Mama's precise, courteous, quietly stated views—and then they ate and talked of something else. Oh, these family dinners! Those silences between conversations! It was this talking-about-something-else, this polite silence, forever and ever! This wasn't something I could talk about with them between soup and main course, between birthday and Christmas, between youth and aging. I couldn't say to them, "You are always talking about something else." I couldn't say anything because even with me, my husband was always talking about something else, and I suffered the same silences, the same shutting out as my mother-in-law, and sometimes I even thought that we were both to blame, his mother and I, because we didn't know how to go about it: we had not succeeded in getting him to reveal his secret; we had not accomplished our mission, the one real mission of our lives. We simply didn't understand this man. She had given him life and I had given him a child . . . is there any more a woman could give a man? You do agree—she can't give any more? I don't know. One day I began to doubt. And that is what I want to tell you, today, because we have met, because I have seen him, and I feel now that everything has built up inside me and I must tell someone, because I think about it all the time. So I'll tell you now. I'm not boring you? Do you have half an hour? Listen, there may be just time enough.

He might have respected both of us, even loved us to some degree. But neither his mother nor I understood him. That was the great failure in our lives.

You say we need not, indeed it is impossible, to "understand" love? You're wrong, darling. I used to say that, said it for a long time. I said these things were decreed by God. Love just is or is not. What is there to "understand"? . . . What, after all, is the value of human feeling if it's just the product of things we can explain? . . . But then, as we grow older, we learn it's not like that, it's different from what we thought: we do, after all, have to try to "understand" things, including love. No, don't shake your head and smile, it is true. We're human beings: we are conscious of everything that happens to us. Our feelings and passions become tolerable or intolerable through consciousness. It is not enough to love.

Let's not argue about that. I know what I know. And I have paid a considerable price for it. What price? . . . My life, darling, my whole life. The fact that I am sitting here with you in this patisserie, in this lovely crimson salon, watching my husband buying candied orange peel for someone else. Not that it particularly surprises me, him buying candied orange peel. He had such taste in everything.

Who is he buying it for? For the other woman, of course. I don't even like to say her name. The one he went on to marry. Didn't you know he had remarried? I imagined the news would have spread to Boston too; that you might have heard, even in America. It shows how silly we can be. How silly to think our personal affairs, things really close to our hearts, should be matters of world importance. While it was all happening—I mean the divorce and my husband's second marriage—events of genuine world importance were taking place, countries were being divided, people were preparing for war, and one day war did break out . . . Not that it was surprising. When people prepare for something, said Lázár—war, for example—with such assiduity, such determination, such foresight, such calculation, that thing is bound eventually to happen. All the same I wouldn't have been surprised at that time to see banner headlines carrying news of my own personal war, my own battles, my defeats, my occasional victories—an entire survey of the front line that was my life . . . But that's another story. At the time the child was born that was all in the dim and distant future.

Perhaps I could put it this way: that in the two years when we still had the child, my husband made peace with the world and with me. Not a proper permanent peace, not yet, just a kind of amnesty, a cease-fire. He waited and watched. He worked to put his soul in order. He was, after all, a man of unimpeachable soul. As I told you before, he was a man. And more than that: he was a gentleman. I don't mean the sort that goes to gentlemen's clubs, of course, the sort that fights duels or shoots himself because he cannot pay his gambling debts. He never touched cards, in any case. On one occasion, I remember, he declared that a gentleman does not play at cards because he has no right to money that he has not earned. In other words, he was *that* sort of gentleman. He was polite and patient with the weak. With those who were his equals he was strict and mindful of his rank, because he did not recognize any other kind of rank. No social rank, in his opinion, was higher than his own. The only other people he admired were artists. They have chosen the most difficult path, he said. They were God's children. Only real artists, no one else, were superior to him.

And because he was a gentleman, he tried, when the child was born, to alleviate that frightening sense of detachment in his soul that was so painful to me. He made genuinely moving efforts to get closer to me and the child. It was like a tiger deciding to go on a vegetarian diet or to join the Salvation Army. How hard life is, how hard it is to be human . . .

That's how we lived for two years. Not entirely well, not happily. But quietly. Those two years must have cost him dear. It needs a super-human effort to go against one's nature. He sweated blood for happiness. Starting from a position of absolute paralysis he tried to become relaxed, carefree, easygoing. The poor thing! . . . He might perhaps have suffered less if I'd released him psychologically, so all my needs, all my demands for love, could be satisfied by the child. But something was changing in me too, something I didn't understand then. My love for my child was, exclusively, *through* my husband. Maybe that is why God decided to punish me.

What are you staring at me for? . . . You don't believe me? . . . Or maybe you're frightened? . . . Ah, my dear, I know this story of mine isn't exactly charming.

I was mad about the child, lived only for him, and it was only in these two years I felt my life had meaning and purpose . . . but it was because of *him* I loved the child: it was for his sake I loved him, do you understand now? I wanted the child to bind him to me, to bind his entire being. Dreadful as it is to say, but I now know that the child, for whom I remain in perpetual mourning, was merely a tool, a means to force my husband to love me. If I were driven into a confessional and made to stay there till dawn, I could not have found the words to say this to him. But even without words, in his heart of hearts, secretly he knew it, just as I knew it, even without the words, because I did not yet have words for things in life . . . The right words always come too late and we pay a terrible price for them. It was Lázár who had the words then. One day my husband was to provide me with the words, without particularly meaning to, half by accident, the way we discover a secret compartment. But that comes later. In the meantime we carried on, knowing next to nothing of each other. Everything was in shipshape order, on the outside at least. At breakfast time the nurse would bring in the baby, who was dressed in light blue and pink. My husband would talk to me and to the child, then get in the car and drive to the factory. We'd often invite guests for dinner. They'd drink to our happiness, praise our lovely home: me, the young mother, the beautiful baby, and our perfect lives. What were they thinking when they left? The foolish ones were jealous, but those who were wise and sensitive must have breathed a sigh of relief when they left our house, and thought, "Alone at last!" We served excellent food and the rarest foreign wines; we enjoyed quiet, thoughtful conversation. It was just that something was missing, and the guests who could sense this were inevitably happy to leave. My mother-in-law tended to arrive in a state of mild panic and leave as soon as she decently could. We felt all this but did not know it. Maybe my husband did know it; he probably did . . . But there was nothing he could do at the time except clench his teeth and go on being helplessly happy.

I wouldn't let go of him, would not let his soul escape for a second. I clung to him with the child. I silently blackmailed him with my emotional needs. Can these powers bind human beings? . . . Yes, they can; they are the only power. My every moment was dedicated to the child, but only because I knew that while there was a child my husband was mine and only mine. It is the sin God can't forgive. You can't make someone love you, nor can you make yourself love them. Nevertheless you try to impose your will; you strain every muscle and nerve to love. It's the only way, you say? . . . Well, it was the way I loved him.

We lived off the child and fought each other. Our wars were fought not with words but with smiles, conversation, and temper. Then one day it happened. I just grew tired and my energy gave out. It was as if my feet and hands had gone to sleep. Because he wasn't the only one who gave all his energy to his work: I did too.

I tired myself out, in the way people do when they are going to be ill. This was in early fall, many years ago. It was a mild, sweet fall. The child had just had his second birthday and was beginning to be really interesting, an utterly delightful, heartstring-tugging, proper character, a somebody. One evening we were sitting in the garden. The child had been put to bed.

"How about going to Merano for six weeks?" my husband suggested.

Two years earlier it was I who had asked if we could visit Merano in the early fall. I'm superstitious; I like a bit of quackery and believed in the grape cure diet. He didn't come with me the first time, making some excuse to stay behind. I knew he didn't enjoy traveling with me, because he feared the closeness implied by a journey, feared the days when two people are thrown entirely on each other's resources in a hotel room in a strange place.

At home the house, our work, our friends, and the business of our lives came between us. This time he wanted to reward me the best he could.

We went to Merano. My mother-in-law moved into our house while we were away, as was the custom. She looked after the child.

It was a strange journey. It was a honeymoon, a valediction, a process of getting acquainted, a running of the gauntlet: it was all of these at once. He tried to bare his soul for me. Because you can be certain of one thing, my dear: that it was never boring in this man's company. I suffered much, it almost killed me, occasionally I was almost a complete blank, occasionally I felt reborn when with him, but not for one moment was I bored. That's just to set the record straight. So, one day we set off to Merano.

Fall was golden, lush, operatic, glorious. We traveled by car. The trees were hung with yellow fruit. The air was richly scented and ripe; the whole world was a garden at the point of turning. There were people in the streets, rich people, people without a care, swarming everywhere, swimming. Big, fat-bellied wasps were humming in the heat, heavy with light. There were Americans just getting drunk on the sun; there were French women bright as dragonflies and more cautious English visitors. The world had not been boarded over yet; for a moment everything—Europe, life itself—was bathed in intense light. But there was a touch of panic too, a sense of having to enjoy everything at once before it all went. People could feel fate working against them. We were lodging in the best hotel, went to concerts, heard fine music, had two adjoining rooms with a view of the mountains.

What were these six weeks about? What were we waiting for? Were we hoping for something? We seemed to be living in silence. My husband had brought books to read: he had perfect pitch as far as language was concerned and, like a great musician, could tell the false note from the true. He was like Lázár in this respect. We'd sit on the balcony at twilight and I'd read to him: French poems, English novels, heavy German prose. And Goethe and some scenes from Hauptmann's *Florian Geyer*. He loved that play. He had seen it on stage once, in Berlin, and had never forgotten it. He also loved Büchner's *Danton's Death*. And *Hamlet,* and *Richard III.* I was obliged to read him verses by the great Hungarian poet János Arany, from his late *Autumn Crocuses* cycle. Then we'd dress, have supper in one of the best restaurants, drink sweet Italian wine and eat sea crab.

In some ways we were living like nouveaux riches, like people who want to make up for everything they have ever lacked, to enjoy it all, and all at once. People that listen to Beethoven while chewing on a capon and slurping French Champagne in time to the music. But it was also like saying good-bye to something. Those years, the last years before the war, were drenched in this peculiar atmosphere. It was like saying good-bye without quite knowing it. My husband said precisely that: something about Europe. I said nothing. It was not Europe I was leaving. Can we, just the two of us, as women, own up to the fact that, concepts such as "Europe" have little to do with us? What I knew deep in my heart was that I lacked the strength to cut myself off from something more important. I was almost choking with helplessness.

One night we were sitting on the balcony. There were grapes in a glass bowl, and big yellow apples. It was apple-gathering time in Merano. The air was so sweet, so full of the smell of apples, it was as if someone had left the lid off an enormous jar of preserves. Below us a French palm-court orchestra was playing melodies from an old Italian opera. My husband had wine brought to the table; the wine—Lacrima Christi—was dark and stood in a crystal jug. There was sweetness in everything, even in the music, something a little overripe, a touch sickening. My husband felt it too and declared:

"Tomorrow we go home."

"Yes," I said. "Let's be on our way."

Suddenly he spoke up in that melancholy, deep voice of his that always touched me. It was like a solemn instrument of some primitive tribe:

"Tell me, Ilonka, what do you think we should do after this?" he asked.

Did I understand what he meant? He was talking about us, our life together. It was a starry night. I looked at the stars, the autumnal stars in that Italian sky, and shuddered. I felt the moment had come when we had to speak the truth. My hands and feet were cold but my palms were sweating with excitement.

"I don't know, I really don't know. I couldn't bear to leave you. I can't imagine life without you," I said.

"I know, it's very difficult," he calmly replied. "I wouldn't want it, either. Maybe it's not the right time yet. Maybe there will never be a right time. But there's something in our life together, just as there is in this holiday, as in everything in our mutual lives, that is shameful and unbefitting. Is it that we daren't tell each other what that is?"

At last he had said it. I closed my eyes and felt dizzy. I stayed silent like that, my eyes closed.

"So tell me at last, what is it that is driving us apart?" I asked.

For a long time he said nothing, simply thought. He put out his cigarette and lit another. He was smoking strong English cigarettes at that time, the smoke of which always made me feel a little giddy. But that smell was part of him too, like the smell of hay in his linen cupboard, because he loved to scent his clothes with a bitter oil smelling of hay. What extraordinary details constitute our sense of a person!

"I don't feel a great need to be loved," he finally said.

"That's impossible," I said, grinding my teeth. "You are a human being. You have an absolute need to be loved."

"It is precisely this that women don't believe, cannot know, and do not understand," he said as if addressing the stars. "That there exists a type of man who has no need of love. He gets on fine without it."

He spoke without pathos, from a great distance, but perfectly naturally. I knew he was telling me the truth now. At least he believed he was telling me the truth. I started to argue.

"You can't know everything about yourself. Maybe you just don't have the courage to feel. You should be less certain, more humble," I pleaded with him.

He threw away his cigarette. He stood up. He was tall—did you see how tall he was?—a head taller than me. But now he towered over me, leaning against the balcony railings, looking more melancholy than ever with the foreign stars behind him. I wanted to unravel him, to find his secret heart. He crossed his arms.

"What is a woman's life?" he pondered. "Feeling possesses every cell of her, from head to foot. I am perfectly aware of this, but I can only understand it in an intellectual way. I can't surrender myself to feeling."

"And the child?" I raised my voice.

"That's the point," he retorted, his voice slightly shaking. "I'm willing to put up with a lot for the child's sake. I love the child. It's through the child that I am able to love you."

"And I . . ." I began, but did not finish. I did not dare tell him that it was the opposite for me, that the child was a vehicle for my love of him.

We spoke for a long time that night, with many long silences. Sometimes I think I remember every word.

"It's impossible for a woman to understand. A man's life depends on the state of his soul. The rest is all extra, a side product. And the child? The child is this strange miracle," he said, then turned to me.

"This is the right time to make a vow. Let's do it right now. Let's vow to stay together. But try to love me a little less. Love the child more," he pleaded, a little hoarse, almost as if he were threatening me. "Your heart must let me go. That's all I want. You know I have no ulterior motive. I can't live under conditions of such emotional tension. There are men more feminine than me, for whom it is vital to be loved. There are others who, even at the best of times, can only just about tolerate the feeling of being loved. I am that kind. It is a kind of shyness, if you like. The more masculine a man, the more shy he is."

"What do you want?" I cried. "What can I do?"

"Let's make a pact," he said. "Let's do it for the child's sake so we can stay together. You know exactly what I want. Only you can help," he continued, frowning. "Only you can loosen this knot. If I really wanted to leave, I would simply leave. But I don't want to leave either you or the child. However impossible it might prove, I want to try harder. I want us to stay together: together, only not so intensely, not so unconditionally, not so much as a matter of life or death. Because I can't go on like this," he added. "I am very sorry but I just can't." And he gave a polite smile.

Then I asked something stupid.

"In that case, why did you marry me?"

"When I married you I knew almost everything about myself. But I didn't know enough about you. I married you because I didn't know you loved me as much as you do."

He looked almost frightened as he said that.

"Is that a crime?" I asked. "Is it such a crime to love you as I do?"

He laughed. He stood in the darkness, smoking his cigarette, softly laughing. It was sad laughter, not in the least cynical or superior.

"It's worse than a crime," he answered. "It's a mistake."

Then he added, in a friendly way:

"I didn't make that answer up. Talleyrand said it first when he discovered that Napoleon had had the young duc d'Enghien executed. I have to tell you, it's a cliché."

Fat lot I cared about Napoleon and the duc d'Enghien! I understood exactly what he wanted to say. I began to bargain with him.

"Listen," I said. "The situation may not be quite so intolerable. We will both grow old. You might find the warmth of love more comforting once you yourself grow cold."

"But that's precisely it," he quietly replied. "That's the whole point. It is the thought that old age is inevitable, that it's creeping on."

He was forty-eight at the time he said this, forty-eight precisely that autumn. He looked a lot younger, though. It was after our separation that he began to age.

We didn't say any more about it that night. Nor the next day—not ever. Two days later we set off home. On our return we found the child in a fever. He died the following week. After that we never talked about anything personal again. We simply lived together waiting for something. For a miracle, perhaps. But there are no miracles.

One afternoon, a few weeks after the child's death, I came home from the cemetery and went into the nursery. My husband was standing in the dark room.

"What are you doing here?" he asked me roughly. Then he came to his senses and left the room.

"I'm sorry," he said, over his shoulder.

It was he who had fitted out the room. He had personally chosen every piece of furniture and arranged everything about it, right down to the position the furniture was to occupy. True, he hardly ever entered the room while the child was alive, and even then he used to stand confused on the threshold, as if he feared the awkwardness and ludicrousness of an emotional scene. But he asked to see the child each day, in his room, and every morning and evening he had to have a report of how the child had slept and its general state of health.

Afterwards he only once went in there: that was a few weeks after the funeral. In any case, we locked up the room and I had the key, and that's how it stayed for three years, until our divorce came through, nor did we ever open it; everything stayed just as it was the moment we took the child to the clinic. I did sometimes sneak in to clean . . . without anyone knowing, of course.

I was half-crazy in those weeks after the funeral. But I pulled myself together and dragged myself about, if only because I didn't want to collapse altogether. I was drawing superhuman strength from somewhere. I knew it was perfectly possible that he was feeling even worse than I did, that he might be close to a serious breakdown, and that even if he denied it, he needed me.

But something happened between us in those weeks, or rather between him and the world . . . I can't quite find the words for it. Something in him did break. All this, of course, happened without anything being said. Isn't that always the case with serious, even life-threatening, events generally? When a person begins to cry or scream, the crisis is past.

He was calm during the entire funeral too. He said nothing. His calm was infectious. We followed the little white-and-gold coffin in silence, with straight backs and dry eyes. But do you know—he never once came to the cemetery with me to visit the grave? . . . He might have gone there by himself, I don't know.

"When someone starts crying, you know it's a cheat. Everything is over by then," he said to me once. "I don't believe in tears. Pain is silent and sheds no tears."

What was happening to me in those weeks? Looking back now I would say I was working my way up to revenge. Revenge? Against whom? Against fate? Against those who treated him? That would have been stupid. Believe me when I say the child had been treated by the best doctors in town.

People say all kinds of things about times like this. "It was as much as they could bear," they say. That's how it was. It was as much as I could bear. But it happened in stages. Everyone was busy with all kinds of things in those few days when the little one was dying. Their smallest cares seemed to exercise them more than the saving of my child's life. I can't forgive them for this, of course, not even now. I wanted to be revenged on them. But I felt the desire for another kind of revenge too, a revenge not in my mind but in my heart. It was the revenge of indifference. A strange indifference and contempt burned within me then. It was a fierce cold flame. Because it's not true that suffering purifies people; that we become better, wiser, more understanding in the process. We become cold and indifferent. When, for the first time in our lives, we properly understand our fate, we become almost calm. Calm and extraordinarily, terrifyingly lonely.

During those weeks I didn't go to confession as I used to. What would I have had to confess? What was my sin and how had I commit-ted it? I felt I was the most innocent creature that ever lived. I don't feel that way now . . . Sin is not just what the catechism says it is. Sin is not simply that which we commit. Sin is also what we desire but are too weak to do. When my husband—for the first and last time in his life—barked at me in that peculiar hoarse voice in the nursery, I understood my sin. I had sinned, in his eyes, because I was unable to save the child.

You're staring into space. I can see you're confused. You feel that only deeply wounded feelings or acute despair can lead a man to such an unjust accusation. Not for one moment did I feel his accusation to be unjust. "Yes, but think of all you did do," you say. Well, yes, it wasn't something I could be arrested for, whatever anyone thought. I sat at that child's bedside for eight days. I slept there and nursed him. I was the one who went against usual practice and called other doctors when the first, and then the second, failed to help. Yes, I did all I could. But I did it all so my husband should find strength to live, so that he should remain mine, so he should love me—because there was no other way but through the child. You understand? . . . It was for my husband I prayed when I was praying for the child. My husband's life was the life that mattered. That was the only reason the child's life was of importance. That's a sin, you say! . . . What is sin? I didn't know then. I do know now. People who are part of us need to be loved and supported: those closest to our hearts, the love of whom lies deepest in us, they need all our power. It all collapsed when the child died. I knew I had lost my husband because, even though he said nothing, he blamed me. Ridicu-lous and unfair to blame me, you say. I don't know. I find it impossible to talk about.

After the child died, I felt utterly exhausted, and of course I imme-diately fell ill with pleurisy. For months I lay in bed, got better, then relapsed again. I was in hospital. My husband brought me flowers and visited me every day, at lunchtime and in the evening when he came home from the factory. I had a nurse. I was so weak I had to be fed. And all the time I knew that none of this would help, that my husband would not forgive me; that being ill would not relieve me of my guilt. He con-tinued as tender and courteous as ever . . . I wept each time he left me.

My mother-in-law visited me a lot at this time. Once, just before spring, when I had recovered some of my strength, she was sitting at my bedside, quietly knitting as usual. She gave me a friendly smile and murmured confidentially:

"What do you want revenge for, Ilonka?"

"What?" I asked, startled, and felt myself flushing. "What's this talk about revenge?"

"It's something you kept repeating when you were in a fever. 'Revenge, revenge!' you cried. There's no revenge to be had, my dear, only patience."

I listened. I was excited. It was the first time since the child's death that I'd really listened to anything. Then I started speaking.

"I can't bear it, Mama. What did I do wrong? I know I am not innocent, but I simply can't understand where I went wrong, what sin I committed. Am I not part of his life? Should we divorce? If you think it would be better for us to separate, Mama, I'll divorce him. You must know I think of nothing else, that all my feelings are directed at him. But if I can't help him, I'd sooner be divorced. Please advise me, Mama."

She looked at me with a serious, wise, sad expression.

"Don't upset yourself, child. You know very well there's no advice I can give. It's just life: we have to live and put up with it."

"Live?! Live?!" I shouted. "I'm not a tree! I can't live life like some tree. We need something to live *for*. I met him and I grew to love him: suddenly life had meaning. Then everything changed in a strange way . . . It's not that *he* has changed. It's not that he loves me any less now than he did in the first year of our marriage. He loves me, even now. But he is angry with me."

My mother-in-law said nothing. She didn't seem to approve of what I'd just said, but she didn't seek to contradict me.

"Am I right?" I anxiously asked.

"Not in the way you put it," she said, picking her words carefully. "I don't think he is exactly angry with you. Or, to put it more precisely, I don't think it is with *you* that he is angry."

"With who, then?" I asked in a temper. "Who has hurt him?"

"That's a difficult question." The old woman frowned. "It's hard to answer."

She sighed and put her knitting down.

"Has he never spoken to you about his childhood?"

"Oh, yes," I said. "Occasionally. In his own way. With the same odd, nervous laugh he gives whenever he talks of something personal. People, friends . . . But he has never said that anyone had harmed him."

"No, of course not," she said dismissively. "You couldn't possibly put it like that. Harmed him? Life can damage people in so many ways."

"Lázár," I said. "The writer . . . you know him, Mama? He may be the only one who knows anything about him."

"Yes," said my mother-in-law. "He used to adore Lázár. That man certainly does know something about him. But there's no point in talking about him. He's not a good man."

"That's interesting," I said. "I feel the same way."

She picked up her knitting again. She smiled gently and added, almost as an afterthought:

"Don't excite yourself, child. The pain is all too fresh at the moment. But life comes along and miraculously arranges human affairs, including all those things that now seem intolerable. You'll leave the hospital, go home, and another baby will arrive to take the place of the first one . . ."

"I don't believe that," I said, and felt my heart shrink with despair. "I have such a bad feeling. I think we are at the end of something. Tell me the truth: do you think our marriage is a genuinely bad marriage?"

She gave me a sharp look from under half-closed lids, through her glasses.

"No, I don't think your marriage is a bad marriage," she pronounced.

"Interesting you should say that," I bitterly replied. "Sometimes I think it is as bad as it could possibly be. Does Mama know of better ones?"

"Better?" she asked quizzically, and turned away her head as if she were looking into the distance. "Maybe. I don't know. Happiness, real happiness, tells no tales. But I certainly know of worse. For example . . ."

She fell silent. It was as if she were suddenly frightened, regretting opening her mouth. But I wouldn't let her drop the subject now. I sat up in bed, threw off the covers, and demanded she continue.

"For example?"

"Well, yes," she said, and sighed. She picked up her knitting again. "I'm sorry we should have to talk about these things. But if it is any comfort to you, I confess my own marriage was worse, because, frankly, I did not love my husband."

She said this calmly, almost indifferently, the way old people sometimes speak when they are near death, people who know the true meaning of words, are afraid of nothing, and care more for truth than for keeping the peace. I went pale.

"That's impossible," I muttered like an idiot. "You had such a good life together."

"It wasn't a bad life," she replied in a dry voice, knitting away furiously. "I got him the factory, you know. He, in his turn, brought me love: one party always gives more love than the other. But it's easier for those who do the loving. You love your husband, so it's easier for you, even though you suffer for it. I had to pretend to a feeling that had nothing to do with what I really felt. That's much harder. I put up with it all my life, and you see, here I am. That's always the case with life. Romantic, passionate people expect more, of course. I was never passionate. But, believe me, your situation is better. I almost envy you."

She tipped her head to one side and looked hard at me.

"But don't you go thinking I had a hard life. My life was no different from anyone else's. I only tell you this because you asked, and because you are muddled with fever. Well, so now you know. You were asking if your marriage was as bad as it could be. I don't think it is. It's a marriage," she declared, as if pronouncing judgment.

"Would Mama advise us to stay together?" I asked in fear.

"Of course," she answered. "What are you thinking of? What do you think marriage is? A mood? A bright idea? It's a sacrament, one of the laws of life. One shouldn't even think about it," she admonished me, apparently insulted.

We said nothing for a long time. I gazed at her bony hands, her clever, nimble fingers, and the knitting pattern; I looked at her pale, calm face with its smooth features, ringed by white hair. There was no sign of suffering there. Even if she had suffered, I thought, she has succeeded in achieving the greatest of human triumphs: she had passed the test of life with distinction. She has not been broken by it. What more can anyone do? Everything else—desire, dissatisfaction—is nothing compared to this. That's what I told myself. But deep inside me I felt I couldn't simply accept the situation. So I told her:

"I can't deal with his unhappiness. If he can't be happy with me, let him go and seek happiness elsewhere, with someone else. With *her*."

"Who?" my mother-in-law asked me, closely examining the stitches in her knitting, as if there could be nothing more important.

"With his true wife," I answered harshly. "You know. The real one. The one intended for him."

"What do you know about her?" my mother-in-law asked, her voice quiet, still not looking at me.

It was I who was embarrassed again. Whenever I argued with these people, with mother and son, I always felt like a child, someone who had not been granted admittance to the serious adult rooms of life.

"About who?" I asked greedily. "Who is there I should know about?"

"Her," my mother-in-law cautiously responded. "The real wife you were talking about . . . the intended one."

"Why? Is there an intended? Does she exist somewhere?" I asked, very loudly now.

My mother-in-law bent over her knitting. Her voice was quiet.

"There is always an intended one somewhere."

Then she fell silent. And I never heard her talk of this again. She was like her son: there was something final about her.

But then, a few days after this conversation, I had gotten myself into such a condition of terror, I got better. I hadn't understood my mother-in-law's words straightaway. It was hard to feel seriously jealous at first, since she had spoken in general terms, in a kind of symbolic fashion. Well, of course, the intended always must live somewhere. But what about me, *me,* what was my role? I asked as I recovered. Who is his real wife, his intended wife, if not me? Where does she live? What is she like? Is she younger? Is she blond? How much does she know? I was utterly terrified.

I panicked. I quickly recovered, went home, had dresses made, hurried to the hairdresser, played tennis, went swimming. I found everything in order at home . . . so much so I thought someone had moved out of the house. Or it was something else: you know . . . the realization that my life had, in the last few years, been relatively happy—that despite the suffering, the restlessness, and all I had thought intolerable, now that it was gone, all was well, better than it had even been? It was an odd feeling. Everything in the house was in its place, but the rooms felt empty, as if the executor had been through them, as if the most important items of furniture had—carefully, sensitively—all been removed somewhere. It's not furniture that furnishes a house, of course, but the feeling that fills people's hearts.

My husband's life was so detached from mine at this time he might as well have been living abroad. I wouldn't have been surprised to have received a letter from him one day, delivered from the next room.

Before all this he would talk to me about the factory, about his plans, hesitantly as though conducting an experiment. Then he would wait with bowed head and listen to my answer as though he himself were being examined. There was no discussing plans now: it seemed he had no special plans for anything anymore. He didn't invite Lázár, either. A whole year passed and we didn't see him, only read his books and articles.

One day—I remember it perfectly, it was an April morning, the fourteenth, a Sunday—I was sitting out on the terrace, reading a book, the garden, cautiously planted for spring with yellow euphorbia, in front of me, when I felt something happen inside me. Please don't laugh. I have no wish to play Joan of Arc with you. I heard no heavenly voices. But there was a voice, a voice so strong it was like the most passionate feeling you could ever feel. The voice told me that I really couldn't go on living like this, that there was no sense in anything, that my situation was demeaning, ruthless, inhuman. I had to change. I had to perform a miracle. There are dizzying moments in life when we see everything clearly, when we are aware of our power and our potential, when we see what it is we have been too timid or cowardly to do. These are life's decisive moments. They come to us unannounced, like death or conversion. This was one of them.

I shuddered. My whole body tingled: it was like goose pimples. I started to feel cold.

I looked at the garden and my eyes filled with tears.

What was it I was feeling? I felt that I was responsible for my own fate. That my life depended on me. There was no point in waiting for some angelic visitation either in my personal life or in any relationship.

My husband and I had a problem of some sort. I don't understand my husband. He doesn't belong to me, doesn't want to belong entirely to me. I knew there was no other woman in his life . . . I was pretty, young, and I loved him. Lázár was not the only powerful figure in his life, the only one with powers. I had powers of my own. I should use them.

I felt such absolute power surge through me, I could have killed someone or built a whole new world with it. Maybe it is only men who truly feel such power and are conscious of it at the decisive moments of their lives. We women are generally terrified and paralyzed at such times.

But I had no intention of backing down. That day, on Sunday, the fourteenth of April, a few months after the child's death, I made the one and only fully conscious choice in my life. You needn't look at me with those big frightened eyes of yours. Listen carefully. I'll tell you what happened.

I decided to take possession of my husband.

Why aren't you laughing? You mean it's nothing to laugh at? I didn't feel like laughing, either. The prospect of the task daunted me. I was so frightened, I was quite out of breath at the thought. Carrying out this task was the meaning of my life, I thought. I couldn't hold back any longer. There was no way of leaving it for time or chance to sort out; I simply couldn't wait for something to happen, couldn't just accept the alternative of going on as I was until it did. I knew right then that it wasn't I who had decided on a course of action: the action had decided me. My husband and I were engaged in a life-or-death struggle, but we couldn't be separated until something of devastating power came between us. Either this man was going to come back to me, body and soul, without reserve or shame, or I would leave him. He had a secret I knew nothing about and I would get it out of him even if I had to dig it out, tooth and nail; even if it was buried deep beneath the ground like a long-buried bone the dog digs up, or like a body some mad lover wants to disinter. It was either this or I move on. Things could not go on the way they were. It was exactly as I said: I decided to take possession of my husband.

Put it like that and it sounds simple enough. But you're a woman too, so you know it is one of the hardest tasks you can undertake. Sometimes I think it's the hardest of all.

You know how it is when a man decides to do something and over-comes every obstacle, anything that might prevent him carrying out his plan and imposing his will . . . well, yes, this was that kind of situation, that state of mind. Those we love are the world. When Napoleon—about whom I know little more than that he was master of the world for a while and had the duc d'Enghien killed, and that doing that was more than a sin; it was a blunder—have I mentioned that before? What I mean to say is that when Napoleon decided to conquer Europe, his decision was no more momentous than mine was then. It was what I vowed to do that breezy Sunday in April.

An explorer might feel something of the sort when he decides to go to Africa or to the North Pole, caring little about what wild animals or climate he might encounter there, if in so doing he might discover something, find something previously undiscovered or unknown, something no explorer had ever come across before . . . Yes, the project of a woman setting out to discover a man's secret is as enormous as that. But she will get that secret even if she has to go through hell for it. That was what I had decided to do.

Or it could be that it was my decision that decided *me* . . . you never really know how these things happen. People do whatever circum-stances allow them to do. It's like being a sleepwalker, a water diviner, the local witch doctor, someone the tribe avoids out of a superstitious awe. And not just the tribe, either, but the authorities too, because there is something frightening in their eyes, something not to be trifled with. It's as if there were a kind of sign on their brow to show that they are about a uniquely dangerous business and will not rest until it has been completed . . . That was how I felt when, having realized the situation and made a conscious decision, I waited for him to come home that day. That was my state of mind at noon when he returned from his Sunday stroll.

He had been down the valley, walking that dog he was so fond of, the tan-colored Vizsla he took wherever he went. He opened the garden gate and came in. I watched him, arms folded, from the top step of the veranda. It was spring, the light was strong, and the breeze that was tossing the boughs was ruffling my hair. I will never forget that moment, the cold light on the distant landscape, on the garden, and in me too. I felt possessed.

Master and dog came to a wary, involuntary stop, the way people instinctively do when confronted by anything strange, somewhat on the defensive. "Come on, then," I thought calmly. "Come on, all of you—other women, friends, childhood memories, family, the whole hostile human world—come on. I am going to take this man from you." So we sat down to eat.

After lunch I had a slight headache. I went to my room, drew the curtains, and lay down, remaining there till the evening.

I am not a writer, like Lázár, so I can't describe my condition that afternoon, what I was thinking, what thoughts ran through my head . . . All I could see was the task ahead; all I knew was that I could not afford to be weak, that I had to do what I had decided to do. At the same time I knew that no one could help me, that I had no idea how to go about it or where to begin . . . You understand? There were moments I thought I was being ridiculous letting myself in for such an impossible task.

"What can I do?" I kept asking myself over and over again. I mean, I couldn't write to the newspapers asking for advice and encouragement, signing myself "Cheated Wife." I know those kinds of letters and the answers they receive from editors, encouraging the cheated woman not to give up, saying her husband is probably laden down with work, that she should look after the house, use this or that ointment and powder at night because that will keep her looking fresh, and her husband will fall in love with her all over again. Well, that sort of thing would not help me. I knew ointments and powders would not do the trick. And anyway, I had always done a first-rate job of housekeeping, everything in the house being absolutely where it ought to be. And I was beautiful then too, more beautiful that year than ever, perhaps. You goose, you silly goose, I thought, even to think of this. This was something altogether different.

There were no soothsayers or sages I could consult on the matter, I could not write to famous writers for advice, nor was it something I could openly discuss with women friends or members of the family—not this apparently unimportant issue that was nonetheless of ultimate importance to me, which was: how to take possession of a man . . . My mild headache had become the usual raging migraine by the evening. But I took two doses and said nothing to my husband, going out to the theater, followed by supper.

The next day, Monday the fifteenth of April—you see how precisely I remember these days; it's a matter of life or death remembering such things!—I woke at dawn and went down to that little church in the Tabán district I had last visited some ten years before. My usual church was the one in the Krisztina where we also got married. It was where Count István Széchenyi vowed to be true to Crescence Seilern. If you didn't already know that, I am telling you now. The marriage, they say, was not a great success. Not that I believe in such tittle-tattle, but people must always be gossiping.

The church in the Tabán was completely empty that morning. I told the sacristan I wanted to make a confession. I waited for a while in one of the pews of the dimly lit church. Eventually an old, unfamiliar, solemn-looking, white-haired priest appeared, entered the confessional box, and gestured for me to enter and kneel. It was to this unknown priest whom I had never seen before, nor have seen since, that I revealed everything.

It was a confession the like of which you make only once in your life. I spoke of myself, the child, my husband. I confessed I wanted to regain my husband's heart and that I didn't know what to do, that I was calling on God to help me. I told him I had led a moral life, that I never even dreamed of any lover but my husband. I told him I didn't know where the fault lay, in me or in him . . . In other words, I told him everything. Not as I am telling you now. I couldn't talk about everything now, I would even be wary of doing so . . . But in that dim church, that morning, before that unfamiliar old priest, I stripped my soul bare.

The confession took a long time. The priest listened.

Have you visited Florence? Do you know Michelangelo's statue—you know, that wonderful sculptural group with four figures in the Duomo . . . wait a minute, what is it called? Yes, the *Pietà*. The main figure is a self-portrait, the elder Michelangelo. I was there once with my husband; it was he who showed me the statue. He said that the face there was a human face without desire, without anger, a face purged by fire, one that knew everything and wanted nothing, not even revenge, not even to forgive—nothing, absolutely nothing. Standing before the statue, my husband told me that was what we should be like. That this was ultimate human perfection, this sacred indifference, this absolute solitude and deafness to both joy and sorrow . . . That's what he said. As

I was confessing, I stole the odd glance at the priest's face and with tears in my eyes I saw how terrifyingly similar his face was to the marble one in the *Pietà*.

He was sitting with half-closed eyes, his arms folded across his chest. He hid his hands in the folds of his habit. He wasn't looking at me. His head was slightly tipped to one side, listening almost like a blind man, keeping strangely silent, as if he weren't listening at all. It was as if he had heard all this many times before; as if he knew that everything I said was superfluous and hopeless. That was how he listened. He listened hard, gave me his complete attention, his entire strange, squat being. And his face, yes . . . his face was that of someone who knew it all anyway, who knew everything, having heard all kinds of people talk about their suffering and misery, and he still knew something more that could not be said. When I finally stopped, he remained silent for a while.

"You have to believe, child," he said eventually.

"I do believe, Most Reverend Father," I mechanically replied.

"No," he said, and that calm, almost dead-looking face began to come alive, his watery old eyes briefly flashing. "You have to believe differently. Don't spend your time concocting schemes. Just believe. That's all you have to do. Believe," he muttered.

He must have been very old by then, and my long speech must have exhausted him.

I thought he didn't want to, or could not, find anything else to say, so I waited for my penance and absolution. I felt we had nothing more to say to each other. But after a long silence, just as he seemed to be nodding off, he opened his eyes wide and began to talk animatedly.

I listened to him and was filled with amazement. No one had talked like that to me before, certainly not at confession. He spoke in simple words in a natural conversational tone, as if he were not in a confessional box but holding forth in company somewhere. He spoke in simple words, without unctuousness, sighing occasionally as though lamenting, like a kindly, very old man. He spoke as naturally as if the whole world were God's church and all things human belonged to God, so one didn't have to put on special airs for God, turn eyes to heaven or to beat one's breast, only to tell the truth, but the whole truth, the full truth . . . That's how he talked.

Talked, I said? I tell you, he not so much talked as chatted in a relaxed low voice. His accent sounded faintly Slavic. The last time I heard that lilt, that regional dialect, was in Zemplén in my childhood.

"Dear soul," he said. "I would like to help you. Once, a long time ago, a woman came to me who was in love with a man so much she killed him. She did not kill him with a knife or poison, but with her love, because she wanted that man completely, because she wanted to remove him from the world. They fought a great deal. The man got so tired of this that one day he died. The woman knew this. He died because he had had enough of fighting. You know, my daughter, people exercise various forms of power over each other. They have many ways of killing each other. It is not enough to love, dear soul. Love can take a very selfish form. One must love humbly, with faith. Life as a whole only makes sense when there is faith. God gave people love so they might bear the world and each other. But those who love without humility place a great burden on the beloved's shoulders. Do you understand, child?" he asked so tenderly he was like an old teacher teaching a child the alphabet.

"I think I understand," I said, a little frightened.

"You will understand it eventually, but you will suffer a great deal. Passionate souls like yours are proud and suffer greatly. You say you want to possess your husband's heart. You also say your husband is a genuine man, not a fickle womanizer but a serious, pure-hearted man with a secret. What could that secret be? That is what you are determined to find out, dear soul; it is what you want to know. Don't you know that God gave people individual souls, each his or her own? Each soul is full of secrets, each as great as the universe. Why do you seek a soul that God has created secret? It may be the meaning, the mission of your life to put up with it, to bear it. Who knows, perhaps you might injure your husband in the process, even ruin him if you succeeded in laying his soul bare, if you forced him to adopt a life, or to assume feelings, that he feels bound to resist. One shouldn't love by force. The woman I was talking about was young and beautiful, like you, and did all kinds of stupid things to recover her husband's love; she flirted with other men to make him jealous, she lived a fast life, tried to make herself still more beautiful, spent a fortune on Viennese outfits, high-fashion dresses, the way unfortunate women sometimes do when there is no faith in their hearts and they lose their spiritual balance. That having failed, she rushed out into the world, to clubs, to parties, everywhere where there are crowds and bright light, where people seek to escape the emptiness of their lives and their vain and hopeless passions, places where people go to forget. How hopeless it all is," he said quietly, almost to himself. "There is no forgetting."

That's how he talked. I was all ears now. But it was as if he hardly noticed I was there. He was muttering away as if to someone else, the way old people mutter. It was as if it were the world he was trying to convince. Then he went on:

"No, there is no forgetting. God will not allow us to forget the questions life poses to us in a storm of passion. You are in a fever, child. A fever of vanity and selfishness. It may be that your husband's feelings toward you are not precisely what you would have them be; it may be he is simply a proud or lonely man who cannot, or is afraid to, show his feelings, because they were badly wounded once. There are many such wounded people in the world. I cannot absolve your husband, dear child, because he too lacks humility. Putting two such proud people together can lead to a lot of suffering. But there is such greed in your soul at the moment it reminds me of sin. You want to dispossess another man of his soul. That's always the case with lovers, it's what they want. And that is a sin."

"I didn't know it was a sin," I said, still kneeling, and started to shiver and tremble.

"It's always a sin when we are not satisfied with what the world freely offers us, when people offer us something of themselves, when we greedily want to rob them of their secrets. Why can't you live more modestly? With fewer emotional needs? . . . Love, real love, is patient, dear child. Love is endlessly patient and can wait. The course you have embarked on is impossible and inhumane. You want to take possession of your husband. But that is after God has arranged your mortal life to be the way it is. Can you not understand that?"

"But I am suffering, Most Reverend Father," I said, and was afraid I might burst into tears.

"Then suffer," he replied quite flatly now, almost indifferently.

"Why do you fear suffering?" he asked after a while. "Suffering is a fire that will purge you of greed and vanity. What is happiness? . . . And what gives you the right to be happy? Are you sure that your desire and love are so selfless they deserve happiness? If they were, you would not be kneeling here now, but would be living the life intended for you, going about your tasks, willing to do what life bids you do," he said sternly, looking hard at me.

It was the first time he had looked at me with those small, bright, glittering eyes. Having done so, he immediately turned away and closed them.

Then, after a long silence, he spoke again.

"You say your husband is angry with you because of the child's death?"

"That's what I feel," I answered.

"Yes," he said, and turned the matter over in his mind. "It's possible."

It was clear the proposition did not take him by surprise; that he thought almost anything was possible where relationships between people are concerned. Almost as an incidental afterthought, he asked me:

"And you have never blamed yourself?" His voice was flat again, mere conversation.

His accent was marked, a little Slovakian. I don't know why, but his regional accent was almost consoling in that moment.

"How can I answer such a question, Reverend Father? Who can answer a question like that?"

"Now look here," he suddenly said, so informally, so gently that I wanted to kiss his hand. He spoke with zeal, in the simple rural manner that only old village priests can manage. "I can't know what is hidden in your soul until you tell me, and what you have confessed to me today, child, is just some kind of strategy or ploy. But what God is whispering in my ear is that it is not the whole truth. What he is whispering is that you are full of self-accusation on this or that count. I could be mistaken, of course," he added to excuse himself, and suddenly stopped there and fell silent. I could see he was regretting something.

"But that's good," he said after a while, his voice faint, almost shy. "If it is self-accusation, it is good. Because then you might eventually be healed."

"What should I do?" I asked.

"Pray," he simply said. "And work. That is what religion commands us to do. I know no more than that. Are you sorry for your sins? Do you regret them?"

"I am sorry and do regret them," I garbled.

"Five Our Fathers and five Hail Marys," he said. "I absolve you."

Then he began to pray. He wanted to hear no more from me.

Two weeks later, one morning, I found the lilac ribbon in my husband's wallet.

Believe it or not I never went through my husband's wallet or pockets. I never took anything from him. He gave me everything I asked for, so why should I steal? I know, many women steal from their husbands out of a sense of obligation, almost as an act of virtue. Women generally do a great deal in the name of virtue. "I'm not that kind of tramp," they say, and get on with doing that which they have no taste for. But I am not that sort. I'm not boasting, I'm simply not.

And I was only looking into his wallet that morning because he rang to say he had left it at home and was sending one of his clerks for it. That's no reason, you will say, of course. But there was something odd about his voice, something hurried, almost excited. He sounded anxious on the phone. You could tell from his voice that this little act of forgetfulness meant something to him. This is the kind of thing a person hears not with the ears but with the heart.

It was the crocodile-skin wallet he was carrying just now, the one you've just seen. Did I tell you I gave it to him? . . . He faithfully used it too. Because I should tell you quite clearly, that man was faithful and true. He kept faith, even with mere objects. He wanted to keep and look after everything. It was the bourgeois in him, the noble bourgeois. Nor was it only objects he wanted to preserve, but all he found delightful, beautiful, valuable, and meaningful in life—you know, the lot: good habits, ways of doing things, furniture, Christian ethics, bridges, the works people had constructed with enormous labor, ingenuity, and suffering, geniuses and laborers both . . . And it was all part of the same thing to him: he loved this world and wanted to preserve it from danger. Men call this culture. We women don't use big words like that when talking to each other. It's enough to remain wisely silent once they start quoting Latin. We know the true essence of things. All they know are concepts. The two are usually quite different.

But back to the crocodile-skin wallet. He looked after that too, because it was beautiful, because it was finely made, and because I gave it to him. When it needed mending, he had it mended. He was a stickler for detail. One time he said—laughing as he said it—that he was a true adventurer, since you could only have adventures if you had order about you and took care of things . . . You are amazed? Yes, I was often amazed when he talked like that. Living with men is very difficult, darling; they have souls, you see . . .

Would you like a cigarette? . . . I'm going to light one, because I feel a bit agitated. Remembering that lilac ribbon always brings back that tremulous, anxious feeling.

As I was saying, there was something about his voice that day. He wasn't in the habit of phoning home about such minor matters. I offered to take it in to the factory myself at lunchtime, if he needed it. But he thanked me and rejected the offer. "Put it in an envelope," he said. "The clerk will be there in no time."

So now I set to examining the wallet, every last little nook and cranny of it. It was the first time in my life I had done something like that. Believe me, I was pretty thorough.

The outermost section had money in it, his Institute of Engineers card, 8 ten-fillér stamps and 5 twenty-fillér ones, and besides that there was his driver's license and a season ticket for the baths, complete with photograph. The picture had been taken ten years ago, just after a haircut, when men tend to look ridiculously younger than they are, as though they had just failed their school exams. Then there were a few of his calling cards, with just the name, no crest, no position. He was very particular about such things. He would not have any heraldic device stitched into his linen or engraved on the silver. It was not that he despised them, but that he was careful to conceal them from the world. There was only one kind of rank among people, he used to say, and that was character. He would come out with things like that sometimes, matters of pride and sensitivity.

There was nothing important in the outer pockets of the wallet. It was all very orderly, like his whole life, like the drawers of his desk, like his wardrobe, like his notes. There was always order around him, so, naturally, there was order in his wallet too. Maybe it was only his heart that was not completely in order, that did not work in perfect harmony, you know . . . people who are very particular about external order may be covering up real disorderliness inside. But this was no time for meditation. I burrowed my way through his wallet like a mole through crumbling earth.

In the innermost pocket I found the photographs, including the child's photograph. The boy was just eight hours old in the picture. He had a lot of hair and, wouldn't you know it, he was clenching his little fists and raising his arms. He was three kilo eighty and fast asleep . . . That's when they took the picture. How long do you think that goes on hurting? As long as we live? That's what I think.

That was what mattered to me most when I searched through the innermost pocket of that wallet; that and the lilac ribbon.

I took the ribbon out, felt it, and, naturally, sniffed it. It had no smell. It was an old ribbon, dark lilac. It smelled of crocodile skin. It was four centimeters long—I measured it—and one centimeter wide. It had been tidily cut with a pair of scissors.

I was so frightened I had to sit down.

I stayed sitting like that with the ribbon in my hand, my heart still firmly resolved to possess my husband, to conquer him the way Napoleon wanted to conquer England. I sat like that, badly shaken, as if I had just read that my husband had been arrested on the outskirts of town because he had robbed or killed someone. I was like that woman married to the "Monster of Düsseldorf" who discovered one evening that the police had taken her husband away because that hearty fellow, that exemplary father, a man who paid his taxes on the button and who liked to go out for a drink after supper, tended to disembowel people he met on the way. It was like that for me the moment I spotted and took out the lilac ribbon.

You think I was being hysterical? No, darling, I'm a woman: both criminal and master detective, both saint and spy, everything at once when it comes to the man I love. I'm not ashamed of it. That's the way God made me. That is my mission on earth. The room was spinning around me. There was good reason for it to be spinning—several good reasons, in fact.

One reason was that I knew nothing about the ribbon, had never

seen it before. Women just know such things. I'd never worn such a ribbon ever, on any dress or hat of mine. I made a point of not wearing
such solemn, funereal colors. That much was certain, no point going on
about it: the ribbon had nothing to do with me. It wasn't a ribbon my
husband had snipped off any hat or dress of mine so that he might trea-
sure it as a token of me. More's the pity, I thought and felt.

Another reason—and this is why I felt pins and needles in both hands
and feet—was because the ribbon was not only not mine, it was not my
husband's, either. What I mean is, whatever object, whatever material a
man like my husband holds in such high regard that he keeps it in his
wallet for years, that he rings home about from the office in excitement—I hardly need say it was the ribbon he was ringing about, since
he wouldn't have felt a burning need for money or calling cards, or
proofs of membership, not in the morning, in the factory—that object
was more than a souvenir or memento to him. No, this was criminal
evidence. Hence my numbness.

What it meant was that my husband was carrying round some kind
of token that was of more importance to him than I was. That was what
the lilac ribbon meant.

Could it have meant something else? The ribbon hadn't faded, simply looked a little worn in the peculiar way dead people's possessions
often do. Have you noticed how the hats and handkerchiefs of the dead
tend to age, practically from the moment the wearer dies? They lose
color somehow, like leaves torn off the branch, and the green begins
immediately to fade as green watercolor does . . . It seems there is a certain electricity that runs not only through people but also through all
their belongings; something that radiates the way the sun does.

The lilac ribbon was barely alive in those terms. It was as if it had
been worn a very long time ago. The person who'd worn it might
already be dead . . . or at least dead to my husband. That's what I was
hoping. I gazed at it, sniffed it again, rubbed it between my fingers,
questioned it . . . but the ribbon did not give up its secret. It remained
obstinately silent, with all the defiance of an inanimate object.

And yet at the same time it was perfectly alive. It was superior, dense
with schadenfreude. It was as if a mischievous goblin had stuck out its
apoplectic lilac tongue to mock and ridicule me. What it said in goblin
language was: "See, I have ventured behind the neat, well-arranged

façade of your life. I had an existence then and continue to exist now. I am what is hidden, the secret, the truth."

Did I understand what it was saying? . . . I felt so agitated, so cheated, so shaken! Such fury and curiosity burned in me that I would not have balked at rushing into the street to find the woman who had once worn it in her hair or her corset . . . I was red with fury at being so insulted. See, even now my face is quite hot, flushed and red, just thinking of the lilac ribbon. Wait, lend me a little powder, let me make myself presentable.

There. Thank you, I feel better now. Well, the clerk soon appeared and I tidily put back everything in the wallet: the calling cards, the proofs of identity, the money, and the lilac ribbon that was so important to my husband that he rang home excitedly from the factory in the morning and had to send a clerk for it . . . And then I stood there, the great decision made in my heart, blazing with indignation, understanding nothing of life.

Or to be more exact, I did know something about it.

My husband was neither an oversensitive youth nor a pathetic, aging lecher. He was a mature man, so his actions were rational and comprehensible. He was not the sort to carry a woman's lilac ribbon around in his wallet in secret without having a reason for it—that much I understood. If that was the secret, I understood it as perfectly as we do the secrets of our own lives.

So if he does something like this, if he carries a sentimental trifle around for years, there must be a serious, proper reason for it. In which case the person to whom this little rag once belonged must be of supreme importance to him.

More important than I was, for sure. He didn't carry my photograph around. You might say—I can see you are about to say it even though you're keeping quiet—that he didn't need a photograph of me because he saw quite enough of me, day and night. Yes, but that's never enough. He should see me even if he is not there beside me. And should he reach for his wallet, it should be to take out my photograph rather than some other woman's lilac ribbon. Don't you think? . . . There you are, you see. It's the least a man can do.

There I was, smoldering, as though someone had set fire to my quiet family home with a careless match. Because whatever lay there behind the façade of our lives, whatever might have happened, it was still a solid and substantial thing, a genuinely mutual form of life, complete with roof and foundation . . . It was the roof that single burning match had landed on.

He didn't come home for lunch. We had a dinner invitation. I dressed to kill that night, straining every sinew to be beautiful. I wore a white dress, the one I kept for grand occasions. It was made of silk, like a wedding dress. It was ceremonial and dignified. I spent a whole two hours at the hairdresser in the afternoon. And even then I did not sit on my laurels but went into town to buy a rosette made of lilac ribbon, a ribbon in the shape of a violet, a sweet, idiotic little trifle of the kind quite fashionable that year. You could get it in various shapes and sizes. I pinned the ribbon, the color of which was precisely the same shade as the ribbon my husband carried around in his wallet, to the white dress, just where it opened. I took such care dressing for the evening I might have been an actress at a premiere. By the time my husband arrived home I was in my fur stole. He changed quickly, because he was late. Just this once it was I waiting patiently for him.

We sat in the car without speaking. I could see he was tired, his mind elsewhere. My heart was beating fast but at the same time I felt a terrifying, solemn calm. All I knew was that that evening would decide the course of my life. I sat beside him graciously, my hair beautifully arranged, in my blue-fox fur and white silk dress, scented and deathly serious, the bunch of lilac ribbon right above my heart. It was a grand house we were visiting, with the Swiss guard at the gate and footmen down the hall. Having taken off his coat and handed it to the valet, he glanced at the mirror, saw me there, and smiled.

I was so beautiful that evening that even he noticed.

He threw off his undercoat and adjusted his tie in the mirror with a distracted, slightly nervous movement, as though he were disturbed by the solemn-looking valet's presence. Men who dress quickly and don't particularly care about clothes tend to fiddle with their bow ties, because they are forever slipping to one side or another. He gave me a smile in the mirror, a very sweet, courteous smile, as if to say, "Yes, I know you are very beautiful. Maybe the loveliest of all women. The trouble is that that doesn't help. The problem lies elsewhere."

But he didn't say anything. I, for my part, was wondering whether I was more beautiful than that other woman, the one whose ribbon he so carefully looked after. Then we entered the grand hall, where a whole host of guests were already assembled: famous men, politicians, the leading figures of the country as well as well-known beautiful women, all chatting to each other as though they were relatives, as though whoever they were talking to already knew everything, everything that had been hinted at and suspected, all of them fully initiated. Initiated into what? Into the delicate, decadent, exciting, stuffy, superior, hopeless, cold conspiracy that constitutes an entire world, the world of society. It was a vast hall with columns of red marble. Between the guests scuttled servants, their legs clad in britches and white stockings, bearing crystal trays loaded with cocktails and highly colored, bitter-as-poison liqueurs. I merely sipped at one of those bitter drinks, because I can't take alcohol: it immediately makes me feel dizzy. In any case I had no need of intoxicants that evening. I felt an irrational, ridiculous, quite childish sort of tension, as if fate had marked me out for a difficult personal task, as if everyone were watching me, particularly me, all these beautiful, interesting women and those clever, powerful men . . . I was continually giggling. I was very charming to everyone, behaving as if I were an eighteenth-century princess in a powdered wig. And you know what? People really were talking about me that evening . . . It's impossible to resist life radiating from someone in my position. Suddenly I saw myself standing among the red marble columns in the middle of the hall with men and women standing around me, myself as the focal point, people bowing to me, my every remark a triumph. I was radiant with a terrifying confidence that night. Oh yes, I was a real success . . . But what is success? Success is willpower, or so it seems: an enormous willpower, which burns everything and everyone that comes into contact with it. And all this simply because I had to know whether there was anyone anywhere who had once worn a lilac ribbon on her dress or her hat, someone who might matter more to my husband than I did . . .

I had never touched cocktails before and I left them alone that night too. Later, at supper, I drank half a glass of acrid French Champagne. I was behaving as though I were a little tipsy . . . but in a strangely sober fashion; it was a clearheaded kind of intoxication.

We were waiting for supper to be set and had formed groups in the hall, as on a stage. My husband was standing in the doorway to the library talking to a concert pianist. Now and then I felt him glance at me, and I knew these were anxious looks he was casting, not understanding my popularity, the sudden, complete, irrational social success I was enjoying, pleased with it but worried at the same time. He looked puzzled, and I was proud sensing his confusion. I was certain of my task now, and I knew the evening would be mine.

These are the most remarkable moments of life. Suddenly, a world opens up and everyone's eyes are on you. I would not have been surprised to have people propose to me that night. I should tell you that that world, the other world of high society and the international set, is hopelessly alien to my nature. It was my husband who introduced me to it, and I always felt stagestruck. I tiptoed through it with great care, the way you might in an amusement park, in the haunted house with the moving floors . . . I was frightened in case I should slip and fall. Whole years went by with me being overpolite and overrestrained in company, or, conversely, overnatural . . . In other words, I was scared, cold, overfriendly, in fact everything except what I really am. It was as though I were in the grip of some terrible cramp before, but that evening released me. I was no longer cramped. I saw everything through a faint mist— the light, the people's faces. I wouldn't have been surprised to find people bursting into applause for me.

Then I felt someone was staring at me. I turned round slowly and looked for the person whose gaze seemed so physical, so electric. It was Lázár. He was standing by a pillar talking to our hostess, but his eyes were on me. We hadn't seen each other for a year.

The footmen opened the mirror-covered double doors and people started filtering into the dimly lit, candle-illuminated dining hall, everyone moving as though they were part of a theatrical procession.

Lázár came over to me.

"What's the matter with you?" he asked, his voice choked back, almost formally.

"Why?" I asked, my voice a little hoarse, still dizzy with success.

"Something is different with you," he said. "I just wanted to say I am sorry now for the cheap trick we once played on you. Do you still remember it? . . ."

"I remember," I said. "Please don't give it a thought. Geniuses love to play."

"Are you in love with someone?" he asked, perfectly calm, perfectly serious, looking me straight in the eye.

"Yes," I replied just as calmly, just as solemnly. "With my husband."

We were standing in the doorway of the dining hall. He looked me over from head to foot. Very softly and with enormous sympathy, he whispered:

"Poor soul."

Then he gave me his arm and led me to the table.

He was one of my neighbors at supper. The other was an aged count who had no idea who I was and kept paying me overblown compliments. Next to Lázár, on his left, was seated the wife of a famous diplomat, who spoke only French. The food too was French. Between courses and pieces of French conversation Lázár turned to me and said in a very low voice, naturally, without any prevarication, as though we were simply continuing a discussion begun much earlier:

"And what have you decided to do?"

I was slowly working my way through the poultry and the sauce. I leaned over the plate with knife and fork in hand, smiled at him, and answered as lightly as if it were the merest chitchat.

"I have decided to take possession of him. I mean to take him back."

"That's impossible," he said. "He has never left you. That's precisely why it's impossible. You can take back those who have been unfaithful. You can take back those who have gone away. But those who have never really, properly arrived, that's impossible. It can't be done."

"Then why did he marry me?" I asked.

"Because he would have been lost if he hadn't."

"Lost in what way?"

"Emotionally. He felt something that was much stronger than he was and he felt unworthy of it."

"Emotionally?" I asked quietly in a level voice while still leaning over the table but so that no one else could hear me. "The emotion that bound him to the woman with the lilac ribbon?"

"What do you know about that?" he asked and sat up straight.

"Only as much as I need to know," I said truthfully.

"Who mentioned this to you? Peter?"

"No," I replied. "Don't you think we know everything about those we love?"

"That's true," he solemnly agreed.

"And you?" I asked him, astonished at my steady voice. "Do you know the woman with the lilac ribbon?"

"I . . . ?" he muttered and bowed his bald head. He looked at the plate, clearly discomposed. "Yes, I know her."

"Do you see her sometimes?"

"Rarely. Practically never." He gazed into the air above him. "It is a very long time since I last saw her."

He began drumming nervously on the table with his long, bony fingers. The diplomat's wife was asking something in French and I responded to something the old count had said; he—who knows why?—had tried to amuse me with a few Chinese mottoes. But I found it hard just then attending to his Chinese mottoes. Champagne arrived, and fruit. Once I had taken a first sip of the pale pink Champagne and the count had managed to extricate himself with some difficulty from the conversation about Chinese mottoes, Lázár turned to me again.

"Why are you wearing that lilac favor this evening?"

"You noticed it?" I asked, and picked a grape from the bunch.

"Immediately—as soon as you entered the room."

"Do you suppose Peter has noticed it too?"

"Be careful," he warned me. "That is a very dangerous game you are playing."

Like fellow conspirators we both glanced over to Peter. There was something haunting in the great hall, in the flickering candlelight, in the hushed tones of our conversation, in the words we used and even more in the mood they conjured. I sat up straight, unmoving, looking fixedly ahead, and smiled as if my neighbors at table had been amusing me with wonderful jokes and fascinating stories. Needless to say, I was interested in what was being said. Never before or since have I heard anything that interested me more than what Lázár was saying that evening.

When we rose from the table Peter came over.

"You were laughing a great deal during supper," he said. "You look pale. Would you like to come out into the garden?"

"No," I said. "There's nothing wrong with me. It's just the light."

"Come with me to the conservatory," said Lázár. "We can get some black coffee there."

"Take me along," said Peter, nervously smiling. "I could do with a laugh myself."

"No," I said. Lázár agreed.

"No. The rules of this game are different from the last. It's the two of us playing this time, and we're not letting you join in. Go and talk to your countesses."

It was at that moment my husband noticed the lilac ribbon. He blinked at it shortsightedly as was his custom and involuntarily leaned toward me as though he were examining something. Then Lázár took my arm and led me away.

I looked back from the entrance to the conservatory. My husband was still standing in the dining-hall doorway while the table was being cleared behind him, myopically staring at us. There was so much sadness, helplessness, and, yes, despair, in his face that I had to stop and look back. I thought my heart would break in the looking. Maybe I never loved him so much as at that moment.

So we sat in the conservatory, Lázár and I . . . I hope this story isn't boring you? Do say if it is. But I won't bore you much longer. That evening flashed by like a dream, you know.

The conservatory was full of scents, muggy, hot, exhausting, like a jungle. We sat under a palm and through the open door could see the brilliantly lit halls inside . . . Somewhere far off, in a corner of the third room, there was music: quiet, delicate music. Guests were dancing. There was a game of cards going on in another room. It was a grand occasion, splendid and soulless, like everything in that house.

Lázár was smoking a cigarette, listening, watching the dancers. I hadn't seen him for a year and now he seemed like a complete stranger . . . He radiated such extraordinary loneliness, he might as well have been living at the North Pole. Loneliness and calm. A sad calm. I suddenly understood that he had stopped wanting things: he didn't want happiness, he didn't want success, maybe he no longer wanted even to write. All he wanted was to know the world, to understand it, to get to the truth of it . . . He was bald and always looked as though he were politely bored. At the same time there was something of the Buddhist monk about him, his slightly slanted eyes inscrutably watching the world so you couldn't tell what he thought of anything.

Once we had drunk our black coffee he spoke.

"May I be honest with you?"

"I'm not afraid of anything," I answered.

"Listen," he said harshly. "No one has a right to interfere in somebody else's life. I'm not an exception. But Peter is my friend . . . not just in the cheap, casual sense of the word. I have very few friends. This man, your husband, has kept the magical memories of our youth, along with its secrets. What I want to say may sound a little dramatic."

I sat there serene, white as a statue, like the benevolent ruler of a tiny nation. I was carved in stone.

"Carry on," I encouraged him.

"Well, then, let me put it in the crudest possible way. Forget it!"

"That is indeed crude," I said. "But I don't understand. Forget what?"

"Peter, the lilac ribbon, and the person with the lilac ribbon. Do you understand? I'm putting it crudely, the way they do in the movies. Forget it . . . You don't know what you're doing. You are poking your fingers in a wound that had begun to heal. It no longer bleeds. The blood has started to clot. It has a very delicate crust. I've been observing your lives for five years now, watching this situation develop. You want to probe the wound now. But I warn you, if you probe it, if you scratch it with your nails, there will be blood everywhere . . . Something—indeed someone—in him might bleed to death."

"As dangerous as that?" I asked, watching the dancers.

"I believe so," he said, carefully thinking it over. "As dangerous as that."

"Then I simply have to do it," I said.

There was something in my voice, a certain hoarse ringing or tremulousness . . . He took my hand.

"Be patient. Bear with it," he pleaded. He was quite agitated now.

"No," I said. "I will not bear with it. I have been cheated for five years. It's worse for me than for women whose husbands are faithless, besotted, skirt-chasing fools. For five years I have been struggling with somebody to whom I could not put a face, someone who lives with us, in the house, like an apparition. Well, I've had enough of it. I can't help my feelings. Let my enemy be flesh and blood, not a phantom . . . You once said that the truth was always simpler than it appears."

"It is simpler," he tried to soothe me, "and infinitely more dangerous."

"Then let it be dangerous," I said. "What could be worse than living with someone who is not mine? . . . Who is harboring some memory and seeks to free himself from what he feels and remembers through me, simply because he deems the memory and feeling, that desire, to be unbefitting to him? . . . Didn't you yourself tell me that? Well, let him own up to the unbefitting desire. Let him go to her and give up his rank, his dignity."

"That's impossible," he said, his voice cracking from excitement. "He'll perish in the process."

"Either way we perish," I calmly replied. "The child died of it. I am practically a sleepwalker now. I know I'm moving toward the edge, to the border between life and death. Please don't meddle, please don't raise your voice, or I will fall. Help if you can. I joined my life to his because I loved him. I thought he loved me . . . For five years I have lived with a man who has never given me his whole heart. I've done all I can to make him mine. I struggled to understand him. I consoled myself with impossible explanations. He's a man, I said. He's proud. He's a man of his class, a lonely man. But this was all lies. Then I tried to bind him to me with the strongest possible human tie, the child. I failed. Why? Can you tell me why? . . . Is it just fate? . . . Or is it something else? . . . You're the writer, the clever man, the accomplice, the witness to Peter's life . . . why are you quiet now? Sometimes I think you had a hand in all this, in all that has happened. You have power over Peter's soul."

"I had once," he said, "but I had to share it with someone else. You should be prepared to share it too. That way everyone might survive," he said, but he was uncertain and confused.

I had never seen this apparently confident but lonely man so uncertain. The Buddhist monk was now just an ordinary man who would happily have run away rather than answer such painful, dangerous questions. But I wouldn't let him go.

"You know better than I do that there is no sharing in love," I said.

"That's a cliché," he retorted in bad temper, and lit a cigarette. "You can share anything. Especially in love."

"What remains of my life if I share?" I asked so passionately that I frightened myself. "A house? A social position? Somebody I dine with, at whose hands I receive the occasional gift of tenderness the way you give an invalid a spoonful of medicine? . . . Do you suppose there is anything more humiliating, more inhumane, than sharing this kind of half-life with somebody? When I want someone, I want all of him," I said, almost loudly.

So I went on: despairing, a little theatrical perhaps. Passion always has a touch of theatricality.

Just then someone passed through the conservatory, someone in military uniform . . . He stopped, startled, looked back, and hurried on, shaking his head.

I felt ashamed. In a quieter, more apologetic tone, I repeated.

"A whole person, someone not to be shared with others. Is that so impossible?"

"No," he said, examining the potted palm with great care. "It's simply very dangerous."

"And our lives, our life together, is that not dangerous the way it is? . . . What do you think? It's deadly dangerous," I declared, and now, having put it like that, I went pale, because I felt it was true.

"The nature of life," he replied, now courteous and cool, like someone back in his element, leaving the world of passion, returning to the milder climate of precise thoughts and concepts, employing the appropriate formulations. "Deadly dangerous is what life is. But people live with danger in various ways. There are those who live as though they were proceeding along an eternally level plain, walking stick in hand. And there are those who are constantly wanting to leap headfirst into the Atlantic. Dangers are for surviving," he said very seriously. "It is the most difficult thing, sometimes the most heroic thing, anyone can do."

There was a small fountain in the conservatory, the water warm to the hand. We listened to its living music as well as the music inside, the music of worldly fashion, a primitive belching.

"I don't even know," I said after a while, "who it is I am supposed to share him with. A person or a memory?"

"That's not important," he said, shrugging. "It's the memory of someone rather than a living being. There's nothing the other one wants, it's just . . ."

"Just that she exists," I said.

"Yes," he answered.

"In that case we have to get rid of her." I stood and started looking for my gloves.

"Of whom? The person? . . ." he asked and slowly unwillingly stood up.

"The person, the memory, the life," I said. "Can you conduct me to this person?"

"I won't," he said. We moved toward the dancers.

"Then I'll find her by myself," I said. "There are a million people in this city, several million in the country. I have no evidence to go on, only the lilac ribbon. I have never seen her photograph; I don't know her name. And yet I am as certain as a water diviner of finding water on an endless plain. Or a prospector who can feel the ore beneath his feet . . . I am absolutely sure I will find her, this someone, this memory or flesh-and-blood being who is an obstacle to my happiness. Do you doubt me?"

He shrugged. He looked at me carefully, with his sad, searching eyes.

"Maybe," he said. "I generally believe in people who let their instincts have free rein. I believe in all their miracles and mischief . . . I believe you will find someone among all those millions, who will answer your call the way one shortwave radio station responds to another. There's nothing mysterious in this. Powerful feelings reach out to each other . . . But what do you think will happen then, when you have succeeded?"

"Then?" I asked uncertainly. "Everything will be clearer then. I have to look her in the face, take stock of her . . . And if it is indeed she . . ."

"She?" he asked impatiently.

"Just she," I retorted, just as impatient. "The other one, the enemy . . . If it is indeed she who prevents my husband's happiness, if she is the reason why my husband cannot be entirely mine, because of some desire that ties him to her, some memory, some sentimental misunderstanding, whatever it is . . . well, then, I'll leave them to their fates."

"Even if it means the end of Peter? . . ."

"Too bad. If that's what finishes him off, let him lump it," I angrily replied.

We were already in the doorway of the great hall.

"He has done everything possible. You have no idea how much

effort it has been for him these past years. You could move mountains with the strength he has spent in denying that memory. I think I know everything there is to know about it. I marveled at it sometimes. He tried to do the most difficult thing in the world. Do you know what he was doing? He was consciously trying to alienate himself from his feelings. It was like someone talking and reasoning with a stick of dynamite, persuading it not to go off."

"I don't believe you," I answered in confusion. "That's impossible."

"Almost impossible," he solemnly replied. "And yet he tried. Why? . . . To save his soul. To save his self-respect, without which no man can live. And he did it for you too; and when the child came along, he did it for the child, straining every nerve and sinew . . . Because he loves you. I hope you understand that?"

"I know," I said. "I wouldn't be fighting for him if he didn't . . . But he doesn't love me completely, unconditionally. There's someone between us. Either that other person goes or I go. No doubt this person in the lilac ribbon is powerful, and terrifying? . . ."

"Should you find her," he said, blinking and looking into the far distance, "you will be amazed. You will be amazed how much simpler the truth is than you imagine, how much closer to hand, more ordinary, and at the same time more grotesque and dangerous."

"And on no condition will you tell me her name?"

He said nothing. I could tell from his eyes and voice that he was uneasy, unable to decide.

"Do you like going to your mother-in-law's house?" he suddenly asked.

"My mother-in-law?" I asked, astonished. "Of course, delighted to. But what has that to do with anything?"

"All I am saying is that Peter feels at home at his mother's house too," he mumbled. "When people are looking for something, they always look at home first . . . Life sometimes arranges things as artfully, as arbitrarily, as in detective fiction . . . You know how it is: the police are feverishly looking for clues here and there, sticking pins into the wall, while the letter they are looking for is lying in front of them, on the victim's desk. But nobody thinks to look there."

"Should I be seeking help in finding the woman with the lilac ribbon from Peter's mother?" I asked, ever more confused.

"All I can say," he answered cautiously, not looking at me, "is that before you set off into the wide world to look for Peter's secret, you should look round Peter's other home, his mother's. I am sure you'll find something there to help you. The parental home is always, to some extent, the scene of the crime. You'll find everything you need to know about a man there."

"Thank you," I said. "Tomorrow morning I will visit her and have a look around . . . Only I don't understand what I am supposed to be looking for."

"It's the way you wanted it," he said, as if disclaiming all responsibility.

The music began to howl. We entered the hall among the dancers. Men talked to me; then, after a while, my husband took my arm and led me away. We went straight home. This all happened on the fifteenth of April, on Monday evening, in the fifth year of our marriage.

I slept deeply that night. I was like a burned-out element. The electricity sometimes runs through things and burns the resistance away. The soul darkens. When I woke and went into the garden—it was early spring and the mornings were warm with a touch of the sirocco, so some days I had breakfast set in the garden—my husband had already gone. I breakfasted alone, sipping bitter tea, not feeling hungry.

There were newspapers lying on the table. For lack of anything else to do, I read one of the headlines. A small state had just disappeared off the map. I tried to imagine how the people in that foreign country might feel, waking up at dawn to discover that their lives, their customs, everything they believed or had sworn by, had disappeared from one day to the next, had ceased to matter, and that they were now on the threshold of something entirely new—maybe better, maybe worse, but something that, at any rate, was utterly different from the country they knew, which might just as well have sunk beneath the waves, and that was where they had to live thenceforth, under entirely new conditions, underwater. I thought about it, and also about myself, and what I wanted . . . What divine commandment had I received, what was the message from heaven? What was the meaning of this continuous excitement in my heart? What was my anxiety, my humiliation, my sorrow compared to the anxiety and sorrow of those millions upon millions of people who were waking this morning to find they had lost what was most precious to them, that had been the center of their lives, the sweet, secret, familiar order of their homeland? . . . But I kept leafing distractedly through the papers, unable to give world affairs my full attention. I asked myself what right I had in a world like this to worry so intensely about myself, to be so obsessed by what would happen to me and whether I had any right to care so much about my own life . . . With so many millions of people living in fear and misery, should I really be worrying about whether I really owned every last little bit of my husband's heart? What was my husband's secret, or my personal happiness, compared to the world's secrets, the world's misery? What was I doing playing detective in a world that is savage enough, frightening and mysterious enough, already? . . . But these were pseudo-questions, you know, pretenses . . . One woman's feelings don't amount to an entire world. Then I thought back to what the old priest had said, and wondered if he was right. Maybe I didn't have enough faith, enough humility . . . Perhaps there was something arrogant about me, something unworthy of a Christian, a woman, indeed of a human being; something arrogant about this crazy project, this amateur-detective attempt to scrape away the surface of a private world and reveal my husband's secret; something unworthy about trying to find that certain mysterious person with her lilac ribbon. Perhaps . . . but I was so overwrought at the time I can no longer explain my feelings clearly.

I sat in the garden, the tea got cold, the sun was shining. The birds were already restless, chattering away. Spring was coming on. I thought how Lázár didn't like the spring: all that fecundity, all those emissions, he said, affect the gastric juices and upset the balance between feeling and reason . . . That's what he said. And then I remembered all we had talked about just a few hours ago at night, with the music in the background, beside the fountain, in that rich, cold, grand house, in the suffocating jungle smells of the conservatory. I remembered, and now it seemed as though it were all just something I'd read.

Do you know the feeling you get when you are beyond pain and despair, beyond the most tragic events, and suddenly become very sober, indifferent, almost cheerful? For example, when the person you loved best is being buried, and you suddenly remember that you have left the refrigerator door open back home and the dog is probably eating the cold meat you had saved for the wake? . . . And the very moment when everyone is singing and standing around the coffin, you start arranging things, whispering, as calm as you like, something about the refrigerator? . . . Because we are quite capable of that: we live between such infinitely divided shores, in a world of such vast distances. I sat in the sunlight and it was as if I were contemplating someone else's bad luck, thinking quite coldly and rationally about all that had happened. I recalled what Lázár had said, word for word, but his words did not strike me now with the force they had then. The tension of the previous day had dissolved. I recalled sitting in the conservatory with the writer but it was as if it hadn't been me. I thought of the lilac ribbon the way you might of a piece of society gossip. By the end, the content and nature of my life might have been summed up by others over tea or supper as follows: "Do you know the Xes? . . . Yes, the industrialist and his wife. They live on the hill at Rózsadomb. Things aren't going well for them. The wife has discovered that her husband is in love with someone else. Just imagine, she found a piece of lilac ribbon in his wallet, then it all came out . . . Yes, they're separating." That would have been a way of putting it, what had happened to me, to us. How often had I heard this kind of thing about other couples, stray remarks overheard in company, and not even bothered with it . . . Could it be that one day we too would become subject to society gossip, my husband and I and the woman with the lilac ribbon?

I closed my eyes, leaned back in the sunshine and, like the wise woman of some primitive village, tried to imagine the face of the lilac-ribboned woman.

Because that face had a life—in the next street, somewhere in the universe. What did I know about her? What can we know of anyone? Five years I had lived with my husband, believing I knew everything about him, knowing his every habit, every gesture: the way he hurriedly washed his hands before meals, never even glancing at the mirror, combing his hair with one hand; the way he'd suddenly be smiling an absentminded, furious smile, never telling me what he'd been thinking of; and more—all we learn of another's body and soul through intimate contact, however frightening, indifferent, moving, depressing, wonderful, or dull that might be. I believed it was all there was to know.

Then one day I discovered I knew nothing about him . . . knew less, in fact, than Lázár, that strange, disappointed, sarcastic figure who exercised such power over my husband's soul. What kind of power? . . . Human power. It was different from mine: greater than my powers as a woman. I can't explain it, can only feel it, and have always felt it, from the moment I first saw them together. But that very same man had just told me the day before that he was now obliged to share his power with the lilac-ribboned woman . . . And now I knew that whatever wonderful or terrible things were happening in the world, it was pointless accusing myself of selfishness, lack of faith, or lack of humility, pointless comparing my problems to those of the world of nations, the problems of those millions suffering their various tragedies, because there was nothing I could do—selfish and petty as I was, obsessed and blind as I was—except get out on the street and search out the woman I had to confront face-to-face, the woman I had to talk to. I had to see her, to hear her voice, look into her eyes, examine her skin, her brow, her hands. Lázár said—and now, closing my eyes in the sunlight, I heard his voice again as clearly as if he were sitting opposite me and we were at the party with the music, back in the dizzying, unreal atmosphere of our conversation—that the truth was dangerous but at the same time far more commonplace, closer to hand, than I could imagine. What might that "commonplace" truth be? What did he mean by that?

In any case, had he suggested where to look, had he given me a clue as to where I might find her?

I decided to visit my mother-in-law that very morning and have a serious talk with her.

I was flushed with heat. Once again I felt as if I had stepped into a hot, dry stream of air. I tried to cool down by deliberately thinking rational thoughts. I was burning up the way I was that moment I first opened—oh so long ago, the same time the previous day—the secret pocket in my husband's wallet. Lázár had told me not to touch anything and to wait . . . Could it not all have been some horrific vision? Maybe the incriminating evidence, the lilac ribbon, was of less significance than I imagined? Or maybe it was just Lázár playing games again, the same peculiar, incomprehensible game he had been playing that evening some years ago? Could it be that life was no more than a terrible, extraordinary game to him, something to conduct experiments on as he pleased;

that he was a chemist working with dangerous acids and corrosives, who wouldn't care if one day he blew up the world? . . . There had been something cold about his eyes, in that ruthless, objective, calm, indifferent, and yet infinitely curious gaze of his, when he said I should go to my mother-in-law's house and "look for clues" to Peter's secret there . . . And yet I knew he was telling the truth, not playing games. I knew that the danger he warned me about was real.

There are days, you know, when one doesn't really want to leave one's room. When the sun, the stars, your environment, everything, speaks to you, when everything is pressingly relevant and wants to say something. No, not just about the lilac ribbon and what lay behind it in my mother-in-law's house or elsewhere. It's reality: the truth they're after.

Then cook came out into the garden to give me the housekeeping book and we did our sums and discussed dinner and supper.

My husband was earning a lot of money at the time, and he gave me as much as I wanted without bothering to keep track of it. I had a checkbook and could spend as and when I liked. Naturally, I was very careful, particularly at that time, to buy only the essentials. But "the essentials" is a rather general concept . . . I was obliged to notice that for me, "the essentials" meant many things that, just a few years ago, would have been mere vanity—impossible luxuries. Our fish came from the most expensive delicatessen in town, our poultry was ordered, unseen, by phone. It was years since I had visited the market either with or without cook. I couldn't tell you how much it cost for the first fruit of spring, I simply demanded the staff should buy the best and most expensive . . . My sense of reality was a little confused back then. And that morning, with the housekeeping book in my hand, the book in which that greedy magpie of a cook had scribbled whatever figures she fancied, for the first time in years it occurred to me that all the unhappiness and despair I felt, everything I took to be of primary importance, might be the product of money and the wicked, terrifying spell it exercised over me . . . I thought that if I were poor I might worry less about my husband, about myself, and about things like lilac ribbons. Poverty and sickness have this miraculous power of completely changing one's priorities; one's sentimental and psychological values go out the window. But I was neither poor nor sick in the strictly medical sense of the term. That was why I told cook:

"Prepare some cold chicken with mayonnaise tonight. But I only want breast of chicken. And lettuce salad."

Then I went into the house to dress and get out into the world in search of the woman with the lilac ribbon. That was my mission. I didn't plan it. There was nothing I specifically intended to say or do: I was simply obeying an internal command.

I was walking down the street, the sun was shining, and of course I had not the least idea where I was going or what I was looking for. I should call on my mother-in-law, I knew that much. However vague this sounds, I had not the slightest doubt that I would find the person I was looking for. The one thing I couldn't know was that Lázár, with one word, almost his last word, had already set things up, and that I would stumble on the secret straightaway: I would simply dip into the tangled web of the world and pluck it out.

And yet I felt no surprise when I found her. Such a cheap word, "found" . . . I was just an instrument then, a performer in the play of fate. Whenever I think back now, I grow dizzy and feel a deep humility. I marvel at how everything turned out to be in such remarkable order, every detail immediately and closely following the one before it, everything fitting together with pinpoint precision. It was as if it had all been arranged by someone, perfectly timed, mysterious yet reassuring . . . I really learned the meaning of faith then. I had been like those people of little faith, abandoned on a stormy sea . . . but now I discovered that the world that looks so chaotic on the surface has an inner order, an order as rational and miraculous as music. The situation of which our personal destinies were a part, the destinies of three people, suddenly resolved itself: destiny was fulfilled. And every aspect of it suddenly became beautifully clear. It was like coming upon a tree bearing poisoned fruit. I was left simply staring.

But then I believed I was the active force, busy doing something, so I did just as Lázár suggested and took a bus to my mother-in-law's house.

I thought I was simply doing a quick sweep, taking stock of the place. I might even stop there for a while to take in something of the clean air of her blameless life: it might help me recover a little from the horribly stifling experiences that had so occupied mine. I might tell her what I knew, do a little sobbing, and ask her to strengthen and console me . . . If she knew anything of Peter's past she would tell me. That's what I thought. I sat on the bus and imagined my mother-in-law's house as a sanatorium on a high mountain. It was as if I were finding my way there from a fetid marsh. That was the mood in which I rang her bell.

She lived in the inner city, on the second floor of a hundred-year-old tenement building. Even the stairwell smelled of English lavender water. I might have been in a linen cupboard. As I rang and waited for the elevator, that cool scent hit me and I felt an overwhelming nostalgia for a different life, a cooler, leaner life free of passion. My eyes filled with tears as the elevator rose. And I still didn't know that the power that had arranged all this was, in these moments, simply directing me. I rang the bell and the maid opened the door.

"What a shame," she said once she recognized me. "The dear lady is not at home."

Suddenly, with a well-practiced movement she caught my hand and kissed it.

"Please don't," I said, but it was too late. "Forget the formalities, Juditka. I'll wait for her."

I smiled at the calm, proud, open face before me. This was Judit, my mother-in-law's maid, who had been with her for fifteen years. She was a Transdanubian peasant girl and had joined my mother-in-law's household when there was still a proper staff. She was a scullery maid then, very young, maybe no more than fifteen. When my father-in-law died and they gave up the large apartment, the girl moved into the inner-city apartment with my mother-in-law. In the meantime, Judit, who in marriageable terms was an old maid of thirty by then—or even over thirty years old—had been promoted to the rank of housekeeper.

We were standing in the dimly lit hall, so Judit put the light on. The moment she did so I started trembling. My legs were shaking and the blood drained from my face, but I continued to stand up straight. The housekeeper was wearing a colored cotton-print dress that morning, and a low-cut dirndl—cheap working clothes. She wore a white head scarf. And round her pale, muscular, peasant-servant neck, on a lilac ribbon, hung an amulet, a cheap locket of the kind you get on the market.

I stretched out my hand without hesitating, without thinking, and with a single movement tore the ribbon from her neck. The locket fell to the floor and opened. You know what was the strangest thing? Judit made no attempt to pick it up. She stood erect and, with a slow, easy movement, crossed her arms across her chest. She looked down at me without moving as I bent down, picked up the locket, and examined the two photographs inside it. Both showed my husband. One of them was very old, taken about sixteen years ago. My husband was twenty-two at the time, Judit fifteen. The other was taken last year, the one he was supposed to have had done for his mother, for Christmas.

We stood there a long time, both of us quite still.

"Forgive me," she eventually said, courteously, almost grandly. "We shouldn't just be standing here. Please, do come in."

She opened the door and led me into her room. I entered without speaking. She stood on the threshold, shut the door, and firmly, quite decisively, turned the key—twice.

I had never entered that room before. Why should I have? . . . Believe it or not, I had never really studied her face before or regarded it as important.

I studied it now.

There was a white painted table in the middle of the room, and two chairs. I was weak and was afraid I might lose my balance, so I slowly made my way over to one of the chairs and sat down. Judit did not sit; she stood by the locked door, her arms folded, calm and determined, as if wanting to prevent anyone else coming in and disturbing us.

I took a good look around. I had a lot of time on my hands. I knew that every single object, each tiny scrap, was of paramount importance to me here, here at "the scene of the crime"—that's the phrase that vaguely came to mind, the phrase Lázár had used for the room where I was now sitting. It was an expression I came across each day in the papers, when they reported how the police, having arrested the criminal, would go to the scene of the crime and conduct a thorough investigation . . . I was investigating the room in exactly the same way. Something had happened here, or some place like it, many years ago, an event lost in the mists of time . . . and now suddenly here I was—judge, witness, and perhaps victim too. Judit said nothing. She did not disturb me, understanding precisely how important everything about this room was to me.

But there was nothing surprising there. The furnishings were not exactly poor, but neither were they comfortable. It was the kind of room you see in a convent, a guest room prepared for the better class of secular visitor: the copper bed; the white furniture; the white curtains; the striped peasant rug; the picture above the bed of the Virgin, complete with rosary; the little jug of flowers on the bedside table; the extremely modest but carefully chosen little decorative objects ranged along the glass shelf above the basin. Do you know what this said to me? It said: resignation. It had an air of conscious, voluntary resignation. You could practically breathe it . . . And the moment I breathed it I no longer felt angry, I felt only sadness and a deep, bottomless fear.

Of course I felt all kinds of emotions and sensations in those long minutes. I noticed everything and sensed what lay beyond each individual item, lapping at them like a sea. It was someone's fate: it was a life. Suddenly I felt scared. I could hear Lázár's sad, hoarse voice, clearly and precisely predicting that I would be amazed to find the truth much simpler, much more ordinary, but much more frightening than I ever imagined. True enough, this was all pretty ordinary. And yes, frightening too.

Wait, I want to get things properly in perspective.

Just now I was saying that I detected an air of resignation. But I observed secrecy and outrage too. Don't go away thinking this was a hovel, one of those Pest slums where poor servants find accommodation. It was a clean, comfortable room: a maid's room at my mother-in-law's could be no other. I also said it was the kind of guest room you find in a convent: little cells where the guest not only lives, sleeps, and washes, but is also obliged to consider his soul. Every object in such a place—the whole atmosphere—is a constant reminder of strict commandments issued by a superior being . . . There was no trace of perfume, cologne, or scented soap in the room. Beside the basin lay a common cake of tallow soap, the kind you use for laundry. Next to that some water for rinsing the teeth, a toothbrush, a brush, and a comb. I also spotted a box of rice powder and a facecloth of chamois leather.

That was the sum of this woman's worldly possessions. I took all this in, item by item.

There was also a framed group photograph on the bedside table. Two little girls, two spry adolescent boys, one of them in uniform, and a startled-looking older couple, a man and a woman, in ceremonial dress. In other words, the family, somewhere in Transdanubia. Next to them, fresh catkins in a glass of water.

A tangle of undarned stockings lay in a sewing basket on the table beside an out-of-date tourist brochure whose brightly colored cover showed children playing on the sandy beach of a faintly ruffled sea. The brochure looked worn, its corners turned down: you could see it had been read over and over again. And on the door there hung a maid's black working dress with a white pinafore. That was the total sum of the room's contents.

These commonplace objects implied a conscious self-discipline. You could tell from them that whoever lived here did not need to be taught order, that the order sprang from within, that she was quite capable of teaching herself. Do you know enough about servants' rooms to know what they are stuffed with? Extraordinary objects, all those things their inner lives require: fancy hearts made of candy; brightly colored post-cards; ancient, long-discarded cushions; cheap little china figurines; things thrown away by that other world, the world of their social superiors . . . I once had a chambermaid who collected boxes of the rice powder I had finished with and my empty perfume bottles; she collected this stuff the way wealthy connoisseurs collect snuffboxes, Gothic carvings, or works by the French impressionists. In the world they inhabit, these objects represent what we consider beautiful, as works of art. Because no one can live with just the bare necessities in the real world . . . we need a little superfluity in our lives, something dazzling, something that sparkles, something lovely, however cheap or worthless. Few people can live without the dream of beauty. There has to be something—a postcard, all red and gold, showing a sunset, or dawn in a forest. We're like that. The poor are no different.

But what I was confronted with, in that room behind the locked door, was not like that.

The woman who occupied this room had quite deliberately stripped away all elements of comfort, bric-a-brac, and cheap glitter. You could see she had strictly, ruthlessly, denied herself anything the world might cast away or regard as luxury. It was a severe room. It was as though the woman had undertaken certain vows to live here. But the vows, the woman, the room—none of it was welcoming. That's why it frightened me.

This was not the room of some kittenish little flirt who inherits her mistress's silk stockings and discarded clothes, secretly sprays herself with Madam's French perfume, and makes eyes at the master of the house. The woman facing me was not the normal household demon, the lower-orders lover, the alluring siren of an ailing, decadent, bourgeois home. This woman was not my husband's *sweetheart,* not even if she kept his portrait in a locket suspended on a lilac ribbon around her neck. Do you know what this woman was like? I'll tell you what I felt: I felt she was hostile but my equal. She was a woman just as passionate, sensitive, strong, worthy, vulnerable, and full of suffering as I was, as is everyone who is conscious of her rank. I sat in the chair, the lilac ribbon in my hand, unable to utter a word.

Nor did she say anything. She was not agitated. She stood up straight, as I do. She had powerful shoulders—not slender, certainly not slim, but very well proportioned. If she had walked into the house we were at last night, among all those famous men and beautiful women, people would have looked at her and asked: "Who is that woman?" . . . And everyone would have felt she was someone who mattered . . . Her figure, her bearing, was what people call regal. I have seen a princess or two in my time, but none of them had that regal bearing. This woman had it. And there was something in her eyes, in her face, something about her, in her things, in the look and feel of the room, that—as I say—frightened me. I'm reminded of the phrase I used before: conscious, voluntary resignation . . . But beneath the resignation there was a tense alertness. A readiness. Something that demanded all or nothing. A prowling, untiring instinct, instilled over years, over decades. A close attention that would never relax. Nor was the resignation humble or selfless, but proud—even haughty. Why do people jabber on about the aristocracy being proud, puffed up with self-importance? I have met a great many countesses and princesses, and not one was proud in that sense. On the contrary, they were, if anything, hesitant and a little shamefaced, like all aristocrats . . . But this Transdanubian peasant girl, whose eyes met mine so boldly, was neither humble nor shamefaced. Her gaze was cold and glittering. It was like a hunter's knife. She was self-controlled and had a clear conscience. She said nothing, she made no move, she didn't even blink. She was a woman fully aware that this was the crowning moment of her life. Her whole body, her soul, and her sense of destiny were living that experience.

Did I say a guest room in a convent? . . . Well, yes, that too. But it was also a cage, the cage of a wild animal. For sixteen years she had stalked up and down in her cage, brushing against its bars, or in another cage exactly like this. She was a refined wild animal embodying passion and patience. I had stepped into her cage and now we were watching each other. This woman wouldn't be paid off with cheap little knick-knacks. She wanted it all, life entire, destiny with all its dangers. And she could wait. She was good at waiting, I admitted to myself, and shuddered.

The locket and ribbon were still lying in my lap. I sat there, paralyzed.

"Would you please give me back the picture," she finally said.

When I made no move, she continued:

"I'll let you keep one of them, the one taken last year, if you like. But the other one is mine."

It was her property. She said it as if she were pronouncing judgment. Yes, the other picture had been taken sixteen years ago, before I had met Peter. But she already knew him then, probably better than I ever did. I took one more look at the pictures, then, without speaking, I handed her the locket.

She too looked at the pictures, checking them over attentively as if to make sure no harm had befallen them. She went over to the window and, from under the bed, brought out an old battered traveling case, found a tiny key in her bedside drawer, opened the worn case, and stowed the locket away. She did all this slowly, deliberately, without the least sign of excitement, as if she had all the time in the world. I watched her carefully and registered, as it were in passing, that just now, when she addressed me and asked for the photographs, she did not use the normal class honorifics, no "miss," no "ma'am."

There was something else I felt in those few moments. It's many years ago now and I see it all more precisely. This feeling all but overwhelmed me, telling me that everything that was happening just then was nothing out of the ordinary. It was as if I'd seen it all before. I was, of course, astonished by how right Lázár had been the previous night when he told me directly that the woman with the lilac ribbon, the finding of whom was a matter of life or death to me, would be so close, merely a few streets away, at my mother-in-law's apartment. I was astonished that she was someone I had often met and had even talked to. When I set out that morning, like a woman obsessed, to find my one and only enemy in life, I did not expect my very first venture would lead straight to her . . . No doubt about it, if someone had predicted this yesterday, I would politely have asked them to change the subject, as I don't like to joke about serious matters. But now that it had happened, I was no longer astonished. I was surprised by neither the person nor the room. All I knew about Judit before was that she had been a "splendid support" to my mother-in-law, that she was regarded as practically a member of the family, miraculous evidence of what proper training could achieve. But now I felt I knew much more about her: that I knew everything. Not in words, not intellectually. I mean by instinct, as part of my destiny: I knew everything about her, and myself, despite never having spoken to her in all these years other than bidding her good day, asking whether anyone was home or if I could have a glass of water. I must have been scared of her: her face. There was simply this woman on the other side of the tracks, going about her business, waiting and aging, as I was . . . and there I was on my side, not knowing why my life lacked something, why it was unbearable, or what to make of the feeling that haunted my days and nights, those feelings that worked their way into my bones like some wicked, mysterious radiation, the sense that things were not quite right . . . I knew nothing about my husband or Judit. But there are moments in life when we understand that the most unlikely, the most impossible, most incomprehensible things are actually the simplest and closest to hand. Suddenly life's mechanism is laid bare before us: those we considered important vanish as through a trapdoor and out of the background step figures about whom we know little that is certain but for whom—we suddenly understand—we have been waiting, as they, with their own burden of fate, have been waiting for us, for this precise moment . . .

And it was all exactly as Lázár said it would be: right on my doorstep.

The situation was that a peasant girl had been keeping my husband's photographs in a locket hanging round her neck. She was fifteen when she moved from her village into town, to work for this upper-middle-class family. Naturally, she falls in love with the young master of the house. In the meantime the young master grows up and gets married. The maid and the young master see each other occasionally but are no longer close. The class difference proves ever more a chasm between them. And time ticks on for them both. The man ages. The girl is practically an old maid. She has never married. Why has she not married? . . .

It was as if I had been thinking aloud. She answered me.

"I'll leave the house. I am sorry for the old lady, but I have to go."

"Where will you go, Juditka?" I asked, using the familiar form of her name, which seemed to come easily to me now.

"I'll go into service," she said. "In the country."

"Can't you go home?" I asked, glancing at the photograph.

"They're poor," she said without expression, quite matter-of-fact.

The word echoed in the room like a cracked bell. It was as if, ultimately, this was the reality that underlay everything we could discuss from then on. It was as if some object had flown through the room and we had both followed its path, I out of curiosity, she indifferently, without comment. The word was familiar to her.

"I don't think that will help," I said after a while. "Why should you leave? No one has harmed you and no one will. If you want to go now, why did you stay so long in the first place? Don't you see," I said, as if arguing with her, as if hitting on an important point, "that now that you have stayed so long, you might as well stay on. Nothing new has happened."

"No," she said. "I'm going."

We spoke quietly, two women together, in brief half-sentences.

"Why?"

"Because it's out in the open now."

"What do you mean?"

"I mean, he knows."

"My husband?"

"Yes."

"Did he not know till now?"

"He knew," she answered. "But he has forgotten."

"Are you sure?"

"Yes."

"And who is there to tell him seeing he has forgotten?" I asked her.

"You, ma'am," she stated quite simply.

I put my hand to my heart.

"Look here, my girl," I said. "What are you talking about? That is your fevered imagination talking. Why do you think I would tell him? What could I possibly say?"

By now we were staring at each other with undisguised curiosity, looking into each other's eyes so keenly, so greedily, we were like people who had lived together for years with our eyes closed. Now that our eyes were open, we could not get enough of what we saw. And at the same time we knew for the first time that all these years we had never been brave or honest enough to let our eyes meet. We always looked away and talked of something else. We lived in our respective spaces. It was just that both of us carried a secret, and this secret was the meaning of both our lives. And now we had admitted it.

What did she look like? Maybe I could describe her for you.

But first a glass of water, is that all right? My throat is dry. Miss, just a moment, a glass of water, please. Thank you. Look, they have started putting the lights out already . . . But there isn't much more. Would you like another cigarette?

Well, she had a wide brow, a pale, open face; her hair was a bluish black. It was pinned up in a bun, parted in the middle. She had a snub, Slavic nose. Her face was quite smooth, with fine, clearly defined features, like the face of Mary in mourning in one of those village altarpieces painted by some anonymous, traveling artist. It was a proud face, so pale it was almost white. The blue-black hair framed that white like . . . but I'm not good at comparisons. What can I say? I leave that kind of thing to Lázár. Not that he would say anything: he'd only smile, because he thinks comparisons are below him. It is facts he wants, simple sentences.

So I'll stick to plain facts, if you're not bored.

It was a beautiful, proud peasant face. In what way peasant? It just was. It lacked the patently obvious complexity of expression you invariably find on middle-class faces, that tense, vulnerable air of sourness. This face was smooth, implacable. You couldn't charm it into a smile with cheap compliments and niceties. It was a face alive with memories, memories of ages long since vanished, memories that were probably not even personal. Tribal memories. The eyes and the lips led independent lives. Her eyes were blue-black like her hair. I once saw a puma at the Dresden Zoo. Her eyes were like that.

Those eyes were staring at me now the way a drowning man might stare at someone on the shore, possibly a murderer, or a potential rescuer. My eyes are feline too, a warm light brown . . . I know my eyes were glittering too that moment, searching her face the way beams search when an army is expecting an assault. But it was her lips that were most terrifying. Soft, pouting lips. It was the mouth of a big beast that was no longer carnivorous. Her teeth were a brilliant white, strong and straight. She was clearly a powerful woman, muscular and well proportioned. And now it was as if a shadow had fallen across that white face. But she made no complaint. She answered me quietly and confidentially, in the voice not of a servant but of a woman like myself.

"There are these," she said. "The pictures. He will know now. I'll go away," she obstinately repeated, almost a little crazed.

"Could it be that he hasn't known till now?"

"Oh," she said, "it's a long time since he looked at me."

"And you always wear that locket?"

"Not always," she said. "Only when I'm alone."

"What happens when you are on duty and he is here, visiting?" I asked more confidentially. "Don't you wear it then?"

"No," she replied, equally confidentially,"because I don't want to remind him of it."

"Why not?" I asked.

"Just because," she said, and opened her blue-black eyes wide as if staring down a well, into the distant past. "Why should he remember, now that he has forgotten?"

Very quietly, I asked her, in confidence, wanting to tease out the answer:

"What, Judit? What was there to forget?"

"Nothing," she replied, cold and harsh.

"Were you his lover? Tell me."

"No, I wasn't his lover," she replied, her voice clear and strong, as if she were accusing someone.

We fell silent. There was no arguing with that voice; I knew it was the truth. And you can hate me, you can tell me I was wrong, but at the very moment I relaxed a secret inner voice told me: "It's a pity she's telling the truth. How much simpler it would all be . . ."

"So what happened? . . ." I asked.

She shrugged, clearly flustered, fury, indignation, and despair flashing across her face like lightning over a deserted landscape.

"Will Madam keep it to herself?" she asked in a cracked, raw voice, as if in warning.

"Keep what?"

"If I tell her, will she keep it to herself? . . ."

I looked into her eyes. I knew I had to be true to whatever I promised. This woman would kill me if I lied to her now.

"If you tell me the truth," I eventually said, "that will be the end of it."

"Swear," she said, solemn and uncertain.

She stepped over to the bed and took the rosary from the wall, handing it to me.

"Will you swear?" she asked.

"I swear," I said.

"That you will never tell your husband what you heard from me, from Judit Áldozó?"

"Never," I said. "I swear."

I can see you don't understand this. Thinking back on it now, I'm not sure I understand it, either. But then it all seemed so natural, so simple. . . . I was standing in my mother-in-law's maid's room, swearing to a servant that I would never tell my husband what I was about to hear from her? Is that simple enough? Yes, I think it is.

I swore.

"Good," she said, and seemed to have calmed down. "So now I'll tell you."

There was such exhaustion in her voice! She hung the rosary back on the wall. She walked to and fro, across the room, twice, her steps long and light . . . yes, very like a puma in a cage. She leaned against the cupboard. She was tall now, much taller than me. She threw her head back, folded her arms, and gazed at the ceiling.

"How did you know who it was? . . ." she asked suspiciously, with considerable disdain, talking like a cheap suburban servant now.

"I just knew," I replied in the same way. "I found out."

"Did he talk about it?"

There was a certain familiarity in that "he," but a great deal of respect too. I could see she was still suspicious, wary in case there was something not quite right behind the scenes, worried that I might cheat her. She stood there the way the accused stands before the detective or the prosecutor; there is that helpless sense of waiting and then, under a conclusive "weight of evidence," the collapse and desire to confess, but then the words stick in the throat . . . The criminal worries that the lawyer will trick him, that the lawyer doesn't really know the truth but is just pretending, that he is wheedling a confession out of him, getting at the underlying truth by pretending to be nice, using some psychological sleight-of-hand . . . But he knows he can't keep silent any longer. It's like a process that, once begun, cannot be stopped. Now he actually wants to confess.

"No," I said.

"Fine," she said, and closed her eyes for a second. "I believe you."

A moment of silence.

"All right, I'll tell you," she said, breathing heavily. "He wanted to marry me."

"I see," I said, as if nothing could be more natural. "And when was that?"

"Twelve years ago, in December. And he persisted. For two whole years."

"How old were you then?"

"Eighteen."

So my husband was thirty-six years old at the time. I carried on in my friendly way, as if nothing had happened.

"Do you have a photograph from that time?"

"Of him?" she asked, surprised. "Yes. You have just seen it."

"No," I said. "Of you, Judit."

"I have," she said sourly, more like an ill-tempered servant now. "It happens I have."

She pulled open the dressing-table drawer and picked up a school exercise book covered in checkered paper—you know, the sort we used at school for French conversation and comprehension, notes on La Fontaine, and so forth . . . She leafed through it. There were religious images, advertisements snipped from newspapers . . . I stood up and looked over her shoulder as she turned the pages.

The religious images were of Saint Anthony of Padua and Saint Joseph. But otherwise, everything in the book suggested a remote or close association with my husband. The newspaper cuttings were advertisements for my husband's factory. There was a bill for a top hat sent by a city hat shop. Then there was my father-in-law's obituary. And the announcement, on watermarked paper, of our forthcoming engagement.

She leafed through all this without emotion, a little tired, as if, having looked at such scraps often enough in the past, she was almost bored of them, yet unable to let them go. For the first time I was watching her hands: strong, bony, and long, with carefully trimmed but unvarnished nails. Long, powerful, bony fingers. With two of them she picked up one of the photographs.

"Here it is," she said with a bitter smile, the corners of her mouth turned down.

The picture showed Judit Áldozó at the age of eighteen, just the age when my husband wanted to marry her.

It had been taken somewhere in town, in a cheap studio. Gold letters on the back advertised the fact that the owner was prepared to commemorate all moments of family rejoicing. It was a conventional photograph, posed and artificial: invisible metal rods adjusted the girl's head to the required position, so that she should be looking toward something far away, her eyes startled and glazed. Judit Áldozó had braided the two bunches of her hair into a crown for the occasion, in the style of Queen Elizabeth of Habsburg. Her proud and frightened peasant face looked as if it were pleading for help.

"Give it back," she said harshly, and took it away from me, slipping it back into the checkered notebook as though hiding something private from the outside world.

"That's what I looked like back then," she said. "I'd been here three years by then. He never talked to me. Then one day he asked me if I could read. I said I could. Good, he said. But he never gave me a book. We didn't talk."

"So what happened?"

"Nothing," she said, shrugging. "That's all."

"You just knew?"

"You can tell."

"True," I sighed. "And then?"

She looked up toward the ceiling and leaned against the cupboard. There was the same glazed, slightly startled expression in her eyes as in the photograph, as if she were gazing into the distant past. "So, after three years," she said, speaking more slowly and haltingly now, "he talked to me. It was afternoon on Christmas Day. We were both in the parlor. He spoke for a long time. He was very nervous. I just listened."

"Yes?" I said, and swallowed.

"Yes," she repeated, and took a gulp too. "He said he knew it was very difficult. He didn't want me to be his lover. He wanted us to go away together, somewhere abroad. Italy," she said, and the tension vanished from her face. She smiled and her eyes sparkled as if she had really understood the full meaning of that wonderful word, as if it meant everything to her, more than anyone could say or hope for in life.

We both instinctively glanced at the cover of the dog-eared tourist brochure lying on the table, the sea slightly ruffled, the children playing in the sand . . . That was as close as she got to Italy.

"And you refused?"

"I did," she said, her expression darkening.

"Why? . . ."

"I just did," she snapped back. And then, uncertainly: "I was afraid."

"Of what? . . ."

"Everything," she said, and shrugged.

"Because he was master and you were servant? . . ."

"That among other things," she quietly agreed, and cast me a look that was almost grateful, as if thanking me for saying so instead of her, saving her the agony. "I was always afraid. But not just of that. I felt something was wrong. He was too far above me," she said, shaking her head.

"Were you afraid of your mistress?"

"Of her? . . . No," she said and smiled again. I could see she thought me a little dense, someone completely at sea in matters of the real world, so she began to explain the situation to me as if she were talking to a child.

"I was not afraid of her, even though she knew."

"Your mistress knew? . . ."

"Yes."

"Who else knew? . . ."

"Only she and his friend. The writer."

"Lázár?"

"Yes."

"Did he speak to you about it? . . ."

"The writer? Yes. I went to his apartment."

"Why?"

"Because he asked me to. Your Ladyship's husband."

The use of the term stood out, mocking and remorseless at once. What it said to me was: "To me he is 'he.' That much I know. To you he is just your husband."

"All right," I said. "In other words two people knew, my mother-in-law and the writer. And what did the writer say?"

She shrugged again.

"He didn't say anything," she said. "He just looked at me and listened."

"For a long time?"

"Long enough. He—" again that extending "he"—"wanted to talk to me, to take a good look at me. To persuade me. But he didn't say anything. There were a lot of books in the room. All those books! I had never seen so many books . . . He didn't sit down, just leaned against the stove. He just looked and smoked. He carried on looking at me till it grew dark. Only then did he speak."

"What did he say?" I asked. I could see them clearly, Lázár and Judit Áldozó, standing silently in the darkening room, struggling over my husband's soul without saying anything, with "all those books!" around.

"Nothing. He simply asked how much land we owned."

"And how much is that?"

"Eight acres."

"Where?"

"In Zala."

"And what did he say then?"

"He said, 'That is little. Four people have to live off that.'"

"Yes," I said quickly, confused. I'm not familiar with such things. But I understood enough to know that it was little.

"And then?"

"He rang the bell and said, 'Judit Áldozó, you may go now.' Nothing more. But by then I knew nothing would come of it."

"Because he was against it?"

"He and the whole world. And that's not the only reason. It was also because I didn't want to. It was like a sickness," she said, and slammed her fist on the table. I hardly recognized her. It was as if something in her had exploded. Her limbs jerked as if in an electric shock, as if a flood had hit her. Her words were quiet, but it was as if she were shouting. "The whole thing was like a sickness . . . I didn't eat for a year, only tea. But don't go thinking it was for him I starved," she quickly added, and put her hand to her heart.

"What do you mean?" I asked, astounded. "What does it mean to starve for someone?"

"They used to do it in the village, a long time ago," she said, and looked down as if it weren't quite proper to betray the secrets of the tribe to a stranger. "One person remains silent and refuses to eat until the other does it."

"Does what?"

"What the other person wants them to do."

"And does it work?"

"It works. But it's a sin."

"I see," I said, and she knew that whatever she said now it was likely that I would think she really did "refuse to eat" for my husband. "But you did not commit that sin?"

"No, not I," she quickly answered, and shook her head, blushing, as though she were confessing. "Because by that time I wanted nothing; because the whole thing was like a sickness. I couldn't sleep; I even developed a rash on my face and thigh. And I was racked with fever for a long time. Her Ladyship looked after me."

"And what did she say?"

"Nothing," she replied, dreamily reminiscing. "She wept. But she didn't say anything. When I had the fever, she fed me sweet water and medicine with a spoon. Once she kissed me," she said, her eyes gentle, as though this was the nicest thing that had ever happened to her.

"When?" I asked.

"When the young master went away . . ."

"Where did he go?"

"Abroad," she simply replied. "For four years."

I listened. That was the period my husband spent in London, Paris, in the north, and in Italian cities. He was thirty-six when he returned from abroad to take over the factory. Sometimes he talked about it: his years of wandering, he called them . . . It was just that he never told me that Judit Áldozó was the reason for his four-year absence.

"And then, before he went away, did you talk?"

"No," she said. "Because I was better by then. To tell you the truth, we only spoke once. That first time, before Christmas. That's when he gave me the locket with the photograph and the lilac ribbon. But he cut off a piece of that. It was in a box," she solemnly explained, as though this somehow changed the significance of the gift, as though every detail was very important, including the fact that the locket my husband gave to Judit Áldozó came out of a box . . . But I myself felt that every detail was of great importance then.

"And the other picture? Did you get that from him?"

"The other one? No," and she looked down. "I bought that."

"Where?"

"At the photographer's studio. It hardly cost anything," she said.

"I see," I said. "You got nothing else from him?"

"Something else?" she asked, opening her eyes wide in wonder. "Oh, yes. He gave me a piece of candied orange peel once."

"You like candied peel?"

She looked down again. I could see she was embarrassed by this sign of weakness.

"Yes," she said. "But I didn't eat it," she added, as if in mitigation. "Would you like to see it? . . . I've kept it. Wrapped in a twist of paper."

And she turned to the cupboard, keen to produce her alibi. I quickly extended my hand.

"No, Judit, leave it," I said. "I believe you. And after that? What happened?"

"Nothing happened," she said, as simply as if she were telling any old story. "He went away and I got better. Her Ladyship sent me home for three months. It was summer. Harvest time. But I was on full pay," she boasted. "Then I came back. He was away a long time. Four years. And I felt at peace again. When he came back he no longer lived with us. We never talked again. He didn't write, not once. Yes, it was a form of sickness," she declared, as if going through an argument she had had with herself a long time ago before coming to a wise conclusion that she was determined now to prove right.

"And that was that?" I asked.

"That was that. He got married. Then the child was born. Then it died. I cried my eyes out and felt sorry for Your Ladyship."

"Yes, yes. Let's drop the subject," I replied in a nervous, abstracted manner, clearly rejecting her offer of empathy. "Tell me, Judit. You say you never, but never, spoke after that."

"Never," she said, and looked me in the eye.

"Not even about that?"

"Not about anything," she solemnly affirmed.

I understood that this was the truth and that it was carved in stone. Neither of them was a liar. I began to feel sick with fear, with the shock. I felt generally unwell. There could be nothing worse than the news that they had never spoken since. That they had remained silent for twelve years: that told me everything. And all the time one of them went about with a locket round her neck with the other's photograph in it, and the other carried around a strip of lilac ribbon that he had cut away and hidden in the deepest recesses of his wallet. And one of them got married, taking me as wife, and when he came home not all of him arrived, because someone else was waiting for him. That said everything. My hands and feet were frozen. I began to shiver.

"Just answer me one more question," I said. "I am not asking you to swear to the truth of all this. As far as I am concerned, I swore not to tell my husband and I will keep my promise. So just tell me this now, Judit. Did you regret it?"

"What?"

"Not accepting his offer of marriage?"

She crossed her arms and went over to the window, staring down into the shadowy yard of the inner-city house. After a long silence, she spoke over her shoulder.

"Yes."

The word dropped between us like a bomb: it was as if someone had thrown an unexploded grenade into the room. In the silence we could hear our hearts and the invisible bomb, all of them ticking away. The bomb carried on ticking. It ticked for two whole years, and then it exploded.

There were noises in the hall. My mother-in-law had arrived. Judit tiptoed over to the door and, with one practiced movement, silently turned the key in the lock. The door opened and there on the threshold stood my mother-in-law in a fur coat with her hat on, just as she had arrived from town.

"It's you," she said, and went pale.

"We were chatting, Mama," I said, and stood up.

The three of us stood in the maid's room, my mother-in-law, Judit, and I, like the three Fates in a tableau vivant. The image suddenly came to me and, grief-stricken as I was, I gave a nervous laugh. But I couldn't go on laughing, because my mother-in-law entered the room, paler than ever, sat down on Judit's bed, covered her face with her hands, and started to cry.

"Please don't cry," said Judit. "She has sworn not to tell him."

She gave me a long, slow, lingering look, examining me from head to toe, then left the room.

After dinner I rang Lázár. He wasn't home; it was his servant who answered the phone. About half past four the phone rang: it was Lázár from town. He was silent for a while, as if he were a very long way away, in another galaxy, because he had to think very carefully about his answer to my request, which was, after all, ridiculously simple. I wanted to see him as a matter of priority.

"Shall I come over to you?" he eventually asked rather gruffly.

But there was no point, because I was expecting my husband any moment. I couldn't suggest meeting in a café or *Konditorei* either. Somewhat annoyed, he relented in the end, saying:

"If you insist, I'll go home and wait for you at the apartment."

I immediately accepted the invitation. I really didn't think much about it in the meantime. In those days generally, but particularly in the hours following the conversation in the morning, I was in such an extraordinary state of mind I seemed to be moving at the dangerous fringes of life, in a space somewhere between prison and hospital, in another world altogether, where the normal rules of life—those that govern social and domestic life, simply did not apply. Even the trip to Lázár's house felt like a strange emergency, like being in an ambulance or in a police car . . . Only once I was ringing the bell did the trembling of my hands remind me that what I was doing was something out of the ordinary, something not entirely proper.

He opened the door, kissed my hand, and without saying a word led me into a large room.

He lived on the fifth floor of a new building on the Danube embankment. Everything in the building itself was brand-new, comfortable and modern. Only the décor of his own apartment was old-fashioned, somehow secondhand and provincial. I looked around and was really surprised. However agitated and preoccupied I was, I still took it all in, and was starting to assess various details of the furnishings, because, well, you know how strange we all are, how even when we are being led off to be hanged, we carry on registering things, like a bird in a tree or a wart on the judge's chin as he reads the death sentence . . . So there I was in this apartment. It was as if I'd called at the wrong place. Deep inside me, you know, I had already imagined Lázár's den, and was expecting something exotic, something faintly Wild West, a wigwam perhaps, along with a mass of books and the scalps of his female conquests—or of his competitors. But it was nothing like that. There were bits of nineteenth-century cherrywood furniture, covered with regulation lace doilies, the sort you are greeted with out in the country—you know, those uncomfortable high-backed, fancy chairs, and the glazed sideboard stuffed with all kinds of office-clerk trash: glasses from Marienbad, Prague pottery . . . It was a room that might have been occupied by a middle-income country lawyer who had moved up to the city, whose wife had inherited the furniture and they couldn't yet afford anything new. . . But there was no sign of a woman's touch, and Lázár, as far as I knew, was quite wealthy.

He did not take me to the room with "all those books," the one in which he received Judit Áldozó. He was courteous in every way, the way a doctor is to his sick patient on a first visit. He showed me to a seat and, naturally, did not offer me any refreshment. From the beginning to the end he was attentive, correct, and reserved, as though he had seen all this before and knew, the way that doctors know when addressing a terminally ill patient, that the conversation was pointless, that all he could do was listen, politely nodding and maybe scribble some ineffective prescription, a syrup or a powder, without offering any hope . . . What did he know of the situation? Only that there was no advising people in matters of feeling. I myself suspected this in my own vague way. Sitting there opposite him, I was annoyed to realize that it had been a pointless journey. There is no such thing as "counsel" in life. Things just happen and there's an end of it.

"Did you find her?" he asked without preamble.

"Yes," I answered, since he wasn't someone who needed a wealth of explanation.

"And do you feel better and calmer for it?"

"I wouldn't say so. And that's precisely why I've come to you. I want to find out what happens next."

"I really can't tell you," he replied without emotion. "Maybe nothing. You will recall that I warned you not to pick at the wound. It had healed quite nicely. There was, as doctors say, a decent cicatrix. But now it has been disturbed. It has suffered a small cut."

The medical terms did not surprise me. It felt like a doctor's waiting room or surgery anyway. There was, I should stress, nothing in the least "literary" about this, nothing like what you might imagine being in a famous writer's apartment . . . No, everything was bourgeois, middle-class, terribly modest and orderly. He noticed my eyes flicking around. It wasn't an entirely comfortable feeling sitting opposite him, because I could see he noticed everything. I felt exposed, as if I were on an operating table. I expected it all to finish up in a book one day.

"I need a certain order around me," he explained. "People are so disorderly. Ideally one should be as orderly as a postmaster in one's affairs. I can't concentrate in a disordered environment."

He did not say what it was he could not concentrate on; probably on life in general . . . on surfaces, on depths, on the places where lilac ribbons flutter.

"I have sworn not to say a word to my husband," I said.

"He'll find out anyway," he nodded.

"Who will tell him?"

"You will. It's just not possible to keep it quiet. It's not only words that will tell him, it's your very soul. Your husband will discover everything, and soon."

He was quiet for a moment. Then, without ceremony, he almost snapped.

"What do you want from me, madam?"

"A clear and precise answer," I retorted, and it surprised me how clear and precise I could be. "You were right when you said that something in our lives would explode. Did I set it off, or was it an accident, mere chance? . . . I don't suppose it matters now. In any case, there's no such thing as chance. My marriage has failed. I fought like crazy and sacrificed my whole life for it. I don't know what I did wrong. I found a piece of evidence—a few clues. I finished up talking to someone who told me she was closer to my husband than I was."

He leaned on the table, listened, and smoked.

"Do you think this woman has left a permanent mark on my husband? Do you think she has lodged herself in his heart, in his memory, in his nerves forever? Is that what it's all about? Is that what love is?"

"Forgive me," he said courteously, but with a trace of mockery in his voice. "I am just a writer, and a male one at that. I don't have the answers to difficult questions like that."

"Do you believe," I asked, "that there is one true love that grows to dominate a person's soul so they can't love anyone else?"

"Possibly," he replied, with a proper concern, cautious like the good doctor who has seen a great deal and prefers not to give a careless answer. "Such things happen. Do they happen often? . . . No."

"What happens inside a person when they're in love?" I asked like a naïve schoolgirl. "What do they feel in their soul?"

"Feel in the soul?" he immediately answered. "Nothing. Feelings don't happen in the soul. They work through some different system. But they can pass through the soul and submerge it, the way a flood covers a floodplain."

"Could we stop the flood if we were really wise and clever?" I asked.

"Well, now," he replied, clearly interested, "that is indeed an interesting question. I've given the matter considerable thought. My answer would have to be: yes, up to a point. What I mean is . . . intelligence in itself can neither produce nor end feeling. But it can regulate. Should our feelings become a source of common danger, we might be able to contain them."

"You mean cage them up, like a tiger? . . ." I blurted out.

"Yes, a tiger, if you like," he shrugged. "Once enclosed, our poor wild feelings can stride round and round the cage, roar, grind their teeth, claw at the bars . . . but in the end they'll be broken, their fur and teeth will fall out, and eventually they'll grow melancholy and obedient. That's quite possible . . . I've seen it happen. That's the product of intelligence. You can control and tame emotions. Though one has to be careful, of course," he warned. "One mustn't open the doors of the cage too early. Because the tiger can get out, and if it is not completely tamed, it can cause a great deal of inconvenience."

"Can't you be plainer than that?" I asked. "I need to know quite explicitly."

"I can't be much plainer than that," he retorted. "You want to know if intelligence can overcome feeling. In plain words, the answer is no. But I do offer you some comfort. I suspect that occasionally, with a bit of luck, we can tame our emotions and allow them to atrophy. Take me, for example. I managed to do it."

I can't tell you what I felt at that moment, but I couldn't bear to look into his eyes. I suddenly remembered the evening I first met him and I grew quite red. I remembered that peculiar game . . . I was blushing like a schoolgirl. Nor did he look at me, but simply stood in front of me leaning against the table, his arms folded, looking toward the window as though examining the house opposite. This mutual embarrassment lasted a little while. It was the most awkward moment of my life.

"Back then, when all this was going on," I started again, gabbling nervously, wanting to change the subject as quickly as possible, "you didn't suggest to Peter that he should marry the girl, did you?"

"I was against it," he said. "I opposed it with all my heart. I was utterly against the marriage. At that stage I still had influence over him."

"No longer?"

"No."

"Does that woman have more power over him than you do now?"

"The woman?" he asked, and tipped his head back while his mouth moved silently, as if he were counting, trying to gauge the true balance of power. "Yes, I do believe so."

"Was my mother-in-law of any help then?"

He shook his head as if recalling a bad memory.

"Not a lot."

"But surely you can't imagine," I asked indignantly, "that a woman as proud, as refined, as extraordinary as she is, would have agreed to such an act of madness?"

"I don't imagine anything," he replied with care. "I only know that this proud, refined, extraordinary woman, as you put it, had lived for years in a state of suspended feeling. She lived not so much in an apartment as in cold storage. People as thoroughly frozen through as she was are readier to understand someone desperate for warmth."

"And it was you who prevented Peter warming himself—as you put it—in the fire of this strange attraction?"

"I did so," he explained, like a patient teacher, "because I don't like people who offer a certain warmth to some but roast others alive."

"Did you think Judit Áldozó was as dangerous as that?"

"In herself? . . . That is a hard question. Not in herself, probably. But the situation to which her very being might give rise: that was dangerous, yes."

"And the alternative, the situation which did then arise—you considered that less of a danger? . . ." I asked, trying to keep my voice steady.

"Easier to control, in any case," he replied.

I really didn't understand that. I listened and stared.

"I see you don't believe what a traditional, old fashioned, law-abiding man I am, madam," he said. "We writers may be the only law-abiding people on earth. The middle classes are a far more restless, rebellious bunch than is generally thought. It is no accident that every revolutionary movement has a nonconforming member of the middle class as its standard bearer. But we writers can't entertain revolutionary illusions. We are the guardians of what there is. It is far more difficult to preserve something than to seize or destroy it. And I cannot allow the characters in my books—the characters my readers love—to rebel against the established order. In a world where everyone is in a veritable fever to destroy the past and to build the new, I must preserve the unwritten contracts that are the ultimate meaning of a deeper order and harmony. I am a gamekeeper who lives among poachers. It's dangerous work . . . A new world!?" he declared with such agonized and disappointed contempt that I found myself staring again. "As if people were new!"

"And is that why you were against Peter marrying Judit Áldozó?"

"That wasn't the only reason I couldn't allow it, of course. Peter is bourgeois, a valuable member of the bourgeoisie . . . there are few like him left. He embodies a culture that is very important to me. He once told me, by way of a joke, that my role was to be the chief witness to his life. I answered, equally by way of a joke, but not altogether as jokingly as you might at first think, that I had to look after him out of sheer commercial interest, because he was my reader, and writers have to save their readers. Of course it was not the size of my readership I meant to preserve, but those few souls in whom my sense of responsibility to the world I know continues to exist . . . They are the people for whom I write . . . If I didn't, there would be no sense in anything I wrote. Peter is one of the few. There are not many left, not here, not anywhere in the world . . . I am not interested in the rest. But that was not the real reason—or to put it more precisely, this wasn't the reason, either. I was simply jealous because I loved him. I have never liked surrendering to my feelings . . . but this feeling, this friendship, was much more refined, much more complex than love. It is the most powerful of all human feelings . . . it is genuinely disinterested. It is unknown to women."

"But why were you jealous of that particular woman?" I persevered. I was listening to everything he was saying but still felt he was not being straight with me, that he was avoiding the real issue.

"Because I don't like sentimental heroes," he eventually admitted, as if resigned to telling the truth. "More than anything else, I like to see everyone and everything in its proper place. But it wasn't only the difference in class that concerned me. Women are quick to learn and can make up centuries of evolution in a few moments . . . I do not doubt that with Peter at her side this woman would have learned everything in a trice, and conducted herself as perfectly as you or I did at that grand house last night . . . Women generally are far superior in culture and manners to the men of their own class. Nevertheless, Peter would still have felt like a sentimental hero to himself, a hero who was a hero from the moment he rose to the moment he went to bed, because he was doing something the world did not approve of, embarking on a mission that is entirely human and perfectly acceptable to God and man, but one whose undertaking required him to be a hero, a sentimental hero. And that's not all. There was the woman. This woman would never forgive Peter for being middle-class."

"That I don't believe," I said, feeling stupid.

"I know different." He frowned. "But none of this resolves your problem. What was decided at that point was the fate of a condition, a feeling. What was at stake for Peter in that feeling, what it meant in terms of passion and desire . . . I don't know. But I felt the earthquake, witnessed it at its most dangerous moment. His entire being was shaken, his sense of belonging to a class, the foundations on which he had built his life and the way of life such foundations implied. One's way of life is not a purely private matter. When such a man—one who preserves and articulates the entire meaning of his culture—when such a man collapses, it is not only he who is destroyed but a part of the world to which he belongs, a world that was worth living in . . . I took serious note of that woman. It wasn't that she came from another class. It may be best for everyone, may be the most fortunate course of events, that children of different classes be swept together by the tides of some great passion . . . No, it was something in her character to which I couldn't help responding, something I could not reconcile myself to and to which I could not abandon Peter. She had a certain ferocity of will, a kind of barbaric power . . . Did you not feel it?"

His sleepy, tired eyes flashed suddenly as he turned to me. He proceeded uncertainly, as if seeking the right words.

"There are people who are possessed of a fierce primeval power, who can suck from others, from their entire environment, whatever sustenance makes life possible—just as, for example, there are certain vines or lianas in the jungle that absorb the water, the salts, the nourishment required by the great trees on which they feed, even over a length of hundreds of yards. That's just the way they are: it is their nature . . . You can argue with wrongdoers, you can pacify them, maybe even resolve some of the inner suffering that leads them to take revenge on other people, on life itself. These are the lucky ones . . . But there are other kinds, people like those vines, who are not at all ill-intentioned but simply squeeze the life out of their environment by enveloping it in an embrace so fierce and willful that it proves fatal in the end. It is a barbaric, elemental form of execution. It is rare to find it in men . . . more common in women. The power that emanates from them destroys anything that might be in their way, even strong characters like Peter. Did you not feel this when you were talking to her? It was like talking to a simoom or a tsunami."

"I was simply talking to a woman," I said, and sighed. "A very powerful woman."

"Well, that is true. Women's response to other women is quite different," he readily admitted. "Personally, I respect their power and fear it. This should make it easier for you to respect Peter. Try to imagine the kind of tide he was swimming against in those years, what strength it required for him to tear himself from the invisible embrace of this dangerous power. Because that power wanted simply everything. It wasn't a backstreet she was looking for, a two-bedroom apartment up an alley, a silver-fox wrap, a three-week vacation in secret with her lover . . . She would have wanted everything, because she was a real woman, not an imitation. Did you not feel this? . . ."

"Yes," I said. "She would rather starve."

"I beg your pardon?" he asked, and now it was he who was surprised.

"Starve," I said. "That's what she told me. It's a stupid, wicked superstition. Where people set out to starve themselves, and keep fasting until they see they are going to get their way."

"Did she say that?" he pondered. "There is such a custom in the east of the country. It is a form of will transference." He gave a sudden, nervous, ill-tempered laugh. "So there you are. Judit Áldozó is the most dangerous exponent of it. Because there are women you can take out to supper in the most glittering restaurants, where they can eat crab and drink Champagne, and they present no danger. Then there are others who would rather fast . . . they are the dangerous ones. I am still worried that you might, needlessly, have set her off. She had begun to tire . . . It was a long time since I last saw her, years ago, but then I felt that your lives, your stars, were shifting, that there was a certain indifference, a kind of sponginess . . . Because life is not all inundations and barbaric powers . . . There's more. There is a law of helplessness too. You should honor that law."

"I am in no position to honor anything," I said, "because this is not the way I want to live. I don't understand Judit Áldozó, I don't have her measure. I can't tell what she once meant to my husband or what she means to him now; I don't know what danger she presents . . . I don't believe there are passions whose embers continue burning in one's soul the whole of one's life, all smoke and the odd flicker of flame, like an underground fire down a mine . . . They may exist here and there, but I believe life can put such fires out. Don't you agree? . . ."

"Yes, of course," he replied, rather too readily, and gazed at his cigarette.

"I see you don't believe it," I continued. "Well, I might be wrong. Maybe certain passions are stronger than life or meaning or time. Everything gets burned, everything is consumed in fire . . . Maybe . . . In that case, let them really burn. No more lapping flames but a proper inferno. I don't want to build a home at the foot of a volcano. I want peace, and calm. That's why I'm not sorry this has happened. The way things are, my whole life is an unbearable failure. I have powers of my own; I can wait and exercise my will as well as Judit Áldozó, even if I have to starve myself to no purpose, for no one; even if I carry on eating my supper of cold chicken with mayonnaise . . . I want an end to this unspoken rivalry, this ridiculous duel. You have been a second in the contest; that's why I am talking to you. Do you think Peter still has feelings for this woman?"

"I do," was his unvarnished reply.

"In that case he has no real feeling for me," I said, loudly but calmly. "Then let him do something about it; let him marry her or not marry her, let them ruin each other's lives or let them prosper, but let him find his own peace. I don't want to live like this. I swore to this woman that I would not tell Peter, and I will keep my promise. But I won't be upset if you, on a suitable occasion, in the not-too-distant future—say, in the next few days—should tactfully, or not so tactfully, discuss this with him. Would you do that?"

"If that's what you want," he agreed, without much enthusiasm.

"I very much want it," I said, and stood up, pulling on my gloves. "I see you would like to know what will become of me," I continued. "I will tell you. I will abide by whatever decisions are taken. I don't like dumb shows that go on for decades; I don't like confrontations with unseen opponents hovering in a state of pale, bloodless tension. If there must be a scene, let there be a good loud scene, complete with blows and corpses, with applause and whistling. I want to know who I am supposed to be, what my role is in this drama and what I am worth. If my role is to fail, I will leave the stage. Let things be as they must be. I will take no further interest in Peter's life nor in Judit Áldozó's."

"That is not true," he calmly replied.

"It is true," I said. "It will be true because I will it. If he can't make up his own mind after twelve years, then it's up to me to make it up for him. If he can't work out who is his real wife, I'll decide."

"And who will that be?" he flashed back at me, all ears now, almost cheerful, as he had not been in the course of the entire conversation. It was as if he had just heard a surprising, especially amusing declaration. "Who is that real wife to be?"

"I have already told you," I answered, a little confused. "Why are you smiling like that, as if you didn't believe me? . . . My mother-in-law once told me that there is always a real wife somewhere. That could be Judit Áldozó, or it could be someone else. Well, he can't find her, so I will."

"I see," he said. He gazed at the carpet, clearly not wanting to argue.

He escorted me to the door without saying anything. He kissed my hand, still with that strange smile on his face. He gravely opened the door for me and made a low bow.

But we should pay and go now; they really are wanting to close. Miss, I had two teas and a pistachio ice. No, darling, you are my guest. No protests, please. And don't feel sorry for me, either. It's the end of the month, but this little treat will not ruin me. I lead a carefree, independent life; my alimony always arrives precisely on the first, and it is considerably more than I need. See, it's not such a bad life.

Ah, but you're thinking, it lacks a certain meaning? . . . That's not true, either. Life is very full. Just as I was on my way here to meet you I was walking down a street and it suddenly started to snow. It was pure delight. The first snow . . . I couldn't give myself over to sheer enjoyment before. I was constantly attending to one man and had no time for the rest of the world. I lost the man and gained a world. Do you think that's a poor exchange? . . . I don't know. You might be right.

I don't have much else to tell you. You know the rest. I have divorced my husband and live alone. He lived alone for a while too; then he married Judit Áldozó. But that's another story.

None of it happened as quickly as I imagined it might at Lázár's apartment. I carried on living with my husband for two more years after that. It seems everything in life runs according to some invisible minute hand: one can't "decide" anything a moment sooner than one is meant to, only once all other matters and the situation itself make the decision for you . . . To do it any other way is foolish, an act of aggression, practically immoral. Life decides, suddenly, wonderfully . . . and, once it does, everything seems simple and natural.

After visiting Lázár I went home and said nothing about Judit Áldozó to my husband. By that time, poor man, he knew everything. It was only the most important fact he was missing. And I couldn't tell him, because I didn't know it myself then, and would not know it for some time afterwards . . . Only Lázár knew—yes, then, as I was saying good-bye, when he suddenly went strangely silent. It must have been what he was thinking of. But he said nothing himself, because the most important things are not the kind of things you can say to anyone. People have to learn it for themselves.

The most important thing? . . . Look, I don't want to upset you. You are a little in love with that Swedish teacher, aren't you? . . . Am I right? . . . Fine, I am not asking for confessions. But allow me to keep silent too. I wouldn't want to ruin that lovely, sweeping emotion. I wouldn't want to hurt you in any way.

I don't know when my husband actually spoke with Lázár, the next day or weeks later, nor do I know what was said. But everything worked out the way Lázár said it would. My husband knew everything: he knew I had found the lilac ribbon, and that I knew who wore the locket. He knew I had spoken with Judit Áldozó, who did in fact resign from my mother-in-law's service at the beginning of the next month. She disappeared for two years. My husband hired private detectives to find her, but grew tired of it and fell ill. He called the detectives off. Do you know what my husband did in the two years of her disappearance?

He waited.

I had no idea it was possible to wait like that. It was as if he had been sentenced to forced labor and set to breaking stones in a quarry. He broke the stones with such strength, with such discipline, with so much devotion, in such despair . . . By that time not even I could help him, and if I had to tell the truth while lying on my deathbed, I would have to confess that I didn't actually want to help him. My own heart was full of bitterness and despair then. I watched his terrible spiritual exertion for two years. This smiling, wordless, courteous, ever paler, ever more silent argument with somebody or something . . . You watch how some people rush for the morning mail: it's as if they were a kind of drug addict. They put a hand into the mailbox, feel there is nothing there, and you see their hand emerge, hovering, empty . . . You watch someone's head jerk to attention as the telephone rings. You see his shoulder tense when he hears the doorbell. His eyes flick hither and thither in the restaurant and the theater foyer, always searching, searching every corner of the universe. We spent two years like this. But there was no trace of Judit Áldozó. Later we discovered she had traveled abroad and worked as a maid in an English doctor's house in London. Hungarian servants were in demand in England then.

Her family heard nothing from her, nor did my mother-in-law. I visited my mother-in-law pretty regularly in those two years. I spent whole afternoons there. Her health was deteriorating, poor thing: she had suffered a thrombosis and had to lie immobile for months on end. I used to sit at her bedside. I grew very fond of her. We sat, we read, we knitted and made conversation. It was almost as though we were weaving a tapestry, the way medieval women did while their husbands were away in the war. I knew that my husband's part in the battle was likely to be dangerous. He could be killed any moment. My mother-in-law knew it too. But neither of us could help him now. That was *his* problem now . . . he was alone, his life in considerable danger, and he himself could do nothing but wait.

The two of us, my mother-in-law and I, walked about on tiptoe in the meantime; we lived and wove our tapestry around him. We were like nurses. We talked about other things, sometimes cheerfully, as if nothing had happened. It might have been a peculiar form of tact or just intense embarrassment, but eventually it got so that my mother-in-law never spoke about what had happened. That noon, when she sat down opposite us in the maid's room and wept, we formed an unspoken pact to help each other, as far as possible, promising we would not talk unnecessarily or despairingly about the situation. If we talked about my husband, it was as of a charming, amiable invalid who happened to be in a condition that concerned us but not in immediate danger of his life . . . Yes, as of someone who could still go on a long time . . . Our role was simply to adjust the pillow under his head, to open the odd jar of preserves, or to amuse him by chatting about events in the world at large. And indeed, throughout these two years, my husband and I led a calm and orderly life at home, without very much socializing. My husband had already begun to dismantle everything that might tie us to society and the world outside. Over two years he slowly, with the greatest tact and refinement, made his exit, walking away from his own life, but in such a manner as not to offend anyone. Little by little our acquaintances were cut off and we remained alone. Actually it wasn't as bad as you might think. We spent five days out of the seven at home. We listened to music or read. Lázár never visited us again. He too went abroad, and lived in Rome for several months.

So that's how we lived. All three of us were waiting for something: my mother-in-law for death, my husband for Judit Áldozó, and I for the moment that either death or the return of Judit Áldozó, or some other unforeseen, unavoidable event, should make it clear what I should do with my life and where I belonged . . . You were asking why I did not leave my husband. How could I live with someone who is waiting for someone else, who springs to attention each time the door opens, who has grown pale, is avoiding people, cuts himself off from the world, is sick unto death with some disease of the emotions, who is eaten away with simply waiting? Well, it wasn't easy, not at all. It is not the most pleasant of situations. But I was his wife and couldn't leave him, because he was in trouble and in danger. I was his wife and had made a sacred vow to remain with him and suffer with him, for better or worse, for richer or poorer, as long as he wanted me, as long as he had need of me. Well, he needed me now. He would have wasted away if left alone those two years. We carried on, waiting for some earthly or heavenly sign. We were waiting for Judit Áldozó.

Because the moment he discovered that the woman had left town and gone to England—it was just that no one knew her address in England, neither her family nor her friends—my husband became genuinely ill with waiting, and there is probably no greater suffering than waiting. I know the feeling . . . Later, once we were divorced, I was waiting for him much the same way, for about a year. You know how it is: you wake up in the morning like an asthmatic, gasping for air. You put a hand out in the dark seeking another hand. You can't understand how the other person is no longer there, nearby, in the next house or the next street. You walk down the street but the other person is not there to meet you. There's no point in having a telephone; the papers are full of news that means nothing to you—items of no consequence, such as that a world war has broken out, or that in a capital city of some one million inhabitants whole rows of streets have been destroyed . . . You hear out the news politely, as it goes in one ear and out the other, and say things like: "Really? . . . Imagine! . . . How interesting!" or "How sad!" But you don't feel anything. There is a lovely, wise, sad Spanish book—I've forgotten the author's name; it was the kind of name a toreador might have, a very long name—in which I read that in this sleepy, feverish, magical state, the state experienced by those who wait or are absent from those they love, there is something of the self-induced trance; even their eyes are like the eyes of sick people when they wake from sleep, exhausted, far away, their eyelids slow to rise. People like that see nothing of the world, they just see a face, the one face; nor do they hear anything, just the one name.

But one day they wake.

Take me, for example.

They look around and rub their eyes. They can see rather more than one face now . . . or to be precise, they still see the face but it's as if through a haze. They see a church spire, a copse of trees, a picture, a book, other people's faces: they see the infinite variety of the world. It is an extraordinary feeling. What was unbearably painful and raw to the touch one day no longer hurts. You sit on a bench and feel calm. You think thoughts like "Chicken stew" or *Die Meistersinger von Nürnberg.* Or "I should buy a new bulb for the table lamp." All this constitutes reality, each part as important as the rest. Yesterday all this seemed impossible, pointless and uncertain: yesterday was a different reality. Yesterday you still yearned for revenge or deliverance, you wanted him to ring you or to need you, you wanted him to be carted off to jail and executed. While you still feel this, the other person is out of reach and laughing. While you still feel it, you are in his power. As long as you are crying out for vengeance, he is gleefully rubbing his hands together, because vengeance is desire too: vengeance is dependency. But there comes a day when you wake, rub your eyes, give a yawn, and suddenly discover you don't want anything. You could bump into him in the street and it wouldn't matter to you. Should he ring, you'd pick it up if you felt like it. Should he want to see you and insist you must meet, well, why not? And you know what? All this time, you are relaxed, at ease with yourself . . . there is no tension, no pain, nothing trancelike in it. What happened? You don't understand. Now you no longer want vengeance, no vengeance at all . . . and you discover what real vengeance is, the only, perfect form of vengeance, which is that there is nothing you want from him, you wish him no harm but no good either, he cannot hurt you anymore. Men in bygone days used to write letters to their lovers at such times, addressing them as "Dear madam . . ." And that said everything, you know. What it said was: "There is no more pain to be got out of me." That was the point a wise woman started sobbing. Or not. A wise man may then send a magnificent gift, a bunch of roses or a life annuity . . . why not? You can do anything, now it no longer hurts.

That's how it is. I've been through it. One day I woke and started to live again. I got on my feet and walked.

But my husband, poor soul, did not wake. I don't know whether he is cured even now. Sometimes I pray for him.

So two years passed. How did we spend our time? We carried on living. My husband said good-bye to the world, quit his social circle, stopped seeing people—all without saying a word, like a swindler who is secretly planning to skip the country but keeps working, apparently conscientiously. The other person—his real wife—was abroad. We waited for her. It wasn't a bad life: the fact is, we got on quite well those two years. Sometimes, at table or reading a book, I stole a glance at his face, the way a relative might steal a glance at the face of someone sick, and while they are inwardly horrified at the other's sickly pallor, they smile sweetly and pass a cheerful remark, such as "You're looking much better today." We were waiting for Judit Áldozó, who had vanished from town, the monster . . . Because she knew that was the worst thing she could do. You don't believe me? You think she might not have been a monster? You think she too paid a price, she too fought, she too is a woman, maybe, she too felt something? Am I right? . . . Go on, comfort me, because I would really like to think so myself. She had sat around for twelve years and then she charged off to England. There she learned English, she learned how to eat in polite company, she got to see the sea. Then one day she came home with seventy pounds in her purse, wearing a tartan skirt and cologne by Atkinson. That was the point at which we divorced.

It broke my heart, of course. For a whole year I thought I might die of it. But then one day I woke up and learned something . . . yes, the most important thing a person can learn by herself.

Shall I tell you what that is?

I won't hurt you?

You can bear it?

Well, yes, I bore it. But I am reluctant to tell just anyone, I don't want to take away people's illusions by telling them they have invested all that faith in a false idol, one that begets so much suffering and so much that is wonderful: heroic deeds, works of art, extraordinary human endeavors. I know you are in that condition at the moment. You still want me to tell you? . . .

All right, since you ask. But you mustn't be angry with me afterwards. Look, darling, God has punished—and rewarded—me by allowing me to suffer and not die in the process. What was it I discovered? . . . Well, my dear, it was this: that there isn't a real wife; not a real anything.

One day I woke, sat up in bed, and smiled. I felt no pain at all. Suddenly I understood that none of this was real. That there is no real anything on earth or in heaven. No real wife, no intended, that's for certain. There are only people, and there isn't that certain one-and-only, wonderful, single being, the one fated to make you happy. There are only people, and people have something of everything in them: sugar, salt, the sweet and the bitter, the lot . . . Lázár knew that when we stood in the door and parted, but he said nothing, only smiled, because I had told him that I was going away and would find my husband's intended, his real life. He knew she was nowhere to be found . . . But he didn't say anything, then went off to Rome and wrote a book. That's what all writers do in the end.

My husband, poor soul, was not a writer: he was a solid citizen, an artist without an art. That's why he suffered so much. Then, when one day Judit Áldozó returned, the woman he believed to be his real wife, wearing cologne from Atkinson, saying "Hello" on the phone like an Englishwoman—well, that was when we divorced. It was a difficult divorce, even if I say so myself. I insisted on the piano.

He didn't marry her straightaway, only a year later. How do they get on? Just fine, I think. You saw him a little while ago, buying candied orange peel for her.

It's just that he's aged. Not a lot, but in a melancholy sort of way. Do you think he knows by now? . . . I fear it may be too late by the time he finds out, that life will have passed him by.

Now look, they really are closing the shop.

I'm sorry? . . . What did you say? Why I started weeping when I saw him just now? Why, if there is no such thing as "the intended"—the chosen one, the real wife—and one is completely over it all, why I should have started powdering my nose when I saw he was still using that crocodile-skin wallet? Wait, let me think. I think I have the answer. The reason I felt embarrassed and started powdering my nose was because while there is no such thing as the one-and-only, special intended, and while I have no more illusions, I still happen to love him. Which is different. When we love someone, we can't help our hearts beating a little faster every time someone talks about them, or whenever we see them. What I mean is: everything passes, but love does not. It's just that it no longer has any practical significance.

Let me give you a kiss, my dear. Good-bye. Shall we meet here again next Tuesday? . . . It was such a nice conversation. About a quarter after seven, if it suits you . . . not much later than that. I'll be sure to be here before a quarter after seven.

Part II

See the pair just leaving, there by the revolving doors? That woman there. The blond one in the round hat? No, the tall one in the mink, yes, the tall brunette, without a hat. The one getting into a car. That stocky fellow is helping her into it, isn't he? They were sitting at that table in the corner earlier. I spotted them as soon as we came in, but I didn't want to say anything. They never even saw me. But now that they've gone I can tell you that that was the man with whom I had that stupid, embarrassing duel.

On account of the woman? . . . Well, of course because of her.

I'm not sure I'm putting that quite right. There was definitely some-one I wanted to kill at the time. But maybe it wasn't our stocky friend. He was nothing to do with it really. He was simply the nearest object.

Can I tell you who this woman was? . . . Oh, I can tell you all right, old man. That woman was my wife. Not the first, but the second. We've been divorced for three years. We divorced immediately after the duel.

Another bottle of wine? After midnight this place suddenly empties out and grows rather chilly. Last time I was here I was still an engineer-ing student—it was at the time of the carnival. These famous old rooms were full of women then: colorful, glittering creatures of the night, laughing all the time. I didn't come back for many years. Time passed;

they dolled the place up, and the customers changed too. Nowadays it's the cosmopolitan crew out for a night's entertainment . . . you know, what they call cosmopolitan. I had no idea my wife was a regular here, of course.

Nice wine. As pale green as Lake Balaton before a storm. Cheers.

Will I tell you the story? If you like.

It might not be a bad thing if I did once actually tell it.

Did you know my first wife? No, I don't think so, because you were in Peru then, building the railroad. You were lucky to find yourself in a big wild country straight after finishing the course, when we both got our diplomas. I must confess I envied you sometimes. If fate had taken me abroad I might have been happier than I am now. As it worked out I stayed at home, taking care of things . . . Well, one day I got tired of all that, so I'm not taking care of anything now. What was I taking care of? Was it the factory? A way of life? I really don't know. I used to have a friend, Lázár, the writer, do you know him? You've never heard of him? Aren't you the happy man! I knew him well. At one time I thought he was my friend. This man kept arguing that I was a rare representative of a vanishing form of life, the pick of my class, a model citizen. According to him, that was why I stayed at home. But I can't even be sure of that.

It is only facts you can be sure of; they are what matter . . . All those explanations we give to account for the facts are pure, irredeemable fiction. Literature. I should tell you that I am no longer a great admirer of literature. I used to read a lot in the past, everything I could lay my hands on. I suspect it is bad literature that fills men's and women's hearts with lies and false feeling. It is the false teaching of dubious books we have to thank for most of the contrived tragedies of human life. Self-pity, false sentiment, all those artificial complications are, to a great extent, the direct consequence of fake, ignorant, or simply mischievous fiction. You find it under banner headlines in the press and in smaller articles on other pages: the seamstress who drinks lye because the joiner has left her, or the female representative involved in an accident after she'd taken Veronal, all because the famous actor failed to turn up for a date. The glorious fruits of literature! Why are you looking at me like that? Surprised? You want to know what I most despise? Literature? The tragic misunderstanding that goes under the name of love? People in general? That's a hard question. I don't despise anyone or anything, I have no right to. But in what remains of my life I intend giving myself over to a passion. A passion for truth, that is. I will not have people lying to me anymore, neither books nor women, and I will have no patience at all with the lies I tell myself.

You say I have suffered. That I've been hurt. That's true. It might have been that woman you saw just now, my second wife, who hurt me. It might have been the first. Something went wrong in any case, and whatever it was it was a dreadful emotional experience. I've become quite solitary as a result. I am angry. I have no faith in women, in love, or in people. What a ridiculous, pathetic creature, you must be thinking. You'd like tactfully to remind me that there are plenty of people who are both happy and passionate; that there is love and patience and participation and forgiveness. You'd like to accuse me of lack of courage, of impatience with the people I happened to have met, of not having the guts, now that I am this solitary wild creature, to admit that it was all my fault. Look, old man, I have heard and considered all these charges. You could torture me and put me on the rack and I'd still think what I think, feel what I truly feel. I have examined the lives of people close to me, I have looked through the windows of other people's lives; I have not been too shy or too reserved, I searched and listened. I myself thought the fault was mine, that it was in me. I explained it in terms of greed, selfishness, lust, social constraints, the ways of the world. Explained what? Failure. That well of loneliness into which everyone is eventually plunged, the way a traveler might stumble into a ditch at night. We are men: nobody is going to help us in this respect; we have to live alone and have to pay the full price of everything down to the last penny. We have to put up with loneliness, with being who we are, and we have to do so in silence. These are the laws of life as far as men are concerned.

And family? I can see you want to ask me about that. Don't I think the family is, in abstract terms, the highest meaning in life, a superior kind of harmony? Life is not about happiness. Life is about supporting your family, bringing up your children as honorable people, and not expecting either gratitude or happiness in return. But I want to give you a straight answer, and my answer is, you are right. It's just that I don't believe family "makes you happy." Nothing can "make" you happy.

The family is a vast project, so enormous and important, both for us personally and for the world at large, that it's worth putting up with all the incomprehensible cares of life, all that superfluous pain, for its sake. Nevertheless, I don't believe in "happy" families. I have seen families where there was a certain harmony of purpose, a proper set of human relationships, families where each member's life ran a little against the grain of the others, where every member of the family led a separate life, but where the whole, all the members of the clan, despite fighting each other tooth and nail, still lived for each other and somehow held together.

Family . . . a big word. Yes, one's family might sometimes be the whole point of life.

But that doesn't solve anything. And in any case I never had a family in quite that sense.

So I kept listening and paying attention. I listened to fashionable sermons about how loneliness was a middle-class disease, sermons with twisted ideas that kept referring to "society"—that magnificent thing, society—a society that embraces and elevates the individual so that suddenly he has a purpose in life, because he knows he is not living simply for a narrowly defined family but for the far better, all-but-superhuman concept of society. I listened very hard to such tirades. I thought about their application not just in theory but in the here and now, where I could properly grasp their implications, in life itself. I considered the lives of "the poor"—they, after all, constitute the largest element of society, are in themselves a society. Did they enjoy a fuller, richer, more vital kind of life for the knowledge that they were part of a union—the steelworkers' union, for example—or of a self-employed workers' pension scheme? Were they happier for the knowledge that they had representatives in parliament, people who could speak, and write articles, on their behalf? Surely it is just as vital to know that there are an infinite number of steelworkers and self-employed in the world who would like to lead better, more humane lives; that their worldly condition improves only in gradual stages, after bitter conflict, after countless unsatisfactory compromises under which their pay is no longer 180 pengő but 210. Looking down, everything seems bottomless. When you're near the bottom, you're very glad of anything that improves your horrible condition. But that's not happiness. Nor did I find happiness among people whose employment or vocation placed them at the heart of social affairs. No, what I found there was resentment, sadness, dissatisfaction, rivalry, fury, struggle, resignation, and idiocy: the clever and foolish constantly at war with each other. I found people who believed in amelioration: that, very slowly, after many unpredictable twists and turns, given time, there would be some improvement in human life. It's nice to believe this. But believing it, or even feeling assured of it, doesn't make anyone less lonely. It's not true that it is only the middle class who feel alone. A peasant on a distant farm can be as lonely as a dentist in Antwerp.

Then I went on to read, and believed for a while, that it was the mere fact of civilization that created loneliness.

The idea was that joy had somehow drained from life in the process, though now and then it might emit the odd spark. Deep in the human heart there lay the memory of a bright, sunlit, happy world where even duty was pleasure, where struggle was delight and everything was worthwhile. Maybe the Greeks were happy—for all that they slaughtered each other, murdered strangers, and put up with extraordinarily long and terrifyingly bloody wars, they were nevertheless radiant with a cheerful communal feeling. They were happy in a deeper, preliterary way; even the tinkers were happy tinkers . . . But we, according to the idea, don't have a proper cultural life: our civilization is uniform, secretive, mechanical. Everyone has a share in it, but nobody is truly happy. Everyone can have a tubful of hot water to bathe in, everyone can gawk at pictures, listen to music, make long-distance telephone calls; our laws defend the rights and interests of the poor as well as of the rich—but just look at our faces. Wherever we live, whether it be in small communities or in wider society, our faces are troubled. How suspicious we look, how tense; how much unresolved insecurity and furious antagonism there is among us. It's all the product of anxiety and loneliness. You can offer various explanations for loneliness, and every explanation would address some specific associated question, but not one of these answers would give you a convincing reason . . . I know mothers with six children who suffer loneliness, mothers whose faces wear the same furious antagonistic expressions, and I know middle-class bachelors who take off their gloves with an affected, careworn laboriousness, as though they were somehow forced to do so. As for politicians and prophets, they divide us into far more artificial groups and subgroups, and the more they try to educate children in the ways of this new world, the more unremitting the sense of essential loneliness becomes. You don't believe me? I know. I could talk about this forever.

If I had the gift of eloquence, if I were a priest, or an artist, or a writer, so that people listened to me, I would beg them, encourage them, to look for joy. Let's forget loneliness. Let it go. It may be no more than illusion. It's not a question of society. It is a matter of something we learn in early childhood. It's a matter of awakening. People just look glazed: it's as if they were wandering about in a trance. Glazed and suspicious. It seems I have no gift of joy myself.

But once, just once, I did come across a face without that glazed look, a face that did not wear that intense, dissatisfied, suspicious, sickly pall of tension.

Yes, it's the one you saw just now. But the face you saw was only a mask, a dramatic mask for a character in a play. When I first saw it, the face was open, full of expectation and patience, radiant and open, the kind of face that must have been there at the world's beginning, before people had eaten of the fruit of knowledge, before they knew pain and fear. The face grew more solemn later, graver and more solemn. The eyes became more watchful; the lips, those open lips she forgot to close, did close, and hardened. Her name was Judit Áldozó. She was a peasant girl. She came to us when she was fifteen as my parents' servant. We never had a relationship. Do you think that might have been the problem? I don't think so. People say such things, but life is not very forgiving of incidental comment, of wisdom after the event. In all likelihood it is no accident that we never became lovers before I took her to wife.

But she was my second wife. You want me to tell you something about the first. Well, my friend, that first one was a splendid creature. Clever, honest, beautiful, cultured. You see, I am talking about her as though I were advertising her in some column. Or as though I were Othello when he set off to murder Desdemona, "so delicate with her needle . . . she will sing the savageness out of a bear . . ." Should I add that she loved music and nature? Because I can talk about her and remain perfectly calm. It's the way retired head gamekeepers out in the country advertise their younger sisters in the local press, small physical imperfections included. But this one, my first wife, had no physical faults. She was young, beautiful, and sensitive . . . So what was the problem? Why couldn't I live with her? What was lacking? Sensual pleasure? I'd be lying if I said that. I had as much pleasure with her in bed as with any other woman, including those with a vocation. I don't believe in the Don Juan ideal; I don't believe it is right to live with several women at the same time. Our task is to create a perfect musical instrument out of just one, the kind of instrument on which any song can be played . . . Sometimes I feel sorry for people, the way they snatch and grab at things so stupidly, so hopelessly . . . one sometimes wants to smack their hands and tell them: "Don't snatch! Don't grab! Sit down properly and have some manners. You'll get what you want if you wait your turn!" Really, they are just like greedy children. They don't know that contentment in life is sometimes simply a matter of patience, that the harmony they are so feverishly seeking and which they think of, wrongly, as happiness, depends entirely on one or two points of technique . . . Why don't schools teach you about relationships between men and women? Why not? I'm not joking. It's a perfectly serious question. Contentment depends as much on such things as on morals and grammar. It shouldn't be treated as a frivolous subject . . . I mean, there should be intelligent people—poets, doctors—to introduce one to the ways of joy, to the various possibilities of coexistence between men and women before it's too late. I don't mean "sex education": I mean joy, patience, modesty, and satisfaction. If I do feel a contempt for some people, it is chiefly on account of their lack of courage in such things—the lack of courage that leads them to conceal the secrets of their lives, not only from the outside world but from themselves.

Don't misunderstand me. I myself am no fan of the "confession," all that sickly, crippled displaying of oneself and the slobbering and frothing at the mouth that goes with it. But I do like truth. It is truth we most like to hear, of course, because superfluous self-revelation is the province of invalids, egotists, and people of an effeminate nature. Nevertheless, it is better to listen to the truth than to speak lies. Unfortunately, wherever I've looked in life, it was chiefly lies I heard.

You ask me what I mean by truth, by healing, by the ability to feel joy? I'll tell you, old man. I'll tell you in two words. Humility and self-knowledge. That's all there is to it.

Maybe humility is too grand a concept. For humility you need grace too, and that is an exceptional state of being. In everyday life we can achieve what I am talking about by exercising a certain modesty and striving to discover our own true desires and inclinations. And by seeking a compromise between our desires and the world as it exists.

I see you are smiling. You are thinking that if everything is so simple, if there really is some universal template, why isn't my life a success? Well, you see, in the end there happened to be these two women, and I tried to live first with one, then the other; I mean really live, as a matter of life and death. I can't complain about them as people, as marvelous people in fact. All the same, I failed, failed with both, and here I am, alone. Self-knowledge, humility, all those great oaths and promises; it was all in vain. I failed, and now all I can do is sit here and sermonize . . . That's what you are thinking. Am I right?

In that case I had better tell you what my first marriage was like and why it failed. My first wife was perfect. I can't even say that I didn't love her. She had but one small fault, and it wasn't something she could do anything about. It wasn't any kind of psychological problem—nothing of the sort. Her problem was that she was a middle-class girl, poor thing, a middle-class woman. Don't misunderstand me: I myself am middle-class. I am conscious of being so, a conscientious member of that class, someone who knows its faults and limitations, content to shoulder the responsibilities of middle-class existence. I don't like drawing-room revolutionaries. One should keep faith with those to whom one is tied by origin, education, interest, and communal memory. It is the middle class I have to thank for everything: my upbringing, my way of being, my desires, the very finest moments of my life, and that common culture which offers such a dignified entry to such moments . . . Because there are many who say this class has had its day, that it has grown feeble, that it has fulfilled its mission, that it can no longer take the leading role in human affairs the way it did in the past. I can't speak about that. I don't understand it. I have a feeling that the middle class is being buried a bit too enthusiastically, a little too impatiently; I think there may be some power left in it, that it might still have a role in the world. Perhaps the middle class will form the bridge on which the forces of revolution meet the forces of order . . . When I say my first wife was a middle-class woman, that is not a criticism; I am simply establishing a certain condition. I too am middle-class, quite hopelessly so. I keep faith with my class. I will defend it when it is attacked. But I won't defend it blindly or from a prejudiced position. I want to see quite clearly what it was I received as my portion of social destiny. I have to know, in other words, what our faults were, and to discover whether we have been attacked by a kind of social virus that has drained us of vigor. Not that I ever talked about this with my wife.

So what was the problem? Wait a minute. Let me get my thoughts in order.

First and foremost, it was that I was a middle-class man, fully acquainted with the rituals of my class. I was rich. My wife's family was relatively poor. Not that being middle-class is a matter of money. My experience is that it is precisely the poorest members of the class, those with the least financial security, who are most urgently preoccupied with maintaining middle-class standards and values. No one rich ever needs to cling so attentively, so desperately, to social customs, to points of etiquette, to respectable behavior, to all those things the poorest of our kind, the petite bourgeoisie, needs to underwrite its very existence at any given moments of life. There is the assistant manager in the office who watches everything like a hawk, careful that his accommodation, his wardrobe, and all the minute details of his life should keep firmly in step with his salary . . . The rich are always open to a kind of minor risk-taking. They are prepared to wear a false beard or to shinny down a drainpipe in order to escape, even if only for a little while, the prison of ennui that goes with property. I am secretly convinced that the rich spend every hour of the day being utterly bored of themselves. But the middling man, the middle-class citizen, who holds an office without a great salary or a reservoir of money, will perform acts of heroism fit for a knight errant simply to maintain his position in the existing hierarchy, which means preserving both his rank and his system of values. It is the petit bourgeois who upholds the sacred rituals. From the moment he is born to the moment he dies, he constantly has to be proving something.

My wife was well brought up. She was taught languages, she had the ability to make sharp distinctions, between good music and a sentimental tune, between literature and cheap hackwork. She could tell you precisely why a painting by Botticelli was beautiful and what Michelangelo had in mind with his *Pietà*. But wait—let me be accurate about this. She learned most of it from me—travel, reading, the art of intimate conversation. The education she received at home and at school, the culture she absorbed there, remained in her only as the memory of strict teaching. I tried to dissolve the tensions implicit in learning such things by rote; I wanted to transform school learning into warm, living experience. It wasn't easy. She had remarkable powers of hearing in both the physical and the psychological human sense. She sensed that I was teaching her and was offended. People are offended by all sorts of things. It doesn't take much. Say one man knows something because of his good fortune in being born who he is and has had the opportunity of inquiring into the mysteries that constitute real art, while the other has only learned it in class. That's an offense. It happens. But it takes us a whole lifetime to learn this.

For the lower managerial class, culture is an inseparable part of the whole package: not experience but accomplishment. It is the top layer of the middle class that provides the artists, the creative types. I was a member of that group. That's not a boast but an admission. Because, in the end, I did not create anything. Something was missing in me . . . what was it? Lázár called it the Holy Spirit. But he never explained what he meant by that.

But back to the problem with my first wife. What was it? Hypersensitivity and pride. It's what lurks under every human frailty, every complaint, every mishap. We are afraid because pride prevents us accepting the gift of love. It takes great courage to allow oneself to be loved unconditionally. Courage is required, an all-but-heroic courage. Most people can neither give nor accept love, because they are cowardly and vain and afraid of failure. They are ashamed of giving themselves, and are even more ashamed of surrendering to someone else in case that means revealing a secret . . . the sad, human secret that one needs tenderness and cannot live without it. I believe that to be true. At least I did believe it, for a long time. I don't argue it so much nowadays, because I'm getting old and have failed.

In what respect did I fail? I failed in precisely the respect I'm talking about. I lacked the courage to accept the tenderness of the woman who loved me. I resisted. I even looked down on her a little for it, because she was different from me—*une petite bourgeoise* with different tastes, wanting a different pace of life—and I was afraid I would eventually have to give in to some high-minded and extremely complex form of blackmail meant to drag the gift of love from me. I did not know then what I know now . . . I didn't know that there was nothing positively shameful about anything in life. Cowardice is the one shameful thing, cowardice that prevents us giving and accepting the feelings of others. It's practically a matter of honor. And I believe in honor. One can't live in disgrace.

Your health! I like this wine, though there is a faint air of sweetness about the taste. I've got rather fond of it recently and tend to open a bottle most nights. Can I offer you a light, old man?

Briefly, then, the problem with my first wife was that our pace of life was different. There is something in the lower-middle-class soul that is always somewhat stiff, startled, artificial, horrified, overfond of pretense, and easily offended, especially once it is removed from its home and natural habitat. I can't think of another class whose children creep through life in such a state of startled suspicion. As concerns that woman, the first one, she might have given me everything a woman can give a man if only she had been a little more fortunate in her birth, had she been born one rung up or one rung down: in other words, if she had been born into a state of greater psychological freedom. She was aware of everything, you know, and understood everything . . . She knew what flowers to display in the old Florentine vase in the spring and in the fall; she dressed correctly, with proper modesty; I never had the least reason to be embarrassed by her in society; she always answered and spoke precisely as she should; our household was exemplary; our servants went about their tasks without fuss, as she taught them to. We lived model lives. But there was another part of life, a more obscure corner of it, the corner that is reality, that is like a cataract or a jungle, that was less than perfect. I'm not thinking of the bedroom exclusively . . . though, naturally, I include it. The bedroom is a jungle too, after all. It contains the memory of an experience so primitive and absolute that its meaning and content is life itself. If we tend and weed this jungle, we produce a beautiful, cultivated, charming place, full of scented flowers, attractive trees and shrubs, and ringing, rainbow-colored fountains, but leave nothing of the jungle to which we desire to return but no longer can.

It's quite a role to play, being a respectable citizen, a solid bourgeois, as they say. No one pays a higher price for culture than we do. It is a grand dramatic role, and as with every heroic part, you have to pay every penny of the cost. You need courage, the courage required for happiness. Art is an experience for an artist. For the solid citizen art is a miracle of training. You probably didn't talk too much about this in Peru, where life is a matter of whatever bubbles up and displays itself as species. But I lived in Pest, in the exclusive suburb of Rózsa-domb. People should take the climate into which they are born into account.

Then a lot of things happened I can't talk about. The woman is still alive and lives alone. I see her sometimes. We don't meet, because she still loves me. You know, she wasn't the sort of woman from whom one separates, to whom you send alimony punctually on the first of the month, and a gift of furs or jewelry at Christmas or her birthday, and think you have done your duty by her. This sort of woman still loves you, nor will she ever love anyone else again. She is not angry with you, because her outlook is that once people have loved each other, there isn't, nor can there ever be, real anger. Fury, the desire for vengeance, yes; but anger, that long-simmering, expectant sort of anger . . . no, that's impossible. She may no longer be waiting for me. She is living and slowly dying. She will die in good taste, in properly refined fashion, as befits her class, quietly, and without fuss. She will die because there is no new way of lending meaning and content to her life, because she cannot live without feeling that she is needed by someone, by the one, special, individual being who has absolute need of her. She might not know this. She might think she has come to some sort of compromise. Some time ago, I ran into a woman with whom I had had an overnight fling, a friend from my first wife's school days, who had recently returned from America. It was the night of the carnival: we met and, almost without being invited, she came back to my apartment. Some time in the morning she told me that Ilonka had spoken about me once. You know how diligent girlfriends can be . . . Well, she told me every-thing, as they all do. She told me, there in her friend's ex-husband's bed, the morning after just having met me, that she had always been jealous of Ilonka, that she had seen me once in a café in town, where she was sitting with my first wife, and I'd suddenly come in and bought some candied orange peel for my second wife, and that I took my money from a brown crocodile-skin wallet. That wallet was a gift from my first wife on my birthday. No, you can wipe that ironic, detective-like smile off your face, I really don't use it anymore. So that's how it was. And these two women, my first wife and her friend, had thoroughly discussed everything. What my wife said to her friend was that she loved me very much, had almost died when we parted, but then grew reconciled to it, because she had discovered I wasn't her one, true, intended love; or, more precisely, that given all the other possibilities, I was one of the many who were not her true, intended loves; or, still more precisely, if greater precision is possible, that there was no such thing as the one, true, intended, real love. That's what her friend told me in the morning, in my bed. I rather looked down on her because she knew all this and still leapt into my bed. When it comes to love I have my doubts about female solidarity, but just then I felt a little contemptuous of this woman, and subtly, politely, I threw her out. I thought I owed that much to my first wife. But I kept thinking about it. As time went by I started to feel that Ilonka was lying. It's not true that one's real love, the intended one, does not exist. That is, after all, what I was for her, that unique being. For me, on the other hand, there wasn't anyone of such overwhelming importance, not her, not my second wife, nor the rest. But I didn't know that at the time. We are such slow learners.

There's nothing more I can tell you about my first wife.

That part no longer hurts, and I don't feel guilty thinking about it. I know we killed the marriage: I myself, life, chance, the death of the child—all these played a part in killing it. That's the way life kills. The stuff you read in the press is crude exaggeration, cheap muck. Life is more complicated, and prodigiously wasteful. It doesn't care about this or that Ilonka . . . collectives and aggregates are what interest it: all the Ilonkas, all the Judits, all the Peters. What it wants to tell us, to articulate to us, concerns the lot of them, as a package. It's no great revelation that this should be the case, but it takes a long time to learn it and reconcile oneself to it. I kept thinking, and eventually all feeling, all passion vanished. Nothing remained except responsibility. That's all that ever remains for a man, whatever the experience. We move among the living and the dead, and are responsible . . . There's nothing we can do to help. But I wanted to talk about my second wife. Yes, the one who has just left with the stocky gentleman.

Who was the second? No, that was not a middle-class woman, old chap. She was a prole. A working-class woman.

Do you want to know about her? Fine, I'll tell you. And I want to be perfectly truthful with you.

She was a servant. She was fifteen when I first met her. She worked in our household, as a maid. I don't want to bore you with adolescent love affairs. But I'll tell you how it began and how it ended. As to what came between, I myself am not sure about that yet.

It began with the fact that no one in my family dared love anyone else in it. My father and mother lived a theoretically connubial existence; in other words, it was pretty abominable. They never raised their voices. It was all: "What would you like, my dear?" "What can I do for you, darling?" That was how they lived. I don't even know whether it was a bad life. It's just that it wasn't a good life. My father was proud and vain. My mother was a respectable middle-class woman in every sense of the word. Responsibility and discretion. They lived, died, loved each other, gave birth to me, and brought me up as if they were both priest and congregation at some kind of superhuman sacrament. Everything was ritual with us; breakfast and supper, social life, the contact between parents and children—even the love between them, I believe, or what tends to be called that, took the form of an impersonal rite. It was as though they had constantly to be accountable for something. Our lives were strictly planned. There are new and powerful states that prepare four- and five-year plans they carry out, with a ruthless, furious devotion, not caring whether their citizens like it or not. Because what matters to them is not the happiness of this or that individual but the happiness, at the end of those four or five years, of the collective, the nation, the people. There are many recent examples of this. And that is the way it was with us at home, only not with four- or five-year plans, but with forty- or fifty-year ones, quite irrespective of each other's and our own personal happiness. Because all those rituals, all that work, the engagements, even death itself, had a deeper meaning: the preserving of order in the ranks of both class and family.

When I consider my memories of childhood I sense an anxious, grim sense of directedness behind everything. We worked like robots, going about our rich, refined, ruthless, emotionless, robot work. There was something we had to save, something we had to prove, every day, in everything we did. We had to prove we were of a certain class. The middle class. The guardians. We were doing an important job. We had to embody the notions of rank and manners. We were to suppress the revolt of the instincts, of the plebeians; we were not to run scared, not to succumb to the desire for individual happiness. You ask whether this is a conscious project. . . . Well, I wouldn't exactly say my father or mother sat down regularly at the dinner table every Sunday to announce that week's program of action or make speeches in which they outlined the next fifty-year family plan. But I couldn't exactly say that we merely accommodated ourselves to the idiotic demands of class and occasion, either. We knew perfectly well that life had singled us out for a difficult series of tests.

It was not only our home, our carefully wrought way of life, our dividends, and the factory we had to protect, but the spirit of resistance that constituted the imperatives and deeper meaning of our lives. We had to keep up our resistance to the attractive powers of the proletariat, the plebs who wanted to weaken our resolve by continually tempting us to take various kinds of liberties, whose tendency to revolt we had to overcome, not in the world, but also in ourselves. Everything was suspect: everything was dangerous. We, like others, were careful to make sure the delicate machinery of a persnickety and ruthless society should continue to work undisturbed. We did this at home, judging the world on appearances while suppressing our desires and regulating our inclinations. Being respectable requires constant exertion of effort. I am referring here to the creative, responsible layers of the middle class—in other words, not the pushy lower orders who simply want a more comfortable, more diverse kind of life. Our ambition was not to live in greater comfort, or more diversely. Under all our acts, manners, and forms of behavior there was an element of conscious self-denial. We experienced it as a kind of religious vocation, being entrusted with the mission of saving a worldly, pagan society from itself. The task of those who perform this role, under oath and in accordance with the rules of the order, is to maintain that order and to keep secret that which should remain secret when danger threatens the objects of their care. We dined with that responsibility in mind. Every week we dutifully went to a performance—to the Opera House or to the National Theater. We received our guests, other responsible people, in the same spirit: they came in their dark suits, they sat down in the drawing room, or at the candlelit dining table with its fine silver and porcelain, where we served good, carefully chosen food and made empty conversation about sterile subjects, and believe me, there was nothing more sterile than our conversation.

But these empty conversations had a function, a deeper purpose. It was like speaking Latin among the barbarians. Beyond the polite phrases, the banal, meaningless arguments and ramblings, there was always the deeper sense that we responsible middle-class people had come together to observe a ritual, to celebrate an honorable compact, and that the codes we were speaking in—because every conversation was about something else—were ways of keeping a vow, proof that we could keep secrets and compacts from those who would rise against us. That was our life. Even with each other, we were constantly having to prove something. By the time I was ten years old I was as self-conscious and quiet, as attentive and well behaved, as the president of a major bank.

I see you're looking amazed. You didn't know this world. You are a creative man, someone who makes things happen. You and your family have only just begun to learn this lesson. You are the first of your family to move up a class . . . You are ambitious. I had only memories, traditions, and duties. For all I know, you might not understand any of this. Please don't be cross if you don't. I'm doing the best I can.

The apartment was always a little on the dark side. It was a nice apartment, a proper house with a garden, always something being built and improved. I had my own room upstairs where I lived, my tutor or governess sleeping in the room next door. I don't think I was ever completely alone, not in all my childhood. I was taught to be amenable both at home and at school. They tamed the wildness in me, the human part, so I should be a proper member of my class and put on a decent show. That may be why I so obstinately, so desperately, craved solitude. I have been living alone now, without even a single servant, for some time now. There's just a woman who comes in occasionally when I am not at home, who tidies my room and generally disposes of the flotsam and jetsam of my life. At last there is no one breathing down my neck, checking on me, keeping an eye on me: no one to whom I am responsible . . . There are considerable joys and satisfactions in life. They often come late, in the wrong, unexpected forms. But they do come. When, having left the family house, after two marriages and divorces, I found myself alone, I felt—for the first time in my life—a kind of melancholy relief on having at last achieved something I actually wanted. It was like serving a life sentence in prison, then being released on account of good behavior . . . for the first time in decades you sleep without fearing the guard patrolling the night corridor who looks in on you through the peephole in the middle of the night. Life has its blessings, even blessings like this. You have to pay heavily for them, but in the end life hands them to you on a plate.

"Joy" is not quite the right word, of course. Comes the day, and suddenly life goes quiet. It is no longer joy you desire, but at least you no longer feel cheated and annihilated. When that day comes, you see quite clearly that you have seen it all and have had your punishments and rewards, both precisely in the proportion you have deserved. If you lacked the courage, or were simply not quite heroic enough to strive for something, you did not get it. End of story. So it's not joy really, just resignation, acceptance, and calm. In due course it comes your way. It's just that you have had to pay dearly for it.

As I was saying, back in the family house we were not only conscious of our class roles, but were prepared to play them. Whenever I think of childhood I see darkened rooms. The rooms are full of magnificent furniture, like in a museum. It's a place in constant need of cleaning and tidying. Sometimes the cleaning makes a lot of noise and involves electrical equipment and open windows, at other times the process is silent and unseen, employing rented staff, but it always entails somebody, a servant or someone in the family, stepping into the room to tidy something away, to blow a speck of dust off the piano, to smooth something out, or to rearrange the folds of a curtain. The apartment was always being jealously tended, as if everything in it—the furniture, the curtains, the pictures, our very habits—were somehow objects on exhibit, artifacts in a museum that needed constant attention, repair, and cleaning, and we had to walk through the halls of this museum on tiptoe because it was inappropriate to walk and talk without restraint among exhibits that insist on a holy hush. There were so many curtains: even in the summer they soaked up the light. The chandeliers hung from the high ceilings, their eight-armed illumination somehow aimless in rooms where everything swam in an indistinct gloom.

Glazed cabinets lined the walls, full of relics that both staff and family passed in a state of awe, objects one never touched or picked up or examined closely. There were gilt-rimmed pieces of Alt Wien porcelain, Chinese vases, paintings on ivory, portraits of unknown men and women, ivory fans never used for fanning people, tiny items made of gold or silver or bronze; pitchers, animals, miniature dishes, none of which were ever used. One cabinet contained the "family silver" the way a casket might contain the bones of a saint. The silver dining service was hardly ever used, which was also the case with the damask tablecloths and the fine china; they were all there to be guarded according to the secret rules of the house, preserved for an incomprehensible, hard-to-imagine, special ritual when there would be twenty-four places at table. But the table never was laid for twenty-four. We had guests, of course, and then the silver service, the damask, the porcelain, and the glass exhibits would be brought out, and the dinner or supper would be conducted with such anxious, careworn ceremony you might have thought the company was far less concerned with eating than with conducting a terrifyingly complex operation in which no one should commit any kind of faux pas or break a plate or glass in the course of conversation.

The facts themselves will be familiar to you in your own life; I am talking about the feelings that constantly welled up in me when I was there, in the rooms of my parents' house; feelings in childhood and even later, as an adult. Yes, there were guests for supper or simply calling by; we lived there and "used" the place, but under the practical, everyday aspect of living there, the house had a deeper meaning and purpose: that meaning and that purpose were locked in our hearts like a last line of defense.

I will always remember my father's room. It was a long room, a real hall. The floors were covered with thick oriental rugs. There were a great many pictures on the walls, of all kinds: expensive paintings in gilt frames, paintings showing distant, never-seen forests, oriental ports, and unknown men of the last century, mostly with beards and dressed in black. An enormous writing desk stood in one corner of the room, the kind known as a diplomat table, over three yards long and some five feet wide, complete with a globe of the world, a copper candelabrum, a tin inkpot, an attaché case of Venetian leather, and a mass of ornaments and mementos. Then there was a collection of heavy leather armchairs gathered around a circular table. By the fireplace surround two bronze bulls were engaged in combat. The pediments of the bookcases displayed other bronze items, eagles and bronze horses, and a tiger half a yard in length, looking ready to spring. That too was made of bronze. And all along the walls a range of glazed bookcases. They contained a vast number of books, four, maybe five thousand, I don't know exactly how many. Literature had its own bookcase, as did religion, philosophy, and social science, the works of English philosophers bound in blue buckram, and sets of all kinds bought from an agent. No one actually read these books. My father spent his time reading the newspapers and accounts of travel. My mother did read, but only German novels. Book dealers occasionally sent us their latest acquisitions and we got stuck with them, so the valet would have to ask Father for the keys and arrange the newly accumulated volumes in the cases. They were careful to lock the cases, of course, ostensibly so that the books should be protected. The truth is they were locked so as to prevent anyone ever taking a book out on a whim, which rash action might result in them being confronted by the secret and possibly dangerous material it might contain.

This room was referred to as Father's "study." No one in human memory had ever actually studied there, least of all my father. His study was the factory and the club he frequented in the afternoons with other manufacturers and financiers, where he would enjoy a quiet game of cards, read the papers, and debate matters of business and politics. My father was undoubtedly a clever man with a sound sense of the practical. It was he who had developed the factory from the workshop set up by my grandfather and expanded it into a major enterprise. It grew in his care until it became one of the country's leading businesses. This required strength, art, foresight, and a deal of ruthlessness—in fact, everything required by any enterprise where one man sits in a room on the top floor deciding what should go on in all the other rooms of all the other floors on the basis of instinct and experience. My father had sat in that particular room of our factory for forty years. It was where he belonged, where he was honored and feared, his name being mentioned with respect throughout the business community. I have no doubt at all that my father's commercial morals, his concepts of money, work, usefulness, and capital, were exactly those the world, his business partners, and his family would have expected of him. He was a creative sort of man: in other words, not one of those tightfisted, ugly capitalists who sit on their money and squeeze all they can out of their employees, but someone naturally bold and entrepreneurial who respected work and aptitude and paid talent better than he did mere mechanical ability. But all this—father, the factory, the club—was yet another form of association: that which was sacred and ritualistic at home was the same, only less refined and more secretive, at work and in the world at large. The social circle founded by my father among others would accept only millionaires as members, always just two hundred of them, no more. When a member died, the circle chose a replacement with the same care and delicacy as did the Académie Française its own members or the order of Tibetan monks the new Dalai Lama among the upper classes of Tibet. Everything—the selection process and the invitation—was carried out with the utmost secrecy. The select two hundred felt, despite title or rank, that they constituted a power in the state greater than even that of a governmental department. They were the alternative power, the invisible partner with which official power was obliged to parley and come to agreement. My father was one of them.

We knew this at home. I never entered the "study" without a sense of awe and self-consciousness. I'd stand before the diplomat table at which no one in human memory had ever been known to work, a desk that only the valet spent time at, every morning arranging and dusting the ornaments. I would gaze at the bearded, unknown men in the portraits, imagining that these dour people with their piercing eyes would, in their own day, have been a member of just such a solemn association of two hundred as my father and his friends at the club were; that they'd have ruled over mines and forests and factories, and that there existed some unwritten compact between life and time, a kind of eternal blood-brotherhood that meant they were stronger and more powerful than other men. The thought that my father was of their company filled me with a certain anxious pride. An anxious sense of ambition, I should say, because I did want to take my father's place among them at some stage. It took fifty years for me to learn that I was not, nor was fitted to be, one of them; it was not until last year that I stepped out of their ranks, the ranks to which they had admitted me, so that I might "withdraw," as they put it, from "any kind of business involvement," though that was not something I could possibly have known back then. That was why I gazed so wide-eyed at Father's "retreat," why I pored over the titles of books no one read, why I began vaguely to suspect that something barely perceptible but significant, something perfectly unremitting, was being enacted behind these strict outward signs and appurtenances, and that this was how it had to be, how it was and always would be, and yet there was something not quite right about the whole thing, even if only because no one actually talked about it . . . For whenever conversation, whether at home or in company, turned to the subject of work, to money, to the factory, or to the society of two hundred, my father and his friends fell noticeably quiet, stared stonily into space, and began to speak of something else. There was a limit, you know, a border with an invisible barrier . . . but of course you know. I'm telling you this now because once I start I feel like telling you absolutely everything.

I couldn't even say our lives were frigid or entirely without warmth. Our major family occasions were lovingly, punctiliously, commemorated. There were four or five "Christmases" each year. These occasions, which were not officially red-letter days, were more important in the family's unwritten Gregorian calendar than Easter or Christmas itself, though the family did in fact have a properly kept written calendar where births, wedding anniversaries, and deaths were duly noted, noted so precisely and in such detail that even a registrar would have examined them with admiration. This book, the book of the clan, the golden book—call it what you will—was in the exclusive care of the head of the family. My great-grandfather had bought the book a hundred and twenty years ago, Great-Grandfather in his furs and braids, the founder of the dynasty, the first worthy begetter in the family, who had been a miller out on the Great Hungarian Plain. It was he who first inscribed the family name in the gilt-edged, black-leather-bound volume packed solid with ivory paper. *"In nomine Dei."* He was "Johannes II" . . . miller and founder. It was he who was first given a state rank.

Once, and once only, did I write in that book, and that was when my son was born. I will never forget that day. It was a beautiful sunlit day in late February. I returned from the hospital in a helpless state of joy and pain, a state one experiences but once in life, when one's son is born. My father was no longer alive. I went into my study, a room I used as infrequently as my father used his, looked out the locked book in the lowest drawer of the diplomat table, opened it, took out my fountain pen, and very carefully inscribed the letters "Matthias I" along with the date and time. It was a great moment, a symbolic moment. How much there is of vanity, of the second-rate, in the range of human feeling! This was the family marching on, I felt. Suddenly everything had a meaning: the factory, the furniture, the pictures on the wall, the money in the bank. My son would take my place in the house, in the factory, in the society of two hundred . . . But that was not to happen. I have thought long and hard about this. We can't be sure that having a child, an heir, is the solution to the deeper crisis in any individual's life. The law says it does, of course, but life is not a product of law.

That's how we lived. That was my childhood. I know, there have been far worse. But this is all relative. It was Judit Áldozó I really wanted to talk about, but here we are talking about my childhood.

We celebrated all anniversaries, particularly the family ones. There were Father's birthday, Mother's name day, and others like these, all of them redder-than-red red-letter days, complete with gifts, music, dinner, toasts, and flickering candles. Our nurses would dress us up in little sailor's costumes made of velvet, with lace collars—you know, *à la milord*. All these occasions were conducted in perfect order, according to unwritten military regulations. Father's birthday was the grandest occasion, of course. We had to learn verses by heart. The entire household gathered in the parlor, everyone dressed to the nines, eyes sparkling, the servants shiftily, raptly, kissing my father's hand and thanking him for something, I really don't know what. Most likely for the fact that they were servants and my father was not. Who knows? They kissed his hand nonetheless. Then came a grand dinner or supper. The most precious plates and the best silver cutlery were fished out of the family vaults. Relatives arrived to celebrate the birthday of the illustrious head of the family with due deference and, naturally, seething envy. We were the head of the clan. Poorer relatives received a monthly donation from Father, a proper stipend or pension. None of them thought it enough in

private. There was an old lady, a certain Auntie Maria, who so complained about Father's meanness that she always refused to join us at the
highly ornate celebratory dinner. "I'll be just fine in the kitchen," she
said. "A small cup of coffee in the kitchen will do me." That's how
poorly she thought of the money my father voluntarily gave her each
month, even though there was absolutely no obligation that he should
give her anything. We had to drag her into the dining room and give her
the best place at the table. It is very hard striking a balance between the
desires and demands of poor relatives. The fact is that it's impossible. It
requires great spirit, an exceptionally great spirit, to suffer the success of
a close relative. Most people are incapable of it, and it would be a foolish
man who would be angry to see the whole family turn against him, the
successful one, in a spirit of wounded sensibility, or mockery, or hostility. Because there's always someone in the family with money or reputation or influence, and the rest, the tribe, gather round this individual
to hate and rob him. My father knew this, and he gave them as much as
he thought right while indifferently tolerating their hostility. Father
was a strong man. The possession of money made him feel neither sentimental nor guilty. He knew exactly how much each person should
have and would not give more. Not in terms of feeling, either. His
favorite sayings were "They'll get that" and "They'll not get that." It
was a carefully considered judgment every time. And once he had pronounced his verdict he stuck by it, as to a papal decree. There was no
arguing with him. I am sure he too was lonely, and had to forgo many
things he desired or that would have pleased him, in the interests of the
family. But he suppressed such desires and stayed strong—firm on his
feet. "They're not getting that," he said sometimes after a long silence
when my mother or some other member of the family put a request to
him, the party in question having already mentioned it several times and
dropped various hints. No, Father was not tightfisted or hard-hearted.
He simply knew people and understood money, and that's all there was
to it.

Cheers.

Excellent wine this, old man. What wit, what strength this wine has!
It's just the right age, six years old. Six is the best age for dogs and for
wine. White wine is dead after seventeen years: it loses color and aroma,

and is no more animated than the glass it's stored in. I discovered this very recently, in Badacsony, from a vintner. You should not be impressed when snobs offer you very old wine. All this takes time to learn.

Where was I? Oh yes, the money.

Tell me, why are writers so slipshod when it comes to the question of money? They write about love, glory, fate, and society; it's just money they never mention, as if it were some kind of second order of existence, a stage property they deposit in their characters' pockets so that the action may proceed. In real life there is much more tension about money than we are willing to admit to ourselves. I am not talking about the economy now, or poverty: in other words, not about basic concepts, but about actual money, the everyday, infinitely dangerous and peculiar substance that, one way or another, is effectively more explosive than dynamite; I mean those few coins or fistfuls of banknotes that we manage to grasp or fail to grasp, that we give away or deny ourselves, or deny someone else . . . They don't write about that. Nevertheless, the everyday anxieties and tensions of life are made up of a thousand such common conspiracies, misrepresentations, betrayals, tiny acts of bravado, surrender, and self-denial: tragedies can develop from the sacrifices involved in working to a tight budget, or else avoided, if life offers another way of resolving the situation. Literature treats economics as though it were a kind of conspiracy. That's exactly what it is, of course, though in a deeper sense of the word—real money exists *within* the spaces of abstractions such as "the economy" and "poverty." What really matters is people's relationship to money, a character's timidity or bravado concerning money: not Money with a capital *M,* but the everyday money we handle morning, afternoon, and evening. My father was rich: in other words, he respected money. He spent a dime with as much care as he would a million. He once spoke of not respecting someone because the individual was forty but had no money.

It shook me when he said this. I thought it heartless and unjust.

"He is poor," I defended him. "He can't help it."

"That's not true," he sternly replied. "He *can* help it. After all, he is not an invalid, he's not even ill. Whoever gets to forty without having made any money—and he, in his circumstances, could undoubtedly have made some—is a coward or lazy or simply a bum. I can't respect such a man."

Look here, I am over fifty now. I'm getting older. I sleep badly and lie on the bed half the night in the dark with my eyes wide open, like a beginner, like someone practicing to be dead. I am a realist. Why, after all, should I fool myself? I am no longer in debt and owe nothing to anyone. My only obligation is to be true to myself. I think my father was right. One doesn't understand such things when one is young. When I was young I considered my father a ruthless, unbending man of finance whose god was money, and who judged people—unfairly—according to their capacity for making it. I despised the concept and felt it to be mean and inhumane. But time passed and I had to learn many things: romance, love, courage and fear, sincerity, and everything else—in other words, money too. And now I understand my father, and I can't find it in myself to blame him for the severity of his judgment. I understand that he looked down on those who were neither ill nor invalid and had passed the age of forty but were too cowardly or lazy or shiftless to have made money. Naturally, I don't mean a lot of money, since there is considerable luck involved in that: great guile, sheer greed, or blind chance. But the kind of money that lies within a person's power to get—that is to say, given one's opportunities or horizons in life—that is wasted only by those who are cowardly or weak. I don't like refined, sensitive souls who, faced with this fact, immediately point to the world, to the wicked, heartless, greedy world that wouldn't allow them to spend the twilight of their lives in a pretty little house with a watering can in their hands, tending their garden on a summer evening, with slippers on their feet and a straw boater on their heads, like any small investor who has happily retired from working life to rest on the rewards of industry and thrift. It's a wicked world, wicked to everyone equally. Whatever it gives, it sooner or later takes away, or at least tries to take away. Real courage consists of the struggle to defend the interests of oneself and one's dependents. I dislike the mawkish sensibility that blames everyone else: those ugly, greedy financiers, those ruthless investors, and the "terribly crude" idea of competition that prevented them turning their dreams into small change. Let them be stronger, more ruthless if they will. That was my father's code. That's why he had no time for the poor, by which I don't mean the unfortunate masses, but those individuals who weren't clever or strong enough to rise from their ranks.

That is a pretty heartless perspective, you say. It's what I myself said for a long time.

I don't say that now. I have absolutely no desire to pass judgment on anyone. I just go on living and thinking; it's all I can do. The truth is, I have not made a single penny in all my life. I barely looked after that which my father and his fathers passed on to me. Mind you, that is no easy matter, either, looking after money, because there are vast powers out there constantly at war with the concept of private property. There were times I fought these powers—enemies both visible and invisible— as vigilantly and fiercely as my ancestors, the founders of our fortune. But the truth is that I was not myself a maker of fortune, because I was no longer really in touch with money. I was of the penultimate genera- tion, whose only desire is to keep what they have been given out of a sense of honor.

My father would sometimes speak of "poor people's money." His respect for money was not based on mere accumulation. He told me that a man who is no more than a factory hand all his life but who, by the time he has finished, owns a small plot, a little house, and a few fruit trees, and can live there on what he has earned, is a more heroic figure than any general. He respected the miraculous willpower shown par- ticularly by the poor—the healthy and the exceptional among them— who, through fierce, stubborn effort, succeeded in grabbing a share of the good things of the world. They had a patch of the earth they had the right to call theirs; there was a house they had bought with their own pittance: they had a roof over their heads. He admired these peo- ple. Apart from them he admired nothing and no one. "He was good for nothing," he'd say sometimes and shrug when the fate of the weak and helpless was described to him. The conviction with which he pro- nounced "good for nothing" was itself a form of contempt.

As a matter of fact I myself am a miser and always have been. I am like anyone who is no longer capable of building and creating and is reduced simply to looking after that which he has inherited from his family. My father was not a miser, he simply had a respect for money: he made it, he accumulated it, and then, when the time was right, he calmly spent it with full confidence in his own judgment. I once saw him write out a check for a million, his hand assured as he put his simple signature to it, as if it were no more than a tip to a waiter. And when the factory burned down and the insurers weren't paying because it had been caused by some kind of negligence, my father decided to rebuild it. He could have left it and shared the proceeds, then lived in comfort on the interest. He was no longer young by this time. He was over sixty. There would have been plenty of good reasons for not rebuilding. It was perfectly within his means to live an independent life, to spend his remaining days strolling about, reading books, and going to see things. But he didn't hesitate a moment: he settled with the investors and the foreign engineers, then wrote out the check and handed it over to the engineer who would build up and head the new venture. And he was right. My father died two years after that, but the factory is still there, still productive, doing useful work. That's as much as we can hope for in life, that we leave something useful behind us, something people value.

Ah yes, but none of this is of much consolation to the builder and maker, you think. I know—you are thinking of the loneliness. The deep, dense loneliness that is the lot of any creative spirit, a product of the restricted atmosphere in which he must move, the oxygen he must breathe. Well, yes. Busy people are lonely people. But we can't be altogether certain that this loneliness is the cause of suffering. I have always suffered more from close human presence and social life than from genuine loneliness. There are times when we regard loneliness as a punishment: we are like children left alone in a dark room while the adults carry on chattering and enjoying themselves next door. But one day we too grow up to be adults and learn that loneliness—genuine, fully conscious solitude—is not a punishment, not a wounded, sickly retreat from life, not isolation, but the one and only truly fitting condition for man. And then it becomes less hard to suffer it. It is like breathing pure mountain air.

That's what my father was like. That is what the world was like back then. Money, work, order: it was a solid bourgeois world. It was as if the house and the factory were ordained to us forever. The rituals associated with work and life were organized, as it were, from a position outside life. It was quiet at home. I learned that quiet early, the keeping silent. People who talk a great deal have something to hide. People who hold their peace are sure of something. That was another thing I learned from my father. As a child these lessons were a source of suffering for me. I felt something was missing from our lives. Love, you say . . . The love that is ready to sacrifice itself. Look, it's far too easy to say that. Later I discovered that love, poorly articulated, clumsily demanded, kills more people than poison, car accidents, and lung cancer. People kill each other with love as with some invisible death ray. They want ever more love and demand constant acts of tenderness; they want it all, all to themselves. They want the whole heart; they want to suck the life energy from their surroundings and are as greedy for it as those enormous plants that drain water, scent, and light from other shrubs. Love is a monstrous selfishness. Is there anyone alive capable of surviving under that reign of terror called love? Look around you, look through the windows that you pass. Look into people's eyes, listen to their complaints, and you will discover everywhere the same despairing anxiety. They can't live with the demands that love imposes on them. They put up with it for a while, they bargain with it, but eventually it exhausts them. Then follow stomach upsets, gastric ulcers. Diabetes. Heart murmurs. And death.

You have seen peace and harmony? Once, in Peru, you say . . . Well, yes, it may be possible, in Peru. But here, in our more temperate climate, the miraculous flower is not allowed to bloom. It may put out a few petals now and then, but it quickly languishes. Maybe the climate of civilization is too much for it. Lázár once told me that civilizations based on the machine must churn out loneliness like a conveyor belt. He also told me the abbot Paphnucius was less lonely in the desert, on top of his column, with guano in his hair, than a million citizens of the great metropolis crowded into cafés and movie palaces on a Sunday afternoon. He was lonely too, but conscientiously so, like a monk in a monastery. The one time anyone got close to him he quickly ran off. I suspect I know this better than he does, or the person who got close to him. But these are private matters, other people's affairs, and I have no right to speak of them. Back home, a lofty, solemn, sacramental kind of loneliness pervaded everything. The loneliness of my childhood sometimes comes back to me like the memory of a sad, frightening dream . . . you know, the kind full of anxiety, the sort one dreams before a test. My childhood was a matter of eternal preparation for some desperately important, dangerous exam. It was an examination in responsible citizenship. We were forever studying. We crammed. We learned by rote. Each day there was a new exam paper to face. We were constantly tense: our acts, our words, even our dreams were fraught with tension. We were walled in by a loneliness so dense even the servants and those who only dropped in at the house for a few minutes—mailmen, delivery boys—they all felt it. Childhood and adolescence were spent waiting in dim, curtained rooms. By the time I got to eighteen the loneliness, anxiety, and waiting had exhausted me. I longed to try something I hadn't tried before, something not entirely within the rules. But I had to wait a good while before that happened.

That was when Judit Áldozó entered my fortress of loneliness.

Here, have a light. How do you get on with the tobacco habit? It's a struggle, isn't it? Myself, I couldn't go on—not with the smoking but with the struggle. There'll be a day when that too has to be faced. One adds up the facts and decides whether to live five or ten years longer by not smoking, or to surrender to this petty, shameful passion that no doubt kills but, until it does so, offers you such a peculiar calming yet exciting experience. After fifty years it becomes one of life's major questions. My answer to that question was angina and the decision to carry on exactly as before until I die. I'll not stop poisoning myself with this bitter weed, because it's not worth it. You say it's not so difficult to give up? Of course it's not that difficult. I've done it before, more than once, while it was worth it. The trouble was, I'd spend the whole day "not smoking." That's something else I'll have to face one day. People should resign themselves to certain weaknesses, to their need for a soporific of some sort, and be prepared to pay the price. It's so much simpler that way. Yes, but then they say: "You should have more courage." My answer to them is: "I may not be the bravest of men, but I am courageous enough to live with my desires."

That's what I think, anyway.

You're looking at me very skeptically. I see, you want to ask whether I always had the courage to follow my desires? As regards Judit Áldozó, for instance? Indeed I had, old man. And I proved it. I paid my whack, as they say on the street. It cost me my peace of mind for the rest of my life, and someone else's peace of mind too. It may be that one can't do much more than that. And now you want to know whether it was worth it? That is what you call a rhetorical question. You can't judge the great decisive moments of life by the standards of a commercial transaction. It's not about whether something was or was not worth it: sometimes people have to do things just because it is their fate to do so, or because that is the given situation, or because their blood pressure demands it, or because their entire body insists on it. It's bound to be some combination of all those factors at work . . . Whatever the case, the result is that they don't act like cowards, they just go ahead and do it. Because nothing else matters. The rest is theory.

So I did it.

Let me tell you what it was like the morning when Judit Áldozó first appeared at the door of our dingy yet magnificent abode. She was like the poor girl in the fairy tales—she arrived carrying nothing more than a small bundle of possessions. Folk tales are generally pretty reliable. I had just returned from the tennis courts, had stepped into the hall, thrown the racket onto a chair, and stood there flushed, about to pull off my sleeveless knit sweater, the kind people wear for exercise. That was the moment I noticed that there was a strange woman standing in the gloom beside the Gothic chest. I asked her what she wanted.

She didn't answer. She was clearly confused. I thought at the time she must have been disoriented by the unfamiliar setting, and put her silence down to a simple case of embarrassment not uncommon with servants. Later I found out it wasn't the unfamiliar setting or the arrival of the young master that confused her but something else. It was the encounter. The fact of our meeting, and that I had looked at her and something happened. I too knew that, of course, knew something had happened that moment, but not as deeply as she did. Women, strong, instinctive women, and she was one, know precisely what is important or decisive the moment it happens, while men, such as ourselves, are always likely to misunderstand events or explain them away. This woman immediately knew, the moment she met me, that our fates were inextricably linked. I knew it too, but I chose to talk about something else.

But not straightaway, because she hadn't answered my question and I felt a little insulted, inclined to be high-handed. We stood dumbly in the hall for a few moments, facing and staring at each other.

We gazed at each other the way people do when coming across something rare and strange. What I was gazing at that moment was nothing like a new servant. I was gazing at a woman who, in some way, for completely mysterious reasons, because of certain impossible factors, would play a major role in my life. Do people realize when this happens? I'm sure they do. Not intellectually but with their whole being. And at the same time they go on thinking other things in an absentminded sort of way. Consider for a moment how unlikely a situation this was. Imagine that, in those moments, someone had come up to me and told me that this was the woman I would one day marry, but that much would have to happen before that came about; that I would first marry someone else, another woman, who would bear me a child, and that the woman standing opposite me then in the dingy hall would go abroad, vanish for years, then return, at which point I would divorce my wife and marry her instead; that I, the persnickety bourgeois boy, the rich, polished gentleman, would marry this insignificant servant girl clutching her bundle while anxiously staring at me just the way I was staring at her . . . scrutinizing her as if I were seeing something I had never seen before, something I really had to take into account . . . Well, all this seemed most unlikely back then. If anyone had predicted it, I would have laughed at him and dismissed the very idea. But now, afterwards, from the distance of a few years, I'd like to answer my own question as to whether I knew how it would work out. And also the issue of whether we know when we meet someone that the meeting is of vital importance, a turning point in our lives . . . Is there a moment when someone steps into the room and we know, yes, this is the one? The one intended, just for us, exactly as in novels?

I don't know the answer. I can only close my eyes and recall the moment. And as I do so, I see that, yes, something happened back then. An electric charge? A form of radiation? A secret intuition? These are just words. But of course people don't communicate their thoughts and feelings through words only. There are other forms of communication between people, other ways of conveying a message. The term people tend to use now is "shortwave." Apparently human intuition is no more

than a form of shortwave transmission. I don't know . . . I have no desire
to con you, nor indeed myself. For that reason the best I can say is that
the moment I first saw Judit Áldozó I was transfixed, and however
impossible the situation, I stood there facing this unknown servant figure quite unable to move. So we carried on gazing at each other for
quite some time.

"What's your name?" I asked her.

She told me. It sounded faintly familiar. "Áldozó" is much like the
word *áldozat,* meaning sacrifice, so there was something ceremonial in
it. Even her given name, Judit, had a biblical ring. It was as if she had
stepped out of history, out of some biblical condition of solid simple
materiality: like eternal life, real life. It was as if she had arrived not
from a village but from some deeper level of existence. I was not much
concerned with the propriety of my actions. I stepped over to the door
and turned on the light so I could see her more clearly. Even my sudden
movement failed to disturb her. Readily and obediently, not like a servant now, but in the manner of a woman acceding to the desires of the
one man entitled to demand anything of her, she turned to one side
toward the light so I might examine her more closely. She stood there in
the lamplight. It was as if she were saying: "There you are, take a good
look. This is me. I know I am beautiful. Look as hard as you want, take
your time. You will remember this face even on your deathbed." So she
stood there calm, immobile, her bundle in her hand, like an artist's
model, silent and willing.

And I carried on gazing at her.

I don't know whether you got a decent look at her just now. I alerted
you too late. You only saw her body. She is as tall as I am. Her height is
in perfect proportion to the rest of her. She is neither fat nor thin, but
exactly as she was at the age of fifteen. She has never put on weight, nor
ever lost any. You know, there are powerful inner laws that govern the
way these things balance out. It was as though her metabolism burned at
a constant, steady flame. I looked into her face and found myself blinking at the beauty of it, like someone who had lived for many years in a
fog and suddenly found himself in bright sunlight. You couldn't see her
face just now. But she has been wearing a mask for a long time anyway,
a cosmopolitan mask made up of mascara, paints, and powders, false
eyes emphasized with eye shadow and a false mouth drawn on with lip-

stick. But then, in that first startled moment, her face was still new and unscarred, untouched, direct from the Maker's hand. The touch of her Creator was still fresh on her cheeks. Her face was heart shaped, beautifully proportioned. Each part of it echoed the other to perfection. Her eyes were black, a special kind of black, you know, as if there were a touch of dark blue in it. Her hair was blue-black, too. And one could immediately tell her body was as well proportioned and quite certain of itself. That was why she could stand in front of me with such poise. She had emerged out of anonymity, out of the depths, out of the vast crowd, arriving with something extraordinary: proportion, assurance, and beauty. Of course I was only faintly aware of all this. She was no longer a child, but was not quite a woman yet, either. Her body had developed but her soul was just waking. I have never met a woman since so absolutely certain of her own body, of the power of her body, as Judit Áldozó was then.

She was wearing cheap city clothes, black shoes with low heels. Everything about her was so consciously and modestly assembled. She was like a peasant girl who had dressed for town and didn't want to be put to shame by city girls. I looked at her hands. I was hoping to find something unattractive in them. I hoped to find stubby fingers and palms rough and red from agricultural work. But her hands were white, her fingers long and graceful. Those hands had not been broken by labor. Later I discovered she had been spoiled at home, that her mother never put her to hard manual work.

There she stood, content to have me gaze at her under the bright lights. She looked directly into my eyes with a simple curiosity. There was nothing flirtatious about her, neither her eyes nor her posture. There was no invitation. She was not a little tart who finds herself in the big city and makes eyes at young gentlemen hoping to ingratiate herself to them. No, she was a woman willing to look a man in the eye because she thinks she might have something in common with him. But she didn't overdo it, not then nor later. The relationship between us was never a fixed one of necessity for her. When I could no longer eat, sleep, and work without her, when she had got under my skin and penetrated my reflexes like a fatal poison, she remained calm and perfectly self-possessed, irrespective of whether she came or went. You think she didn't love me? . . . I too thought so for a while. But I don't want to judge her too harshly. She loved me, but in a different way, in a more cautious, more practical, more grounded sort of way. That, after all, was what the situation allowed. That's what made her a working woman, and me a middle-class boy. That's what I wanted to tell you.

And then what happened? Nothing, old man. Phenomena like my time under the spell of Judit Áldozó are not to be explained in terms of "events," the way things happen in novels or plays. The key events of our lives take place in time, in other words, over a period, very slowly. They hardly appear to be events at all. People go on living . . . that is the nature of events, of any act of importance to us. I can't tell you that Judit Áldozó appeared in our house one day and that the next day, or six months later, this or that other thing happened. I can't even claim that as soon as I saw her that first time I was immediately consumed by a passion that deprived me of both sleep and appetite, that left me dreaming of a stranger, a peasant girl, who now lived in close proximity to me, who entered my room on a daily basis, whose conduct was ever the same, who answered any question I put to her, who lived and matured the way a tree does, who conveyed any information of importance in her own characteristically simple and surprising manner, who trod the same earth and breathed the same air as I did . . . Yes, it was all as I describe it, but none of these conditions constitutes an event. In fact, for a long time, there were simply no events.

Nevertheless I recall that initial period in keen detail. The girl did not hold a particularly important position in our household and I rarely saw her. My mother trained her to be a housemaid, but she was not to serve us at the table, because she knew nothing of our family rituals. She tended to trail after the servant as he was cleaning, like a clown in a circus imitating the main act. I would occasionally bump into her on the stairs or in the drawing room; sometimes she even came to my room and greeted me, stopping on the threshold to deliver some message. I should have said that I was thirty-two years old when Judit Áldozó joined us. Thirty-two years old, and an independent adult in many respects. I was a partner in the factory, and my father, albeit carefully, was training me to stand on my own feet. I had a substantial income, but I did not move out of the family home. I lived on a separate floor, in two rooms. I had my own personal door. In the evenings, if I had no other business, I would dine with my parents. I tell you all this to show I had few opportunities to meet the girl. And yet, from the moment she first entered the house and I spotted her in the hall, a certain tension existed between us, a quite unambiguous tension.

She always looked me straight in the eye. It was as if she were always asking me a question. She was not some house-trained domestic kitten, not an innocent fresh from the village, the kind who lowers her eyes when meeting the young master of the house. She did not blush or preen. Whenever we met, she would stand a moment as if someone had touched her. Just like the moment when I turned on the light to see her better that first time, where she obediently turned her face so I could see it better. She looked straight into my eyes, but in such a strange way . . . not in a challenging manner, nor inviting, but seriously, quite solemnly, her eyes wide open as if she had asked me something. She was always looking at me with those wide-open, questioning eyes. It was always the same question. There is a fundamental question in all of creation, said Lázár, a question that lies at the very root of consciousness: it is the question "Why?" It was the same question Judit Áldozó was asking me. Why am I living; what is the meaning of it all? . . . It did sort of come down to this. The only odd thing was that it happened to be me that she was putting the question to.

And because she was terrifyingly beautiful, full of dignity, and utterly complete in her virginal fierceness, like a masterpiece of creation, a unique, perfect specimen of which only a single design and prototype existed, her beauty did, of course, exercise an influence in our house, in our lives, constituting an insistent, silent, uninterrupted music. Beauty is probably a form of energy, the way heat, or light, or sheer willpower are forms of energy. Nowadays I am starting to think there is something constructed about it—not in terms of cosmetics, of course, since I have no great respect for beauty artificially arrived at, something pinched and poked into existence, the way people pamper animals. No, there is something behind beauty, which is, after all, compounded of fragile, mortal matter that suggests a fierce will. It takes the heart and all the other organs, intelligence and instinct, bearing and clothing, to bind together the fortunate, miraculous formula that makes up the compound that ultimately leads to and has the effect of beauty. As I said, I was thirty-two years old.

I can tell from your expression that you are asking the age-old, worldly-wise male question "What was the problem?" Isn't it the simplest thing for a man to follow his instincts and inclinations? A thirty-two-year-old man is, after all, aware of the facts of life. He knows that there is no woman he may not bed providing she is free, that there is no other man in her heart and thoughts, that there is no physical issue or matter of culture between them, and that they have the opportunity of meeting and getting to know each other. It's true. I myself knew it was true, and frequently put that knowledge to use. Like any man of my age whose appearance is not altogether repulsive and is, on top of that, possessed of means, I met many women who made themselves available to me, nor did I refuse their offers. A man of promise is as much the center of attention as an attractive woman. It's not a matter of personality: women too get lonely, have desires, and want affection and entertainment: every European capital has a surplus of women, and, well, I was neither ugly nor stupid. I lived a life of refined gentility, and it was generally known that I was rich. What with all this, I did exactly as any other man in my position would. I am sure that, following the preoccupations and confusions of the first few weeks, one kind word would have tamed her and inclined her affections to me. But I never did say that kind word. From my point of view, this familiarity, if the presence of a young servant in one's parental home might be regarded as familiarity, roused my suspicions, and presented a danger. It became mysterious and exciting only once I realized that it was not as a lover I desired her, not as someone to bed, like all the others before, that I was not interested in purchasing and consuming fifty kilos of human flesh. No. So what did I want? It took me some time to find out. I didn't bother her, because I was hoping for something from her. Expecting something. Not a brief thrill. But what, then? The answer to a question I had been asking all my life, that's what.

In the meantime we carried on in our usual ways, as befitted us. Naturally, I even considered removing this girl from our family circle, educating her, establishing a healthier relationship with her, buying her an apartment, taking her as a lover, and going on like that as best we could. Mind you, I have to tell you that this occurred to me only much later—years after, in fact. And it was too late then—by that time the woman was aware of her power, was highly capable and altogether stronger. That's when I fled from her. In the first few years I simply felt something stirring at home. I'd return in the evening to a deep silence, silence and order, as in a monastery. I'd go up to my apartment, where the servant had prepared everything perfectly for the night, some cold orange juice in a thermos flask, my reading matter, and cigarettes. I had always had a big vase of flowers on my writing desk. My clothes, my books, my ornaments, everything was just where it ought to be. I'd stand still and listen. The room was warm. I wasn't always thinking of the girl, of course; I didn't always feel compelled to consider that she was nearby, sleeping somewhere in the servants' quarters. A year passed, and then another: I simply felt there was some meaning to the house. All I knew was that Judit Áldozó lived there and that she was very beautiful. Everyone recognized that. The servant later had to be dismissed, as did the cook, a lonely, older woman, because she had fallen in love with Judit and had no other way of expressing her love but by grumbling and quarreling. Not that anyone ever said as much. Maybe only my mother knew the truth, but if so, she kept it to herself. Afterwards I puzzled for ages about her silence. My mother was an intuitive woman and had plenty of experience: she knew everything without having to say it. No one else in the household knew about the secret passion of the servant and the cook, only my mother, who, I am sure, had no special experience of love, nor understood such perverse and hopeless desires as the old cook had for Judit; maybe she never even read about such things. But she understood reality: she recognized truth. She herself was an older woman by then: she knew everything and marveled at nothing. She even knew that Judit presented a danger in the house, danger not only to the servant and the cook . . . She knew she presented a danger to everyone who lived in the house. Not my father, though, because Father was old and sick by then, and in any case they did not love each other. My mother did, however, love me, and later I wondered why, when she knew everything, she hadn't got rid of the source of danger in time. A whole life had gone by, or almost vanished, before I finally understood.

Lean closer. Just between us, the truth is, my mother welcomed this danger. She might well have feared that I faced a danger that was greater still. Can you guess what danger that might be? Not a clue? The danger of loneliness, of the terrifying loneliness that constituted our lives, the lives of my mother and father, the loneliness of the whole triumphant, successful, ritual-observing class we belonged to. There is a certain human process that is more to be feared, that is worse than anything . . . It's the process whereby we become cut off from each other, when we become little more than machines. We live according to stern domestic codes, work to an even stricter code of duty, surrounded by a social order governed by a thoroughgoing strictness that produces orderly forms of amusements, preferences, and affections, so our entire lives become predictable, knowing what time to dress, to take breakfast, to go to work, to make love, to be entertained, to engage in social refinements. There is order everywhere, a mad order. And in the grip of that order life freezes about us, as around an expedition that is prepared for a long journey to lush shores, but finds both sea and land icebound, so that eventually there is no plan, no desire, just cold and immobility. And cold and immobility are the definition of death. It's a slow, irresistible process. One day a family's entire life turns to consommé. Everything becomes important, every least detail, but they can't see anything of the whole and lose contact with life itself . . . They take such care in dressing in the morning and for the evening you'd think they were preparing for some dangerous ceremony like going to a funeral or a wedding, or to a court to be sentenced. They maintain their social contacts, have guests over, but behind it all looms the specter of loneliness. And while there is a sense of waiting or expectation behind the loneliness, something for heart and soul to hold on to, life remains tolerable and they go on living . . . not well, not as human beings should, but there is at least a reason to wind up the mechanism of one's life in the morning and to let it tick on into night.

Because hope persists for a long time. People are very reluctant to resign themselves to lack of hope, to the thought of being alone; mortally, hopelessly alone. Very few can live with the knowledge that there is no end to loneliness. They carry on hoping, snatching at things, taking refuge in relationships to which they bring no genuine passion, to which they cannot surrender and so take recourse to distractions, to giving themselves artificial tasks, feverishly working or traveling with grand itineraries, or investing in big houses, buying the affections of women with whom they have nothing in common, becoming collectors of ornamental fans, or precious stones, or rare beetles. But none of this is of the least help. And they know perfectly well, even as they are doing these things, that they don't help. And yet they carry on hoping.

By that time, they themselves have no idea what it is they have invested their hopes in. They are fully aware that more money, a more complete collection of beetles, a new lover, an interesting circle of friends, and garden parties even more splendid than your neighbors', none of them help . . . That is why, first and foremost, in the midst of their suffering and confusion, they are desperate to maintain order. Their every waking moment is spent in ordering their lives. They are continually "making arrangements"—seeing to some contract or attending some social event, or making a sexual assignation . . . As long as they are not alone, not for a second! As long as they never have to catch a glimpse of their own loneliness! Quick, bring on company! Fetch the dogs! Hang those tapestries! Buy those shares, or those antiques! Get a new lover! Quick, before the loneliness has to be faced.

That's how they live. It's how we lived. We took a great deal of trouble dressing. By the time he was fifty my father dressed with as much care as a church elder or a Catholic priest preparing for mass. His servant knew his habits to a T and by dawn had prepared his suit, his shoes, and his tie as if he were a sacristan. It was all because my father—by no means a vain man and never too particular about his appearance before— resolved to be dignified in his old age and, from that moment on, decided to pay minute attention to his clothes, with not a speck of dust on his sleeve, not one unwonted crease in his trousers, not one stain or crinkle on his shirt or his collar, his tie perfectly knotted . . . yes, just like a priest dressed for mass, as careful as that. And then, having dressed, the second ritual of the day began: breakfast. Then the car waiting to take him somewhere, the reading of the papers, the mail, the office, the efficient and respectful clerks rendering accounts, the meetings with business contacts, the club and the social round . . . and all this conducted with such constant close attention to detail, such anxious care, it was as if there were someone watching all this, someone to whom he himself had to render accounts of every part of his sacred duties. That is what my mother feared. Because behind all this ritual, this dressing up, this tapestry collecting and club calling, behind the socializing and entertaining, the terror of loneliness had raised its head like an iceberg in a warming sea. Loneliness, you know, tends to appear in certain modes of individual and social life like an illness in an exhausted body. It's the kind of condition that doesn't suddenly leap to attention. The real crises—sickness, breakups, the terminal things—don't just turn up to be announced or established or noticed at any particular hour of any particular day. By the time we have noticed them, those decisive moments of our lives, they are usually already past, and there is nothing left for us to do but accept them and send for the lawyer or the doctor or the priest. Loneliness is a form of sickness. Or, more precisely, not a form of sickness, but a condition in which whoever is fated to suffer it finds himself displayed in a cage like a stuffed animal. No: sickness is the process that precedes loneliness, a process I'd compare to slowly freezing over. My mother wanted to save me from that.

Life, you know, becomes increasingly mechanical. Things chill down. The rooms are as well heated as ever they were, your temperature remains normal, your blood pressure is exactly as it was, you still have money in the bank or in your business. Once a week you go to the opera or to the theater, preferably where they are playing something cheerful. You eat light meals at the restaurant; you mix your wine with sparkling water because you have taken note of all the healthy advice. Life presents no problems. Your local doctor—that is if he is only a good doctor not a true one; the two are not the same—shakes your hand after the half-yearly checkup and says you're fine. But if he is a true doctor—that is to say, a doctor bred in the bone, in the way a pelican is nothing but a pelican and a general is a general even when he is not engaged in a battle and is simply trimming his hedge or doing the crossword—if he is a doctor of this sort, he will not be satisfied with shaking your hand after the half-yearly examination, because despite the fact that your heart, your lungs, your kidneys and liver are all in perfect working order, he recognizes your life is not so, and can sense the chill of loneliness as it works through you, exactly the way a ship's delicate instruments can detect the mortal danger of the approaching iceberg even in warm waters. I can't think of another analogy, that's why I return to the iceberg. But maybe I could just add that the chill is of the kind you feel in the summer, in houses emptied of occupants who have departed for their holidays, having sprinkled camphor here and there and wrapped their furs and carpets up in newspapers, while outside it is summer, scorching hot summer, and behind the closed shutters the lonely furniture and the shadowed walls have soaked up all the cold and loneliness that even inanimate objects register, that everyone feels is there, that all who are lonely, objects as well as people, breathe in and radiate.

People remain alone because they are proud and will not dare accept love's slightly jealous offerings; because they are fulfilling a role that seems more important than love; because they are vain; because every proper member of the bourgeoisie, everyone who is truly bourgeois— that is to say, a solid respectable citizen—is vain. I don't mean the petit bourgeois, people who regard themselves as respectable because they have money or because somehow or other they find themselves socially elevated to some position of rank. They are just churls in bourgeois dress. I mean the creative guardians of that proper and respectable class, the truly solid bourgeoisie.

There comes a time when loneliness begins to crystallize around them. They begin to feel the cold. Then they turn ceremonial, become artifacts like Chinese vases or Renaissance tables. They turn to ceremony, start to collect stupid, pointless titles and distinctions, do everything they possibly can to achieve dignity and grace, filling their days with all kinds of complicated affairs in order to earn a medal or ribbon or a new title, such as vice president, or president, or honorary president, of this, that, or the other. That is what loneliness means, the being there. Happy people have no history, we are taught; happy people have neither rank nor title, no superfluous role in the world.

That's why mother feared for me. Maybe that is why she tolerated Judit Áldozó in the house even after she noticed the danger her whole being radiated. As I said, nothing "happened" . . . I might qualify that by saying, "regrettably" nothing happened. It was just that three years went by. Then one evening, at Christmas, I was on my way home from work and decided to call in on my then lover, a singer, who was alone at home that afternoon in the lovely, warm, and boring apartment I had fitted out for her, and I gave her a present that was as lovely and as boring as she, the singer, was, and indeed as all the other lovers and apartments and presents that I had frittered away my time with had been. But as I was saying, I came home, because the family was to dine at my place that evening. And then it happened. I entered the drawing room. The Christmas tree was on the piano, fully decorated and sparkling, otherwise the light was dim, and there was Judit Áldozó kneeling in front of the fire.

It was Christmas, the afternoon, and being in my parents' place, in the hours before the Christmas Eve dinner, I felt tense and alone. I also knew that this is how it would always be from now on, for the rest of my life, unless something miraculous happened. At Christmas, you know, one always tends to entertain a faint belief in miracles, not just you and I, but the whole world, all humanity as they say, for that, after all, is why we have festivals, because without miracles we cannot live. This afternoon had, of course, been preceded by many other such afternoons and evenings and mornings, days when I had seen Judit Áldozó without feeling anything unusual. If you live by the sea you are not always thinking that you could sail to India, or that you could drown yourself in it. Most of the time you just live there, read, and go in for a swim. But that afternoon I stood in the dimly lit room and gazed at Judit. She was wearing her black housemaid's uniform, just as I was wearing my gray industrialist's suit, preparing to go to my room and put on my black dinner suit evening uniform. That afternoon I stood in the twilit room, looked at the Christmas tree, the kneeling female figure, and suddenly understood all that had happened in the last three years. I understood that the decisive events of our lives are moments of stillness and silence, and that behind the visible, sensible events there lies another level, where something lazy is slumbering, a sleeping monster lodged under the sea or deep in the forest, in the heart of man, a dozy monster, some primeval creature, that rarely shifts itself, that yawns and stretches but rarely reaches for anything, and that this too is you, this monster, this otherness. And that there is a kind of order under the commonplace events in life, the kind you find in music or mathematics . . . a slightly romantic kind of order. Is that so hard to understand? It's how I felt. As I said before, I am an artist without a medium, a musician without an instrument.

The girl was arranging the kindling in the grate and felt me standing behind her, watching her, but she did not move. She did not turn to face me. She knelt and bent forward, a position that registers, that means something emotionally. A woman kneeling and bending forward, even when she is working, cannot but register as a sentimental phenomenon. I couldn't help laughing. But it wasn't a frivolous laughter, simply good-natured, like someone rejoicing that even in those overwhelming, decisive, crucial moments we can't forget that there remains in us and in our relationships with each other a kind of vulgar humanity, a sort of stumbling awkwardness associated with grand passions and feelings of pathos brought on by certain movements of the body, such as, for example, those of that woman kneeling in that dimly lit room. I know it's regrettable. Ridiculous. But great and powerful feelings that are part of the world's self-renewing energy, to whose workings every living being is a slave or a cog in the machine, must always be combined with the ridiculous in order to become the dazzling phenomena they are. That was another thought that occurred to me in that moment. And, naturally, I recognized not only the feeling that I desired this body, but also the tension and apprehension of the fact that this was fated to be, that while there was something low and contemptible in this fact, it was, nevertheless, a fact: that the truth was that I desired her. It was no less true that it wasn't her body alone I desired, the body that was just now displaying itself in this almost buffoonish manner, but that which lay beneath the body, her condition, her feelings, her secrets. And because, like many wealthy and relatively idle young men now, I had spent a great deal of my time among women, I was also aware that there are no permanent or long-lasting sentimental arrangements between men and women; that sentimental moments renew themselves from within and when they vanish, they vanish into thin air due to habitual proximity and indifference. I understood that this lovely body, that solid rump, that slender waist, the broad yet proportionate shoulders, that charming, slightly bent neck with its chestnut-colored down, and those fleshy, pleasantly formed legs, this female body, was not the most beautiful in the world, and that I myself had known, taken possession of, and carried into bed, bodies better proportioned, lovelier, and more exciting than hers—but that this wasn't the point. I understood equally well that the ebb and flow of desire and satisfaction, of longing and nausea, were constantly at work in people, attracting and repelling them, and that there was no answer to it, no peace to be found. I understood all this, though not as clearly or with as much certainty as I do now, being older. It may be that I maintained some hope, some hope at the bottom of my heart, that there would be a body, one single, unique body, that would move in perfect harmony with mine, that would succeed in quenching the thirst of desire and the nausea of satisfaction and result in a condition of relative peace, in an idyll that people generally refer to as happiness. But I wasn't to know at that age that there's no such thing in real life.

In real life it does happen, though rarely, that the tension of desire and the succeeding nausea is not followed by an equivalent dose of inward self-monitoring, the depression of satisfaction. There are also people who are like pigs, to whom it's all the same: desire and satisfaction all occur on some indifferent plane of being for them. Maybe they are the satisfied ones. I do not desire that kind of satisfaction. As I say, I didn't know all this for certain back then: I might have hoped a little, and I certainly looked down on myself a little, laughed at the whole situation and the feelings associated with it, the feelings that were so strongly associated with that ridiculous situation. There was much I didn't know then, and I had no inkling that there was little ridiculous about situations where our physical and psychological conditions yield to a relationship with another person. I had no idea about that.

I addressed the girl. I can't remember what I said now, but I can see the whole scene as clearly as if someone had filmed it all on 16mm for a family movie, the kind of record that sentimental people make of a honeymoon, or the first steps of a toddler . . .

This is what I see: Judit slowly gets to her feet, draws a handkerchief from the pocket of her apron, and wipes her hands clear of ashes and wood dust. I see this with pinpoint clarity. Then we immediately start talking, in low voices, quickly, as if afraid that someone might step into the room. We are conspirators, thief and accomplice.

There's something I have to say to you now. I'd like to tell it, honestly, exactly as it was, and as I am sure you will understand, this won't be easy. Because what I am about tell you is not a dirty story, old man, not the story of a seduction—oh, no. My story is somewhat darker than that, and is only mine insofar as I am the chief actor in it. The fact is, there were greater powers exerting pressure on us, greater powers pressing through us.

As I was saying, our voices were low. That's quite natural when you think about it: I was the master, she the servant, and our conversation was confidential in a house where she was part of the staff. What we were talking about was private and of great importance, and someone really could have walked in at any moment—my mother, or perhaps the servant who wanted Judit for himself. Both the situation and my natural tact dictated that we should talk in low voices. She too felt this, of course, and knew she had to whisper.

But I felt something else too. I felt it from the moment we started talking. I felt there was something else going on here. This wasn't just a case of a man talking to a woman he finds attractive, someone from whom he wants something, someone he wants to possess for his pleasure. It wasn't even that I was in love with this firm-bodied, beautiful young woman, or that I was crazy for her, dripping with lust; that the blood had so rushed to my head that I would have tried anything, including force, to get her, to possess her, to make her mine. All this is pretty tedious, I know. It happens in every man's life, and not just once. Sexual hunger can, as you know, be as agonizing and as relentless as the hunger for food. No, there was another reason for all this whispering. I had never before felt the need to be so on my guard, you know. Because I wasn't speaking only about my own affairs; it was a direct encounter with another person, as a person. It was why I had to keep my voice down. It was serious stuff, more serious than a romantic tale about a young gentleman and some pretty young domestic. Because when the woman stood up and, without the least sign of having been flustered, started wiping her hands down and looking me in the eye with deep attention, with those big round eyes of hers—she was already in her evening uniform, in a black dress with white apron and white cap, and looked just like the housemaid in an operetta, laughably so—I felt that the relationship I was offering was based, not only on desire, but, first and foremost, on a kind of conspiracy against somebody or something. And she too felt it. We immediately started speaking about what concerned us. There was no preamble, no beating about the bush. We spoke, almost exactly, as you might expect two conspirators to speak in a palace or some important office where valuable documents and secret papers are stored. One is an employee of the office, the other a visitor, and now, at last, they have finally found a couple of minutes to discuss their joint venture. They talk in whispers, as though they were talking about something else. They are both very excited, but one still behaves as though she were simply going about her work while the other behaves as though he just happened to be passing through the room and had hesitated for a word. They don't have much time. At any moment the boss or some nosy official might enter, and if seen together, both might immediately arouse curiosity and their plot be discovered. That's why we went straight to the point, and why Judit Áldozó stole the occasional glance at the fire, because the larger bits of wood were damp and did not immediately catch light. So she knelt before the fire again and I knelt down by her side and helped her adjust the yellow copper andirons and made sure the fire was properly lit. But all the time I was talking.

What did I say to her? Wait a moment, I need a cigarette. No, I won't bother. I don't tend to count my cigarettes this time of day. In any case a lot of this is not particularly important.

But then, it seemed to me, everything was distinctly important, everything I said, and everything that might result from it. I had no time to court her or woo her. It was all beside the point, anyway. I simply said I would like to live with her. My declaration did not surprise her. She calmly heard me out, then looked directly at me with a solemn look on her face, without any sense of astonishment. Afterwards I felt she was weighing me up, as if wanting to calculate my strength, the way a peasant girl will size up a local lad showing off in front of her, telling her he can lift this or that heavy object, a full sack of wheat, that sort of thing. It was not my muscles she was weighing up, but my soul. As I say, now, in retrospect, I feel there may have been something mocking in her examination of me, a silent, gentle mocking, as if she were saying: "You're not all that strong. You'll need greater strength if you want to live with me. I'd break your back." That's what I read in her look. I felt it, so I spoke a little faster and still more quietly. I told her that it would be very difficult, because the situation was impossible, my father would never agree to the marriage, and there were likely to be all sorts of other problems too. For example, I said, it was likely that such a marriage would lead to serious tensions between myself and my family as well as the world beyond, and that, if we were being honest, we could not entirely ignore the world of which we were a part, the world that had made us what we were. And it was likely that such tensions, starting, as it were, from such a point of weakness, would sooner or later have a bad effect on the relationship between us, too. I told her I had seen this kind of thing before. I had known people of my own social rank who had married below them, and that these marriages always turned out for the worse. I spouted rubbish like that. Of course I meant it seriously, speaking not out of fear, just wanting to be straight with her. And, understanding that I was being honest, she looked at me earnestly and made a gesture to let me know she thought as I did. It was as if she were encouraging me to look for more reasons that would immediately make it clear how impossible, how hopeless the idea was: she wanted me to go on arguing as convincingly as possible that it was quite insane. And I, for my part, carried on finding such reasons. She did not say a word, not a single word, or, to be precise, she only spoke once I had finished, and even then very briefly. She let me speak. I myself don't understand how, but I spoke for an hour and a half, there by the fireplace, while all the time she remained in that kneeling position, me sitting beside her in the low armchair, the English leather one. I stared into the fire while talking: no one came in, no one disturbed us. There is a kind of hidden order in life, the way a situation arises in a man's life just at the point when something has to be decided or done, so circumstance conspires to bring it about: places, objects, the people closest to hand, all unconsciously combine to produce the moment. No one disturbed us. It was already evening. My father had arrived home, and they would certainly have been looking for Judit to arrange the dishes and cutlery in preparation for supper. We were all used to dressing for the evening meal, but no one disturbed us. Later I understood that this was not as extraordinary as you might think. Life arranges everything to perfection when it wants to put on a show.

In that hour and a half, for the first time in my life, I felt as though I were speaking frankly and directly to someone. I told her I wanted to live with her; that I suspected, but did not know for sure, that I couldn't marry her. The vital thing, I said, was to live together. I asked her if she remembered meeting me the first time she entered our house. She said nothing, only nodded to indicate that she did. She looked extraordinarily beautiful in the low-lit room as she knelt by the fire in the flickering red light, her hair sparkling, her head bent slightly to one side on that slender neck as she listened to me, poker in hand. She was very beautiful, very much part of my life. I told her she should leave the house, resign, give some excuse, then go home and wait for me somewhere, and that in a few days I'd settle what business I had in hand, then we could go off to Italy together, and stay there, maybe for years. I asked her if she wanted to see Italy . . . She didn't say anything, but silently indicated that she did not. Quite likely she didn't understand the question: it was as if I had asked her whether she wanted to see Henry IV. She didn't understand. But she did listen very closely. She kept her eyes on the fire, kneeling straight-backed, like a penitent, so close to me I had only to stretch out my hand to touch her. I did in fact take her hand, but she withdrew it, not in a flirtatious manner, not as though she were offended, just as a perfectly natural, simple form of rejection, with the slightest movement, as if wishing to correct some-thing I had said. I saw for the first time then that she was, in her own way, an aristocrat through and through, that her natural nobility was part of the fabric. It surprised me, but at the same time I immediately accepted it. By that time I knew it was not rank, not the privilege of birth that divided people, but character and intelligence. She knelt in front of the fireplace in the pale red light, like a princess, willowy, at ease, not haughty but not humble either, without betraying a trace of confusion, without the merest tremor of her eyelids, as though this con-versation were the most natural thing in the world. And there above her rose the Christmas tree. Well, you know, when I thought about this later I couldn't help laughing, though it was a rather dry laugh, I can tell you . . . Judit beneath the Christmas tree, like some strange, incompre-hensible gift.

And because she said nothing all this time, I myself eventually fell silent. She hadn't answered me when I asked her if she wanted to live with me, nor when I asked if she wanted to come to Italy with me and stay, perhaps for years. And because I couldn't think of anything else to say, and because, when it came down to it, having spoken to her and tried everything, like a buyer putting an offer to a stubborn vendor, making a low offer first, then, on seeing the other is resolute and seeing the deal stalling, offering the entire asking price, I asked her if she would be my wife.

She did answer this.

Not immediately, true. Her first response was unexpected. She looked at me angrily, almost with hatred. I could see some great emo-tion passing through her entire body like a terrible cramp. She began to shake: she was kneeling in front of me, shaking. She hung the poker back on its hook next to the bellows. She crossed her arms across her chest. She looked like a young novice ordered to kneel by some severe teacher. She stared into the fire with a fierce solemnity, her expression clearly tortured. Then she stood up, smoothed her front, and said simply:

"No."

"Why?" I asked.

"Because you are a coward," she said, and gave me a long look, examining me head to foot. Then she left the room.

Your very good health!

So that's how it began. Then I went out. The shops were already closing, people were hurrying home with Christmas parcels under their arms. I stopped at a little jeweler's selling cheap little trinkets. I bought a gold locket—you know, one of these cheap bits of tat in which women keep the pictures of their dead or current lovers. I found an identity card with a photo in my wallet, a season ticket of some sort that had just expired, tore off the photo, put it in the locket, and asked the man to wrap it up exactly like a normal present. When I got home, Judit opened the door. I pressed the parcel into her hand. Soon after that I went away, not returning home for years, and it was only much later I found out she had been wearing the locket round her neck on a piece of lilac ribbon ever since then, never removing it, only when washing or when she needed a new ribbon.

After that, everything went on as though nothing had happened that fateful Christmas afternoon, as if we had never had such a conversation. Judit served us at table that evening, together with the servant, as usual. Naturally I knew by then that I had been in a delirious state that afternoon. I knew it in exactly the same way madmen know when they are in a fury, beating their heads against the wall, wrestling with their nurses, or removing their own teeth at night with a rusted nail: they know as they are doing these things that even as they are frothing at the mouth and doing them, they are engaged in shameful acts deeply unworthy of themselves and of society. They know this not only after the event, when the fury has left them, but in the very act of doing those crazy, hurtful things. I too knew it even as I was sitting by the fire that afternoon, knew that what I was saying and planning was sheer madness for a man in my position. Later I always thought of it as a kind of fit, losing control and willpower, my nerves and all the organs of sense, working autonomously. The critical and moderating faculties go numb at moments like that. I am absolutely sure that what I experienced that Christmas Day afternoon under the Christmas tree was a nervous breakdown, the only serious nervous breakdown of my entire life. Judit knew it too; that was why she listened so intently, as if she were one member of the family noticing the signs of breakdown in another. Of course she knew something else too: she knew and understood the cause of the breakdown. If any member of the family had been listening to me that afternoon—it needn't have been a member of the family, a stranger would have done—they would immediately have sent for the doctor.

All this came as a surprise to me, because I normally gave everything proper consideration. Maybe a little too much consideration. Maybe that is what had been missing in my way of life: the ability to make sudden decisions, or spontaneity, as they call it. I never did anything just because an idea had occurred to me; never acted on the spur of the moment simply because of a rush of feeling, because an opportunity presented itself or because someone demanded it of me. In the factory and the office I was known as a man of considered judgment, someone who'd think things over slowly and carefully before making an important decision. So I was more surprised than anyone else that I was having this breakdown, because I knew, even as I was talking, that I was talking nonsense, and that nothing would be as I planned it, that I should have done it all differently, been subtler, more careful, or more forceful. You know, till that moment, I had pursued love according to the law of cash-and-carry, like the Americans in wartime: you pay, you take away . . . That was how I thought it was supposed to go. It wasn't the most high-minded kind of thinking, but it was, if nothing else, healthily selfish. This time, though, I had neither paid for nor taken away the thing I desired, but had allowed myself to plead and prevaricate, in a quite hopeless fashion, in a situation that was undoubtedly humiliating for me.

There's no explaining delirium. Everyone is seized by it at least once in life . . . and it may be that life is much poorer if it never once grips us and batters us like a storm, if our foundations are never once shaken by it, so the earth does not shake and the roof tiles all stay on, if its howling fury never once blows away everything that reason and character had kept in order. That's what happened to me . . . You ask me if I regret it? No, I answer, I don't regret it. But I wouldn't exactly say it gave meaning to my life. It was just something that happened, like a bout of sickness, and once someone gets over a heavy bout of it, it is best to send him abroad to recover. That's exactly what I did. Such traveling is, of course, a form of escape. But before I went away I wanted to be sure of something, so I asked my friend Lázár, the writer, to invite her over just once, so that he could see her and talk with her, and prevailed on Judit to accept the invitation. I know now that she was right, that I was a coward, and that that is why I did what I did. It was like sending her to the doctor, you see, so that he might examine her and declare her healthy . . . After all, she was in some ways like someone I might pick up in the street and include in my field of operations, as they have it in the military. She heard me out, disapprovingly, but did as I asked, without protest. She was sullen and certainly insulted. It was as if she had said: "Fine, I'll go to the doctor if you insist and subject myself to an examination." But go she did.

Yes, Lázár. It was a strange relationship between us.

We were contemporaries, school friends. He was already thirty-five by the time fame caught up with him: before that he was practically unknown. He used to write odd little articles for hopeless magazines in a tone that made me think he was laughing at his readers, that he had an endless contempt for the whole enterprise, for writing, for publication, for the reader, and for criticism. You could never work out what he really thought about anything. What did he write about? About the sea, about some old book, about some character, everything brief, no more than two or three pages in some magazine that appeared in an edition of no more than a few hundred, a thousand at most. These pieces were so personal you might have thought they were written in the private language of some strange tribe observing the world or what lay behind the world. This tribe—or so I felt when I first read his writing—was one of those vanishing tribes of which only a few members remained to speak the language, the mother tongue of Lázár's articles. Apart from that he spoke and wrote a calm, passionless, beautiful Hungarian, pure and regular. He used to say to me that he read the works of the great nineteenth-century poet János Arany first thing at morning and last thing at night, the way a man might brush his teeth. But what he wrote was a kind of news from his other country.

And then, suddenly, he was famous. Why? It was impossible to explain. Hands reached out for him, he was in demand, first in literary salons, then on platforms in public debates, then in the press—you saw his name everywhere. People started imitating him: papers and journals were full of Lázár-style books and articles, none of them written by him and yet of all of which he was the hidden author. Then, even more surprisingly, the general public too began to take an interest in him, which was something no one understood, since his writing contained nothing that might amuse or console or delight people: he never seemed to be trying to establish any contact with his readers. But they forgave him that too. Within a few years he occupied the leading position in the peculiar competition that constitutes the worldly side of intellectual existence: his work was constantly discussed, his texts analyzed and picked over as though they were ancient Oriental manuscripts, subjects for high scholarship. None of this changed him. Once, at one particularly successful moment, I asked him what he felt. Didn't the sheer noise around him offend his ears? For, naturally enough, there were critical voices too, jealous voices screaming at him, full of hatred and false accusation. But all this cry and countercry merged into a single sea of sound, out of which his name rose, sharp and clear, like the sound of the first violin in the orchestra. He heard my question through and turned it over in his mind. Then he replied most solemnly: "It's the revenge of the writer." That was all he said.

I knew something about him that others didn't know: I knew he loved to play. Everything was play to him: people, situations, books, the mysterious phenomenon generally referred to as literature. Once, when I accused him of this, he shrugged and said that the deep secret at the core of art, in the artist himself, was the embodying of an instinct for play. And literature? I asked. Literature is, after all, more than that, literature offers answers and moral values . . . He heard me through as seriously and courteously as ever, and replied that this was true enough, but that the instinct that fuels human behavior is the instinct for play and that, in any case, the ultimate meaning of literature, as of religion, and, indeed, of all the arts, is form. He avoided my question. The mass of readers and critics naturally cannot know that a person can play just as solemnly with a kitten chasing a ball of wool in the sunshine as with a problem of knowledge or ethics, engaging with both with an equal inner detachment, concentrating entirely on the phenomenon or thought before him, giving his heart to neither. He was a player in that sense. People didn't know this about him . . . And he was the witness, the observer in my life: it was something we often discussed, perfectly openly. Every man, you know, has someone who fulfills the role of defense lawyer, custodian, and judge, and at the same time his accomplice, in the mysterious and terrifying trial that is his life. That figure is his witness. He is someone who sees and understands perfectly. Everything you do is done partly with him in mind, so when you succeed at some venture you ask yourself: "Would he be convinced by it?" This witness hovers in the background throughout our entire life. He is not a comfortable playfellow in that sense. But there is nothing you can do to free yourself of him, and maybe you don't even want to try.

Lázár, the writer, fulfilled that role in my life: it was with him I played the strange games of youth and adulthood, games that would have been incomprehensible to anyone else. He was the only one who knew, and of whom I alone knew, that it didn't matter that the world regarded us as adults, as a serious industrialist, as a famous writer; that it was beside the point that women regarded us as excitable or melancholy or passionate examples of manhood . . . what really mattered was this capricious, brave, ruthless desire to play, which distorted and yet at the same time, at least for ourselves, lent beauty to the hollow, ritual theater of life.

Whenever we found ourselves together in society we were like two evil conspirators, understanding each other without secret signals, immediately engaging in our game.

There was a variety of games. We had our "Mr. Smith" game. Shall I explain it so you understand how it was with us? The rules of this game were that we had to go straight into it, without any warning, when we were in company—that is to say, in the company of various Mr. and Mrs. Smiths—so they should not suspect anything. So we would meet somewhere with others present, and immediately get started. What does one Mr. Smith say to the other Mr. Smith should they be speaking in company about, say, the recent collapse of the government, or the Danube flood that swept through entire neighbor-hoods, or the divorce of the famous actress, or the well-known politician caught with his hands in the public purse, or how the fellow caught up in that scandal shot himself at a well-known beauty spot? Mr. Smith would hem and haw and say, "Well, fancy that," then go on to add some thumping commonplace, such as "Wet stuff, water!" or "If people will insist on putting their feet into water, they must expect to get wet!" Or something like "Well, it takes all sorts." It's what the Smiths have been saying since the dawn of time. When the train arrives they say, "It's arrived." Should the train stop in Füzesabony, they solemnly announce, "Ah, Füzesabony!" And they are always right. And maybe that is why the world is so hopeless, so dreadful beyond comprehension: it is because the clichés are always true, and only an artist or a genius has the gall to rap a cliché over the knuckles, to expose what is dead and against life in them, to show that, behind the truisms beloved of our respectable and matter-of-fact Mr. Smith, there lurks another truth, an eternal truth that stands the world on its head and sticks its tongue out at Füzesabony and is not a bit surprised when the morally bankrupt high official is dis-covered in a pink nightie by the security police, his body dangling from a window . . . If the subject happened to be a political debate, Lázár or I would answer Mr. Smith without hesitation, saying: "Well, as ever, one of them is right, but the other is not altogether wrong. Let's give every-one a chance." Lázár and I perfected the Mr. Smith game so that all the real-life Mr. Smiths never once noticed and carried on precisely as before.

Then there was the "In our day . . ." game, and that was pretty good too. Back in our day, you should know, everything was better: sugar was sweeter, water more fluid, the air more like proper air; women didn't run around flinging themselves into men's arms but spent the day paddling and bathing in the river, right till sunset, and even after the sun set they'd stay there paddling in the river. And when men saw a pile of banknotes in front of them, they didn't try to grab it but pushed it away, declaring: "Go on, take it away, give it to the poor. Yes, sir, that's what men and women were like in our day." We played a lot of games like that . . .

This was the man to whom I sent Judit Áldozó so that he might give her the once-over. As I said, it was just like sending her to the doctor.

Judit called on Lázár in the afternoon. I met him in the evening. "Look," he said. "What's the point? The matter is already settled." I listened to him with suspicion. I was afraid he was just playing another game. We were sitting in a city-center café, like the one we're in now. He kept turning his cigarette holder—he always used long cigarette holders when smoking, because he was constantly suffering from nicotine poisoning, forever contemplating complex plans and inventions that would help humankind escape the painful consequences of this particular poison—gazing at me so earnestly, studying me with such attention, that I grew ever more suspicious. I wondered if this was another of his straight-faced jokes, a new game in which he was only pretending that this affair was deadly serious, and that soon enough he would laugh aloud at me, as he so often did, and go on to prove that there was nothing important or deadly serious about it, and that it was just another of those Mr. Smith games. After all, it is only the lower orders who believe the universe revolves around them and that the stars carefully arrange themselves with their fate in mind. I know he considered me a bourgeois—not in the contemptuous sense of the word that is so fashionable now; no, he recognized that it takes considerable effort to maintain a bourgeois existence, and would not look down on my origins, my manner, or my values, because he too had a high opinion of the middle classes. It was just that he considered me a hopeless case. He felt there was something hopeless in my situation. The bourgeois is always trying to escape, he said. But he didn't want to say any more about Judit Áldozó. Courteously but firmly he changed the subject.

Afterwards I often thought back to this conversation the way a sick man remembers learning the real name and nature of his disease when he first visited the famous doctor. The great doctor goes about his examination in a thorough, careful manner, using every kind of instrument, then airily begins to talk of something else, inquiring whether we did not fancy a voyage, or have seen the latest fashionable play, or been in touch with some mutual acquaintance. The only subject he does not touch upon is the one we are most anxious to hear about. That is, after all, why we are there, why we have suffered the tension and discomfort of the examination: it is because we wanted to be certain of something, because we ourselves do not know whether our condition is unusual, whether it is a general malaise or just a collection of insignificant symptoms, since we have been aware for some time that our anxious and troubled state is a sign of something wrong in our constitution, in the very rhythm of our life, all the while hoping that it could all be put right at a stroke, faintly but unambiguously suspecting that the great man knows the truth but isn't telling us. So there's nothing to do but wait until we discover for ourselves the truth the doctor kept from us, discover it through the development of further symptoms, through various other signs of danger, and through the manner of our treatment. In the meantime everyone really knows the score: the sick man knows he is very sick; the doctor knows not only that he is very sick but that the patient himself suspects as much and, furthermore, that the patient is quite aware that the doctor is keeping something from him. But there is nothing anyone can do about this; all both can do is to wait until the sickness takes some particular course. Then a cure of some sort may be attempted.

That's how it was with Lázár the evening after Judit's visit. He talked about all kinds of things—about Rome, about new books, about the relationship between literature and the seasons. Then he stood up, shook my hand, and said good-bye. That was when I felt it had not been a game. My heart was thumping with tension. I felt he had left me to my fate, that I had to deal with things by myself from then on. That was the moment I first began to respect the woman who had had such an effect on Lázár. I respected her and feared her. A few days later I went away.

A long time passed. I have only vague memories of it. It was, you might say, the development section of the drama. I wouldn't want to bore you with the details of that.

I traveled for four years, all over Europe. My father had no real notion of the reason for my absence. My mother might have known, but she kept quiet about it. For a long time I noticed nothing unusual. I was young and the world, as they say, was mine.

There was peace then . . . though not proper peace, not really. We were between two wars. The borders were never completely open, but the trains did not stop too long at the variously colored international barriers. People asked each other for loans, not only people but countries, as if nothing had happened, going about their lives with miraculous confidence. And, what was still more miraculous, they received the loans—long-term loans—and they built houses, big ones, small ones, and generally behaved as though they had seen the back of painful, terrible times forever, as though it were an entirely new era, so that now everything was as it should be: they could plan far ahead, bring up their children, and give themselves over to individual pleasures that were not only delightful but even a touch superfluous. That was the world in which I started traveling—the world between two wars. I can't say that the feeling I set out with, and which I experienced at various stopping places on my journey, was one of absolute security. We behaved like people who had, to their surprise, been robbed of everything: our whole lives were tinged with suspicion during the brief period between two wars in Europe: we, all of us, individuals and nations, made enthusiastic efforts to be generous and great-hearted, but—secretly, at any rate—we carried revolvers in our pockets and would occasionally reach, in a panic, for our wallets in the pocket above our hearts. Not just for our wallets, probably, but for our hearts and minds too, because we feared for them also. Nevertheless, one could at least travel again.

Everywhere people were building new houses, new estates, new towns, and, yes, new nations too. I headed north first, then south, then west. Eventually I spent several years in the cities of the West. The things I loved and in which I most earnestly believed were most directly to hand there. It was like when we learn a language at school and then travel to the country where the book language is the mother tongue of real people. In the West I lived among the members of a truly civil society, people who clearly did not regard membership of their class as a form of acting or sloganeering, nor a chore, but simply lived in the manner befitting those who had inherited the house they lived in from their ancestors, a house slightly too small, a little too dark and old-fashioned perhaps, but the house they best knew, one not worth demolishing in order to build another. Their way of life was as it was, needing the odd spot of repair and upkeep. We, at home, were still busy building that house, a home worthy of the civic being; between palaces and cottages we were constructing a wider, more compendious way of life in which everyone might feel at home: Judit Áldozó, myself, both of us.

Judit was only a shadow in my thoughts during those years. At first she was primarily the memory of a fierce, fevered condition. Yes, I had been ill and beside myself, ranting. My eyes were not clear. I had become deeply conscious of my loneliness; a freezing wave of loneliness had swept into my life. Fearing loneliness, I fled from it to a person whose being, whose energy, and whose smile suggested that this loneliness might be shared. That was what I remembered. But then the whole world opened up and it proved very interesting. I saw all kinds of statues, gas turbines, and other forms of loneliness; I saw people who felt joy hearing the music of a single line of verse; I saw economic systems that promised dignity and generosity; I saw vast cities, mountaintops, beautiful medieval wells, little German towns, their main squares surrounded by sycamores; cathedral towers, beaches with golden sand and dark blue oceans; women bathing naked on the shore. I saw the world. The memory of Judit Áldozó couldn't compete with the wonders of the world. She was less than a shadow compared to this new reality. Life showed me, and promised me, everything in those years. It offered me liberation from the narrow confines and melancholy clutter of our house. It stripped me of the clothes I had to wear in order to perform my parts back home, and let me lose myself in the traffic of the world. It offered me women too, an army of women, the women of the entire world, from Flemish brunettes with hot-dreamy looks, through bright-eyed French women, to meek German girls . . . all kinds of women. I moved in the world. Women revolved around me as they do around every man, sending messages, calling: the respectable who promised me their entire lives; the flirtatious who offered lives of simple, sensuous, wild abandon—nothing permanent, but something long enough, something more mysterious than a quick fly-by-night affair.

"Women." Have you noticed the wary, uncertain way in which men pronounce the word? It is as if they were speaking of a not completely enchained, ever rebellious, conquered but unbroken tribe of discontents. And, really, what does the everyday concept "women" signify in the hurly-burly of existence? What do we expect of them? . . . Children? Help? Peace? Delight? Everything? Nothing? A few moments of pleasure?

We carry on living, desiring, meeting, and falling in love, and then we marry, and, with that one woman, we experience love, childbirth, and death, all the time allowing our heads to be turned by a neatly formed ankle, and ready to face ruin for the sake of a hairdo or the hot breath emanating from another's lips. We lie with them in middle-class beds, or on sofas with broken springs, in cheap no-questions-asked hotels, down filthy side streets, and feel a very brief satisfaction. Or we grow drunk on high-flown sentiment with a woman, weepy and full of vows. We promise to face the world together, to assist each other, to live on a mountaintop, or in the heart of some great city . . . But then time passes, a year, or three years, or two weeks—have you noticed how love, like death, has nothing to do with clocks or calendars?—and the grand plan to which both the woman and the man have agreed is not carried through, or only partially carried through, not quite as either had imagined. And so the man and woman part, with anger or with indifference, and once again they set out, full of hope, ready to start again with someone new. Alternatively, they might stay together out of sheer exhaustion, draining the lifeblood from each other, and so sicken, killing each other little by little before dying. But then, in that very last moment, just as they are closing their eyes, what is it they understand? What had they wanted from each other? They seem to have done nothing except conform to an old, blind law, the law of love, at whose bidding the world must constantly renew itself, because the world requires the lust of men and women to perpetuate the species. So was that all? What, poor things, had they been hoping for? What have they given each other? What have they received? What a terrifying, secret audit! Is the instinct that draws one man to one woman personal? Isn't it just desire, always, eternally, simply desire, that occasionally, for some brief interval, is incarnated in a particular body? And this strange, artificial excitement, the fever in which we live: might that not have been nature's fully conscious way of preventing men and women feeling utterly alone?

Look around you. There's no escape from sexual tension: it's there in literature, in paintings, on the stage, and out in the street . . . Go into a theater. There are men and women sitting in the auditorium watching men and women conspiring onstage, chatting, making promises, and taking vows. The audience coughs and croaks and is clearly bored . . . but let the words "I love you" be spoken by the actors, or "I want you," or anything that refers to love, possession, parting, and to the happiness or misery associated with them, the auditorium immediately falls deathly silent: thousands upon thousands, all over the world, are holding their breath. Writers spend their lives cooking such things up: they use the emotion to blackmail the audience. And wherever you go, this whipped-up excitement continues unabated: perfumes, bright dresses, expensive furs, half-naked bodies, skin-colored stockings. It's the same desire at work—the desire to show off a silk-stockinged knee or, in the summer, on the beach, to go practically naked, because this way the feminine presence becomes more teasing, more exciting, not to mention the makeup, the scarlet basque, the blue eye shadow, the blond highlights, all the cheap rubbish they apply and pamper themselves with—it's all so unhealthy.

I was almost fifty before I understood *The Kreutzer Sonata*. It seems to be about jealousy, but that is not the true subject. Tolstoy's masterpiece talks about jealousy presumably because Tolstoy himself was painfully sensitive and had a jealous nature. But jealousy is nothing more than vanity. Jealousy is pitiful and contemptible. Oh, yes, I know the feeling quite well . . . all too well. I almost died of it. But I am no longer jealous. Do you understand me? Do you believe me? Look at me. No, old man, I am no longer jealous, because—at considerable cost—I overcame that vanity. Tolstoy still believed in some kind of balm for it, so he assigned to women a role that is half animal; they should give birth and dress in sackcloth. But that is the sickness, not the cure. The alternative, of course, is no better. It proposes women as bits of décor, masterpieces of emotion. How can I respect, how can I give my heart and mind to, someone who, from the moment of rising to the hour of lying down, does nothing but dress and preen herself as if to say, "Here I am . . ." Someone who apparently wishes to make herself attractive to me by means of feather, fur, and scent. But that is too simple. It's more complicated than that. She wants to be attractive to everyone, you see; she wants to lodge the spore of desire in the whole world's nervous system. Movies, theaters, the street, the café, the restaurant, the baths, the hills: everywhere it's the same unhealthy excitement. Do you think nature really needs all this? No, dear boy! Not at all. Only one social arrangement, one mode of production, requires it: it's the one in which women regard themselves as items for sale.

Of course you're right, I don't myself have a better answer, a better system of production and social exchange . . . all the alternatives have failed. I have to admit that in our system, a woman constantly feels obliged to sell herself, sometimes consciously, more often subconsciously. I don't say every woman is conscious of being a commercial object . . . but I daren't believe that exceptions *don't* prove the rule. I don't blame women: it's not their fault. This presentation of the self as something "on offer" can feel like death, especially the foolishness, the haughtiness, that ironically flirtatious performance of giving herself airs when a woman feels under pressure because she is surrounded by others more beautiful, less expensive, and more exciting. What is a woman to do with her life, both as woman and as a human being, when, as today, women outnumber men in every part of Europe, when competition has assumed a terrifying intensity? They offer themselves, some virtuously, with downcast eyes, like tremulous, highly delicate bouquets who continue trembling in private in case time passes and no one carries them away; others more consciously, setting out each day like Roman legionaries fully aware of their imperial mission to vanquish the barbarian . . . No, my friend, we have no right to condemn women. The only right we may have is to pity them, and perhaps not even them, but ourselves, we men, who are incapable of solving this long, painful crisis in the great free market of civilization. It is constant anxiety. Wherever you go, wherever you look. And it is money that is behind all the human misery—not all the time, maybe, but in ninety-nine cases out of a hundred. That is the subject the saintly, wise author of *The Kreutzer Sonata* never mentions, not once, in his furious indictment . . .

The story is about jealousy. Tolstoy cursed women, fashion, music—all the bewitchments of social life. The one thing he fails to mention is that inner peace is not to be achieved by changes in social order, or by changing the means of production, but by ourselves alone. How? By overcoming vanity and desire. Is that possible? . . . It's all but impossible. Maybe later, at some stage in the future, it may happen. Time does not diminish desire; but fury, jealousy, greed, the hopeless excitement and disgust that are key elements in desire and its satisfaction, might gradually fall away or wear away. One simply grows tired, you see. There are times even now when I am glad to feel old age knocking at the door. What I sometimes desire now are rainy days when I can sit by the fire with a glass of red wine and an old book that speaks of past desires and disappointments.

But back then I was still young. I spent four years traveling. I woke in women's arms, with my own hair tangled and matted, in the rooms of other cities. I learned my craft to the best of my ability. I was lost in the beauty of the world. I didn't think about Judit Áldozó. At least not often, not consciously, only the way one thinks, when abroad, of streets back home, of rooms, of people one has left behind; people who emerge from the golden glow of memory in a state so refined they're practically dead. There was, I reflected, one hour of madness when I, a lonely, middle-class young man, met a wild, beautiful young woman and we fell to talking in the midst of that loneliness . . . then I forgot it all. I traveled. The years of wandering passed, then I went home. Nothing happened.

It was just that, in the meantime, Judit Áldozó was back there, waiting for me.

She did not say as much, of course, when I got home and we met once more. She took my coat, my hat, and my gloves and gave me a polite, reserved smile such as is due to the young master of the house when he returns after an absence: it was the official smile a servant gives. I addressed her correctly, smiling and unflustered. I stopped just short of patting her cheek in good-humored paternal fashion . . . The family was waiting for me. Judit went off with the servant to prepare the dinner that was to welcome the lost prodigal. Everyone was effusive with delight, as indeed was I, glad to be finally at home.

My father had retired that year, and I took over the factory. I moved away from home, rented a villa on a hillside near the city. I saw less of my family now—weeks went by without meeting Judit. After another two years my father died. My mother left the big house and let the old staff go. Judit was the only one she kept with her, she being house-keeper in all but name by then. I visited Mother once a week, for dinner on Sunday, and saw Judit on those occasions, though we never talked to each other. Our relationship was warm and courteous. I occasionally addressed her in a more familiar way as "Juditka," "Judi," in a spirit of kindly, slightly patronizing benevolence. It was the way one might talk to a still-young but rapidly aging spinster. Yes, there was a moment, back in the long-distant past, one mad occasion, on which we had talked of all kinds of things, the kind of things a person can, later, only smile about. It was youth and foolishness. That's what I thought each time I recalled it: it was the way I chose to view it. It was very comfortable. False but comfortable. Everything was in its proper place: everything was as it should be. And so I got married.

It was a polite and pleasant existence with my wife, though later, after my son died, I felt cheated. Loneliness was eating me away, infecting everything around me. I was becoming seriously ill with it. My mother suspected as much but didn't say anything. Years passed. Lázár became ever less of a presence. We met occasionally, but we no longer played our old games. We must have grown up, I suppose. To grow up is to become lonely. Lonely people either fail and become resentful, or come to some good-natured accommodation with the world. Since I was lonely *within* a marriage, within a family, it wasn't easy coming to a good-natured accommodation. I gave my time to work, to society, and to travel. My wife did everything she could for the sake of a happy and contented life together. She labored feverishly at it, the way a man labors at breaking stones: there was even an air of desperation about her efforts. I was unable to help her. Once, a long time ago, I tried the experiment of taking her away to Merano. It was on the way there I discovered it was hopeless, that there would not be an accommodation. My life—what I had made of it—was certainly tolerable but almost entirely without meaning. A great artist might be able to cope with such loneliness. He'd pay a terrible price for it, but his work might offer him some compensation. No one else could do his work for him, after all. His work would offer something simple and lasting: people would regard it as something miraculous. That's what they say. It was what I imagined. I spoke to Lázár about it once and he was of a different opinion. He said that the sense of loneliness is bound to lead to premature defeat. There was no escape. Those were the rules. Do you imagine that is so? I myself don't know. All I know is that I wasn't an artist, so I felt all the more alone, both in my life and in my work. My work was of no vital importance to humanity. I was a manufacturer of utilitarian goods, my job being to provide certain necessities of a civilized life on a production line. Production was a perfectly honorable enterprise, but it was machines, not I myself, that produced the goods: it was what my workforce was employed to do; what they were tamed, taught, and disciplined to achieve; it was their purpose. What was it I did in this fac-

tory my father had built up and which his engineers had constructed? . . .
I'd go in at nine like most senior management, chiefly because I had to
set an example. I read through the mail. My secretary informed me who
had tried to contact me by phone and who else wished to speak to me.
After that, the engineers and salesmen arrived, told me how things
stood, and asked me for my opinion concerning the possibility of man-
ufacturing some new line. The brilliant, hand-picked engineers and
clerks—mostly handpicked by my father—were always ready with new
plans. I heard them through, raised some minor problems, suggested
modifications. Most of the time I simply agreed and approved. The factory went on producing what it produced morning, noon, and into the
evening; the salesmen made sales and demanded their commission; I
spent the entire day in my office. All this amounted to a moderately useful, necessary, honest activity. We did not cheat ourselves, our customers, the state, or the world at large. The only person being cheated was I
myself.

That was because I believed that work was an inevitable, unconditional part of my life. "It is my working life," as people say. I observed
the faces of those near to me. I listened to what they said, and I tried to
answer the central question as to whether work was fulfilling for them,
or whether they secretly felt exploited; that the best part of them, their
very essence, was being drained out of them. From time to time there
were those less satisfied with their working conditions, people who
tried to do everything better or simply differently, not that doing things
"differently" always meant a better or more appropriate way. But at
least they wanted to do something different. They wanted to change
the world in some way. They wanted to find new meaning in their
work. And that is the point, I think. It's not enough for people to earn a
living, to support their family, and to do an honest job . . . no, people
want more than that. They want to realize their ideas, bring their plans
to fruition. It's not just bread and jobs; it is a vocation they want. Without that, life has no meaning. They want to feel needed, not just because
they supply the necessary manpower in a factory or fulfill an office to
other people's general satisfaction . . . they want to achieve something,
something others could not achieve. Of course it is only the talented
who really want this. Most people are lazy. Maybe, in even their souls
there flickers the vague thought that life is not entirely about wages,

that God had some other purpose for them . . . but that was all so long ago! And they—this remainder who can remember no sense of purpose—are in the majority. And they hate the talented. They regard those who want to live and work differently from them, those who don't rush from the robotic life of the workplace to the robotic life of the home as soon as the bell rings, as ambitious, as creeps. They find all kinds of refined, convoluted ways of crushing talented people's enthusiasm for solitary work. They mock, they tease, they raise obstacles and spread rumors about them.

I witnessed all this in my office whenever my workers, engineers, and business contacts came to see me.

And I? What did I do? I was the boss. I sat there like a sentry. I took great trouble to be dignified, humane, and just. At the same time, of course, I also made sure that the factory and my staff provided me with what befitted, and was required by, my position. I was very punctilious in working the proper hours at the factory: to put it more precisely, I worked as hard as those I employed. I strove to serve capital and profit in the appropriate manner. But I felt absolutely hollow inside. What was my sphere of action in the factory? I was free to accept or reject ideas, I was free to change working practice, I was free to seek new markets for our products. Did I take pleasure in the handsome profits? "Pleasure" is the wrong word. I took satisfaction at having fulfilled my public obligations, and the money enabled me to live a blameless, fashionable, generous, and disinterested kind of life. At the factory, and in business generally, people regarded me as the very model of a respectable businessman. I could afford to be liberal, to offer a living wage, and more than a living wage, to a good many . . . It's nice being able to give. It was just I myself who took no real joy in it. I lived in comfort, but my days were spent doing honest work. My hands were not idle; at least the world did not regard me as either indolent or a waste of space. I was the good boss: that's what they said in the factory.

But all this meant nothing; it was just a tiresome, careful, conscientious way of filling time. Life remains hollow if you don't fill it up with something exciting, some project with a hint of danger. That project can only be work, of course. It is the other kind of work, the invisible work of the soul, the intelligence and talent, whose productions enrich and humanize the world and lend it the air of truth. I read a great deal.

But you know how it is with reading too . . . you only benefit from books if you can give something back to them. What I mean is, if you approach them in the spirit of a duel, so you can both wound and be wounded, so you are willing to argue, to overcome and be overcome, and grow richer by what you have learned, not only in the book, but in life, or by being able to make something of your work. One day I noticed that the books I read had ceased to have anything properly to do with me. I read as I might in some foreign city, to fill the time, the way you go to visit a museum, gazing at the exhibits with a kind of courteous disinterest. I read as if I were fulfilling an obligation: a new book appeared that everyone was talking about, so I read it. Or there was some old classic I had missed reading and so felt my education was incomplete, that something was missing. That was the way I read . . . There had been a time when reading was an experience. I grabbed new books by well-known authors with my heart in my mouth; a new book was like meeting someone new, an encounter fraught with risk, that might result in happiness and general benefit, but was also potentially threatening: it might produce unwelcome consequences. By now I was reading the way I worked in the factory, the way I went to social occasions two or three times a week, the way I went to the theater, the way I lived at home with my wife, courteously, considerately, with the ever more pressing, ever more upsetting, ever louder, ever more urgently demanding questions pounding at my heart that led me to wonder if I was seriously ill, in great danger, sick unto death, or the subject of some developing plot or cabal, certain of nothing, fearing that one day I might wake to find everything I had worked for, this whole painstaking, careful, orderly enterprise—the respectability, the good manners, and the culminating masterpiece, our polite coexistence—collapsing around me . . . That was the fraught emotional state I was constantly living in at the time. And one day I discovered in my wallet, the brown crocodile-skin wallet I had been given by my wife, a faded lilac ribbon. That was when I realized that Judit Áldozó had been waiting for me all these years. She had been waiting for me to stop being a coward. But many years had passed since our conversation that Christmas.

As for the lilac ribbon—I don't have it anymore, it vanished along with the wallet and everything else in life, like the people who had once worn such significant objects of superstition—I found it in the deepest pocket of the wallet, where I kept nothing except a lock of my little dead son's hair. It took me some time to understand what the lilac ribbon was doing there, how I had come into possession of it, and when Judit might have smuggled it into the wallet. My wife had gone away to a spa, leaving me alone in the house, and my mother had sent Judit down to oversee the spring cleaning. I must have been in the bathroom when she slipped into my bedroom and hid the ribbon in my wallet, the wallet having been left lying on the table. At least, that is what she told me later.

What did she mean by it? Nothing. All women are superstitious when it comes to love. What she wanted was for me to have something of hers permanently about my person, something she herself had worn on her body. That was her way of binding me, communicating with me. Bearing in mind her position and our relationship, this was an act of genuine subversion. She undertook it because she was prepared to wait.

When I understood this—the lilac ribbon did communicate something of it in its own eloquent way—I felt strangely irritated. I was annoyed by this minor act of sabotage. You know what it's like when a man discovers that all he has planned has come to nothing, that everything has been knocked sideways. Now I discovered that this woman, who lived just a few blocks away, had been waiting ten years for me. But beyond the irritation I also felt a certain calm. I wouldn't want to make too much of the feeling. I hadn't in fact made plans, nor did I prepare new ones. I didn't say to myself: "You see, that was what you've been covering up all these years, the thing you weren't prepared to admit, that there is somebody or something more important than your normal way of life, your role in society, your work, and your family: some twisted passion you have been denying . . . but the passion remains and is waiting for you and won't let you go. And that's all right. Now the tension is over. Your life and work were not entirely meaningless after all. Life still wants something of you."

No, I couldn't say I thought this, but the fact is that the moment I found the ribbon the tension was gone. Where to locate these vital psychological processes: in the nerves, in our minds? My mind had long forgotten the episode, but my nerves still recalled it. And now, when she sent me that signal, such a well-mannered, servantlike signal— women are like servants in love; all of them would prefer their love letters on paper decorated with motifs of brightly colored roses, entwined hands, or pairs of amorous doves, and would, ideally, stuff the pockets of their intended with locks of hair, handkerchiefs, and other superstitious mementos!—now, finally, I was at peace. It was as if everything had suddenly been endowed with a mysterious purpose: my work, my life, and yes, even my marriage . . . Does this make sense?

I do understand now. The thing is, there are some things that simply have to happen in life: everything has to find its place. But that is a very slow process. Decisions, ideals, intentions are of little help here. Have you noticed how difficult it is to arrange the furniture in a room so it is perfect, so you never want to move it again? It takes years, and you think everything is just where it should be, while all the time you have the vague, uncomfortable feeling that it is not quite right after all, that maybe the armchairs are not in their proper places and perhaps there should be a table just where that chair is now. And then, eventually, after ten or twenty years have passed, years in which you have never felt fully comfortable, when the furniture and the space available for it seem to have been at odds for ages, you suddenly see how it should be, you spot the mistake, you understand the secret inner dimensions of the room, push the furniture a little this way or that and find, or so you think, that everything has finally found its place. And for a few more years you feel convinced that the room is finally perfect, a complete success. But then—say, after ten more years—you grow dissatisfied again, if only because you change, as we all do, as does our spatial awareness, so that there never can be perfect, final order. That's how life is: we develop strategies to tackle it, and for a long time we believe the strategies are the appropriate ones, so we go to work in the morning, take a walk in the afternoon, and engage in cultural activities in the evening. Then, one day, we discover the only way we can continue to bear or make sense of it is by turning the whole thing on its head, and we can't begin to understand how we could have tolerated the idiotic system as it was. That's how things change around us and in us. And it is all temporary, even the new order, the inner peace, because it is part of the process of change and works according to its laws, so eventually it too stops working . . . And why? Maybe because we ourselves come to a stop sometime. As does everything that is of any consequence to us.

No, this was not what they call a "grand passion." It was simply that someone brought me to understand that she lived nearby and was waiting for me. It was a cheap way of doing it. A servant's way. It was like a pair of eyes gazing at me in the darkness. It was my secret, and the secret lent a certain bearing, a certain tension to my life. I didn't want to betray the secret; I didn't want to be faced with painful, idiotic, murky situations. I simply felt a little calmer after that.

That is until, one day, Judit Áldozó disappeared from my mother's household.

The story I am telling you extends over years, and much of it has grown indistinct and lost importance . . . It's the woman I want to talk about now, this proletarian creature. I want to concentrate on the important parts and ignore the parts involving the police, if you don't mind. All such stories involve the police or a magistrate somewhere along the line. Life punishes one a little, as you may be aware . . . Lázár told me that once and I took it as an insult at the time, the idea of it, but later, once proceedings started, I understood. Because we are not innocents in the eyes of life, and one day we find ourselves on trial. Whether life finds us guilty or not guilty, we ourselves know we are not innocent.

As I said, she disappeared, disappeared as completely as if she had been sewn into a sack and thrown into the Danube.

They hid her disappearance from me for a while. My mother had been living alone for ages and Judit had looked after her. One afternoon I went to visit my mother and a strange person opened the door. That's how I knew.

I understood that this was her only way of telling me. After all, she had no contact with me and had no legal hold on me. You can't resolve a matter of decades in one dramatic scene or with a loud argument. Something eventually has to be done one way or another. Maybe something had happened in the meanwhile and I didn't know about it. The three women in my life—my mother, my wife, and Judit—said nothing about it. I was their common interest, something they could arrange between them in some fashion; I just needed to be informed of the result. The upshot was that Judit left my mother's household and traveled abroad. But even this I only found out later, once a policeman friend of mine had made a few inquiries at the passport office. She had gone to England. I also found out that this was no spur-of-the-moment, snap decision, but a course she had been considering for some time.

The three women had kept their silence. One of them went away. Another—my mother—said nothing, simply suffered. The third—my wife—waited and watched. By that time she knew everything, or almost everything. She acted in a circumspect manner, the way her culture, condition, and intelligence dictated. I can't tell you how remarkably tactful she was! What should a refined, cultivated woman do when she discovers her husband is in deep trouble, and that the trouble is long-standing, that he has become detached from her; that, in effect, he is detached from everyone, that he is lonely, hopelessly drifting, and that perhaps, just perhaps, there is a woman somewhere with whom he might share this oppressive loneliness for the brief span of his life? Naturally, she fights. She waits, watches, and lives in hope. She does everything possible to enjoy the best possible relationship with her husband. Then she grows tired. Then she begins to lose self-control. There are moments when any woman turns feral . . . her very soul screams out in wounded pride and sheer animal passion. Then she calms down, grows resigned, if only because there is nothing she can do.

No, hang on a moment; I suspect she never does grow resigned . . . But these are merely details, shreds of emotion. In the end there is nothing to be done. One day she lets the husband go.

Judit vanished and no one spoke of her anymore. As I told you, it was as though she had been stitched into a sack. The silence about her, about a woman who had, after all, spent most of her life in my mother's house, was so conspicuous it was as though they had dismissed a lazy tradesman. Now she was here, now she was gone. Servants come and go. What is it that moaning housewives say? "I tell you, they are all well-paid snakes-in-the-grass. Isn't it strange how they have everything they need, but nothing is enough for them?" True, nothing was enough for Judit. One day she woke, recalled the something that had happened, and she wanted it all, everything. That's why she left.

I fell ill. Not immediately, only some six months after her departure. It wasn't a devastating illness, only a life-threatening one. The doctor could do nothing; no one could do anything. By that time I felt even I could do nothing. What ailed me? It's hard to say. Of course the simplest thing would be to claim that the moment this woman left—a woman whose youth had been spent in my vicinity and whose body and soul constituted a kind of personal invitation to me—my suppressed feelings for her ignited like a fire down a mine. All the combustible material was there, stored in the pit of my soul . . . That sounds all very pretty. But it's not entirely true . . . Should I say that, beyond my astonishment, beyond the alienating shock, I also felt a subtle, somewhat surprising sense of relief? That too is part of the truth, even if not the whole truth, as it is also true that at first it was my vanity that felt most bruised. I knew for a fact that she had gone abroad because of me, and secretly I was relieved: it was like having some wild animal hidden in the house and discovering one day that the beast had chosen to kick over the traces, that it had escaped and returned to the jungle. But at the same time I felt offended, because I thought she had no right to leave. It was as if some personal possession had decided to defy me. Yes, I was vain. But time passed.

One day I woke to find that I missed her.

That is the most miserable feeling. Missing someone. You look around and you don't understand. You reach out a hesitant hand for a glass of water or a book. Everything is in its place, your life is in order—objects, people, the well-known routine, the world—and you go on as before. It's just that there is something missing. You rearrange your room . . . was that the problem? No. You go away. The city you have long wanted to see is waiting for you in all its pomp, its rich solemnity. You wake early in a strange town, hurry down to the street equipped with street map and guidebook, locate the famous altarpiece at the famous church, admire the arches of the famous bridge; the waiter at the restaurant, full of local pride, brings you the famous local dish. There is a wonderful local wine that goes straight to your head. Great artists who once lived here have left a generous profusion of masterpieces for the city of their birth. You stroll past windows, doorways, under arches whose beauty and majesty has been the subject of world-famous scholarly books. Day and night the streets jostle with beautiful women and girls with lovely eyes. Those who live here are proud, proud of their beauty and refinement. You are the subject of their glances—some friendly, some gently mocking your loneliness, and inviting—meaningful feminine glances, eyes that sparkle. In the evening there's the sound of music by the river, people singing by the light of paper lanterns, couples dancing and sipping wine. And in the midst of this rich mosaic of song and flattering light, there is a table set for you too, and a woman who makes charming conversation. Like a conscientious student, you take care to see everything and make the best of your time: as soon as the sun rises, you set out on your daily walk, your guidebook in your hand, furiously concentrating, anxious to be fully occupied as if you were afraid of missing something. Your sense of time is quite transformed. You are meticulous in your portioning of time, waking at the precise moment you intended. It is as if someone were waiting for you. And clearly, that is the point, though you dare not confess it to yourself for a long time: you really do believe that there is someone waiting. That is why you are so meticulous. And if you are observant and precise enough, if you get up early enough and go to bed late enough, if you see enough people, if you take trips here and there or visit particular places, you may just meet the person waiting for you. Of course you know that hoping so is childish. There's nothing left for you but to trust in an infinitesimal chance. All the police know is that she has gone away, to somewhere in England. The British embassy are no better informed. Either that or they are not letting on. A mysterious universal screen, which stretches across the whole world, obscures her from your view. There are forty-seven million people in England, and London is one of the most densely populated cities in the world. Where to look for her? And if you did find her, what would you say to her? But you continue waiting.

Do you fancy another glass? A good clean wine, this, leaves you fresh and clear in the morning, no headache. I know it well. Waiter, another bottle, please!

This place is so cold, so full of smoke. But that is when I feel happiest here. There are only the all-nighters left now. The lonely and the wise, the hopeless and the despairing, those to whom nothing much matters as long as they can be somewhere where the lamps are lit and there are strangers sitting close by, where they can stay lonely until they have to go home. It's hard going home at a certain age, after certain experiences. The best thing is to be in a place like this, among strangers, alone, with no ties. Gardens and friendship, said Epicurus: there is no other way. I think he was right. But one doesn't need too much garden, either—a few potted plants on a café terrace. And friends: one or two are enough.

Waiter! Ice, please. Drink up.

Where was I?

Ah, yes, that time. Waiting time.

The only thing of which I was aware was that people had started watching me. First my wife. Then people in the factory. Then people at the club, in the world at large. My wife was seeing little of me by that time: occasionally at dinner and less in the evening. We hadn't had guests for a long time. At first I was nervous about turning down invitations, but then it became a habit, and I couldn't bear to have guests over. It seemed so painful, so unreal . . . being home, keeping house, you know what I mean. Everything was lovely and orderly, just as it should be: the rooms, the treasured paintings, the ornaments, the servant and the chambermaid, the porcelain, the silver, the fine food, the fine drink . . . it was just that I didn't feel I was the master of my own household. I didn't even feel at home. I couldn't believe, not for one moment, that this was my real home, a home where I could receive visitors. It was like being in a play, my wife and I constantly proving something to our guests, that this was a real home, a proper place. But it wasn't! Why? There's no arguing with facts. On the other hand, there's no point explaining them, either, not when they are as simple and as undeniable.

We were being left to ourselves. The world has keen ears. All it needs is a few signs, a few gestures, and the delicate spy network of envy, curiosity, and malice soon begins to suspect something. It's enough to turn down a few invitations or not return an invitation early enough, an invitation you once had accepted, and the whole social fabric is abuzz with coded communications to indicate that someone is about to desert the ruling hierarchy, aware that such-and-such a family or couple is "having problems." This "having problems" affects the disintegrating family as it might an invalid quarantined on account of his infection; it's as if the local doctor had pinned a notice in red letters on the front door of the house. The affected family is treated with a little more delicacy, with a touch of mockery and reserve. What people are hoping for is scandal, of course. There's nothing they long for more keenly when it comes to others than the prospect of complete collapse. They are positively in fever for it, a fever that is a form of plague. You step into a café or a restaurant alone and they are whispering: "Have you heard? They're having problems. They're getting divorced. The man seduced his wife's best friend." This is what they are hoping for. And should you go somewhere with your wife, they still have their eyes on you, as they huddle together, muttering in a knowing way: "They still go around together, but it doesn't mean anything. They're just keeping up appearances." And slowly you realize that they're right, even if they don't know the truth, even if every part of the evidence is based on ignorance and lies. In matters of importance, of human interest, society possesses a mysteriously reliable awareness. Lázár once told me, half-jokingly, that there's nothing as true as calumny. Generally, people have no secrets from each other. They pick each other's secrets up on a kind of shortwave, he said, a shortwave that penetrates the deepest recesses of our hearts, and their words and actions are merely consequences of this. I believe he was right. That was precisely how we lived. A gentle disintegration followed. It was as if I had been preparing myself for emigration, you understand. You go around thinking that your workplace, your family, suspect nothing, but the truth is that everyone knows you have already been to the embassy to apply for a visa and a ticket. Your family carries on talking to you as patiently and as warily as they would with a madman or a criminal, as someone worthy of pity, but the fact is that the police and the ambulance have already been put on alert, that these are the conditions under which you must live.

One can't help knowing this and becoming suspicious. One acts with circumspection, weighing every word. There is nothing more difficult than deconstructing a situation that has taken time to construct. It is as complex as trying to demolish a cathedral. One can be sorry for so many things . . . but of course there is no greater sin against one's partners and oneself than allowing one's emotions free range in a crisis.

It takes a long time to understand your rights in life: to understand to what degree your life is your own, to what degree you have given that life over to feeling and memory. You see how hopelessly I am a prisoner of my own class? For me the whole thing was like a complex legal matter entailing a separation. It was a quiet act of rebellion against my family and my worldly situation. And indeed it was a legal matter, not only concerning the divorce and the alimony. There are other laws people are bound to. At such times you spend whole nights asking your-self: What have I received? What have I given? What do I owe? And it's not just at night you ask yourself such questions, but in broad daylight, in crowds, out in the street. Terrible questions. It took me years until I understood that beneath all one's obligations, there existed a right, a right according to an unwritten law not made by man, but by the Creator, which was the right to die alone. Do you see?

It is an important and substantial right. Everything else is a form of debt. You owe a debt to your family and to society, from which you have received considerable benefits; you owe something to your feelings, to your memories. But there comes the point when your soul overflows with the desire for solitude, when all you want is, quietly, with a proper human dignity, to prepare yourself for the end, for the last human task of all: for death. When you get to that point you must be careful not to cheat, because if you do, you lose your right to act. As long as you are acting out of selfishness, out of a desire for comfort or a sense of grievance; as long as desiring solitude is a form of vanity, you are still in hock to the world and to all those who represent the world for you. But there comes a day when the soul completely fills with desire for solitude, when you want nothing but to cast from your soul everything superfluous, false, or secondary. When a man sets out on a long, dangerous journey, he is very careful what he packs. He examines every item from every possible point of view. He measures and judges the worth of everything, and only then does he find a place for it in his modest pack. Only when he is sure he is certain to need it. Chinese hermits, who leave their families when they reach roughly sixty, take leave of them like this. All they take is one small pack. They leave the house at dawn, silently, with a smile. It is not a change that they want; no, they are heading for the mountains to find solitude and death. It's the last human journey. That is what you have a right to. The pack you take with you for such a journey must be light—something you can carry with one hand. It will contain nothing unnecessary, not a single item of vanity. It is a very powerful desire at a certain age. Once you hear the lapping sound of loneliness you immediately recognize it as something familiar. It is as if you had been born by the sea, then spent the rest of your life in noisy cities; but one night you hear it again in your dreams: the sea. And you want to live alone, to live without a purpose, to render up everything to those who have a right to it, and then to leave; to wash your soul clear and wait.

Solitude is hard at first: it's like being sentenced. There are times when you find it unbearable. And perhaps that severe sentence might seem lighter if you could, after all, share it with someone, it doesn't matter who: with rough companions, anonymous women. There are such times, times of weakness. But they pass, because slowly the loneliness enfolds you, takes personal possession of you, like a mysterious force of life—like time, time in which everything happens. Suddenly you understand that everything that has happened has happened according to its own timetable. First came curiosity, then desire, then work, and finally, here comes loneliness. There's nothing you want now: you have no hope of consolation in a new woman, no hope of a friend whose wise counsel might heal your soul. You find all human talk vanity, even the wisest. There is so much selfishness in every human feeling. It's all empty promises, refined forms of blackmail: all helpless, hopeless attachment! Once you know this, you no longer hope for anything from people; you don't expect women to be of help, you recognize the price and terrifying consequences of money, power, and success, and you no longer want anything of life but to huddle up in some mean corner, without companionship, assistance, and comfort, and listen to the silence that slowly begins to lap at your soul as it does at the shores of time . . . Then, and only then, you have the right to leave: because leaving is something you do have a perfect right to.

Every man has the right to prepare himself for his own leave-taking, for a solitary death in his own sepulchral silence; to void his soul for the last time, to turn his soul into as empty and hallowed a place as it was at the beginning of time, in childhood. That was the way Lázár one day took the road to Rome. I myself have only now arrived at the point of loneliness. I too had a long road to travel. I must admit I had hoped for another way. But there isn't another way. In the end, or shortly before the end, one must be alone.

But first I married Judit Áldozó. That's just how things worked out.

One day, at four in the afternoon, the telephone rang in my room. My wife picked it up. By that time she knew everything: knew that I was sick with the delirium of waiting. She treated me like a helpless invalid, ready to sacrifice everything for my sake. But when it came to herself, to her own condition, she was quite incapable of genuine sacrifice: she fought it to the bitter end. She wanted to keep me. But by that time the other woman had proved stronger, and I went away with her.

She picked up the receiver and asked something. I was sitting with my books with my back to the phone, reading. I could tell from the shakiness of her voice that something important was happening, that this was the moment at which the waiting and the tension had come to an end, the moment we had all been preparing for all those years. She came over to me with the phone in her hand, silently put it down on the table, and left the room.

"Hello," said a familiar voice, Judit's voice. She said it in English, as if she had forgotten Hungarian.

Then silence. I asked her where she was. She gave me the address of a hotel near the railway station. I put the phone down, found my hat and gloves, and went down the stairs, my head full of all kinds of thoughts, except the thought that this would be the last time I would go down these particular stairs. I still had a car then, the car always parked in front of the house. I drove over to the slightly shady, third-class hotel. Judit was waiting in the lounge among her luggage. She was wearing a checkered skirt, a pale-blue woolen jumper, expensive gloves, and a traveling hat. She sat so comfortably in the lounge of that third-class establishment it seemed the whole situation—her departure and homecoming—was part of some long-discussed mutual arrangement. She extended her hand to me, quite the lady now.

"Should I stay here?" she asked, looking round, indicating the hotel, uncertainly, as if she had decided to let me make all the decisions.

I slipped the porter some money and told him to put her luggage in my car. She followed me without a word, sat beside me in the passenger seat. Her luggage was nice—leather cases, English manufacture, complete with the labels of not entirely familiar foreign hotels. I remember how, in those first few moments, this handsome luggage filled me with a sort of monstrous satisfaction. I was happy because I had no need to feel embarrassed by Judit's luggage. I headed for the grand hotel on the island and booked a room for her. I myself took a room on the Danube embankment and phoned home from there, asking to have my clothes and suitcases sent on. I never entered our house again. For six months we managed like this, my wife at home, Judit at the island hotel, I at the hotel on the embankment. Then the divorce came through, and I married Judit the next day.

I had no contact with the world at all during those six months. I broke all those contacts I had been so careful to maintain not so long ago. It was like breaking with a family. I went about my business at the factory, but as for the rest, the social circle, and that turbulent form of the world we call society, I saw neither hide nor hair of them. I continued to receive invitations for a while, invitations issued in a spirit of false generosity, of barely hidden schadenfreude and curiosity. Everyone wanted to see the rebel, the man who had kicked over the traces. They wanted to drag me through salons where the conversation was always of something else but where they kept a wary ironic eye on you as though you were some sort of madman who might any moment say or do something shocking: such guests are a little frightening but can entertain the company. People who called themselves my friends sought me out with an air of mysterious solemnity: they seemed to have made a grave promise to "save" me. They wrote me letters, visited me in my office, and talked to me soul-to-soul. Eventually they all took offense and left me to my fate. In no time at all people talked of me as if I had committed fraud or some other crime.

Nevertheless, these six months were a calm oasis in my life. The truth is always simple and calming. Judit lived on the island, and we dined together every evening. She was patient and prepared to wait. She was in no hurry. Sometimes people understand something and know it's not worth hassling or panicking, because everything will happen in due course anyway. We observed each other like opponents before a duel. At that time we still thought this duel would be the chief concern of our lives . . . a life-or-death affair, and that at the end of it, however scarred and patched by then, we would declare an armistice, a gentlemen's agreement. I had surrendered my social rank, my class loyalty, my family, and indeed the woman who loved me, for her. She had not given up anything for me, but she was perfectly prepared to sacrifice everything. She had made the move. She had acted. One day it happens: expectation turns to action.

It took me a long time to understand what the true state of affairs between us was. It took her a long time too. There was nobody near us, around us, who might have warned us. Lázár was living abroad by that time like a person who had been offended in some way and had chosen to die. And then, one day, he actually did die, in Rome, at the age of fifty-two. There wasn't anyone left to act as a witness to my life, to watch over me or constrain me.

From the moment we met in that third-class hotel near the station, we lived like émigrés, émigrés who had arrived in an utterly alien country in which they tried to emulate its manners, to assimilate, to blend in with the great mass of people, doing everything possible not to stand out, and if possible not to give in to sentimentality, not to think of the homes they had left and those they had loved. Neither of us spoke about it, but we both knew that whatever lives we had lived before were now finished, quite over. We waited and watched.

Should I tell you the story just as it happened? I'm not boring you? I'll stick to the essentials as far as I know them. After the initial shock when I was left alone in my embankment hotel and my baggage had been brought over, I fell asleep. I slept a long time, exhausted. It was late in the evening when I woke. The telephone had not rung, not once; neither Judit nor my wife called. What could they have been doing in those hours when one of them finally knew for certain that she had lost me and the other had cause to believe that she had won this small, silent war that had started so long ago? They sat at opposite ends of town, each in her room, thinking, naturally, not of me but of each other. They knew there never was a complete end to things, that their own duel was just approaching its most difficult period. I slept as if drugged. It was evening before I woke and rang Judit. She answered calmly. I asked her to wait, told her that I was on my way, that I wanted to speak to her.

It was that evening I first began to really know this extraordinary woman. We went to a restaurant in the city center, somewhere I was unlikely to bump into anyone I knew. We sat down at the set table, the waiter brought the menu. I ordered the food and we talked in hushed voices of ordinary things. Throughout the meal I was watching Judit's movements. She knew I was watching her, and occasionally broke into a mocking smile. She never quite lost that mocking smile. It was like saying: "I know you are watching me. Well, watch closely. I have learned what there is to learn."

And indeed she had learned to perfection, maybe even a little too well. This woman, if you please, had made herself study, in a few bare years, everything that people regard as correct behavior, good manners, and social graces—all that we had received as a given and had learned by simply being creatures of our environment and education: properly trained animals. She knew how to enter, how to greet people, how not to look at the waiter, how not to take notice of the service, while at the same time understanding how one should be served by maintaining an air of studied superiority. Her manner of eating was correct to a fault. She handled her knife, her fork, her napkin, everything, like someone who had never dined any other way or used different cutlery, under different circumstances. I marveled at her dress sense too, not just that first night but the rest of the time. Not that I am an expert in women's fashions; it is just that, like any other man, I know whether the woman I am stepping out with looks right in her clothes or has made an error of taste, given way to some personal quirk. She, in her black dress and black hat, was so beautiful, so simply and terrifyingly lovely, that even the waiters gawked at her. The way she moved, the way she took her place at the table, drew off her gloves, and listened, smiling and nodding over her shoulder, as I read her the menu, agreeing on the choice of food, then immediately changed the subject of conversation, charmingly leaning toward me: all this was one hideously difficult test, a test she passed that first night, like the brilliant student she was, with flying colors.

I, for my part, was full of anxiety, inwardly willing her on, and once she passed I was wild with joy, satisfied and relieved. It was, you know, as when we understand that nothing happens without a reason. Everything that had happened between us had happened for a reason, and what it showed was that this woman was a truly extraordinary being. I immediately felt ashamed on account of my earlier anxiety. She herself sensed this, and sometimes—slightly mockingly, as I have already said—she smiled at me. She behaved like a lady in the restaurant, like a woman of the highest rank who had spent her life in places like this. No, wait—she behaved much better than that. Upper-class ladies don't eat as faultlessly as she did, cannot hold their knives and forks with such refinement or maintain such firm discipline of gesture and posture. People born into a rank tend to rebel a little against the constraints of rank. Judit was taking her exam, not so as you'd notice, of course, but she was following all the rules.

It began that evening and so it continued all the days after, over months and years—every evening, every morning, in company or alone, at table or in society, and later in bed, in every possible situation—the terrifying, hopeless, endless exam that Judit passed each day with flying colors. In theory it was wonderful: it was just that we both failed the practical examination.

I made mistakes too. We watched each other like tigers and trainers in the middle of a performance. Never, not once, did I utter a single word of criticism of Judit; I never asked her to wear something else, to behave or speak in the least differently. I never "educated" her. I received her soul in its maturity, as a gift, the way it was created, and then as whatever life had made of it. I didn't expect anything out of the usual of her. It wasn't a "lady" or a glittering socialite I yearned for. I hoped for a woman with whom I might share a lonely life. But she was terrifyingly ambitious, as ambitious as a young, newly appointed officer in the army wanting to conquer and take occupation of the world, one who spends all day mugging up, practicing, training for the part. She wasn't scared of anything or anyone. There was only one thing she feared: her own hypersensitivity to offense, some mortal wound to the pride glowing in the depths of her life, her very being. That is what she was afraid of, and everything she did by word, silence, and deed was a form of defense against it. It was something I could never understand.

So we dined at the restaurant. What did we talk about? Well, London, naturally. How did the conversation go? She answered questions exactly as though she were sitting an exam. The answers came pat: "London is a great city. It has a vast population. The poor cook with mutton fat. The English think and act with deliberation." And then, among the clichés, suddenly something to the point: "The English know it is necessary to survive." When she said this—it might have been the first personal observation she had ever addressed to me, the first truth she had discovered for herself and revealed for my benefit—the light in her eyes suddenly flashed, then went out. It was as if she couldn't contain herself and had voiced an opinion, but immediately regretted it, as if she had given something of herself away, unveiled a secret, demonstrated that she too had a view of the world, of herself, of me, and of the English, and that she had been forced to speak out about it. People don't talk about their experiences in the presence of enemies. I sensed something strange in that moment, but I couldn't have said what . . . She fell silent for a moment. Then she was back with the clichés again. The exam clock was running. *"Yes, the English have a sense of humor. They love Dickens and music."* Judit had read *David Copperfield*. And what else? She answered calmly. She had brought along the latest Huxley as travel reading. *Point Counter Point* was the title. She was reading it on the way and was still reading it . . . she could lend it to me if I liked.

So that's how things were. There I was, sitting with Judit Áldozó in a city restaurant, eating crab and asparagus with a heavy red wine, chatting about the latest novel by Aldous Huxley. Her handkerchief, open before me on the table, had a heavy, pleasant scent. I asked her what scent she used. She mentioned the name of an American beauty product, her English pronunciation perfect. She said she preferred American scents to French ones because the French were a little overpowering. I gave her a skeptical look. Was she teasing me? But no, it was no joke, it was serious, that was her honest opinion. She gave her opinion the way some people pin down facts based on experience. I didn't dare ask her how a Transdanubian peasant girl came by such experiences, how she could be so certain that French perfumes were "a little overpowering." And in any case, what else did she do in London apart from being a maid in an English family home? I knew London a little, and had some experience of English households, and I knew that being a servant in London was not a lofty station. Judit looked steadily back at me, expecting more questions. And even then, on that first evening, I noticed something I was to keep noticing right to the end, every evening.

You won't guess what it was.

She would accept any suggestion I made. Shall we go here? Shall we go there? She simply nodded: Fine, let's go. But then, once we were in the car and on our way, she would quietly say: "But maybe we could . . ." And we would finish up not at the restaurant I had chosen but at another that was by no means better or finer. And if I chose something from the menu, they would bring the dish, she'd taste it, push it aside, and say, "Maybe it might be better if . . ." And then the willing waiters would bring some other dish and different wine. She always wanted something different. And she always wanted to go somewhere different. I thought it might be fear and confusion that caused these sudden changes of mind, but slowly I realized the true problem was that the sweet was never sweet enough, the salty never salty enough for her. She would suddenly push aside the roast chicken roasted by the best chef in the best restaurant and declare quietly but firmly, "It's not quite right. Bring me something else." Cream wasn't creamy enough for her, the coffee never strong enough, never, at any place.

I thought she might be capricious. Never mind, just observe and keep observing, I thought. So I observed. I even found it amusing, this caprice, this volatility of hers.

But then I discovered the volatility had deep roots, so deep I could shed no light on it. Poverty was somewhere at the bottom of it. Judit was struggling with her memories. I was sometimes moved by the sheer intensity of her desire to be stronger, more disciplined than her memories. But now that the barriers were down, the barriers raised between her and the world by poverty, some tide had burst its banks in her. It wasn't that she wanted more, something better and more glamorous than what I offered: what she wanted was something *different*. Do you understand? She was like an invalid who imagines she might feel better in another room; or that there might be a different doctor, wiser than her own, that she might consult; or that there was a medicine on sale somewhere that was more potent, more effective than the medicines she had so far taken. It was always something *else* she wanted: always something different. Occasionally she apologized for it. She didn't really say anything, just looked at me. It was at these moments I felt closest to her proud, wounded soul. She would look at me all but helplessly, as if she could not help her poverty and her memories. And then a voice started speaking inside her that was louder than this silent pleading. The voice wanted something else. It started straightaway, that first evening.

What did she want? Revenge and all that goes with it. In what form? She herself did not know. She probably hadn't worked out her battle plan. It does no good shaking the foundations of the sagging, sunken, inert structure into which people are born. Occasionally there is an accident, some particular human contact, some chance encounter or event: we wake, take a look round the world, and are suddenly surprised to find we have no home to go to. We don't even know what to look for or how to limit our desires; what it is we actually desire. We can no longer see the horizon: the image we had has been blown out of shape. All at once nothing satisfies, nothing will do. Yesterday we were happy with a bar of chocolate, a brightly colored ribbon, or any simple pleasure such as sunshine or health. We drank clean water from a damaged old cup, happy that the water was cold and quenched our thirst. In the evening we might have leaned on the rails of a corridor in the tenement courtyard listening in the dark to music playing in the distance and been almost happy. We might have looked at a flower and smiled. The world offered wonderful satisfactions now and then. But then comes an accident and the soul loses its inner peace.

What did Judit do? She instigated, in her own fashion, a kind of class war against me.

Maybe it was not against me, not personally. It was just that I embodied a world for which she felt an infinite longing, a world she so desperately, so feverishly envied, and tried, in a cold fury, with such unfortunate results, to enter, so that when at last she found a repository for these longings—that is to say, in me—she quite lost her equilibrium. At first she was anxious and fussy. She sent back her food. Then, to my quiet surprise, she started changing hotel rooms. She exchanged the little en suite apartment overlooking the park for a bigger one that had a view of the river, with separate bedroom and dressing room. "It's quieter here," she said, like a fussy traveling diva. I listened to her complaints with a smile. Naturally I paid her bills and said nothing. I gave her a checkbook and asked her to pay for everything herself. After only three months, the bank informed me—with surprising speed—that the sizable account I had opened for Judit had nothing left in it. How, and on what, had she spent the money, which for her would have represented a substantial sum, a small fortune? It wasn't a question I ever addressed to her, of course: quite likely she would not have been able to answer. The harness of her soul had snapped, that's all. Her wardrobe overflowed with expensive clothes selected, surprisingly, according to the best of taste, mostly entirely superfluous feminine fripperies. She shopped in the best stores, without a thought, paying by check: hats, dresses, furs, fashionable novelties, first smaller, then bigger items of jewelry. She craved these things with an extraordinary hunger, a hunger somewhat unnatural in her position. Most of the things she never wore. She was like a starved creature set in front of a laid table, who doesn't care that nature very quickly sets a limit to our desires or that surfeit might lead to sickness.

Nothing was good enough. Nothing was colorful, sweet, salty, hot, or cold enough. Her soul was excitedly seeking something to quench her thirst as quickly as possible. She spent the morning exploring the most expensive central stores, desperately concerned that the shop not overcharge her for the item she desired. What item? Another fur? Another colorful, fashionable trinket of the season? Yes, all this; and then there were the impossible, crazy things, things bordering on the outrageous. One day I was forced to say something. It stopped her dead in her tracks, like someone arrested in the middle of a riot. She looked around as if waking from a dream and began to cry. She cried for days. Then, for a long time, she bought nothing.

But then she went through another strange period of silence, as if looking far into the distance, remembering. I was moved by her silence. She was with me whenever I wanted her. She was like a thief caught in the act: ashamed, obedient, on her best behavior. I decided not to mention it again, not to warn her. Money was of little importance, after all: I was still rich at the time, and knew by then that it was pointless saving money if by doing so I lost mysef. Because I too lived dangerously in those months; all three of us did, Judit, my wife, and I. We were in mortal danger in the strict sense of the word: everything to which we had clung had collapsed; our lives had turned into a floodplain, a tide of dirty water washing everywhere, drowning our memories, our security, our homes. Now and then we could raise our heads above the water and look around for the nearest shore. But there was no shore to be seen anywhere. Everything has to adopt a form at some stage, even rebellion. Eventually everything is reduced to cliché. Of what value was money in this quiet earthquake? Let the money be washed away with the tide along with the rest; with calm, with desire, with self-respect, with vanity. There comes a day when everything suddenly seems very simple. So I said nothing to Judit, but let her do whatever she wanted. I gave her everything, just like that. For a while she resisted the shopping plague, moderated it, stared at me in panic, exactly like a servant accused of greed, infidelity, or extravagance; and then she set out on her mad dash round town again: dressmakers, antiques dealers, fashion stores.

Hang on a minute, I've got a headache. Waiter, a glass of water! And an aspirin. Thank you.

Talking about it now, I feel the same dizziness as I did then. It was

like leaning over a huge waterfall. And there is no safety barrier anywhere, not a hand to reach out for. Only the water roaring and the call
of the deep, and you suddenly feel that profound, frightening urge . . .
suddenly you know you need every ounce of your strength to turn
around and walk away again. You can still do something. You just have
to take a step backwards, to say a word, to write a letter, to do something. Down there waits the roaring water. That's how it feels.

That's just what I was thinking of when I got this headache. Today I
can see all this clearly, at least a few moments of it. For example, when
she told me that she had a lover in London, a Greek teacher of singing.
That was near the end, once she had decided to come home. But first she
wanted clothes: shoes, decent luggage. The Greek music master bought
her everything she wanted. Then she came home, took a room near the
station, picked up the phone, and rang me, saying "Hello" in English, as
though she had forgotten Hungarian.

What effect did this news have on me? I'd like to be honest with you,
so I am trying to recall, to look into my heart, to check my recollection,
and can only answer in a single word: none. It is hard for people to
understand the true significance of actions and relationships. Someone
dies, for example. You don't understand it. The person is already buried, and you still feel nothing. You go about in mourning with a ceremonial solemnity, you look straight ahead of you when you are in
society, but then, when you're at home, alone, you yawn, you scratch
your nose, you read a book and think of everything except the dead
man you are supposedly mourning. On the outside you behave one
way, properly somber and funereal; but inside, you are astonished to
note, you feel absolutely nothing, at most a kind of guilty satisfaction
and relief. And indifference: a deep indifference. This lasts a while, for
days, perhaps for months. You cheat the world: you are indifferent on
the sly. Then one day, much later, maybe after a year, when the dead
one has long decomposed, you are just walking along and suddenly you
feel dizzy and have to lean against the wall because the event has finally
gotten through to you: the feeling that had tied you to the dead one.
The meaning of death. The fact, the reality of it, the knowledge that it
is useless to scrape away the earth with your fingers and uncover what is
left of him: you will never again see that smile, and all the wisdom and
power in the world is incapable of raising the dead man to make him

walk down the street toward you with a smile on his face. You can lead an army and occupy every corner of the globe, but it's still useless. And then you cry out. Or maybe not even that. You just stand in the street, pale, aware of a loss so great it seems the world has lost all meaning. It is as if you were left totally alone, the only man on earth.

And jealousy. What does that mean? What is there behind it? Vanity, of course. Seventy percent of our body is made up of fluids; only the remaining thirty percent is constituted of the solid matter that makes up a human being. In the same way, human character is comprised of seventy percent vanity, the rest made up of desire, generosity, fear of death, and a sense of honor. When a man in love walks down the street with bloodshot eyes because a woman—just as vain as he is, just as needy, just as lonely, just as desperate for happiness, just as unfortunate a creature as everyone else—has found brief solace in another man's arms somewhere in town, it is not that he wants to save the woman's body or soul from some imagined danger or humiliation: it's his own vanity that he wishes to preserve from harm. Judit told me she had a Greek music master for a lover. I nodded politely, as if to say "Yes, I see," and changed the subject. And indeed, right at that moment, I felt nothing. It was much later, once we had divorced, once I knew that other people loved her too, once I was alone, that I remembered the Greek music master, and groaned in fury and despair. Well, then, I thought, I would kill them both, both Judit and the Greek music master, if I ever laid hands on them. I suffered like a wounded creature, a wild animal shot in the thigh, all because a woman with whom I had nothing more to do, whose society I avoided because we had failed each other in every respect, had at some time in the past an affair with a man whom she, Judit, would only faintly remember now, the way one remembers a dead man one hardly knew. But then, at the moment she actually confessed to the affair, I felt nothing. I carried on peeling an apple with a polite, agreeable expression on my face, as if this were precisely what I expected to hear and I were content to get the anticipated news.

That was how we got to know each other.

Then, eventually, Judit had had enough of all that my money could buy her. She had bolted her food like a greedy child, and now she was sick. Disappointment and indifference followed. She woke up one day offended—not by me, not by the world at large, but by the realization that no one can pursue their desires for long without due punishment. I found out that back in her childhood at home, on the farm, they were as unspeakably, as impossibly, as shamefully poor as sociological studies sometimes describe. They had a little house and a few acres of land, but debt and the size of the family meant they had to sell. After this there remained nothing but a shack and a yard. And that's where they lived, her father, her mother, and her paralyzed sister. The children were scattered about the world: they were engaged in service. She spoke about her childhood without emotion, in a matter-of-fact way, but it took her a long time to speak about poverty. She never tried to make me feel guilty; she was too much of a real woman for that—in other words, she was wise and practical in the essential things. People don't blame fate for death, sickness, and poverty, they accept and bear it: she simply stated things. She told me how in winter they lived underground, she and the family. Judit would have been six when famine drove them from their home to another part of the country, where they took jobs harvesting melons. She didn't mean "living underground" in a figurative sense: she meant really underground, digging a deep ditch in the earth, covering it with reeds, and spending the entire winter there. She also told me, in great detail—and I could see this childhood memory meant a lot to her—that there were dreadful frosts that year, so the meadow mice had to scamper all over them and take refuge with them in the ditch. It was very unpleasant, Judit recalled, in a faraway voice but without complaint.

So you see, there was this beautiful woman sitting opposite me with expensive furs round her neck, her fingers glittering with jewels in the dazzling restaurant, so not a man could pass by without running a brief glance up and down her, and all the while she was quietly telling me how unpleasant it had been living underground in the great frost with thousands of mice running over their makeshift beds. At times like this I sat in silence beside her, looking at her, listening to her. I wouldn't have been surprised if she had slapped me across the face sometimes, not for any particular reason but simply because she happened to remember something. But Judit simply continued talking, as matter-of-fact as ever. She knew more about poverty, the world, and living with others than all the sociological textbooks put together. She never blamed anything or anyone; she simply remembered and observed.

But as I say, one day she had had enough of her new life. She was sick of it. Maybe she had recalled something. Maybe she understood that she couldn't be compensated for all that had happened to her and the others, to countless millions of people, by rushing round the shops: that there was no solution to be found on the individual level. Great matters are not settled by personal means. The personal is hopeless, superfluous. There is no personal recompense for what has happened and goes on happening to people at large, for what happens now and has happened for a thousand years. And all those who break free for a moment, emerge from the shadows, and bathe in the light: even in their happiest moments they harbor the guilty memory of their betrayal. It is as if they had committed their souls for eternity to those left behind. Did she know all this? She never talked about it. People don't talk about the reasons for their poverty. She remembered poverty as one of the natural world's natural phenomena. She never blamed the rich. If anything, she blamed the poor, recalling them and everything that constituted poverty in slightly mocking fashion. As if the poor could somehow help it. As if poverty were a form of sickness, and all those who suffered with it might have somehow avoided it. Maybe they didn't look after themselves properly; maybe they overate or didn't wear the right clothes in the evening when it was cold. It was the accusing way close family speak of the chronically sick, as if the dying man suffering from acute anemia with only weeks to live might have done something about it. "He should have started taking his medicine earlier," "He should have let someone open the window," "He shouldn't have stuffed himself with poppy-seed cake!" If only the poor man had done all this, he might have escaped the anemia that was killing him! That was something like the way Judit regarded the poor and poverty. It was as if she had said: "Someone should have done something about it." But she never blamed the rich. She was too worldly-wise for that.

She was more worldly-wise than is wise, and now, when the goods of the world were laid out before her, she suddenly felt sick, because she had tried to cram in too much of it. But it was her memories that did it, really. Memories are more potent than indulgence. They are always more potent.

She wasn't a delicate creature, but her memories still got the better of her. I could see her struggling against her weakness. Ever since the world began, there have been healthy and sick, rich and poor. We can alleviate poverty, we can strive for greater equality, we can put limits on our greed, our profiteering, our rapacity, but we can't turn a dullard into a genius by education, can't teach the cloth-eared the heavenly beauties of music, nor can we teach temperance to the overfed. Judit never talked in terms of justice: she was too worldly-wise for that. The sun rises and sets, she thought, and you will always find the poor somewhere. She had risen from the ranks of the poor simply because she was beautiful, a woman, and because I desired her. But she was growing wise to me too. For her, it was like emerging from a trance. She started looking round. She started to listen.

Apart from our first meeting she had rarely looked directly at me. People don't gaze into the eyes of an idea, into the eyes of supernatural beings that determine their fates. There must have been a certain glow, a kind of dazzling luminosity, around me in those early years that meant she had to blink and squint when she raised her eyes to meet mine. The effect wasn't due to my personality or social rank, nor to the fact that I was a man or that I was in any way a special being. To her I had been a secret code that she dare not crack because such codes are the key to happiness and misery. I was, for her, the condition to which a person might aspire her entire life. But when the possibility of that condition arose and was achieved, she recoiled, was disappointed, and became vengeful. Lázár was very fond of one of Strindberg's plays, the one called *A Dream Play*. Do you know it? . . . I have never seen it. He would often quote lines from it and recall particular scenes. He said there was a character whose one wish was that life should present him with "a green tackle box": you know the kind of green box in which a fisherman keeps his hooks, lines, and bait. Well, this character grows old, life passes him by, and eventually the gods take pity on him and send him the box. The character looks at the box he has longed for all his life, moves to the front of the stage, examines the box more closely, and, with deep sadness, declares, "It's not green enough . . ." Lázár quoted this sometimes when talking about human desire. And as Judit and I slowly grew more familiar I began to feel that I was "not green enough" for her. For a long time she did not dare see me as I was. People are always scared of seeing on an ordinary human scale things they have intensely desired or have raised into an ideal. We were living together by this time, and the intolerable tension that had infected our earlier, more feverish years had gone: now we perceived each other as people, as man and woman, complete with physical weaknesses demanding simple human cures . . . and yet she still liked to regard me in a way I never saw myself. It was as if I were the priest of a strange religion or the scion of some aristocratic family. I saw myself merely as a lonely man nursing a few hopes.

The café is almost empty. There's this cold smoke everywhere. We can go too, if you like. But I'll just get to the end of the story first. Give me a light. Thanks. Having started, I might as well finish—if I don't bore you. I was talking about hope, and I should say how I discovered the truth and how I could live with it. Shall I go on?

All right, then, listen. I'm listening too. I am looking deep into my soul as I speak. I am all ears. I said I wanted to tell you the truth, so that is what I am obliged to do.

You see, dear boy, I was hoping for a miracle. What kind of miracle? Well, simply that love might prove to be eternal; that its mysterious, superhuman power might overcome loneliness, dissolve the distance between two people, and break down any artificial barriers that society had erected in the form of education, money, history, and memory. I felt in mortal danger and was looking for a hand to grasp. I longed for reassurance that there really was such a thing as empathy, as companionship: that all this was still humanly possible. So I reached out for Judit.

Once the first phase of confusion, tension, and anxious waiting had passed, we naturally turned to each other for love. I married her and waited for the miracle.

I imagined the miracle to be quite simple. I thought the differences between us might dissolve in the great melting pot of love. I lay down in bed with her as if I had finally arrived home after a long exile, at the end of a voyage. Home is much simpler, but more mysterious and more important, than abroad, because not even the most exotic foreign place can offer the experiences a few familiar rooms can. I mean childhood. It is the memory of expectation that lies at the bottom of all our lives. It's what we recall when, much later, we see the Niagara Falls or Lake Michigan. We see the light and hear the sound of surprises, joys, hopes, and fears locked away in childhood. That is what we love, what we are forever seeking. And for an adult, perhaps only love can conjure something of that tremulous hopeful sense of waiting . . . love—in other words, not just bed and all that bed entails, but those moments of searching, waiting, and hoping that throw two people together.

Judit and I lay down in bed and made love. We made love passionately, expectantly, in wonder and hope. We were probably hoping that what the world and mankind had ruined might be put right by the two of us eye-to-eye in this other, purer, more ancient realm, in that eternal country without and beyond borders. I mean in bed. Any love preceded by an extended period of waiting—though maybe it's not exactly romantic love when just a few cinders remain unconsumed by the purgatorial fires of waiting—hopes for a miracle from both the other and itself. Neither Judit nor I was exactly a youngster by then, but we were not old, just man and woman, in the complete, most basic sense of those words. We reach an age when it is not purely sexual satisfaction we desire of each other, not full-blown happiness or release, but a simple and solemn truth that vanity and falsehood had previously hidden from us, hidden from us even when we were in love: it is the truth that we are human beings, we men and women, and that we share a common enterprise or responsibility on earth, a responsibility that may not be quite as personal as we think. Being human beings is not a responsibility we can avoid, but we can, and do, tell an awful lot of lies in trying to fulfill it.

Once people are old enough, it is the truth they want, and they want it in bed, too, in the sheer physical underworld of it. It isn't beauty we most want—after a while we stop noticing the beauty, anyway. It's not that the other should be wonderful, exciting, wise, experienced, curious, lusty, and responsive. So what is it that matters so much? It is the truth. In other words, it is exactly the same thing as matters in literature and in all human affairs. This truth is a compound of spontaneity, readiness, and the willingness to be surprised by the miraculous gift of joy that arrives unplanned, unintended. Even when we are being selfish, wanting only to receive, it is the ability to give, to give in an almost distracted, vaguely conscious way, as it were, without planning, without mad ambition. It's what I think of as "bed truth." No, old man, there is no Soviet-style *pyatiletka,* no Five-Year Plan, nor Four-Year Plan, either. The feeling that drives two people together can have no plan.

Bed is jungle, wilderness, a place full of surprises, teeming with the unexpected; there is the same unbearable dank heat, the same extraordinary flowers and lianas with their deathly scent and their ability to twine around you; the same glowing eyes of the same beasts of prey watching you in the half-light, the heraldic beasts of desire and obsession, ever ready to pounce. Jungle and half-light, strange cries in the distance—you can't tell whether it is a man screaming by a well, his throat ripped open by some predator, or nature itself screaming, nature, which is human, animal, inhuman at once—bed entails all that. This woman knew all there was to be known. She had the secret knowledge: she knew the body. She knew self-control and loss of self-control. Love for her was not a series of occasional meetings but a constant return to a familiar childhood base: a blend of homecoming and festival; the dark-brown light over a field at dusk, the taste of certain familiar foods, the excitement and anticipation, and, under it all, the confidence that once evening came, there would be nothing to fear in the flight of the bat, just the road home at dusk. She was like a child tired of playing, making her way home because the light in the window was calling her to a hot dinner and a clean bed. That was love as far as Judit was concerned.

As I said, I was hopeful.

To hope is to fear what you desire, the things in which you neither trust nor genuinely believe. You don't place your hopes in what you already have: what is possessed simply exists, as if by default.

We traveled for a while. Then we came home and rented an out-of-town property. It was Judit, not I, who arranged all this. The next natural step would be to introduce her to "society," if she wanted it. I was looking to bring home intelligent people who were not snobs, who might regard what had happened as more than food for gossip. "Society," that strange world of which, only a little while ago, I had been a perfectly respectable member—the world in which Judit had only recently been a servant—followed our lives with keen interest and, in its own way, accepted what had happened. People always need something to spice up their lives. When it comes, they immediately sit up, their eyes begin to sparkle, and soon they're on the phone from morn till night . . . It wouldn't have surprised anyone in society if the papers had discussed "the affair" in their leading articles: they brought up the subject, they talked about it, they analyzed it in the minutest detail as if it were a crime of some sort. And who knows? They might have been right according to the rules on which society depends. People don't tolerate the agonizing boredom of cohabitation for nothing; it's not for nothing they continue squirming in the sharp-jawed snares of a relationship that has long ago lost interest; and, surely, something must lead them to accept the necessary self-denials involved in the social contract. Nobody, they feel, has the right to seek satisfaction, peace, and joy as an individual while they, the majority, a great many of them, have agreed to censor their feelings and desires in the interest of the grand sum of censorship—civilization. That is why they snort and grunt and set up kangaroo courts and advertise their verdicts in the form of gossip each time they hear someone has dared to rebel, seeking individual recourse against loneliness. But now that I am alone, I sometimes wonder whether they are so wrong in censuring people who venture outside the rules.

I'm just raising the question, you know. Just between the two of us, now it's past midnight.

Women don't understand this. Only men understand that there is something else beside happiness. This difference may be that great hopeless gulf in understanding between men and women, the gulf that's always there, each and every time. Women—real women—have only one true home: the place occupied by the man to whom they are attached. For men there is another home: the great, eternal, impersonal, and tragic place symbolized by flags and borders. I don't mean to say that women feel no loyalty to the community into which they are born, to the language in which they take oaths, lie, and shop, to the land where they grew up; nor do I say that loyalty, fidelity, the readiness for self-sacrifice, sometimes even for downright heroism on behalf of the man's other realm, lie beyond them. But women never really die for a country: they die for a man. Every time. Joan of Arc and the others are the exceptions, masculine women. There are ever more of these now. Women's patriotism is much quieter than men's. They have fewer slogans. They agree with Goethe, who said that when a peasant cottage burns down, that is a genuine tragedy, but when one's homeland is devastated, that is, on the whole, a symbolic loss. Home, for women, is always that peasant cottage. That's the home they jealously guard, the home they live and work for, the home for which they are ready to perform every sacrifice. In that cottage there is a bed, a table, a man, and any number of children. That is woman's true home.

As I was saying, we loved each other. And now I want to tell you something, in case you didn't know: love, true love, is always fatal. What I mean is, it does not aim at happiness, at an idyll, at a hand-in-hand eternity of sentimental walks under flowering lime trees, with a gentle light burning on the veranda behind, the house swimming in cool scents. Life can be that, but not love. Love burns with a fierce, more dangerous flame. One day you discover a desire in yourself to encounter this all-consuming passion. It is when you no longer want to keep anything for yourself, when you don't want love to offer you a healthier, calmer, more fulfilled kind of life, but you just want to *be;* you know, to exist in a total sense, even at the cost of perishing in the process. This desire comes late in life: some never feel it, never encounter it. They are too cautious, but I don't envy them that. Then there are the gluttons, the curious, who have to sample everything and can't pass any opportunity by. They are genuinely to be pitied. There are also the obsessed, the desperate: love's pickpockets, who, quick as lightning, dip their hands into your heart to steal a feeling, discover some secret physical suscepti-bility there, then immediately vanish into the darkness, melt into the crowd, snickering with malicious delight. Nor must we forget the cow-ards, the calculating, who even in love work out everything strategi-cally, as if love were a matter of economics and production deadlines, people who live according to a precise agenda. Most folk are like this: they are true wretches. And then there comes a day when someone really understands what life desires of love, why life has given us sensi-bility. Does life mean well? Nature is not benign. Do you think it means to make you happy with this feeling? Nature has no need of human pipe dreams. All nature wants is to beget and destroy: that is its business. It is ruthless because its plan is indifferent to the human predicament, beyond the human. Nature has gifted us with passion, but it insists that the passion be unconditional.

In all true life there comes a moment when a man is so deep in pas-sion, it is as if he had cast himself into the waters of Niagara without a life belt. I don't believe in love that begins like a picnic, a holiday excur-sion complete with rucksack and singing and sunbeams breaking through the boughs . . . You know, that flood of spring-is-here feeling most people experience at the start of a relationship . . . I am deeply suspicious of it. Passion does not celebrate holidays! It's a dark force that builds and destroys worlds and waits on no answer from those it has touched, nor does it ask them whether they feel good as a result. Frankly, it doesn't care either way. It gives everything and demands everything: it is that unconditional passion of which the deepest stratum is nothing less than life-and-death. There is no other way of experiencing passion . . . and how few make it that far! People comfort and cosset each other in bed, tell whopping lies, and pretend to feel all kinds of things, selfishly robbing the other of what they fancy, possibly throwing some superfluous tidbit of joy the other's way in return . . . But they have no idea that this is not passion. It is no accident that history has regarded great lovers with the same awe and veneration as heroes, as brave pioneers who have risked all by voluntarily embarking on a hopeless but extraordinary human enterprise. Yes, true lovers run every kind of risk, literally, in every possible sense. It is a joint enterprise, in which the woman is as much the guiding force as the man, just as heroic, just as full of valor as a knight setting out to seek the Holy Grail, that being the whole point of the crusade, of the battles, of the wounds received, of the final vanquishing . . . What else should lovers want? What other purpose has that ultimate, unconditional sacrifice toward which fatal passion drives all those it has touched? Life articulates itself through this power, then immediately turns away from those it has sacrificed, completely indifferent to them. All ages and all religions honor lovers for this reason. Lovers bind themselves to the stake when they are in each other's arms. The true lovers, I mean. The courageous, the few, the chosen. The rest simply hope to find a woman the way they might a beast of burden, or to spend a few hours in sweetly pale and comforting arms, either to flatter their male or female vanity, or to satisfy the legal demands of a biological urge . . . But that's not love. Behind each lover's embrace stands the figure of Death, whose shadows are no less powerful than those wild flashes of joy. Behind every kiss looms the secret desire for annihilation, for an ultimate happiness that is no longer in the mood for argument but knows that to be happy is to cease entirely and surrender to feeling.

Love is feeling without an end in view. Maybe that is why lovers have always been honored by old religions, by ancient epic poems, and in song . . . Deep in unconscious memory people recall how love was great once, when it was not just a form of social commerce or a way of whiling away time, a game or an amusement to be compared with bridge or a society ball. They recall that there was once a frightening task all living beings had to accomplish, that task being to love, love being the full articulation of life, the most complete experience of existence and of its natural consequence, nonexistence. But people don't learn this till very late. And how unimportant are the virtues or moral standing or beauty or fine qualities of the partner in this enterprise! To love is to know joy as completely as it can be known and then to perish. But all those people, those hundreds of millions of people, carry on, hoping for help, waiting for their lovers to perform some act of charity on their behalf, a show of tenderness, patience, forgiveness, comfort. And they have no idea that what they receive in this way is unimportant: it is they themselves who must give, only they, give unconditionally—that is the meaning of the game.

That's how we set out on love, Judit Áldozó and I, when we started life in the house just outside town.

That, at least, is how *I* set out. That was the kind of thing I felt. And I hoped. I still went into the office, but I felt so detached from everything I was like a crook who knows he must be discovered one day, and that when that day comes, he will have to leave his job and all that goes with it . . . What did I discover? I discovered I no longer had anything to do with the part I played in the world, but I kept proper hours and followed the rules as strictly as ever. I was first to arrive at the factory, and the last to leave, at six, when there was only the doorman left in the place, and I carried on walking across town, just as before. I used to visit the old *cukrászda* and would sometimes see my wife there—"my first wife," I almost said, my real wife. Because I never once felt that Judit was my wife. She was the other woman.

What did I feel when I saw the first, my real wife? I didn't feel sentimental. But the blood always drained from my face. I gave her an embarrassed greeting and firmly looked away. Because the body remembers, you know, it never forgets. It's like a sea and a shore that once belonged together.

But that isn't what I wanted to talk about now, now that I have told you almost everything. The end of this story is as stupid as anything you will hear from the most stupid or ordinary man. Shall I tell you anyway? Well, of course, now I have started you will want me to finish.

Look, old man, we lived for a year under these highly unlikely physical and psychological circumstances. I lived for a year as if I were living in the jungle among wild beasts and poisonous plants, with snakes beneath each stone or bush. That year might well have been worth it. Worth what had preceded it and what was to come.

As to what preceded it, you know most of that now. What happened next took even me a little by surprise. I can see you are thinking that one day I discovered that Judit had been cheating on me. No, old man, I wasn't to know that until much later. She only betrayed me once she had no other choice.

It took me a year to discover that Judit Áldozó was stealing from me.

Don't look at me with that incredulous expression. I don't mean it figuratively. It wasn't my feelings she was robbing me of, it was the money in my wallet. I mean in the usual sense of the word, the way the police report it in their notebooks.

When did she start stealing? Oh, immediately, from the very first moment. No, wait. Let me think. No, it wasn't at the very beginning. At that stage she was merely deceiving me. I told you how, at the beginning of the relationship, when we were still living in the hotel, I opened an account for her at my bank and provided her with a checkbook. The account was very soon overdrawn. It was almost impossible to understand this flood of spending, this waste. Yes, she bought a great many things, furs, accessories, but I never looked to see what she was doing. I never cared about the quantity or quality of her shopping, only about her feverish acquisitiveness. It was the pathological fury of the overcompensation that worried me. To put it bluntly, a letter arrived from the bank one day to inform me that her account was exhausted. Naturally, I deposited more money in it, but somewhat less this time. A few weeks later the account was drained again. At that point I warned her, but only in a light, joking manner, not seriously, that she had no idea of our material circumstances. Her ideas of money and property had changed in England: here, at home, we were more modest, less steeped in wealth than she imagined. She dutifully heard the sermon through. She did not ask for more money. Then we moved into the house with the garden and I gave her a monthly allowance that was far more than necessary for housekeeping and her own requirements. We never spoke of money again.

But one day I opened a letter in which the bank informed Judit that, on such and such a date, they had credited her account with twenty-six thousand pengő. I kept looking at the letter and rubbing my eyes. In those first few moments I felt a rush of blood to the head: I was jealous! I imagined Judit must have brought the money with her from England, where she had had a lover of some sort—not the Greek music master about whom she had told me, but someone else, God knows whom, a milord who had paid her handsomely for her services. This feeling, this idea, hurt so much that I beat my fist against the desk. Then I set off for the bank. There I discovered that Judit had not brought this sum with her from England, but had paid it in, in small installments. She had made her first deposit the day I presented her with the checkbook.

"Women!" you say, and smile. Yes, that's what I myself said at first, and gave a smile of relief. It now seemed certain—and the order and date of the deposits showed as much—that Judit had asked me for the money but had secretly stowed it away so I shouldn't know. I thought she was busy with her shopping sprees, carelessly throwing money about everywhere. Indeed, she did throw it about, but not entirely carelessly. As I later discovered, she drove a very hard bargain when she was shopping, and had the receipts made out for bigger sums than she actually paid. Women of the street do this to their dim, happy-go-lucky admirers. When I understood that it was my money that Judit was hoarding, I smiled in relief.

I put the bank statement back in the envelope, stuck down the flap, and left it for Judit. I said nothing about my discovery. But then a new kind of jealousy grew in me. I was living with a woman who kept secrets. She kept secrets the way false women do, the kind that dine with their husbands and families, full of airy charm, but even while happily chatting to those who believe in them, accepting sacrifices and gifts from the man who trusts them, are by the end of the afternoon date already plotting how to sneak into a strange man's house and shamelessly spend several hours insulting every decent human feeling, betraying those who trust them and take care of them. Please understand that I am an old-fashioned man and have nothing but the deepest contempt for women who break up marriages. My contempt is so deep that I can't find any fashionable excuse. No one has a right to the sort of sly, filthy, cheap affair such women call happiness, not at the price of secretly or openly wounding other people's feelings. I have been both the sufferer and the instigator of such repulsive affairs, and if there is one thing in my life I utterly regret and feel ashamed of it is the breakup of my own marriage. I have sympathy for every kind of sexual misadventure, for those caught in the terrifying currents of physical desire: I even understand the most extreme, twisted forms of it. Desire speaks to us in a thousand voices. I understand all that. But only unattached people are free to cast themselves into those deep waters. Anything else is deception and treachery, worse than conscious cruelty.

People who feel something for each other can't live with secrets in their hearts. That's what cheating means. The rest is almost coincidental . . . a purely physical matter, usually on some melancholy impulse, nothing much. But these calculated affairs, in carefully chosen hours, in carefully chosen places, lacking all spontaneity . . . how sad, how cheap they all are. And behind it all there is this wretched little secret. It stinks out the relationship. It's as if there were a corpse rotting somewhere in one of the rooms, under a couch.

That's how it was the day I discovered the bank statement. Judit had a secret. And she did a good job of keeping it from me.

She did a good job though I watched her like a hawk. I couldn't have watched her more closely if I had hired a team of private detectives to observe her. We lived graciously, intimately, according to the rules of male-female cohabitation, and we lied to each other. She lied that she had no secrets from me; I lied by pretending to believe her. I watched her and kept thinking. At one stage I even thought to change my tactics, to surprise her and corner her, force her to confess. Such a confession might clear the air, the way an opportune summer storm clears away days of stifling heat. But I might also have feared a confession. That this woman, with whom I was sharing my fate, was keeping something from me was a genuinely frightening thought. Twenty-six thousand pengő for a woman who had spent her childhood in a ditch with mice scrambling all over her, a servant, was more than a lot of money: it was a fortune. And the money grew and multiplied. If it were only a matter of the ancient, nagging female practice of artfully putting aside some money from the housekeeping to use as pocket money, of filtering off a small sum from joint expenses . . . well, that might have been something to smile at. All women do this, because all women are worried that their husbands don't really understand the necessities of life: their instinct is that men can only earn, not save. All women prepare for a rainy day. The women who do this are as honest as the day is long in other respects, but when it comes to money, they cheat their husbands, stealing from them like domestic magpies or petty thieves. They know that the greatest secret in life is to preserve: jam, people, money—anything important enough to keep. And so they cheat and filch. It's the female version of the heroic exploit: a petty but tenacious wisdom. But it wasn't pennies and dimes that Judit was stowing away. Quietly, regularly, sweetly, Judit was robbing me, showing me fake bills, hoarding away money.

We lived graciously and quietly. Judit stole and I watched her. It was the beginning of the end.

One day I found out it wasn't just money she was robbing me of but the secret something that is a basic condition of anyone's life: self-respect. Look, I know this idea of self-respect is really little more than vanity. It's a male word. Women shrug when they hear it said. Women, in case you didn't know, do not "respect" themselves. They may respect the man they are with, their social or family rank, or their reputation. All this is transference, formality. But when it comes to themselves, and that strange phenomenon compounded of character and self-knowledge crudely glued together that we refer to as "I," women regard it with a generous, slightly condescending cynicism.

I discovered that this woman was consciously, systematically robbing me—that's to say she did everything to carve out for herself as large a slice of the loaf we shared as she could inconspicuously manage. I mean the loaf I thought was there for the both of us, and what is more, a loaf made of the finest bread she'd ever eaten. But I learned this not in the bank that regularly, and with the best of intentions, continued informing Judit of the very happy state of her account. No, old man, it was in bed I learned it. And that was so painful . . . well, indeed, this is the thing we men mean when we say we cannot live without self-respect.

It was in bed I learned it. I had been observing her for a while by then. I thought she was stowing the money away for her family. She had an extensive family, men and women, people at the back of beyond, trawling about in the depths of something very like history, at a depth I could comprehend with my mind but not in my heart, since my heart lacked the courage to explore secrets that lay that deep. I thought it might have been this mysterious, subterranean confederacy of relatives that had put Judit up to robbing me. Maybe they were all in debt. Maybe they were desperate to buy land . . . But you want to know why she never said anything? I asked myself that question. My immediate answer was that the reason she said nothing was because she was embarrassed by her poverty, because poverty, you know, is a kind of conspiracy, a secret society, an eternal, silently taken vow. It is not only a better life that the poor want: they want self-esteem too, the knowledge that they are the victims of a grave injustice and that the world honors them for that the way it honors heroes. And indeed they are heroes: now that I am getting old I can see that they are the only real heroes. All other forms of heroism are of the moment, or constrained, or come down to vanity. But sixty years of poverty, quietly fulfilling all the obligations family and society imposes on you while remaining human, dignified, perhaps even cheerful and gracious: that is true heroism.

I thought she was stealing for her family. But no, Judit wasn't sentimental. She stole for herself, with no particular purpose, with the solemn diligence and circumspection of a thousand-year-old wisdom that tells you that seven fat years are not long, that masters are not to be relied on, that fortune's wheel is forever turning, and if clownish good fortune has happily deposited you in the top seat at the table, it's best to dig in, since you never know when the lean years will come calling. She stole for prudence's sake, not out of generosity or compassion. If she had wanted to help her family, she had only to say the word to me. She knew that perfectly well. But Judit had an instinctive fear of the family, particularly now that she had set her foot elsewhere, on the master's territory. Her embattled, acquisitive nature knew nothing of compassion.

And in the meantime she was watching me, her husband. What was I doing? Am I not getting bored of it all? Am I going to send her away?

If I do, she must certainly stow away as much as she can, as quickly as she can. She watched me at table and she watched me in bed. And when I first noticed it, I blushed in embarrassment. The room was dark, and that might have been lucky for Judit. People don't know their own limits. If I hadn't kept a grip on myself I might have killed her. Might have. Pointless to talk about it.

It was a mere glance, all of it, in a tender, intimate moment, when I had closed my eyes and suddenly opened them again. I saw a face in the dim light, a familiar, doomed face that was very carefully, very subtly, smiling at me in mockery. Then I knew that this woman, with whom, now and at other times, before, I believed I was sharing moments of unconditional giving, for whom I had exiled myself from the realm of human and social contracts, this woman was actually watching me, just at such moments, with gentle but unmistakable mockery. It was as if she were observing me, examining me, saying: "What is the young gentleman up to now?" and "Ah, he's gentry." And then she served me. I realized that Judit, both in and out of bed, did not love me: she served me. Exactly as she did when she was a maid fresh to the household, cleaning my clothes and polishing my shoes. Exactly the way she later served me my food when I occasionally went to my mother's for dinner. She served me because that was her role in respect of me, and one can't change these great, fixed, human relationships by force. And when embarked on her strange battle against my wife and me, she never once believed, not for a moment, that this relationship, this role in life that drew us together yet kept us from each other, could really be dissolved or changed from within. She did not believe that she would ever have any other role in my life than to serve, to be the servant, to play the maid. And because she knew all this, not just in her mind but with her entire body, in her nerves, in her dreams, in her past, in her very genes, she never argued much, but simply did as the laws of her life dictated. I understand this now.

Did it hurt? you ask.

Terribly.

But I did not send her away. Not immediately. I was too vain. I didn't want to acknowledge the pain she caused me. I let her serve me for a while, in bed and at table; I allowed her to carry on stealing. I never told her, not even later, that I knew about her sad, shady little dealings, nor did I mention that, in unguarded moments, I had caught her mocking, superior, curious eyes looking at me in bed.

There are certain affairs that must be seen right through to the end, right to the end when there is nothing else left—to the point of annihilation. I saw it through. Then, after a while, when I discovered something else, I quietly told her to leave. She went without complaint. There was no scene, no argument. She took her belongings—there were a considerable number of belongings by then, including the house and a great deal of jewelry—and left. She left as silently, as without comment, as she had arrived at the age of fifteen. She looked back from the threshold with the same silent, interrogatory, indifferent look she gave me that very first time in the hall.

The most beautiful thing about her was her eyes. Sometimes I still see them in my dreams.

Yes, that stocky fellow took her. I even fought a duel with him . . . these are such pathetic things, but sometimes there's no other way.

Look here, old man, they want to throw us out.

Bill, please, waiter. It says . . . but no, don't even think of it! This was my treat, if you please. No buts. You were my guest.

No, I don't fancy going to Peru with you. Once somebody has grown as solitary as I have, what's the point of going to Peru or anywhere else? You see, one day I realized that no one can help me. It is love people want . . . but there's no one who can help with it, never. Once a man understands this, he becomes strong and solitary.

So this is what happened while you were in Peru.

Part III

ව ව ව

What are you looking at, darling? Photographs? You carry on. At least you have something to do while I make the coffee.

Wait, let me put my housecoat on. What's the time? Half-past three? I'll just open the window for a moment. No, don't get up, stay in bed. Look how bright the moon is. It's quite full. The town is absolutely quiet at this time, fast asleep. In half an hour, at four, the trucks will start rumbling, bringing vegetables and milk and meat to market. But Rome is properly asleep now in the moonlight. I don't tend to sleep at this time, because I have been waking at three with a pounding heart for a while now. What are you laughing at? I don't mean a pounding heart as when we are making love. Stop laughing! The doctor says it is at this time the heart rate changes, you know, as when you change gear from first to second in the car. And another man—not a doctor—once told me that three in the morning is when the earth's magnetic field changes. Have you any idea what that means? I don't, either. He had read it in a Swiss book. Yes, it was him, the man whose photograph you are holding. He said it.

Don't move, darling. If only you knew how beautiful you are when you lie in bed, your head propped on your arm, your hair falling over your eyes! You have to go to the museum to see men's bodies as splendid as yours. And your face too, yes . . . what can I say? It's the head of an artist. Why are you looking at me so suspiciously? You know I adore you. Because you are gorgeous. Because you're an artist. Because you are my one and only. You're a gift from God. Wait, don't move, let me kiss you! No, just here, in the corner of your eye! And your brow! No, relax. You're not cold? Shall I close the window? It's mild out in the street, and those two orange trees under the window are shining in the moonlight. When you're not here at night I often lean on the window-sill till dawn and watch the moonlit Via Liguria, this sweet and lovely street. See? There's someone stealing along by the houses, just as in the Middle Ages. Do you know who it is? You mustn't laugh at me. Just because I'm in love with you, just because I think you are the only one in the world for me forever, my dear, it doesn't mean I'm silly. It's old age slinking along the Via Liguria under my window, and not just here, but all over Rome and everywhere else, all over the world.

Old age is a thief and a murderer. One day he enters the room. He has blacked his face up with soot, like a burglar. With both hands he tears the mop of hair off your head, hits you across the face with his fist and knocks out your teeth, steals the light from your eyes, the sound from your ears, all the nice tastes in your stomach . . . No, all right, I won't go on. Why the mocking laughter? I still have a perfect right to love you and, see, I am not being miserly with it, I am gorging myself on all the happiness you give me. One can never have enough of such sweetness and happiness. I'm not ashamed of it, I freely confess I couldn't live without you now. But don't worry, I won't follow you on my broom to the Capitol! The day will come when I no longer have the right to love you, because I am aging. An old belly, wrinkled breasts. Don't go comforting me. I know the script. By then all you could give me would be alms. Or like alms. Or the kind of extra people pay their employees as overtime. Why do you look at me like that from the corner of your eyes? You'll see, that's just how it will be. I've learned to go when it's time to go . . . Would you like to know who taught me that lesson? Yes, the man whose photograph you are holding.

What are you asking? Wait, the early vegetable van is making such a racket. Was he my husband? No, my sweet, he was not my husband. It's that other one there, the one in the fur coat, in the corner of the album, who was my husband. He was not my second husband, the one whose name I now bear, but the first. He was the true one, my intended. That's if such a thing exists. The second simply married me. To put it more precisely, I paid to have him marry me, because by that time I had crossed the border and needed papers and passport. It's a long time since I parted from the first. Where is the photograph of the second? I don't know. I haven't kept it, because later I didn't even want to see him, not even in my dreams. Whenever I dreamt of him I suffered, as if I had dreamt something improper—women covered head to toe in hair, that kind of thing. What are you staring at? There's no man anywhere whose life has not been touched by women. Some woman is bound to cross his path. And there are men . . . men whose lives are like one of those houses that form a through passage from one street to another. One woman simply passes his key on to the next woman. He was like that. It's the same with women. Every woman has, at some time, had a man knocking at her door. There are modest men who tap gently and ask, "May I . . . just for a moment?" The sillier kind of woman starts screaming in outrage, declaring, "What nerve!" or "Why just a moment?" And then they slam the door. Ah, but later they regret having been so peevish. They start looking through the crack in the door, watching in case the presumptuous fellow should still be standing there, hat in hand. As soon as they see he has gone they are in a foul mood. And later—sometimes much later—they start shivering at night, because everything around them has gone cold, and they suspect it might have been a mistake sending the man on his way, since it wouldn't be so bad to have a man in this cold room, in this cold bed, warming it up, close, within touching distance, and no matter if he lies, no matter if he is rude, as long as he's there. Like you? Thank heaven you're still here next to me. You were so brazen I couldn't get rid of you. What are you grinning at? Thank heaven, I say. Don't you go snorting like that, mocking and grinning, you bastard.

Enough of your sniggering. Do you or don't you want me to go on?

Well, of course they came knocking at my door, a considerable number of them, I should say. But this, my second husband, he was only my husband on paper.

In '48, you see, I arrived in Vienna with nothing but two suitcases, because I had had enough of democracy. The suitcases were all that remained of the good life, them and the jewels.

This man, my second husband, had been living in Vienna for some years by then. He made his living by getting married, then divorced. As soon as the war was over, he strolled into Vienna, because he was a smart guy, you know, clever enough to leave beautiful Hungary while the going was good. He had the right papers, though heaven knows how he got them. He married me, asking forty thousand for the privilege. And then he wanted another twenty thousand for the divorce. I paid it by selling jewels. But you know that. After all, there were some jewels left for you, weren't there? There, you see. It's good to economize. Everything was fine with him, the only problem being that one day he came to the hotel where I lived alone and insisted it wasn't just a marriage of convenience, that he had connubial rights. I kicked him out, of course. They are so common nowadays, you know, these marriages of convenience: women marry to get hold of the papers they need abroad. There are some marriages of convenience in which three children quickly appear, one after the other. You have to be really careful. As I said, I kicked him out. By way of farewell he asked for the silver cigarette case he saw on the bedside table. I never saw him again. He went off looking for new brides.

My real husband? That's the one in the fur coat, the one you're looking at. What do you think of him? Do you reckon he looks like a proper gentleman? People certainly referred to him as a gentleman. It's just that, you know, it's hard to tell the difference between gentlemen and those who just pretend to be one and turn out to be fake. There are rich gentlemen with good manners, and there are less-rich gentlemen whose manners are nothing special, but still they're gentlemen. There are a great many rich, well-turned-out men. But gentlemen are few. So few they're hardly worth mentioning. They're as rare as that peculiar creature I once saw in the London Zoo: the okapi. Sometimes I think that no one really rich could ever be a real gentleman. You might find a few among the poor, maybe. But they're as rare as saints. Or okapi.

My husband? I told you, he was very much like a gentleman. But he wasn't entirely, unquestionably a gentleman. You know why he wasn't? Because he took offense. When he got to know me. I mean, when he really and truly got to know me. He took offense and divorced me. That's how he failed the test of being a gentleman. It's not that he was stupid. He himself knew that any man you can offend, or who takes offense, isn't a proper gentleman. There are gentlemen even of my kind. Yes, they're rare, because we were as poor as the field mice with which we slept and lived in my childhood, but they're gentlemen.

My father harvested melons in the wet country, the Nyírség. He was what they call there a Canadaman. We were so poor we had to dig a shelter in the ditch and live there through winter, together with the field mice. But whenever I think of my father, you know, I picture him as a gentleman. Because you could never offend him. He had an inner calm. When he was angry, he struck out, of course, and his fist was hard as stone. Sometimes he was helpless with anger because the world despised him, because he was a beggar. At such times he kept silent and kept blinking. He could read, and could sign his name in his own fashion, but he rarely used book knowledge, or any knowledge. He just kept silent. I do believe he was thinking, but only briefly. Sometimes he'd get hold of liquor, cheap pálinka, and drink himself senseless. But when I put all the pieces together and think of him, this man, my father, who lived with my mother and their children in a ditch full of mice, I think of him as a gentleman. One winter, when he had no shoes, the postman gave him a pair of galoshes with holes in them, and he went about in them, wrapping his feet in rags. I can tell you, he never felt offended.

My first husband, my real husband, kept his shoes in a shoe cupboard, because he had so many fine shoes he needed to have a cupboard made for them. And he was always reading books, damned clever books. For a long time I thought it was impossible to offend a man so wealthy that he even had to have a shoe cupboard. It's not for nothing I mention the shoe cupboard. When I first entered the service of my husband's family, it was the shoe cupboard I liked best. I liked it but it scared me too. I didn't have any shoes for a long time when I was a child. I was over ten years old when someone gave me a pair that fitted and actually belonged to me. It was a used pair given to the cook by the deputy sheriff's wife. It was the kind people wore during the war, low-heeled shoes, the sort you buttoned up. They were too tight for the cook, and one winter morning when I was fetching milk for the house she took pity on me and gave me these marvelous shoes. Maybe that was why I was so glad to have this great trunk, the one I left back in Pest when I skipped the democracy after the Russian siege of Budapest. The trunk was still in one piece after the siege, complete with the shoes. I was so happy . . . Well, that's enough about shoes.

Here's the coffee. Wait, I'll bring some cigarettes too. These sweet American cigarettes make me gag. Yes, I understand you need the cigarettes for your art. Night shifts in the local bar require cigarettes too. But careful of your heart, my angel. I couldn't bear it if any harm befell you.

How did I come to be employed in that gentleman's household? Well, it wasn't a wife they were advertising for, you may be sure of that. It was only much later I became a wife there, a wife and a lady, with the full complement of old honorifics: "honorable" lady, "excellent" lady, "most excellent" lady . . . I was hired as a servant, a general maid.

What are you looking at? I'm not joking.

As I said, I was a servant. Not even a proper servant, just a scullery maid, essentially a cleaner. Because this was an elegant house, my sweet, a house proper for gentlefolk. I could tell you a great deal about it and what went on there, how they lived, their habits, their dinners, their conversations, their boredom. For years I went about on tiptoe there, hardly daring to breathe. I was scared. It took years, you know, before I was admitted into the inner rooms, because I knew nothing about what to do and how to behave in such refined company. I had to learn. At first I was only allowed to work in the bathroom and the toilet. They wouldn't even let me near the food in the kitchen, I could only peel potatoes or help with the washing up . . . It was as if my hands were considered filthy. They had to be careful in case anything I touched got dirty. But maybe it wasn't them: not them, not the master, not the cook or the serving man, no. It was me. I felt my hands were never clean enough for an elegant house like that. I felt like that for a long time. My hands were often red then, creased, hard, and full of sores. Not as soft and white as they are now. Not that they ever criticized my hands. It was just that I did not dare touch anything, because I feared I'd leave a mark. I certainly never dared touch their food. You know the way doctors put on a thin gauze mask when they are performing an operation, because they're worried about infecting the patient. I held my breath when handling their things . . . the glass from which they drank, the pillows on which they slept. You, you may laugh, but even when I was cleaning the toilet bowl after them I was careful that the lovely white porcelain should not be dirtier for me having touched it. This fear, this anxiety, lasted for years. It was a very superior household.

I can see what you're thinking! You think fear and anxiety were done with the day my luck turned and I became lady of the house, an "honorable" and "most excellent" so-and-so. No, little one, you're wrong. It didn't stop. That day certainly arrived, but I was just as anxious then as I had been those years before, when I was only a scullery maid. I was never at peace, never happy in that house.

Why not, when that house gave me everything? Everything good: everything bad. Every harm and every satisfaction.

That's such a hard question, sweetheart. The question of satisfaction, I mean . . . Sometimes I think it's the hardest question anyone can ask.

Pass me the photograph. It's a long time since I last looked at it . . . Well, yes, that was my husband. The other? The one who looks like an artist? Who knows? Perhaps he was an artist. Not a real artist, though. Not an artist through and through—like you, for example. You can tell by looking at him. He was always looking at me so solemnly, so ironically, it seemed he couldn't believe in anything, not a solitary thing; in nothing and no one, not in himself, not even in the idea of himself as an artist. He looks tired there, and had aged a little when I took the picture. He himself said he looked secondhand in it. You know, like those pictures in the papers showing before and after. I took it in the last year of the war between two bombing raids. He was sitting at the window, reading. He didn't even know he was being photographed. He didn't like pictures of himself, either photographs or drawings. He didn't like being looked at while he was reading. He didn't like being spoken to when he was quiet. He didn't like . . . yes, he didn't like it . . . when people loved him. What's that? Did he love me? No, my dear, he didn't love me, not even me. He just put up with me for a while, in the room a corner of which you see there. That bookcase and all those books there, they were destroyed soon after I took the picture. The room you see was wrecked. And the house, of which this is the fourth floor. We used to sit there between bombings. Everything you see in this picture has been destroyed.

Here's the coffee. Go on, drink it. Here's your cigarette. Now listen.

I'm always nervous when talking about this, so don't be surprised if I sometimes show it, sweetheart. A lot of things happened to us. We, who lived in Pest throughout the siege and all that came before and after it. It was a mercy you were away from it in the provinces at the time. You are a wise man. So wonderful.

Well, I'm sure everything was better in Zala. But we who were rotting away in the cellars of Pest, waiting for bombs, we had a hard time. You were also wise to find your way to Pest no earlier than '47, by which time there was a government in place and the bars were open. I believe you when you say they welcomed you with open arms. But don't talk about that to anyone. There are a lot of bad people about, and some Jew, a survivor of the labor camps, might suggest you had some reason for lying low in Zala till '47. All right, all right, I'll shut up.

This man, the artistic one, once told me we had all gone mad, all of us who survived the siege. And that we're all in the madhouse now.

Who was this artistic-looking gentleman? Well, he was not a drummer. There is only one drummer in the world that matters, darling, and that is you. He didn't have an Italian work permit . . . the kind of work he did needed no permit. For a while he wrote books. Take that frown off your face, I know you don't like reading. I can't bear to look at you with your brow furrowed like that. Don't rack your brains, you wouldn't have heard of him anyway. What did he write? Lyrics? The kind of song lyrics your band plays in the bar? No, I don't think that was his sort of thing. True, by the time I met him, he was playing with the idea of writing songs for café singers, and he might have if they'd asked him. That's because, by that time, no other form of writing interested him. He might even have been willing to do some copywriting, he felt such contempt for the written word. He loathed his own writing too, not just the stuff others wrote, that anyone ever wrote. Why? I don't really know, but I have my suspicions. He once told me he understood book burning because there has never been a single book that could help people.

Was he crazy? Well, you see, that had never occurred to me. What a clever man you are!

Do you want to know what went on there, in the elegant house where I served as a maid? All right, I'll explain. But listen carefully to what I am about to tell you, because it's no fairy tale: it's what school textbooks call history. I know books and schools were never your style. Nevertheless, listen, because what I am about to tell you has vanished from the world. It's as distant as those stories you hear about ancient Hungarians who went about the world on horseback and tenderized their steak by keeping it under the saddle. They wore helmets and armor, they lived and died in those things. My employers were historical characters, like them, like the great chieftain Árpád, father of the Hungarians, leader of the seven chieftains, as you might remember from your village school. Wait, I'll sit down next to you on the bed. Give me a cigarette. Thanks. So it was like this.

I want to explain to you why I never felt comfortable in that lovely house. Because they treated me very well. The old man, His Excellency, treated me like an orphan, a poor little soul—you know, like a relative with a clubfoot from the poor side of the family forced to take shelter with the rich side. And the charitable family does everything possible not to make the newcomer self-conscious about the sad difference in status. It might have been the charity that was the most annoying thing. It made me so angry!

Mind you, I made my peace with the old master pretty soon. Do you know why? Because he was mean. He was the only one in the family who never tried to be kind to me. He never addressed me as "Judit, love." He gave me no cheap gifts, no hand-me-down clothes from gentlefolk, like the old lady—Her Ladyship—who gave me her ragged winter coat, or the young master, the young master who later married me, who gave me the right to be called Her Ladyship. He himself had some office, such as lord of the City Council, but he didn't care much for titles and never used it. He didn't even like people calling him the usual "Your Excellency." It was to be "Doctor" at all times. But I was already Her Ladyship by then. Not that he bothered with that, either. It amused him when the servants started addressing me as "Your Ladyship." It was a slightly sarcastic sort of amusement at silly people who took such things too seriously.

The old master was different. He tolerated the "excellency" stuff because he was a practical man who knew that the great majority of people were not only grasping but vain and stupid too and that there was nothing you could do about it. The old man never asked. He ordered. If I made a mistake, he growled at me, and I was so frightened

I would drop the tray or whatever I was holding. If he so much as looked at me, my palms would begin to sweat and I trembled. He looked like one of those bronze statues you see in Italian towns, in the square . . . you know, those early-century statues when merchants became proper subjects for bronze . . . potbellied little squirts in frock coats and rumpled trousers. In other words, patriots, patriots who did nothing but get up in the morning and play the patriot till it was time for bed again; the kind of people who earn a statue by founding the local horse abattoir, that kind of thing. And their pants were just as rumpled in real-life cloth as in bronze. The old man would look about him in the manner of those turn-of-the-century statues, giving us his statue look, much like the real merchants, the statues' originals, I expect.

I might have been an insignificant puff of wind as far as he was concerned, not quite human. I was nothing. When I brought the orange juice to his room—they were strange like that, starting the day with orange juice, followed by gym and the punching bag, then a sugarless tea, with proper breakfast only later, a big breakfast enough for two in the morning room, as regularly as Easter mass in the village church at home—when I brought in the orange juice, I wouldn't dare look at the old man as he lay in bed, reading by the bedside light. I was too frightened to look into his eyes.

The old man wasn't, in fact, all that old at the time. Nor was I always nothing to him. I think I can tell you now that he's gone, that sometimes—when I was helping him on with his coat in the dark hall—he went so far as to pinch my ass or pull my ear. In other words, he gave me unmistakable signs that he thought me attractive and that the only reason he wasn't about to proposition me was that he was a man of taste who considered me below his rank. He was not the kind to have an affair with a servant. What I thought was: I'm just a servant in the house. If the old man wants to have his way, if he insists, let's just put up with it and drop the idea of pleasure. I had no right to resist the wishes of such a powerful, stern figure. It was probably what he thought too. He would have been mightily surprised if I did resist.

But it never came to that. He was the master, that's all, so whatever he wanted would have to be. *He* would never have thought of taking me for wife, not in his wildest dreams. Nor would he have wondered, not for a second, if it was right or wrong to have his way with me. That's why I preferred serving on the old man. I was young, healthy, and vigorous, fully aware of my youth and health, and I loathed the idea of being ill. The old man still had a healthy, vigorous mind. His wife and his son—the one who later married me—were already ill. It's not that I thought as much: I just knew it.

Everything in the elegant house was beset with danger. For a long time I just stared and gawked the way I did as a child when I was sick and found myself in hospital. The hospital was quite an experience for me, perhaps the greatest and most beautiful experience of my childhood. A dog had bitten me, here on the calf, and the district medical officer wouldn't have me being tended in the ditch where we were living, bound up in rags, the way we always were whenever we cut ourselves. He sent a gendarme for me and had me carried to hospital by force.

The hospital in the nearby little town was just an old building, but to me it seemed a magical fairy-tale castle.

I was interested in everything and frightened of everything there. Even the smell, that country-hospital smell, was exciting! And attractive too, simply by virtue of being new, a smell different from the smell of the ditch, the burrow where I lived like an animal with my dad, my mother, and the rest of the family: polecat, field mouse, hamster, we were all these things. The hospital was treating me for rabies and gave me painful injections, but what did I care about injections or rabies! Night and day I watched the comings and goings of the world: the suicidal, the cancer-ridden, and the incontinent, all in a common ward. Later, in Paris, I saw a lovely engraving of an ancient French hospital at the time of the revolution, a vaulted hall where ragged people sat in beds. My hospital was just as unlikely a place for me to spend the best days of my childhood, the best being the days when I was in danger of contracting rabies.

But I didn't get rabies. They cured me. At least I didn't get it then, not the way they describe the disease in textbooks. But maybe something rabid remained in me. I sometimes wondered about it later. They say people with rabies are constantly thirsty while at the same time being frightened of water. I felt a bit like that myself whenever things were going well. I have been intensely thirsty all my life, but whenever I found a way of quenching my thirst I recoiled from it in disgust. Don't worry, I won't bite you.

It was this hospital I was reminded of—that and the rabies—when I landed up at the elegant house.

There wasn't a large garden, but it was scented like a rural drugstore. They used to bring home strange herbs from abroad. Everything was from abroad there, you know, even the toilet paper! Don't stare like that! They never went shopping like ordinary mortals, you know. They just rang the wholesaler, who brought them everything they needed—meat for the kitchen, shrubs for the garden, a new record for the record player, books, bath salts, scents, pomades whose smells were so dreamlike, so exciting, sweet, and tantalizing they made me dizzy and quite sick. I practically wept with emotion whenever I cleaned the bathroom after them and smelled their soap and cologne, every lingering smell and scent. And it was all on account.

The rich are strange, darling. As you know, I myself was pretty rich for a while. I had a maid to scrub my back in the morning. I even had a car, a convertible coupe, driven by a chauffeur. I had an open sports car, too, to race about in. And, believe it or not, I didn't feel in the least embarrassed to be moving among them. I was not retiring or bashful. I made myself at home. There were moments I imagined I was really rich. But now I know that I wasn't, not really, not for a second. I simply had jewels, money, and a bank account. I was granted these things by those who could afford them. Or I took it from them, when I had the opportunity. I was a clever little girl, you see. I learned in the ditch, in my childhood, not to be idle, to pick up whatever lay at hand, to smell it, take a bite of it, and to hide it—to hide everything that others threw away. An old enameled pot with a hole in it was just as valuable as a precious stone. I was just a slip of a girl when I learned that lesson. You can never be too industrious.

Now, these rainy days, that's what I always ask myself. Have I been industrious? Have I given things proper attention? I don't suffer from pangs of conscience. On the contrary, I worry in case I've forgotten to take anything I could have. Like you. For example, that ring of mine that you sold yesterday . . . you struck a really good deal, darling. I'm proud of you. I'm not just saying that—after all, no one knows better than you do how to sell jewelry. I don't know where I'd be without you. I say "my" ring, but it was really the ring Her Old Ladyship used to wear. It was a present from the old man for their silver wedding anniversary. I found it by accident in a drawer after the old woman died. I was the lady of the house by then and felt entitled to it. I put the ring on and examined it. And I remembered how many years ago, after first coming to the house, I found a ring on the laundry table among other forgotten things while the old girl was happily splashing about in the bath: an old-fashioned, heavy ring with a fat gemstone in it. I put it on and examined it with such nervous excitement that I started trembling, threw the ring back onto the table, and ran to the toilet, because my whole body was seized with cramps, I felt so sick. It was all because of the ring. But this time, after Her Ladyship's death, I said nothing to my husband. I just slipped it into my pocket. I didn't steal it. It was mine by right, since after his mother's death my husband gave me anything that even faintly sparkled. But it felt good just to take this one ring, the one she proudly wore on her finger, and to put it into my pocket without my husband knowing, without his permission. And I looked after it really well—that is, until yesterday, when you finally sold it.

What are you laughing at? Take it from me, that house was so particular even the toilet paper was imported from abroad. There were four bathrooms: the one for the old lady had pale green tiles, the young gentleman's were yellow, the old boy's dark blue. The fourth was used by the servants. All the bathrooms except ours had matching toilet paper, imported from America. There's everything you want in America— vast industries and plenty of millionaires. I'd like to go there sometime. I heard my husband, the first one, the real one, went there after the war when he decided he wanted no more of the People's Democracy. But I wouldn't want to meet him now. Why? What would be the point? Sometimes it just happens that two people have said everything they could possibly say to each other and have nothing left to say.

Not that you can ever be sure of that. Some conversations go on forever. Wait, I haven't finished!

.   .   .

It was a beautiful house and we servants had our own bathroom, but that just had ordinary white tiles. The paper we used was ordinary white too, a little rough, as I remember. It was a well-ordered house.

The old man was the mainspring of order. Everything went as smooth as clockwork, with the delicate precision of a fine lady's watch bought not two weeks ago. The staff rose at six in the morning. The ritual of cleaning had to be as religiously attended to as mass at church. Brooms, brushes, dusters, rags, the window cloths, proper oils for parquet and furniture—the refined grease with which we treated the floorboards was like those highly expensive egg-based preparations beauty salons produce for the glamorous—and I mustn't forget all the exciting machinery, like the vacuum cleaner, which did not merely suck the dirt from the rugs but brushed them too; the electric polisher that buffed the parquet so bright you could see your face in it. I used to stop sometimes and simply gaze at myself like those nymphs in the ancient Greek reliefs . . . yes, I'd lean over and examine my face, my eyes sparkling, just as absorbed, as startled as that half-boy, half-girl statue I once saw in the museum looking adoringly at his or her charming reflection.

We dressed for cleaning each morning like actors for a performance. We wore costumes. The manservant put on a vest which was like a man's waistcoat turned inside out. Cook was like a nurse in an operating theater in her sterile white gown, her head covered in a white scarf, waiting for the surgeon and patient to turn up. I was like one of those peasant girls in the operetta chorus dressed for gathering berries at dawn in my traditional maid's cap. I was obliged to understand that this dressing up wasn't simply because it was pretty but because it was hygienic and clean, because they didn't trust me, thinking I might be dirty, carrying a lot of germs. Not that they ever said as much to my face, of course! And they may not actually have thought it, not in so many words. It was just that they were wary, wary of everyone and everything. That was their nature. They were suspicious to an extraordinary degree. They protected themselves against germs, against thieves, against heat and cold, against dust and drafts. They protected themselves against wear and tear and tooth decay. They never stopped worrying, whether it was about their teeth or the state of the furniture, about their shares, their thoughts—the thoughts they adapted or borrowed from books. I was never consciously aware of this. But I understood that, from the moment I first stepped into the house, they wanted to be protected against me too, from whatever disease I carried.

Why should I be carrying a disease? I was young and fresh as a daisy. All the same, they had me examined by a doctor. It was a horrible examination; it was as if the doctor himself didn't fancy doing it. Their local doctor was an elderly man, and he tried to joke his way through the minute, painstaking process. But as a doctor—indeed, the family doctor—he essentially approved of the exercise. After all, there was a young man in the house, still just a student, and it was not unlikely that sooner or later the young man would want to get familiar with the new scullery maid, who had, for all purposes, just been plucked out of the ditch. They worried in case he caught TB or the pox off me. I even suspected that the old doctor—an intelligent man—was faintly ashamed of this overscrupulous need for assurance, this just-in-case. Once there proved to be nothing wrong with me, they tolerated me in the house like a decently bred dog that would need no vaccinations. The young gentleman did not contract any infection from me, of course. It was just that—much later—he happened to marry me. That was the one danger they'd never thought to insure themselves against. Not even the family doctor could diagnose it. One has to be so careful, darling. I think the old gentleman, for one, would have had an apoplectic fit if it ever occurred to him that my disease might be transmitted by way of marriage.

The old woman was different. She worried about other things. Not about her husband, not about her son, but about the fortune. She was worried about every detail of it. She regarded the family, the factory, the palatial home, the entire miraculous edifice of it, as a kind of rare antique of which there could only be this one unique example. It was like a Chinese jar to her, one that was worth—how should I know?—millions, perhaps. Once broken, it could never be replaced. She watched over everything, over their whole lives . . . who they were and how they lived. It was her masterpiece, so she worried about it. I sometimes think this worry of hers wasn't entirely groundless—something did break there, and it won't be replaced.

What's that? Are you asking me if she was mad? Well, of course, they were all mad, the lot of them. Only the old man was not mad. And we, the rest of us who lived in the house, the staff—I almost said "the nurses"—were slowly infected by their lunacy. You know, the way the nursing staff in the madhouse, the assistant medics, the head doctor, the director, all are slowly infected by the refined, invisible, concentrated poison of madness. It's what spreads and germinates in the wards where the lunatics are kept . . . you can't detect it under a microscope, but it remains infectious. Anyone healthy who finds himself surrounded by mad people slowly goes as mad as they are. We ourselves were far from normal, we who served, fed, and cleaned them. The manservant, the cook, the chauffeur, and myself: we were the inner circle, the first to catch the madness bug. We aped their manners, partly to mock them, but at the same time we took them seriously and fell under their spell. We tried to live, to dress, to behave like them. We too made a show of offering the food round at the table and talked pretty, making fancy gestures, the way we saw them doing in the grand dining room. When we broke a plate we would say the kind of things they said, like "It's my nerves. I have a terrible migraine!" My poor mother gave birth to six children in a ditch, but I never once heard her complain of a terrible migraine. That's probably because she had never heard of migraine, and as far as she knew it might be some kind of food or drink. But I was soon suffering from migraine myself, simply because I was quick at picking things up. Whenever I broke a dish in the kitchen I put my hand on my brow, put on a pained expression, and complained to Cook, "Wind's in the south, I feel a migraine coming on." And we didn't grin at each other, Cook and I; we didn't stand there splitting our sides laughing, because by now we had both permitted ourselves the luxury of migraines. I was always a quick learner. It wasn't simply that my hands grew pale, like theirs: I was growing pale within. When my mother saw me one day—after three years in service—she burst into tears. Not tears of joy. She wept out of fear. It was as if I'd grown an extra nose.

They were all barking mad, but mad in a way that meant they could talk to each other politely during the day, to fulfill their official obligations in the time allowed, to smile charmingly and do everything that was required of them according to the best fashion. At the same time I felt they might just as easily, at any moment, say something rude or stab the doctor in the chest with the nearest pair of scissors.

Do you know what betrayed the fact that they were mad? I think it might have been their stiffness. The way they moved, their very language, was stiff. There was no sign of flexibility, softness, nothing natural or healthy in their movement. They laughed and smiled the way actors do after much practice: they adjusted their smiles to fit the occasion. They spoke quietly, particularly when they were most furious. Sometimes they spoke so quietly they hardly moved their mouths, merely whispered. I never once heard a voice raised; never once witnessed an argument in that house. The old man grumbled and rumbled sometimes, but he was infected too, because straight after he would practically bite his own tongue off. He hated any spontaneous fit of cursing or rage.

They performed to each other all the time, even when simply sitting, as if they were trapeze artists in a circus, hanging off the bar, acknowledging applause.

At dinner they'd make such a show of offering each other food you'd think they were guests in their own house. "Here you are, my dear," "Do have a taste of this, darling" . . . so it went on. It took some time to get used to it, but eventually I did.

The knocking. That was another thing to get used to. You know, they never stepped into each other's rooms without first knocking. They all lived under the one roof, but they lived their lives a long way from each other: it was as if there were great tracts of land between them with invisible borders that they had to cross to get from one bedroom to another . . . The old woman slept on the ground floor. The old man on the first. The young gentleman, my husband-to-be, slept on the second under the mansard. They even had a special set of stairs built for him so that he might have privacy in his own domain—just as he had his own car and, later, his own servant. They took enormous pains not to disturb each other. That was one of the reasons I first thought they were mad. But when we copied their manners in the kitchen, it was by no means mockery. There was a moment, in the first year or two, when I seemed to wake from the trance and suddenly started to laugh. But when I saw how cross the older servants were—the manservant and the cook, I mean—I regretted it. I had broken some sacred rule and ridiculed all that was most holy. I quickly snapped to and felt ashamed of myself. I understood that there was nothing here to be laughed at. Madness is never a thing to be laughed at.

But it was more than madness pure and simple. It took me some time to realize what it was, what it was they were so desperately trying to preserve; what this never-ending round of frantic cleaning, these hospital rules, and all these manners, with their "if you please" and "May I offer you this or that" was about. It wasn't their money they were protecting, or not simply their money. Because, when it came to money, they were—once again—different from normal people, people not born into money. It wasn't money but something else they were protecting: it was that they were determined to guard, not just the money. It took me some time to cotton on. I might never have if I hadn't met the man whose photograph you were looking at just now. Yes, the one that looked like an artist. He explained it to me.

What did he say? Well, one day he told me that the lives of people like that were dedicated not to preserving, but to resisting. That's all he said. I see you don't understand. But I do—now.

Perhaps if I tell you the whole story, you might understand it too. But I won't mind if you fall asleep in the meantime.

I was just saying that everything in the house smelled of hospitals, the hospital where they treated me for rabies, the one that was the greatest, most marvelous experience of my childhood. What can I say about the cleanliness there? It was *unnaturally* clean. I mean, all that wax we rubbed into everything—the floorboards, the furniture, the parquet— and then the various creams and liquids we applied to windows, to carpets, to the silver and the copper, the stuff we cleaned and polished until it shone . . . it was all unnatural. Whoever stepped into the house, and especially someone coming from a place like mine, immediately started sniffing the air and choking in the artificial atmosphere. The hospital was drowning in the smell of carbolic and disinfectant: here it was detergents, the creams and liquids. And then there were the cigars, the foreign cigars, the lingering smoke of Egyptian cigarettes, the expensive liqueurs, the perfumes and scents worn by the guests. All these had long soaked into the furniture, the bed linen, and the curtains; they had eaten and wormed their way into everything.

The old woman had a mania for cleaning. Despite the servant with his tidying and me with my work, she would call in contract cleaners once a month, people who arrived like the fire brigade, complete with ladders and strange machines, who washed and scraped and fumigated just about everything. We also had a regular window cleaner whose one job was to wash and wipe the windows that we, the resident staff, had already washed. The smell of the laundry room was like an operating theater where they destroy the germs by radiating the place with blue lamps. You've never seen such a superior laundry room! You might have taken it for an expensive, upper-class funeral parlor. I never entered it without a sense of faint religious awe. I was only allowed in when Her Ladyship told me to help the laundress, who washed, ironed, and folded linen. She reminded me of those women back home that wash the dead and sort out dead men's clothes. The family wasn't about to trust me, you can be sure of that! I was a slattern by comparison with the delicate professional summoned to perform the great annual wash! . . . This special laundress used to be summoned by Her Ladyship with an open postcard announcing the joyful news that the dirty washing was waiting for her! . . . And of course she came immediately, delighted to be of use. My help was limited to helping her run the finest shirts, underwear, and damask tablecloths through the mangle. On no account would they trust me with the washing itself! There came a day when the laundress did not appear to summons. Instead there was a postcard written by her daughter. I remember every word of it, since I was the one who took the mail upstairs and, naturally, I read whatever was not in an envelope. This was what the laundress's daughter wrote: "Dear Madam, I regret to inform Your Kind Ladyship that my mother can't come to do the washing because she is dead." She signed it: "Your humble servant, Ilonka." I remember the way Her Ladyship wrinkled her brow as she read the card. She looked cross and shook her head. But she didn't say anything. At that point I stepped forward and volunteered to do the work, and for a while they let me do it, at least until a new laundress was found, one who was a laundress by calling and had the advantage of still being alive.

Everything important in that household was done by qualified tradesmen. "Qualified" was one of their favorite words. If the doorbell broke, it wasn't the manservant who fixed it but a qualified tradesman called in for the occasion. They trusted no one but qualified tradesmen. There was one fellow who came regularly, a man with a ceremonial air, wearing a bowler. He looked like a university professor called out to a council meeting in the provinces. His job was to trim corns. But he wasn't just any old trimmer of corns, the kind people like us sometimes visit in town, slipping off our shoes and extending our feet so they can slice the corn or an extra growth of hard skin away. Heaven forfend! He wasn't even the usual kind of home chiropodist—we would never have allowed one of those in the house. No, this man had a proper business card and you could find his telephone number in the directory. What it said on the card was "Swedish Pedicure." We had a Swedish pedicurist come to the house once a month. He always wore black and handed over his hat and gloves with such ceremony when he entered that I felt quite overcome with awe: I almost kissed his hand. My own feet were frostbitten, on account, as you know, of those damp winters in the ditch, and I had corns and bunions and ingrown toenails that were so painful I could hardly walk sometimes. But I would never have dreamt of asking this foot artist to touch my foot. He brought a bag with him, like a doctor. He put on a white gown, carefully washed his hands in the bathroom, as if preparing himself for the operation, then took an electric gadget from his bag, something like a small dentist's drill, sat himself down by Her Ladyship or the old man, or my husband, and set to work, shaving away the hardened parts of their ineffable skin. So that's our corn cutter. I must say, darling, one of the high points of my life was when I was lady of that refined house and ordered the maid to call the "Swedish pedicurist." I desired to have my refined corns treated. Everything comes to you if you wait long enough. As did this.

There was also the reading. The reading started the moment I brought the old man his orange juice. He lay in bed with the bedside light on and read an English newspaper. The Hungarian papers, of which there were a great many in the house, were only read by us servants, in the kitchen or in the toilet when we were bored. The old woman read the German press; the old man the English, but mostly only those pages that were full of long columns of numbers, the daily updates on foreign stock markets, because while he wasn't a great reader of English, the numbers did interest him . . . As for the young gentleman, he read now the German, now the French papers, but as far as I could see he only read the headlines. I expect they thought these papers were better informed than ours, made a louder noise, and could tell bigger, more whopping lies. I liked reading the papers myself. I'd gather up whole bedsheets full of foreign papers in the various rooms and read them, nervous and awestruck.

There were many qualified tradesmen to see. After the orange juice, if it wasn't the Swedish pedicurist, it was the masseuse. She wore a lorgnette and was quite rude. I knew she stole the bathroom creams and cosmetics. But she pinched cakes too, and the exotic fruits left in the parlor from the day before. She'd quickly stuff her face with two mouthfuls, not because she was hungry but just to deprive the house of something. She simply had what we called sticky fingers. Then she'd enter Her Ladyship's room and give her a thorough pounding.

The gentlemen got massages too, administered by a man they referred to as "the Swedish gymnastics instructor." They went through a few exercises in swimming shorts with him, then the instructor prepared a bath and stripped down so he could splash my husband and the old man with alternate cups of hot and cold water.

I can see you have no idea why he should do this. You have a great deal to learn, sweetheart.

The idea behind the instructor switching between hot and cold water was to improve their circulation. They couldn't have set about their day with the necessary energy required without it. Everything in the house was approached with an eye to order and to scientific rigor. It took me a long time to understand how all these rituals related to each other.

In summer the coach would come three times a week before breakfast to play tennis with them in the garden. The coach was an older man, silver haired, very elegant, like the picture of the English thinker on that old copper engraving in the museum. I'd sneak a surreptitious look at them playing from the window of the servants' quarters. It touched me to see this deeply moving spectacle of two old gentlemen, master and coach, engaged in a courteous game of tennis, discoursing with ball, as it were, rather than with words. My employer, the old man, was a powerful, sun-bronzed figure . . . he kept his tan even in the winter, because every afternoon after lunch he took a siesta under the sunlamp. Perhaps he needed a tanned face to inspire greater respect at work. I don't know, it's just a guess. At his advanced age he was still playing tennis, like the king of Sweden. The white trousers and the bright knit sleeveless jumper really suited him! After tennis they'd take a shower. There was a special set of showers for tennis, down in the basement in a gym with wooden floors, where there were all kinds of gymnastic equipment, including wall bars and some idiotic rowing boat—you know, the kind that has only a seat and oars on springs. They practiced rowing on it when the weather was bad and they couldn't go down to the clubhouse to take a canoe down the Danube. So the Swedish pedicure man left, then the masseur-cum-gym-instructor then the tennis coach . . . or whoever came next. Then they got dressed.

I watched all this from the servants' window, peeking out at them like a village maiden watching those brightly painted, ugly, but moving icons on the wagons of a passing religious fair: there was a mysterious, sanctified feeling about it, something faintly supernatural, not quite human. I often felt like that as I watched the family in my first few years with them.

Unfortunately, it was quite some time before I was allowed in to breakfast, since this was one of the major family rituals. I had to serve my time before I was permitted to minister to them. Of course they never sat down to it uncombed or unwashed, in their night things. They dressed for it with as much care as they would for a wedding. By that time they would have exercised, showered, and bathed, and the manservant would have shaved both my husband-to-be and the old man. They had already leafed through the English, French, and German papers. They listened to the radio while shaving, but not to the news, because they were afraid they might hear something that might spoil their morning appetites . . . They listened to simple, stirring dance music, a kind of jollifying that lifted their spirits and prepared them to face the rigors of the day ahead.

They dressed with great care. The old man had a dressing room with built-in wardrobes. Her Ladyship had something similar, as did my husband. They stored clothes for all seasons there, in slipcases hung with camphor, as if ready for mass. But they had ordinary wardrobes too, where everyday items were kept, stuff they wanted quickly to hand. Even as I'm speaking the smell of those wardrobes comes back to me, making my nose twitch. They had something brought over from England that looked like a cube of sugar but which, when you put your nose to it, filled the room with the smell of autumn haystacks. Her

Ladyship liked the artificial scent of hay in her cupboards and linen chests.

But there weren't just chests and wardrobes, there were shoe cupboards too . . . oh, heavens! It was the high point of my life, you know, as good as a Sunday off, when, at last, they let me loose on the shoe cupboard. There was so much cleaning material there—leather-care cream, a range of polishes—and I set about those shoes without using spit or saliva, using only those marvelous greasy ointments, the alcoholic liquid polish, the soft brushes, the rags! And believe me, I polished every one of those shoes and boots—the old man's, my husband's—until you could see your face in them! But it wasn't just the clothes and shoes that had their own wardrobes and cupboards; so did the linen. The linen chest was divided into compartments according to material and quality, the shirts separated from the underpants! And, my God, what shirts, what underpants! . . . I think it was while ironing my husband's "lawn underpants" that I first fell in love with him! He had his monogram even on his pants, heaven knows why. It was near where his belly button would be, and above the monogram there was the royal crest. The old man was, besides everything else, an adviser at the royal court, not just the head of a city council like his son . . . there was a difference in rank there, a step up on the ladder between baron and count. As I said, it took time for me to come to grips with all this.

But I forget the glove cupboard, where a variety of gloves lay in some mind-numbingly complex order, like preserved herring in a tin box. There were gloves to wear in the street, in town, for hunting, for driving; gray ones, yellow ones, white ones; gloves made of fawn leather, gloves lined with fur for the winter. There was a special drawer full of kid gloves for ceremonial occasions, and another with black mourning gloves for funerals, those grand occasions whenever someone important kicked the bucket. And soft gloves of pigeon gray to wear with the frock coat and top hat, though they never actually put those on, but carried them the way the king carries a scepter. Ah, those gloves! And then there were the jackets and vests of every kind, jackets with or without sleeves, long and short, thick and thin, in every color, of every quality, neat little tweed jackets and the like. There were times in the fall when they dressed for the evening, without a dressing gown, a little sportily, and sat down in front of the fire to smoke. The manservant would put dried pine twigs onto the embers so that everything should be just so, the way it was in the advertisements for brandy in English picture magazines, where you see the lord graciously puffing at his pipe by the hearth, replete with his daily intake of alcohol. And there he is, faintly smirking in his tweed jacket.

There were other jackets too: cream-colored ones they wore for grouse hunting, along with narrow-brimmed Tyrolean hats, complete with chamois feather. My husband had knit cardigans for spring and summer. And of course all kinds of colors and weights for winter sports. But the list is endless.

And to top it all, that smell of must and hay. The first time I lay down in my husband's bed my gorge rose at the smell, this cunning, perverse male smell I remembered from all those years ironing his underpants and tidying his linen cupboard. When I was so happy, so excited by the smell and the memory, I was actually sick. My husband's body smelled the same. It was the kind of soap he used too, you know. That, and the alcoholic cologne with which the servant treated his face after shaving, and the water he washed his hair in: it was all that same autumnal haystack smell . . . hardly perceptible, a mere breath. And somehow it wasn't a human smell, but a haystack, yes, in very early fall, in a French painting of the last century . . . Maybe that was why I started heaving when I first lay down in bed and he embraced me. Because by that time I was his wife. The other one, the first, had gone. Why? Maybe she couldn't bear the smell, either? Or the man? I don't know. There's no one clever enough to explain why a man and woman are attracted to each other and then why they part. All I knew was that the first night I spent in my husband's bed, it was not like sleeping with someone human but with some strange, artificial being. The strangeness of it made me so excited that I was sick. Then I got used to it. After a while I stopped feeling sick whenever he called me to him or we embraced; my stomach was no longer heaving. People can get used to anything, even happiness and wealth.

But I can't really tell you much about being rich, not the real truth, though I can see your eyes have lit up, and you're interested to know what I learned and saw while I was with them. Well, it was certainly interesting. It was like a fantastic journey in a foreign country where they live differently, eat and drink differently, are born and die differently.

I like it better here with you, in this hotel. I feel I know you better. Everything about you is familiar . . . Yes, I even feel more comfortable with your smell. Some people say that living in a stinking machine age—what they call civilization—we are bound to lose our sense of smell, that it will simply wither away . . . But I was born with animals around me, a poor child born among animals, like baby Jesus . . . so I had the gift of smell that rich people have forgotten. My husband's family didn't even recognize their own smell. That was why I didn't like them. I was simply their servant, first in the kitchen, later in the drawing room and in bed. I was always catering to them. But I love you because I know your smell. Give me a kiss. Thank you.

No, I can't tell you everything about being rich, because it would take all night—not just one night, but a thousand nights, and then another thousand, just as in the fairy story, I could talk for a thousand nights, for years on end. So I won't go on to list everything there was in their cupboards, their chests of drawers, how many outfits and accessories they had, but, believe me, it was like a vast theatrical wardrobe, something to fit every occasion, each part, every second of life! It's just impossible to go through all that! I'd rather tell you what they were like inside, in themselves. That's if you're interested. I know you are. So you just lie there and listen.

You see, it became clear to me after a while that all that great pile of things—the treasures and trinkets with which they packed their rooms and cupboards—weren't really necessary. They didn't need them. Certainly, they pushed things to this or that side but really they weren't concerned whether anything could actually be used, and if so, for what. The old man had a store of clothes to suit an aging character actor. But he, you see, slept in a nightshirt, wore braces, emerged from the bathroom with his mustache tied up, and he even had a little brilliantined mustache brush with a tiny mirror on top . . . He liked to walk around his room in a worn old dressing gown whose elbows had worn through even though he had a half a dozen silk ones hanging in his wardrobe, stuff he had been given as birthday or name-day presents by Her Lady-ship.

The old man grumbled a bit but was generally pleased that most things were shipshape. He looked after the money and the factory and adapted well to the role he partly created, partly inherited, though secretly he would have preferred to drink spritzers and play skittles in the afternoon at a nearby inn. But he was smart and knew that whatever a man produces in some ways produces him. It was that man who told me that once, the artistic one, that everything turns against you, and that you're never free, because you are always captive to the thing you created. Well, the old man had created the factory and the money and was resigned to the fact that he was bound to these things and could never escape them. That's why he didn't go to play skittles in Pasarét in the afternoon, but played bridge instead at a millionaires' club some-where in the center of town, no doubt with a wry expression on his face.

There was a kind of bitter, ironic wisdom in the old man that I can't forget. When I brought him his orange juice on a silver tray in the morning, he looked up from his English newspaper that he had been scanning for stock-market news, pushed his glasses up on his brow, and put his hand out for the glass in his shortsighted way . . . but there was a bitter smile playing about his lips under the mustache, the kind people pull when taking some medicine in which they have no faith . . . He dressed with the same expression. And there was something about that mustache. His mustache was cut like Franz Joseph's—Uncle Joe, you know—it was one of those *k und k* jobs, proper empire. It was as if the whole man was a leftover from another world, from a time of real peace, where masters were really masters and servants were really servants, when great industrialists thought in terms of fifty million people at a time, when they manufactured a new steam engine or a modern pan-cake-maker to order. That was the world the old man sprang from, and it was clear that he found the new mini-world too small, too narrow. There was, of course, the small matter of the war.

He had this mocking smile under his mustache, a mixture of self-contempt and general disdain. The whole world was ridiculous to him. That was how he dressed, how he played tennis, sat down to breakfast, kissed Her Ladyship's hand, whenever he was being delicate and courteous . . . it was all somehow contemptible, fit for ridicule. I liked that about him.

I grew to realize that all the stuff they packed the house with was not for use as far as they were concerned: it was just a form of mania. You know how it is when people suffer a breakdown and have to keep repeating certain obsessive acts, like washing their hands fifty times a day and so on? That's the way these people bought clothes, linen, gloves, and ties. I remember ties particularly because I had a lot of trouble with them. It was my job to keep my husband's and the old man's ties in order. Enough to say they had quite a few ties between them. There is no color in the rainbow that was not covered among those ties: bow ties, dress ties, ready-tied ties all hanging in their wardrobes, arranged in color order. I don't suppose it's impossible that there might even have been ties in shades beyond ultraviolet. Who knows?

On the other hand, no one dressed more simply, more soberly than my husband. He never once wore anything conspicuous. You'd never catch him with a loud or vulgar tie. God forbid! He dressed in what they call "best bourgeois taste." I once heard the old man quietly say to his son: "Look at that ridiculous man there, dressing like gentry." He was pointing at someone wearing a short fur coat with a drawstring and a hunter's cap. They avoided anyone that was not of their class, the class that, according to them, constituted civil society. Being respectable members of society, they owed nothing either to those below or above them.

My husband somehow always succeeded in wearing the same clothes: a suit made of heavy charcoal-gray material. And a plain, dark, neat tie to go with it. Of course he changed his outfits with the seasons and according to the customs of the house, society, and universal taste. But when I think of him now . . . he rarely comes to mind, occasionally in dreams, and he's always looking at me as if he's cross about something. I don't understand why! I always see him in a dark suit, a solemn, double-breasted gray suit, like a kind of uniform. The old man was similar. He always seemed to be in an old-fashioned suit with a frock coat that generously covered his paunch. That's what I always imagined him in, anyway, and I think it actually was like that! They took great care that their environment, their very lifestyle, should always be discreet, retiring, colorless. They knew what money meant; even their grandparents were rich, Grandfather being a highly placed bureaucrat and wine grower. They didn't have to learn to be wealthy the way some Johnny-come-lately bumpkins do now, the kind who love nothing better than wearing a silk top hat as they climb into their brand-new American cars. Everything about the house was quiet, like the color of their ties. It was just that, deep down, secretly, they always wanted more. Things just had to be perfect. That was their obsession. That's why the wardrobes were overflowing, why they could never get enough of shoes, linen, and ties. My husband took no notice of fashion: he just knew what was necessary and what was superfluous. It was in his blood. But the old man was still not completely confident in all the ways of high society. I'll give you an example. In one of his wardrobes, on the inside of the door, he had a printed English-language table of what color clothes and what sort of tie it was appropriate to wear on what occasion. On a rainy Tuesday in April, for example, the drill might be to wear a dark-blue suit with a pale-blue striped tie, and so on.

It's really hard being rich.

So I mugged up on it—wealth, that is. I studied with them for years, drinking it all in. I studied wealth as religiously as children study catechism at the village school.

It was only after a while I understood that it wasn't a matter of this or that outfit, this or that tie, not really, but something else. They wanted to be perfect. That was what they were obsessed with: perfection. That's why they were crazy. Perfection seems to be the rich man's plague. It's not a set of clothes they want, it's a clothes store. Nor is one store enough. If there is more than one wealthy person in the house, it takes several stores. Not because they need or use them: just so they should have them available.

Another example. One day I discovered that there was a locked room on the third story of the villa just by the big balcony, a room with a small balcony of its own. It was a room they never used, that had been the nursery. It had been my husband's room when he was a child. For years on end no one entered it except the staff, and even we only went in once a year to clean. It was here that everything associated with my husband's early years slumbered on behind drawn blinds and a locked door. It was like a museum in there, the toys all in place like the paraphernalia and costumes of a bygone age. The first time I went in there, I felt a deep pang of pity. It was early one spring and they sent me to clean it. There was still the sour, sharp smell of the disinfectant they used on everything in the room, especially on the linoleum-covered floor: it was a hygienic sty, somewhere a child had once lived and played and complained of stomachaches. An artist had painted images of animals, fairy tales, dwarfs and Snow White on the white walls. The furniture was pale green, in faded oil colors. There was a beautifully made wooden cot with a net canopy, a marvelous set of scales to weigh the child on, and then, on the shelves, splendid games, teddy bears, building blocks, electric trains, picture books . . . all in exemplary order, as if on exhibition.

It was that pang of pity that did it for me. I hurried to open the window and raise the blinds. I was desperate for air. I still don't quite know how to describe what I felt on first entering that room where my husband was a child. I swear it wasn't the ditch I was thinking of, the ditch where I grew up. Believe me, life wasn't so bad in that ditch. True, it wasn't that good, either; it was simply different, the way everything is in reality. The ditch was reality for me. Poverty is not what adults imagine it is for children, I mean adults who were never poor. For a child poverty is fun as well as misery . . . Poor children like the dirt in which they can roll about and play. And you don't need to wash your hands when you're poor. What would be the point? Poverty is only bad for adults, very bad, worse than anything. It's like the mange or stomach cramps. Poverty is the worst thing . . . And yet, when I stepped into the room, I did not envy my husband. I felt sorry for him instead, for having spent his childhood there, in that operating theater of a nursery. I felt someone brought up like this, in a place like this, could never be a whole person. They could only be a copy of a person, something that resembles a human being.

The nursery was as perfect as the rest of the house. It could not be more perfect. It was like their wardrobes and their shoe cupboards. It was as if everything had to be a place for storing things. Apart from their store of clothes and shoes they also needed their special store of books and pictures. It was like a factory store, really. There was a separate locked room in the attic that served as the official lumber room—

another store. And all these stores were not there only to contain clothes and shoes and books and pictures, but were a form of perfection in themselves, the same obsessive perfection.

I expect there was a kind of store deep in their souls, too, where the obsession was nurtured, mothballed, and kept in proper order. They certainly had more of everything than they ever needed: two cars, two gramophones, two ice-cream-making machines, several radios, and several pairs of binoculars: the kind of opera glasses that people take to the theater, enameled and inlaid with mother-of-pearl, carried in pretty cases; the sort they took to the races for watching the horses; another for hanging round their necks on board ships so they could admire the sunset. I can't be certain, but for all I know they might have had different ones for looking at cliffs, for watching the sun rise, for sunsets, for observing birds in flight, and so on. Everything they bought was intended to make the perfect more perfect.

It was the servant who shaved them, but my husband's bathroom contained half a dozen shaving sets, the latest on the market. There were also half a dozen cutthroat razors in a deerskin case—Swedish, American, and English blades—though he never once touched his face with one of them. It was the same with lighters. My husband bought every lighter going, then threw them into drawers to rust along with other pretty gadgets, because he actually preferred to use a common match. One day he brought home an electric shaver in a leather case but never used it. If he was thinking of buying records to play on the gramophone, he always bought a complete set—the complete works of this or that composer all at once: the complete Wagner, the complete Bach, all the different recordings. There was nothing more important to him than having every single piece of Bach in the collection, every single damn piece—the full set, you understand?

As for books, the book dealer no longer waited for them to decide which book to buy but sent them every new book that came in, anything they might possibly pick up and read sometime. It was the servant's job to cut the pages and then arrange them on the shelves in their cut, but mostly unread, condition. They did read, of course. They read plenty. The old man read books about trade, and liked travelogues. My husband was an extraordinarily cultivated man: he even liked poetry. But all those books the dealers showered us with in the name of courtesy—well, no mortal could ever have read them all, one life just wasn't enough. Not that they sent the books back; no, they didn't feel justified in doing that, because one had, after all, to support literature. And on top of that there was all the worry and tension in case the marvelous novel they had just bought was not the best possible novel, or indeed, God forbid, that there might be a novel somewhere else more perfect than the one they had asked to be sent over last week from Berlin! They were terrified in case some book, some implement, some object that was not part of a set, something substandard and of no value—in other words, something imperfect—found its way into the house.

So everything was perfect there—kitchen, parlor, all the things in all the stores—everything perfect and shipshape. It was only their lives that fell short of perfection.

What was missing in them? Peace. These people had not a moment of peace. That's despite living according to a strict timetable, despite the deep silence of the house and their lives. No voice was ever raised. Nothing ever took them by surprise. It was all calculated, foreseen: the financial crash, diphtheria, every twist and turn in life, right down to death. But still they were not at peace. Maybe they would have found peace if they once committed themselves, if they hadn't been so circumspect. But they didn't have the heart or guts for that. You need courage to live in a more headlong way, without a timetable, hour by hour, day by day, moment by moment, not expecting anything, not hoping for anything, just being. But they were incapable of that, they couldn't just *be*. They could get up in the morning all right, in royal fashion, like kings, brushing their teeth in the presence of their courtiers. They could take breakfast with as much ceremony as the pope says mass here in Rome in that special chapel of his that some old man covered with a lot of naked figures. I was there once. And it was my old employers' breakfast the chapel brought to mind.

Breakfast was a ritual to them. Then they went off to lead useful lives. All day they manufactured marvelous machines and sold whatever it was they produced. Then they invented new machines. The times in between they spent socializing. And at night they returned to rest, because they had spent all day being useful, cultivated, orderly, and well behaved. It is very tiring living like that! You're an artist, so you wouldn't know how tiring it is when, first thing in the morning, someone knows exactly what they'll do the rest of the day, right till midnight. You live only as your wonderfully artistic soul commands you to live, and you don't know in advance what idea might come into your head while you're drumming, how the rhythm of the music might take you so you throw your drumsticks into the air, or respond to a blast from the saxophone player with a burst of drumming. You are an artist. Spontaneous. My employers were utterly different. They fought tooth and nail to keep things as they were. And it wasn't only in the factory they manufactured stuff, but at breakfast and over dinner too. They were busily making the stuff they called culture, which meant discretion: smiling discreetly, blowing your nose discreetly. It was vital for them to preserve whatever culture they produced through work and manners: it was their entire life. The preserving of it was more important to them than the making of it.

Really, it was as if they were living several lives at once. As if they were living their fathers' and sons' lives too. As if they weren't individual, simple, once-and-once-only personal beings, but a move in a long game, which is not any individual's game but the family's, the family of a certain class. That's why they took such care, such anxious care, of those family photographs and family groups. It was like a museum protecting beautifully painted portraits of the famous and long-dead: "Grandfather and Grandmother on the occasion of their engagement." "Father and Mother's marriage." The photograph of a bankrupt uncle in his frock coat or wearing a boater. The picture of a happy or unhappy great-aunt smiling from beneath a veil while holding a parasol. That was them, all of them, together, a slowly evolving, slowly decaying composite person, a prosperous family. It was all utterly alien to me. For me, family was a necessity, a need. For them it was a project.

So that's what they were like. And because they always took the long view and made careful calculations, they could never really feel at peace. The only people capable of being at peace are people who live in the moment. It's the same with the fear of death. Atheists don't fear death, because they don't believe in God. Are you a believer? What's that you're muttering? Yes, I see you nodding to say yes, you are, but how much? I have only ever seen one man who, I was certain, had no fear of death. It was the artist man, that's right—him. He didn't believe in God, so he was afraid of nothing, neither of death nor life. Believers are frightened of death because they cling to everything religion promises them; they believe there is life after death, but also judgment. Our artist friend didn't believe any of that. He said that if there was a God he could not be so cruel as to land people with eternal life. You see how crazy they all are, these artistic types? But respectable families—they fear death as much as they fear life. That's why this family was religious, and prudent, and virtuous . . . Because they were afraid.

I can see you don't understand. They themselves could probably understand it on an intellectual level, they being such cultivated people, but not in their hearts or their guts. Their hearts and guts never had a moment of peace. They were afraid that all the calculations, all the planning, all that keeping things tidy, weren't worth anything: that one day it would all be over. But what did they really think would be over? The family? The factory? The money? No, these people knew that what they were afraid of was nowhere near so simple. What they were afraid of was that one day they'd have no energy left and be too tired to hold things together. You know that Eytie mechanic, the one we took that ancient jalopy of a car to the other day, to see what was the matter with it? Remember how he told us the engine was still running and that there were no cracks in it, but that the whole thing had metal fatigue? It was as if my employers were frightened of developing metal fatigue; that everything they had scraped together would fall apart, and then their "culture" would be done for.

That's enough about them. I could go on forever. Just think of all the secrets stored in their drawers and in those safes that were built into the walls, where they kept deeds and shares and documents and jewels. What are you shrugging for? But my darling, my one and only, these things are not as we proles imagine! The rich are really strange. Maybe there is some dark crevice in their souls where they are hiding something else. It was the key to this safe, hidden in this crevice, that I wanted to steal from them. I wanted to discover what was locked deep in their hearts.

But the rich remain rich even when dispossessed. I saw them after the siege, clambering out of their cellars, chiefly the Christians but then the Jews too, people who had somehow managed to survive, every one of them robbed and dispossessed to the extent that you couldn't imagine having less. Nevertheless—robbed of everything, their houses bombed flat, their businesses in ruins because of the war and what followed it, not to mention the great change you could sense in the air even before it happened, the surprise the Commies were preparing for them—these rich Christians and Jews, the rich, were back in their villas within two years, and the women with their neat little earrings and silver-fox collars were back in the Café Gerbeaud. How did they do it? I don't know. But I'm quite sure that their lives straight after the war were not different from before and during. They were just as fussy about their food and clothes. When the first train set off for abroad and they had received their first travel permit from the Russian high command in Budapest, they were already complaining about having to spend the night in the upper berth of their sleeping car to the shops in Zurich or Paris. You see what I mean? Being rich must be a condition, much like sickness or health. Say you are rich, you might, in some mysterious way, be rich forever, but however much money you have, you never feel properly rich. Maybe you need to *believe* in your wealth in order to be properly rich—I mean, the way saints and revolutionaries believe that they are different. And you can't afford to feel guilty if you are rich: if you felt guilty for a second you'd be finished. The not-truly-rich, those who have visions of the poor while indulging in a beefsteak and drinking Champagne, will eventually lose out, because they are insincere in their wealth. They're not rich out of conviction, they are only pretending, cowardly, sneakily, to be rich. You have to be very disciplined to be rich. You can perform a few charitable acts, but only as a kind of a fig leaf. Listen, darling. I hope one day, when I am no longer around and you meet someone who has more jewelry left than I have, you will not be too sensitive about such things. Don't be cross. I'm just telling you what I think. There! Give me your lovely artistic hand, let me clutch it to my heart. Can you feel it beating? It's beating for a proper prole, you see. Well, there you are. That's me all over.

Enough to say I was a clever little girl and quickly learned all there was to know about wealth. I served them for a long time and learned their secrets. But one day I left them, because I'd grown tired of waiting. What was I waiting for? I was waiting for my husband to desire and miss me. What are you looking at? I waited just as I should under the circumstances. I was strong. I had a plan.

Have another look at his photograph, take a good look. I kept it because
I paid the photographer good money for it, when I was still a maid,
because he was still with his first wife.

Let me adjust the bolster under your head. Go on, relax, stretch out.
You should always relax when you're with me, darling. I want you to
feel good when you are with me. It's exhausting enough for you working all night in that bar with the band. When you are here in bed with
me, you should do nothing except love me, then relax.

Is that something I said to my husband too? No, sweetheart. I did
not mean for him to feel good when he was in bed with me. And that
was the trouble, really. Somehow I couldn't resolve in myself to make
him feel good with me, though he did everything to please me, poor
man, undertook every kind of sacrifice for my sake. He broke with his
family, with society, with all his usual ways. When he came to me it was
really like emigrating, the way some bankrupt man-about-town sets out
on a sea voyage to a faraway land. Maybe that was exactly why I could
never reconcile myself to him; he just wasn't at home with me. All the
time he was with me it was as if he had run away to an exciting, spicy,
hot country like Brazil and married some local woman. Does such a
person ever wonder how he got there? And when he is with that local
woman, even at the most intimate moments, isn't his mind elsewhere?
Isn't he thinking of home? Perhaps. It made me nervous. That was why
I didn't want him to feel too good when we were together, at table or in
bed.

What was that home he was thinking about? Where was it? Was it
his first wife? I don't think so. Home, real home, is not to be found on
maps, you know. But home stands for a great deal, not just good and
lovely things, but hateful, contrary things too. We are learning that lesson ourselves now, aren't we, now that we no longer have a home?
Don't imagine we'll get it back by paying the odd home visit. There'll
be good-byes and tears, some will feel heartbroken, some will strut
about proudly waving their new foreign passports while paying a bill
with their traveler's check . . . But the home we think about when we're
abroad, that has gone for good. Do you still dream of your home in

Zala? I do sometimes dream of the wetlands in the Nyírség, but whenever I do I wake with a headache. It seems home is not just a region, a town, a house, or people but a feeling. What's that? Are there eternal feelings? No, dear, I don't think so. You know very well I adore you, but if one day I stopped adoring you because you have cheated on me or gone off with someone—but that's all impossible, isn't it? Should it ever happen, should I ever have to say good-bye to you, please don't think my heart will break. We'll carry on having charming conversations, if you like . . . but there will be one thing we won't talk about, because that will have been over, vanished into thin air. There's no time for mourning. There is only ever one home in your life, like love, the one true love. And it passes like love, like true love. And it's right it should be like that; otherwise it would all be too much for us to bear.

That first woman, my husband's first wife—she was a refined lady. Very beautiful, very self-controlled. It was her self-control I most envied. That seems to be one of those things you can't learn or buy with money. It's something you're born with. It may be that the stuff these strange people, the rich, are so busy cultivating all the time is nothing more than a kind of self-discipline. Their blood cells, their very glands, are all precisely under control. I hated this capacity in them, and my husband knew I hated it. It was precisely because his first wife was cultured and self-controlled that my husband left her one day. He had grown tired of self-control. I was more than just a woman to him: I was a trial, a rehearsal, an adventure, both hunt and prey, a form of fraud, a sacrilege—like when someone in polite society suddenly spits on the carpet. The devil knows what these things mean. I'll fetch a cognac, a three-star bottle, all right? I've grown thirsty with all this talking.

Drink, my dear. There—you see how I drink? I put my lips to where your lips have touched the glass . . . what surprising, tender, marvelous ideas you have! I could weep when something like this occurs to you. I have no idea how you do it. I'm not saying the idea is entirely original, it might be other lovers in the past have thought of it . . . but it's still a wonderful gift.

There—now I have drunk after you. You see my husband never made tender gestures like this. We never once drank from the same glass while looking into each other's eyes as we are doing now. If he wanted to please me, he would buy me a ring—yes, that nice ring with the turquoise stone, the one you were looking at just now with such fascination: that too was a present from him. What's that, darling? Fine, you can take it, have the ring valued as you did the others, at that first-rate man of yours. You shall have whatever you want.

Shall I tell you more about the rich? There is no way of telling anyone everything about them. I mean, I lived among them for years, but it was like walking in my sleep, in a deep sleep filled with dread. I always worried about saying the wrong thing when I talked to them. I worried in case I listened wrong or touched things in the wrong way. They never shouted or cursed at me, certainly not! They trained and educated me instead, sensitively, patiently, the way the Italian organ grinder out in the street trains his monkey, showing him how to perch on his shoulder and how to preen himself. But they also taught me the way one might teach a cripple, someone incapable of walking, of doing anything the way it ought to be done. Because that is what I was when I first went to them: a cripple. I couldn't do anything properly. I couldn't walk, not as they understood walking, couldn't say hello, couldn't speak . . . and as for eating? I hadn't the foggiest notion how to eat! Even listening was beyond me—listening properly, that is, listening with purpose: in other words, with evil intent. I listened and gawped. I was a fish out of water. But little by little I learned everything they had to teach me. I worked at it and got on. It surprised them how much and how quickly I learned. It was I who left them gawping in the end. I'm not boasting, but I do believe they were quite astonished when they saw how much I learned.

I knew about the family vault, for example. The mausoleum. Oh, lord, that mausoleum! You know how it was back then, when I was still a maid in their house. I saw how everyone was robbing them. The cook made a bit on the side, the servant took backhanders from the salesmen who inflated the prices for brandy, wine, and the best cigars, the chauffeur stole and sold the gas in their cars. All this was to be expected. My employers were perfectly aware of it: it was part of the household budget. I didn't steal anything myself, since I only cleaned the bathroom, where there was nothing to steal. But later, once I had become "Her Ladyship," I couldn't help thinking of everything I had seen in the cellar and the kitchen, and the mausoleum was too much of a temptation. I couldn't resist it.

You see there came a day when my husband—a proper gentleman—

suddenly felt his life was incomplete without a family vault in the Buda graveyard. His parents, the old gentleman and the old lady, were old-fashioned in their death, turning to dust under simple marble tomb-stones without a proper mausoleum. My husband grew quite morose when this omission occurred to him. But he soon recovered and set to work to remedy the fault. He asked me to negotiate with the designer and the clerk-of-works to create the perfect mausoleum. By that time we had more than one car, a summer house in Zebegény and a perma-nent winter residence on exclusive Rózsadomb, not to mention a man-sion in Transdanubia, near Lake Balaton, on an estate that my husband found himself lumbered with as the result of some deal. We certainly couldn't complain we had nowhere to live.

But a mausoleum we did not have. We hastened to correct this over-sight. Naturally we couldn't trust any ordinary builder with the job. My husband took great pains to discover the leading funerary expert in the city. We had plans brought over from England and Italy, whole books, their pages printed on heavy burnished paper . . . you have no idea the amount people have written on the subject of funerary monuments. I mean, after all, to just go and die, that's nothing special—people scrape out a bit of earth and shove you in, end of story. But gentlefolk lead dif-ferent lives, and, naturally, their deaths are different too. So we employed an expert to help us choose a model, and had a beautiful, spa-cious, dry mausoleum built, complete with cupola. I wept when I first saw the mausoleum from within, the sheer glory of it, because, for just a moment, it made me think of the sandy ditch we lived in out on the wetlands. I mean, the vault was bigger than the ditch. With careful fore-sight they had left enough space at the center for six graves, I have no idea for whom. Maybe they were expecting guests, the visiting dead, just in case someone dropped in and needed somewhere to stretch out. I looked at the three spare places and told my husband I would sooner be buried by dogs than lie in this crypt of theirs! You should have seen him laugh when I said it!

And so we were prepared for all eventualities. Naturally the mauso-leum was equipped with electric lights, lights in two colors, blue and white. When everything was ready we called the priest to consecrate this house of dead pleasure. Everything you could possibly think of was provided, darling—gilt letters above the entrance, and, on the elevation, modestly small, the aristocratic family crest, the crest they wore on their underpants. Then there was a forecourt where they planted flowers, with columns at the entrance leading to a sort of marbled waiting room for visitors should they fancy taking a breather before they died. You then passed from the zinc hall, through the wrought-iron gates, into the parlor, where the elders were arranged. It was a proper mausoleum, set up for eternity, as if the dead interred there were not to be thrown out after thirty to fifty years. There they were, including the most illustrious among them, for eternity, until the last trumpet called them forth in their distinguished pajamas and privileged dressing gowns.

I earned an eight-thousand-pengő commission doing the mausoleum, the builder wouldn't give me more. I had an account in a bank and one day, stupidly, I deposited this little extra cash. My husband came across the statement quite by chance, the statement revealing how my little-here and little-there had started to amount to a reasonable sum. He didn't say anything—of course he didn't say anything, what a crazy idea!—but I could see it upset him. He thought a member of the family shouldn't be making a profit on his parents' family vault. Can you credit that? I couldn't understand it myself, not to this day. I only tell you the story to show you how strange the rich are.

There's something else. I got used to everything, I bore it all silently. But they had one habit I really couldn't stand. Even today I have to take a deep breath because I feel sick just thinking about it. It was that one step too far! I have learned a few things in my time, and there is never an end to learning. But I can bear it all; I am resigned to it. You never know, perhaps I might even get used to the idea of getting older. Silently. But that habit of theirs I couldn't bear. I redden when I remember it, red with helpless fury, like a turkey.

You mean bed? Yes, but not the way you think. It was related to bed, but in another way. I mean their nightgowns and their pajamas.

You don't understand. Well, I agree it's hard to explain. What I mean is that I looked around me, amazed at everything in the house: I felt an almost religious awe, the way you do when you see a giraffe in the zoo. There was the colored toilet paper, the Swedish chiropodist, the lot. I understood that such unusual people could not live by ordinary, every-day rules. They had to have food served a different way, the beds made a different way, like no ordinary mortal being.

Naturally, their food had to be cooked differently because their digestive system had to be quite different, like the kangaroo's. I'm not absolutely sure how it was with their intestines, but they certainly digested their food in a way no ordinary mortal does. Not naturally, in the regular way, but in a way that forced them to use peculiar laxatives, strange enemas . . . the whole thing was a great secret.

So I looked on while they did all this, gazing in wonder, mouth open, often with goose pimples. High culture, it seems, is not just a matter of museums but something you find in people's bathrooms and the kitchens where others cook for them. Their way of life did not change, not a bit, not even during the siege, would you believe it? While everyone else was eating beans or peas, they were still opening tins of delicacies from abroad, goose liver from Strasbourg and such things. There was a woman in the cellar, who spent three weeks there, the wife of an ex–minister of state whose husband had fled west to escape the Russians, who stayed here because she had some other man . . . and believe it or not, this woman was on a diet, a diet she maintained even as bombs were falling. She was looking after her figure, cooking some tasty something on a spirit flame using only olive oil because she feared that the fat in the beans and the gristle that everyone stuffed themselves with out of fear and anxiety might lead her to put on weight! When-ever I get to thinking about it, I marvel what a strange thing this thing called culture is.

Here in Rome there are all these wonderful statues and paintings and grand tapestries, like the castoffs of a lost world, the kind we get in junk shops back home. But maybe all the masterworks of Rome offer just one view of culture. It might be that culture is also what happens when people cook for the rich, with butter or oil, with complicated recipes prescribed by the doctor—as if it were not only their teeth and guts that required nourishment but they had to have a special soup for the liver, a different cut of meat for the heart, a particular blend of salads for the gall bladder, and a rare form of pastry with raisins for the pancreas. And having eaten all this, the rich withdraw into solitude so that their myste-rious organs of digestion can get on with digesting. That's culture too! I understood it all, admired it, and full-heartedly approved of it. It was just their way with nightshirts and pajamas I failed to understand. I could never reconcile myself to it. Damn the God that invented such things!

Have patience, I'm about to tell you. After making the bed I had to lay the nightshirt on top of it facedown, folding the bottom end of it back and over, spreading the sleeves. See what I mean? Looked at this way, the nightshirt or pajamas looked faintly Arabic, like some Eastern pilgrim at prayer, stomach to the ground, his arms spread over the sand. Why did they insist on this? I have no idea. Maybe because it's more convenient that way, because it involves one movement less, because you just need to pull it on from the back and there you are, ready for bed, without having to struggle into it and tire yourself out before going to sleep. But I hated this kind of calculation, absolutely loathed it. I simply couldn't tolerate this affectation of theirs. My whole nervous system rebelled against it. My hands shook with fury whenever I made their beds, folding and adjusting their nightgowns, pajama jackets, and trousers the way the manservant taught me. Why?

People are peculiar, you see. They are born that way, even when they're not rich. Everyone is annoyed or driven mad by something. Even the poor who tolerate everything for a while, who resign themselves to everything and bear the weight of the world on their backs with a certain awe and helplessness, accepting whatever comes their way. There comes a moment for them, one that came for me each evening when I was making the bed, putting out their nightwear in the required manner. That was when I understood that soon people would no longer put up with the world as it was. I mean individuals as well as nations. Someone would scream out loud that they had had enough, that things had to change. And that when this happened, people would take to the streets and go on the rampage, smashing and breaking things. Though that's only the circus part, a sideshow. Revolution, I mean real revolution, is that which has already happened inside people. Don't stare at me like an idiot, gorgeous.

I might be talking rubbish, but not everything runs according to the laws of normal logic, not everything people say or do has to make sense. Do you think it's rational or logical that I should be lying with you in this bed? Don't you get it, sweetheart? Never mind. Just keep your mouth shut and carry on loving me. Our logic makes no sense—but here we are.

So that's the nightwear business. I loathed this habit of theirs. But eventually I resigned myself to that too. They were so much stronger, after all. It is possible to hate dominant forms of life just as it is possible to admire them, but you cannot deny them. I grew to hate them. I hated them to the extent that I joined them and became rich myself; wore their clothes, lay down in their beds, started to watch my figure, and, eventually, got to taking laxatives before I went to bed, just like the rich. I didn't hate them because they were rich and I was poor, no, please don't misunderstand me. It would be nice if someone finally understood the true state of affairs.

Newspapers and parliaments are constantly going on about this now. Even the movies are full of it, or so I understood watching a newsreel the other day. Everyone is talking about it. I wonder what has got into people. I can't imagine it's good for people to be talking so crudely, so generally about rich and poor, about Americans and Russians. I don't understand it. They even say there is bound to be a great revolution and the Russians will come out on top, along with the poor, by and large. But a very refined man once told me in a bar—a South American, I think, a drug dealer, so I heard, who supposedly kept a stash of heroin in his dentures—that that was not how it was going to be, that it would be the Americans who'd win out in the end, because they had more money.

I thought a good deal about this. The saxophonist said the same thing. He said the Americans would drill a great hole in the ground and pack it with atom bombs, and then this little guy in glasses, the man who was currently the president over the ocean, would get down on his hands and knees, carrying a burning match, and crawl over to the hole, light the fuse of the atom bomb, and then—whoosh!—the whole caboodle would go up. I thought it a load of nonsense at first. But I can't bring myself to laugh anymore. I have seen a great deal that seemed just as ridiculous but soon became reality. My experience is that, generally, the more stupid the idea, the more certain that, one day, it will be turned into fact.

I'll never forget the gossip in Budapest near the end of the war. One day, for example, the Germans ranged cannons along the embankment on the Buda side of the city. Enormous cannons they were, properly dug in by the bridgeheads. They broke up the pavements and placed machine-gun nests all the way along the lovely chestnut-lined shore. People looked at them anxiously, but there were some smart people who declared there would not be a siege of Budapest because all those terrifying weapons, the heavy artillery by the bridges, the bundles of explosives on the bridges themselves, were all a confidence trick. It was a trick to pull the wool over the Russians' eyes. They didn't really want a battle. That's what they were saying. But it was no trick: at least it didn't fool the Russians. The Russians arrived at the river one day and shot everything to pieces, including the cannons. So I have no idea if what the South American said will come true, but I suspect that, in the end, it will work out exactly as he said, if only because it sounded so ridiculous at first hearing.

I also thought a lot about what this very refined man said about how the Americans would win because they were rich. The rich—now there is something I do understand. My experience was that you had to be very careful with the rich because they are extraordinarily crafty. They possess enormous resilience . . . though heaven alone knows where the resilience comes from. One thing is certain—they are subtle, and it is never easy dealing with them. What I said about their nightwear is evidence of that. People who have you prepare their pajamas the way I was told to prepare them are not ordinary people. Such people know exactly what they want, day and night, and a poor man should cross himself when coming into their presence. Of course I mean only the genuinely rich, not those who just happen to have money. Those are less dangerous. They flash their money around the way a child blows bubbles. And it all ends as it does with soap bubbles: the bubble just bursts in their hands.

My husband was genuinely rich. That might be why he was always so tired.

Pour me another glass, just one finger. No, darling, no, I won't drink from your glass this time. Inspired ideas are not to be repeated. They quickly wear out and lose their magic. Don't take it the wrong way.

Don't rush me, I can only tell it in its proper order.

He was offended, yes, he was terminally offended. That was something I never understood, because I was born poor. There is a strange similarity between the really poor and the really rich . . . you can't offend either of them. My father, who was a barefoot fruit picker in the wetlands, was as impossible to offend as the prince of the Rákóczis. My husband was embarrassed by his wealth: far from him to flash it about! He would have worn any disguise to avoid his wealth being pointed out. His manners were so refined, so quiet, so fearfully courteous that you couldn't offend him with words, with manners, or with acts, since it all washed off his refinement like water off a leaf. They left no scar. No, the only person capable of offending him was himself. And the tendency to offend himself grew in him like some wicked, sickly passion.

Later, when he began to suspect that there was something wrong with him, he started to panic. He was like someone dangerously ill who suddenly loses faith in the famous physician, in the whole range of science and medicine, and turns instead to the woman selling herbal cures because she might be able to help. That was how he came to me one day, leaving his wife and his old life behind. He thought I could offer a kind of herbal cure for him. But I was no herbalist.

Pass me that photo, let me have another look at him. Yes, that's what he was like fifteen years ago.

Have I said I wore this picture round my neck a long time? In a small locket, on a lilac ribbon? Do you know why? Because I'd paid for it. I was just a servant then and bought it out of my wages: that was why I looked after it. My husband never knew what an important matter it was for someone like me to pay money for something for which there is no pressing need, I mean real money, like the change from my wages or a tip. Later I spent money like water—his money—I threw thousands around the way I sent dust flying with my feather duster on mornings when I was still a servant. It wasn't real money to me. But my heart was in my mouth when I bought this photograph, because I was poor and felt it a sin to spend money on things that were not absolutely essential. That photograph was a sin for me, mere vanity. I bought it all the same, sneaking a visit to the famous, highly fashionable photographer in the city center, ready to pay the full price without bargaining. The photographer laughed and sold it to me at cut price. Buying his photograph was the only sacrifice I ever made for that man.

He was reasonably tall, a couple of inches taller than me. His weight was steady. He controlled his body the way he controlled his words and manners. He put on a few pounds in winter, but lost them again in May and remained at that weight till Christmas. Don't think for a moment that he dieted. Forget diets. It was just that he treated his body the way he might treat one of his employees. His body was required to work for him.

He treated his eyes and his mouth the same way. His eyes and mouth laughed separately, as and when they were required. They never laughed at the same time. Not the way you did, my precious, so freely, so sweetly, both eyes and mouth smiling at once, yesterday when you truly excelled yourself and sold that ring—and came home to me with the good news.

That was something he could never do. I lived with him, I was his wife and, before that, his servant. Needless to say, I felt much closer to him as a servant than when I was merely his wife. Even so, I never saw him give a full-hearted laugh the way you do.

He was far more likely to smile. When I met that hunk of a Greek in London, the man who taught me a great many things—don't go bothering me with what he taught me, I couldn't tell you everything, we'd be here till dawn—he warned me never to laugh in company when in England because it was considered vulgar. I should just smile and keep smiling. I tell you this because I want you to know everything you might find useful sometime.

My husband could smile like nobody's business. I was so jealous of it sometimes I felt quite sick just thinking about his smile. It was as if he had learned a high art at some mysterious university where the rich go to get their education and smiling is a compulsory subject. He even smiled when he was being cheated. I tried it on with him sometimes. I cheated him and watched. I cheated him in bed and watched to see what he'd do. There were moments when that was dangerous. You never know how someone will react when they're cheated in bed.

The danger was a deathly thrill to me. I wouldn't have been surprised if one day he grabbed a knife from the kitchen and stabbed me in the stomach—like a pig at slaughter time. It was only a dream, of course: wish fulfillment. I learned the term from a doctor I consulted for a while because I wanted to be fashionable like the others, because I was rich and could indulge myself with a few psychological problems. The doctor got fifty pengő for an hour's work. This fee entitled me to lie on a sofa in his surgery and to regale him with my dreams as well as all the rude talk I could muster. There are people who pay to have a woman lie on a sofa and talk filth. But it was I who did the paying, learning terms like "repression" and "wish fulfillment." I certainly learned a great deal. It wasn't easy living with the gentry.

But smiling was something I never learned. It seems you need something else for that. Maybe you have to have a history of ancestors smiling before you. I hated it as much as I did the fuss about the pajamas . . . I hated their smiles. I cheated my husband in bed by pretending to enjoy it when I didn't really. I'm sure he knew it, but did he draw a knife and stab me? No, he smiled. He sat in the huge French bed, his hair tousled, his muscles well toned, a man in top condition, smelling faintly of hay. He fixed me with a glassy look and smiled. I wanted to cry at such moments. I was helpless with grief and fury. I am sure that later, when he saw his bombed-out house, or still later, when they kicked him out of the factory and expropriated him, he was smiling the same smile in exactly the same way.

It is one of the foulest of human sins, that serene, superior smile. It is the true crime of the rich. It is the one thing that can never be forgiven. Because I can understand people beating or killing each other when they have been hurt. But if they merely smile and say nothing, I have no idea what to do with them. Sometimes I felt no punishment was enough for it. There was nothing I, a woman who had clambered out of the ditch to find myself in his life, could do against him. The world could not harm him, whatever it did to him, to his wealth, to his lands, or to anything that mattered to him. It was the smile that had to be wiped out. Don't those famous revolutionaries know this?

Because shares and precious stones may vanish, but the trace of these things, a kind of residual bloom, will hang around the rich even after they have lost everything. When you take the really rich and strip them to their bare skin, they still retain the aura of wealth, an aura no earthly power can drag from them. The fact is that when you have someone truly rich, someone with fifty thousand acres, say, or a factory with two thousand workers, and they lose it all, they still remain richer than my kind, however well we happen to be doing.

How they do it? I don't know. Look, I was there when wealthy people were having a particularly bad time back home. All the odds were stacked against them. Everyone hated them. Little by little, step by methodical step, they were deprived of everything, all their visible goods, and later, with supreme skill, of their invisible goods too. And yet these people remained as serene as before.

I stood there gaping. I wasn't angry. I did not feel in the least like mocking. I don't want to make a big song and dance about money to you, or to go on forever about the rich and the poor. Don't get me wrong, I know it would sound good if I started shouting at dawn about how much I hated the rich, about their money, their power. I hated them, yes I did, but it wasn't their wealth I hated. It was more that I was afraid of them, or rather that I was in awe of them the way primitive man feared thunder and lightning. I was angry with them the way people used to be angry with the gods. You know about the little gods, those tubby ones, those of human proportions, who talk big, screw around, and are real rogues, those who interfere with the mess of ordinary people's lives, who worm their way into others' beds, into women's lives, who steal the food off the table, gods who behave much as people do. They are not gods like that; they are middling, helpful gods of human size.

That's how I felt when I thought of the rich. It wasn't their money, their mansions, their precious stones that made me hate them. I was not a revolutionary proletarian, not a worker with a proper consciousness, nothing like that.

Why not? It was because of the depths from which I'd risen. I knew more than street-corner orators did; I knew that under it all, right at the bottom of things, there isn't, nor has there ever been, justice; that when you end one injustice, it is immediately replaced by another. More than that, I was a woman, a beautiful woman at that, and I wanted my own place in the sun. Is that a crime? Maybe the revolutionaries—those who thrive by promising that everything will be fine providing we kick out whatever exists and is bad and do something that in other circumstances we would consider bad—maybe they would despise me for it. But I want to be honest with you. I want to give you everything I have, that I still have, not just the jewels. That's why I must tell you that the reason I hated the rich was because it was only money I could take from them. But the rest, the secret and meaning of wealth, that sense of otherness which cast a more frightening spell over me than money did, that they did not give me. They hid it so well that no revolutionary could take it from them. They stowed it away more securely than valuables in the safes of foreign banks, than the pieces of gold buried in their gardens.

I couldn't work out the way they could suddenly change subject and simply talk about something else the very moment when the subject seemed most exciting and painfully relevant. There were moments I was so furious my heart beat in my mouth. I was furious when in love, furious when I had been hurt, furious when I saw injustice, when someone was suffering—sometimes I felt like screaming out in righteous indignation. But they—they stayed quiet and smiled at such moments. It's beyond words as far as I am concerned. Words are never really enough, not when anything really matters, matters as much as birth or death. Words don't do those occasions any real justice. Maybe music can do it, I don't know. Or when we feel desire and touch someone, like this. Don't move. There was a good reason that other friend of mine hid the dictionaries in the end. He was looking for a word. But he couldn't find it.

So don't be surprised. I'm no good at explaining myself. I'm just talking . . . How far off the point talking is when you really want to say something!

Give me the photograph again. Yes, that's what he looked like when I met him. Later, when I last saw him—after the siege—he was just the same. He had changed only the way a well-made object changes with use . . . a little more shiny, a little smoother, a little more burnished if you like. He was aging like a good razor or cigarette holder.

Heaven knows. Maybe I should make an effort to tell you what happened. You know what—I'll start at the end. Maybe that way it will be clearer, leaving out the beginning.

His problem was that he was bourgeois. What's bourgeois? The pictures in Red propaganda show us evil, potbellied figures who spend the entire day studying share prices while driving their workers to exhaustion.

That's the way I pictured them, too, before I found myself among them. But later I understood that the whole business of the bourgeois and the class war was different from what we proles were told.

These people were sure they had a role in the world; I don't mean just in business, copying those people who had had great power when they themselves had little power. What they believed was that when it came down to it, they were putting the world into some sort of order, that with them in charge, the lords of the world would not be such great lords as they had been, and the proles would not remain in abject poverty, as we once were. They thought the whole world would eventually accept their values; that even while one group moved down and another one up, they, the bourgeois, would keep their position—even in a world where everything was being turned upside down.

Then one day he asked to speak to me. He said he wanted to marry me—me, the maid! I didn't quite understand what he was talking about, but at that moment I hated him so much I could have spat at him. It was Christmas and I was squatting by the fire, preparing to light it. I thought it was the greatest insult I'd ever received. He wanted to buy me like he would some fancy breed of dog—that's what I felt. I told him to get out of my way. I didn't even want to look at him.

So he didn't make me his wife then. After a while time passed and he got married. He married a proper lady. They had a child but the child died. The old man died too, and I was sorry about that. When he died the house was like a museum where people only dropped by to take a look. I wouldn't have been surprised if a bunch of schoolchildren turned up one Sunday morning, rang the bell, and said it was an educational visit. By that time my husband was living in a different house, with his wife. They did a lot of traveling. I'd stayed with the old gentleman. The old woman wasn't daft. I was scared of her, but I loved her too. There was some knowledge flickering in her, some age-old female wisdom. She had cures for liver and kidney ailments. She knew about washing and how to listen to music. She knew about us too, about the boy's rebellion, without saying a word . . . she recognized the long-standing tension between us the way only women know, as if by a kind of radar. Women can sniff out the secrets of any man in their vicinity.

So she knew her son was hopelessly lonely because the world into which he'd been born, to which he belonged heart and soul—in his memories, in his dreams, even when he was wide awake—could no longer protect him. It couldn't protect him because it was falling apart, disintegrating like an old piece of cloth, beyond use even as a decorative throw or a rag for wiping. She knew her son was no longer moving forward, no longer on the attack: he was on the back foot, merely defending. She knew that people who stop moving forward and spend their lives on the back foot are no longer alive: they merely exist. The old woman sensed this danger: her ancient female weaving-and-spinning instincts told her as much. She was aware of this secret the way families are aware of a sinister genetic weakness that is not to be spoken of because considerable interests are at stake. No one should know or speak about the fact that anemia or madness had ravaged the family in the past.

What are you looking at? Yes, I am just as neurotic as the rich. And it wasn't being among the rich that gave me my neurosis. I was neurotic in my own way in the ditch back home . . . that is to say if I ever had anything of the kind people call "home." Whenever I say the word "family" or "home," I see nothing, I only smell things: earth, mud, mice, human smells. Then, beyond all that, another smell, one hovering over my half-animal, half-human childhood, over the pale blue sky, the mushroom-smelling wood wet with rain, the taste of sunlight, a smell like metal when you touch it with your tongue. I was a neurotic child too, why deny it? It's not just the rich that have secrets.

But it's the end I want to tell you about, the very last time I saw my husband. Because, sitting with you here at dawn in this hotel in Rome, I feel I know for certain that that was the last time.

Wait, let's not drink any more. A black coffee instead . . . Give me your hand. Put it to my heart. Yes, it's pounding. That's how it pounds every dawn. It's not the black coffee or the cigarettes, it's not even being with you that does it. It pounds because I remember that moment—the moment I last saw him.

Please don't think it is desire that makes my heart pound like this. There is no cheap movie scene involved in that pounding. I have already told you that I never loved him. There was a time when I was in love with him, of course, but that's only because I hadn't yet lived with him. Love and being in love don't go together, you know.

I was foolish and in love, and everything happened just as I had planned. The old woman died and I went to London. Show me that second photograph! Yes, that was my virile Greek, dearest. He taught singing in London, in Soho. He was a real Greek, down to his fingernails, and could flash those beautiful, fiery, dark eyes of his. He could whisper and swear and, when roused, show as much of the whites of his eyes as that Neapolitan tenor we saw at the concert the other day.

I felt very lonely in London. London is a huge, stony desert: even boredom feels endless there. The English have become connoisseurs of boredom: they know how to deal with it. I went there as a maid and quickly found employment. At that time foreign maids were in demand the way African slaves once were. There is a city in England called Liverpool that, they say, is built on the skulls of black men—not that I know that for certain. I couldn't stand being a maid in London for long, because the job was quite different in London than it had been in Budapest. It was better in some ways and worse in others. It wasn't the work so much. The fact that I had to work was no bother. I could barely speak the language, which was a serious concern, but what was worse was that I didn't really feel like a maid in the house, more just a component. A component, that is, not in an English household with an English family, but in some kind of big business dealing with imports. I was an imported article. On top of that it wasn't a real English family I had joined but a rich German Jewish family living in London. The head of the family had fled Hitler to England, bringing his family with him, and was producing warm woolen underwear for the army. He was a thoroughly German Jew—that is to say, as much German as Jewish. He wore his hair close-cropped, and I think—though I don't know this for certain, it's not impossible—had had a surgeon apply some dueling scars to his face, hoping he'd pass for someone who had been a proper card-playing German student. That's what I kept thinking when I occasionally looked at his picture.

They were good people, though, and played at being English with more enthusiasm than the English themselves then wanted or had means to do. The house was lovely. It was in a green outer suburb of London.

There were four in the family, plus a staff of five and a daily charwoman. I was on the door, responsible for letting people in. The staff included a cook and a manservant as back at home, a kitchen maid, and a driver. I thought this was all perfectly proper. Very few of the grand old English families were employing such specialized staff by this time. They'd sold the great family houses, or had them rebuilt, maintaining the obligatory minimum staff in the few grand households where people still preserved old customs.

We all looked out for ourselves. The kitchen maid would not lift a finger to help me in my duties. The manservant would sooner have cut off his hand than help the cook. We were all simply components to keep the machine ticking over. Do you know what made me nervous in all this? It was that I never understood the machine we were serving. We were all components, both masters and servants, but was the machine an accurate Swiss watch or a timed explosive device? There was something unsettling about this quiet, refined, ultra-English mode of life. You know, the way everyone kept smiling, like in English detective fiction, where murderer and victim continue to smile even as they are politely discussing who is to kill who.

And it was boring. I wasn't good at putting up with this fully heated, fully laundered, dry-cleaned, English form of boredom. I never knew when it was proper to laugh. In the parlor, of course, I could only laugh inwardly because I had no right to laugh when my anglicized employers told each other jokes. But it was the same with laughter in the kitchen. I was never sure when it was safe. They liked their jokes. The manservant subscribed to a comic journal and over dinner would read out the incomprehensible, and to my mind idiotic, English jokes. Everyone burst into loud laughter: the cook, the chauffeur, the kitchen maid, and the manservant, all of them. And, as they did so, they craftily watched me with one eye to check whether I understood their marvelous English sense of humor.

Most of the time I only understood enough of the charade to know it was beyond me, and that it wasn't really the joke they were laughing at, but me. The English, you know, are almost as hard to understand as the rich. You have to be very careful with them, because they are always smiling, even when they are thinking the most terrible things. And they can look at you so stupidly you'd think they couldn't count to two. But they are not stupid, and they are remarkably good at counting, particularly when they want to put one over on you. But of course they carry on smiling even then, even as they are cheating you.

The English servants regarded me, the foreigner, of course, as a kind of white Negro, a lower life-form. But even so, I suspect they didn't look down on me quite as much as they looked down on my immigrant employers, the rich German Jews. They looked at me with pity. Maybe they felt a little sorry for me because I couldn't fully appreciate the sparkling humor in *Punch*.

I lived with them as best I could. And waited . . . what else could I do?

What was I waiting for? For my knight in shining armor, my Lohengrin, who would one day leave home and hearth and rescue me? For the rich man who was still living with his rich wife? I knew my time would come, that I just had to wait.

But I also knew that that man would never make a move by himself. I would eventually have to go for him, to grab him by the hair and drag him away from his life. It would be like saving someone from drowning in quicksand. That's how I imagined it.

One Sunday afternoon I met the Greek in Soho. I never found out what his real occupation was. He told me he was a businessman. He had rather too much money and even a car, a car being a much rarer sight then than it is now. He spent the night in clubs playing cards. I think his only real occupation was being Levantine. The English were not surprised that someone could make a living simply by being a Levantine. Smiling and courteous, humming and nodding, the English knew everything about us foreigners. They didn't say anything, just hissed a little when someone offended against their code of good manners. It was, of course, impossible to discover what the code actually was.

My Greek friend was always up to something just off center. He was never jailed, but when I was with him in a pub or a classy restaurant he would take the odd glance at the door as though he were expecting a raid. He kept his ears open. Oh, do put that photograph back with the other one where it belongs. What did I learn from him? I told you: I learned to sing. He discovered I had a voice. Yes, you're right, that wasn't the only thing I learned. What a donkey you are! I told you he was Levantine: forget the Greek part.

Don't interrupt. I just want to get to the end of the story. Tell you what about the end? That it was all in vain, that secretly I never stopped hating my husband. But I loved him too, loved him to distraction.

I understood that the moment I was walking over the bridge after the siege and met him coming the other way. How simple it sounds when put like that . . . There, you see? I've said it and nothing has happened. Here you are in a bed in Rome, in a hotel room, puffing away at an American cigarette with the scent of coffee from the Turkish copper pot wafting around you, it's almost dawn, your head is propped on one arm, and you're looking at me like that. Your lovely shiny hair is tumbling over your brow. And you're waiting for me to go on. Isn't life extraordinary with all its changes? Well, there I was crossing the bridge and suddenly who should I see walking toward me but my husband.

Is that all? Was it as simple as that?

Saying it now, I myself am astonished how much can fit into a single sentence. For example, just saying something like "after the siege." One just says it, right? But there was nothing simple about the siege. You will know that at the end of February the big guns were still booming away in some parts of the country. Towns and villages were burning, people were being killed. But in Pest and Buda by that time we were—in some ways—living like people in great cities normally live. But at the same time, we had another life. We were like nomads before time began. We were wandering Gypsies. By mid-February the last Nazis had been defeated in Buda and Pest and gradually, with the ever-fainter sound of thunder, like real thunder, the front moved on, each day a little farther away. People started emerging from cellars.

You, of course, were out in Zala County, where there was no fighting: if you could have seen how things were in Pest, you'd have thought we had all gone mad. And you would have been right if you judged by appearances alone in those weeks and months after the siege. It was everything you could possibly imagine. Appearances won't tell you what people feel, how people talk when crawling out of the rubble, when they're still humiliated and terrified. You can't smell the foul stench they've had to get used to: the dirt, the lack of washing, the lack of water. We were emerging from filth, from close human contact. I think I'm remembering this all topsy-turvy now, the way it is lodged in my memory. A lot of things get confused when I think back to this time. It's like when the reel breaks in a movie, you know . . . suddenly you lose the thread of the story, dazzled by the flashing gray patterns on the screen.

The houses were still smoking. Buda with all its pretty detail, the Bastion, and the old quarter, were one great dying fire. I happened to be in Buda then. I didn't spend the siege in the cellar of the house I'd been living in, because that had been bombed in the summer. I'd moved to a hotel. Then, once the Russian army had surrounded the city, I moved in with a friend. Which friend? You'll find out in a minute.

It wasn't difficult finding accommodation in Pest then. People usually spent the night elsewhere, anywhere but at home—I mean people who could easily have stayed at home, who didn't have to hide—but everyone was caught up in a great tide of emotion. We were like mythical creatures left over at the end of some festival. People felt they had to hide because it wasn't impossible that some dark force should be out looking for them, pursuing them—the Russians, the Communists— who knows? It was as if everyone was in disguise, guests at a macabre masked ball to which everyone was invited. Persian soothsayers and master chefs, complete with false beards . . . the cast list was uncanny.

But that wasn't the whole story. At first sight it seemed everyone was dizzy with the drink the Nazis had stored in the cellars of hotels and restaurants and had no time to drink on their stampede to the west. You've heard the stories survivors tell of major airplane disasters or shipwrecks, how they find themselves marooned on some mountain- top, then, after three or four days, the supplies run out? Soon everybody—all those ladies and gentlemen with proper manners—is sizing each other up, speculating on each other's edibility. You know the film *The Gold Rush,* where that little funny man with the toothbrush mustache—Chaplin, I mean—is being chased round and round the cabin in Alaska by that enormous prospector because the big man wants to eat the little man? There was that kind of madness in people's eyes, the way they looked at things, the way they talked about there being a bit of food here or there. That was because they had made up their minds, like the survivors of a shipwreck, that one way or the other they would stay alive, even if it meant eating other people. They stowed away whatever could be stowed, wherever they found it.

I had a glimpse of reality after the siege. It was like having a cataract peeled away with a penknife. It took my breath away for a moment, it was all so fascinating.

The Bastion was still alight when we staggered from the cellar. Women were dressed like crones, in rags, covered in soot, hoping to escape the attentions of the Russian soldiers that way. The smell of death, the corpse smell of cellars, rose from our clothes, from our very bodies. Everywhere you went, however near or far, great fat bombs lay by the sidewalks, belching smoke. I walked down the wide avenue past corpses, fallen masonry, and useless, abandoned armored cars. I saw the frail skeletons of wingless Rata planes. I made my way through Kriszti-naváros toward the green at the Vérmező. I wasn't quite steady on my feet, because I was dizzy with fresh air, with winter sunlight, with simply being alive . . . But I plodded on like ten or twenty thousand others, because there was already an improvised bridge over the Danube. It was a hump of a bridge, a camel's back. The Russian military police had rounded up a group of workers to build the bridge in under two weeks, under the direction of Russian engineers. At last, we could move between Buda and Pest again. Like everyone else I rushed to cross the bridge to Pest, because I had to get to Pest at any price. I could not stand being where I was anymore, not the way things were.

What was it I couldn't stand? Was I desperate to see my old house? Of course not. I'll tell you what.

The first morning the bridge was up, I rushed to Pest because I wanted to buy nail-polish remover at my favorite old drugstore in the city center. No, I'm not mad. It was just as I told you. Buda was still in flames. The tenement blocks of Pest were full of gaping holes. I had spent two weeks rotting in a cellar in Buda, along with a crowd of men, women, and children, with people starving and screaming around me, where one old man died of fright, and where everyone was filthy because we had no water. But in all of that, in all those two weeks, nothing tortured me so much as the thought that I had forgotten to bring my nail-polish remover into the shelter. When the last air-raid warning sounded and the siege began, I moved into the cellar with my nails painted bright red. And there I stayed with scarlet nails for two weeks, while Buda was falling around me. My scarlet nails had gone quite black with dirt.

You should know that even back then I had scarlet nails. I was a proper girl-about-town. I know men don't understand this, but what I was most worried about during the siege was not being able to hurry over to my favorite old drugstore in Pest where they sold good peacetime-quality nail-polish remover.

The psychiatrist who charged me fifty pengő per visit for the privilege of lying on a couch in his surgery three times a week and talking dirt—I did it simply because I did everything befitting a middle-class lady—he would most certainly have explained to me that it wasn't filthy nail polish I wanted to wash away, but uncleanness of another sort, the dirtiness of my prewar life. Well, maybe, but all I knew was that my nails were black, not scarlet, and that I had to do something about it. That's why I hurried over the bridge at the earliest possible opportunity.

Once I reached the street where we used to live, a familiar figure hurried past me. It was the plumber, born and bred in the district, a decent older man. Like many others at the time, he had grown a gray beard so that he might look like a proper granddad, someone on his last legs, hoping this might prevent him being carted off to forced labor in Russia, as far as Ekaterinburg. He was carrying a big parcel. I was delighted to recognize him as he was passing. Then suddenly I heard him shout to the locksmith who was living in a bombed-out house on the other side of the street:

"Jenő, run down to the Central Market Hall, they still have stuff there!"

And the other man, the lanky locksmith, shouted back, croaky with enthusiasm:

"Glad you told me. I'll get straight down!"

I stood at the edge of the grass of the Vérmező for a while, gazing after them. I saw the old Bulgarian wino who used to supply the richer houses with firewood for the winter. He emerged from another bombed property and carefully, almost ceremonially, lifted up a gold-rimmed mirror the way the priest raises the host when we celebrate the resurrection. The mirror flashed in the sparkling late-winter light. The old man was proceeding along reverentially, raising the mirror in such awe, you'd think the good fairy had given him the finest present of his life, the thing he had secretly longed for ever since he was a child. It was obvious he had just stolen it. He walked through the ruins in perfect peace, the one great winner in the lottery of life, spotted in the very moment the prize was announced. His stolen mirror made him the luckiest Bulgarian in the world.

I rubbed my eyes for a second, then an instinct took me over to the ruined building he had just left. The door was still there, but instead of the stairs a pile of rubble rose toward the next level. Later I heard that this old Buda house had been hit by over thirty bombs, shells, and grenades. I knew some people who lived there—a seamstress who occasionally worked for me, a vet who looked after my dog, and, on the first floor, a retired high-court judge with his wife, with whom we had sometimes had tea in the Auguszt, the old Buda patisserie. Krisztinaváros, unlike the other Budapest districts, was always more like a small provincial Austrian town than a suburb. People spent years there in cozy security or moved there in search of cozy security. Once there, they made their quiet, gentle vows—vows without any ulterior motive or even meaning—to be respectable members of the class of pensioners and middle-class families who had struggled their way to this haven of modest prosperity. Those who found their way here from below adopted the restrained, respectful manners of the older residents, including the plumber and the locksmith . . . Krisztinaváros was one big law-abiding, well-spoken, middle-class family.

The people who lived in that house, the house from whose ruins the Bulgarian emerged clutching his stolen mirror, were like that. He hurried from there, just as the plumber and locksmith had done. They were all encouraging each other to get busy, because the party wouldn't last forever, because, for now, Buda was in flames and there was no police, no order. And somewhere down at the Central Market Hall there might still be something that hadn't been pinched by the Russians or the rabble.

"Glad you told me. I'll get straight down!" The words rang in my ear. It was like a song, like the voice of a street urchin or a cry from some seething underworld. I entered the familiar house, climbed the pile of rubble to the next level, and found myself in the apartment where the judge and his wife had lived, in the middle room, the parlor. I recognized the room because my husband and I had once been invited by the old couple for tea there. The ceiling was gone, a bomb having fallen through the roof, dragging the upstairs apartment's parlor with it. It was an utter mess—roof beams, tiles, fragments of window frames, a door from the apartment above, bricks and plaster . . . then pieces of furniture, the leg of an Empire table, the front of a cupboard from the Maria Theresa period, a sideboard, lamps, all swimming in a shallow dirty liquid.

It was like a historical cesspool. Under it all I spotted the fringes of an Oriental carpet and a photograph of the judge, the photograph framed in silver, the old man posing in his frock coat, his hair pomaded. I stared at it in awe. It was like being confronted by a religious icon. There was something saintly about the old stiff figure, something dynastic. But I soon grew tired of looking and pushed the photograph aside with my foot. The bomb had wrecked more than one apartment here. Something had turned the flotsam of history into a heap of garbage. The tenants hadn't yet emerged from their cellar. They might have died there. I was about to go back down when I realized I was not alone.

Through the open door linking this room with one of the neighbor's rooms, I saw a man crawling on all fours. He had a box of silver cutlery under his arm. He greeted me without embarrassment, perfectly politely, as if he were merely visiting. The room next door was the judge's dining room: it was from there he emerged. I recognized him as an office worker, someone I knew by sight because he was local too, one of the honest burghers of Krisztinaváros. "Ah, the books!" he sighed in sympathy. "What a shame about the books!" . . . We climbed down together to ground level, me helping him to carry the silverware. We talked freely. He told me he had really come for the books, because the old judge had a substantial library full of literature and legal textbooks, all nicely bound . . . and he so loved books. He thought he'd try to save the library, but the books were beyond saving, he told me with real regret, because the ceiling next door had also fallen in and the books were so badly soaked they had practically turned to pulp, the kind used in paper mills. He said nothing about the silver cutlery. He had picked that up almost as an afterthought, instead of the books.

We chatted on while we clambered down the pile of rubble on all fours. The office worker gallantly showed me the route down, every so often holding on to my elbow and guiding me round the more dangerous, gravelly edges. We rested a moment in the doorway and said goodbye. He ambled down the street with the box of silverware under his arm, the perfect, respectable neighbor.

All these people—the Bulgarian, the plumber, the locksmith, the clerk—were busily going about their work. They were the kinds of people who would later be described as "the private sector," self-employed *maszek*s. They thought there was time enough, if they hurried, to save whatever hadn't already been stolen by the Nazis, our local fascists, the Russians, or such Communists as had managed to make their way home from abroad. They felt it their patriotic duty to lay their hands on anything still possible to lay hands on, and so they set about their work of "salvaging." It wasn't just their own effects they were salvaging, but other people's too, stowing them away before everything disappeared into Russian soldiers' packs or the Communists' pockets. There were not that many salvagers but they were remarkable for their industriousness. As for the rest, those nine million or more others in the country—you know, those they call "the people" now—they—that is to say we, were still paralyzed and looked on passively while the properly interested parties went about stealing in the name of "the people." The fascist Arrow Cross had been robbing us for weeks already. Salvaging was like a highly infectious plague. The Jews were completely stripped of their property: first of their apartments, then their lands, their businesses, their factories, their drugstores, their offices, and, finally, their lives. This was not private sector *maszek* work but the state itself. Then came the Russians. They too went about looting for days and nights on end, going from house to house, from apartment to apartment. Then, when they left, came the Moscow-trained Commies with their handcarts. Now *they* had really been taught how to bleed the people dry.

The people! Do you know what that is? Who they were? Were you and I "the people"? Because today, everyone is heartily sick of them claiming to do everything in the name of "the people": "the people," "the masses," "the proletariat." I remember how surprised I was when one summer, a long time ago, at harvest time, my husband and I were staying on an estate and the landlord's boy, a little boy with blond curls, rushed in at dinner and enthusiastically bellowed: "Mama, Mama! One of the proletariat has just had an accident—the harvester has chopped off one of his fingers!" Out of the mouths of babes, we said patronizingly. Now, everyone is a part of the masses—the proletariat, the gentry, even people like us.

Mind you, we were never so united, "the people" and the rest, as in those few weeks when the Commies first arrived, because the Commies were the experts. When they stole, it wasn't theft but restitution. Do you know what "restitution" means? "The people" had no idea. When the progressives brought in laws that told them "What's yours isn't really yours: it belongs to the state," they simply stared. There seemed to be nothing that was not the state's. It was hard to get your head around that.

The people felt less contempt for the looting Russkies than they did for those enthusiastic purveyors of social justice who one day "saved" a painting by a famous English artist from a foreigner's apartment and next day took possession of an old family's collection of lace, or some class-alien grandpa's gold teeth. When they set about stealing in the name of "the people," everyone just stared. Or spat out of the side of their mouths. The Russians went about ransacking with po-faced indifference. We expected that. They had been through all this once back home, on a really large scale. Russkies didn't argue about restitution or social justice: they just robbed and stripped.

Ah, you see! I am all hot and bothered just thinking about it. Pass me the cologne, I want to splash some on my brow.

You were lying low in the provinces, so you couldn't know what life was like in Budapest. Nothing had happened, and yet, as if by magic, at a whistle from some fairy or demon, the city came alive, just like in those tales where the wicked wizard vanishes in a puff of smoke and the enchanted, apparently dead leap to their feet. The hands of the clock start moving round again, the clock ticks, the spring bubbles up. That war drifted away like a wicked demon: it tramped off westward. And now, whatever remained of the city, of society, sprang to life with such passion, fury, and sheer willpower, with such strength and stamina and cunning, it seemed nothing had happened. The weeks when there was not a single bridge, not even a pontoon bridge, over the Danube, we crossed by boat, as people used to do two hundred years ago. But out on the boulevard there were suddenly stalls in gateways, selling all kinds of nice food and luxury items: clothes, shoes, everything you could imagine, not to mention gold napoleons, morphine, and pork lard. The Jews who remained staggered from their yellow-star houses, and within a week or two you could see them bargaining, surrounded as they were by the corpses of men and horses. People were quibbling over prices for warm British cloth, French perfumes, Dutch brandy, and Swiss watches among the rubble. Everything was up for grabs, for offer, for a quick deal. The Jews were trading with Russian truck drivers; goods and food were moving from one part of the country to another. The Christians too emerged. And soon the migrations began. Vienna and Bratislava had fallen. People rushed to Vienna, getting lifts from Russians with cargoes of lard and cigarettes, returning with cars.

We were still deaf from the half-dead shells they'd been dropping on us, and those big smoke-belching bombs of theirs, but cafés in Pest quickly opened up again. There were places you could get strong, fiercely poisonous coffee. Russian sailors were dancing at tea dances with girls from Józsefváros to the sound of wind-up record players. Not everyone's relatives were yet buried, and you could see the feet of corpses protruding from improvised roadside graves. But there were women in fashionable clothes, fully made up, hurrying over the Danube in boats to meet young men at some wrecked apartment block. Well-dressed middle-class people were taking leisurely strolls to a café that, just two weeks after the siege, was serving veal paprika. And there was gossip—and manicure.

I can't tell you what it felt like. Here was the occupied, burnt-out town still reeking with smoke, full of Russian burglars and criminal sailors who robbed people in crowded streets, and there was I, in a shop on the boulevard, bargaining with the shopgirls for French perfume or nail-polish remover, just two weeks after the siege.

Later—even now—I feel there isn't anyone out there who can

understand what happened to us. It was like returning from the far shore of the underworld. Everything from the past had collapsed and rotted. Everything was gone—that at least is what we thought. Now something new would have to begin.

That's what we thought those first few weeks.

Those first few weeks—the weeks immediately after the siege—were worth living through. But that time passed. Just imagine! For those few weeks there was no law, no nothing. Countesses sat on the sidewalk selling cheap, greasy lángos. A Jewish woman I knew had gone half-mad. She walked the streets all day with crazy, glassy eyes, searching for her daughter, stopping everyone until she found out her daughter had been killed by our own fascists and thrown into the Danube. She didn't want to believe it. Everyone went around believing they were living new lives and that it would all be somehow different from before. The idea of something "different" gave people hope, a hope you could see sparkling in people's eyes. It was as if they were lovers, or drug addicts—people living on the crest of some huge elation. And indeed, pretty soon everything *was* "different." But not in a way we recognized.

What had I imagined? Did I imagine we would be better people, more human? No, I didn't: nothing of the kind.

What we did hope for in those days—because we did hope, myself included, and everyone I talked to was equally hopeful—was that the fear, the suffering, the dread and loathing, all that fire and brimstone, might have purged something from us. Perhaps I hoped we might forget certain passions, some bad habits. Or . . . No, wait, I'd like to tell you just as it was, quite straight.

Maybe there were some reasonable things to hope for. We might have hoped for an end to the great sense of chaos, the sense that everything would be in a mess forever and ever. Maybe some things might simply vanish: the gendarmerie, ostentatious display, the state dog pound, the habit of addressing people by old-fashioned honorifics, that this-is-mine-and-that-is-yours and yours-forever-mine-forever attitude. What would replace it? Oh, we'd have a great party, an enormous, strident nothing where humankind could stroll down the streets, munching lángos, avoiding piles of rubble, and throw out everything that constituted a habitual tie: houses, contracts, manners. No one dared speak about this. We were busy having heaven and hell at the same time. It was how people lived in Eden before the Fall. We had a few weeks of it in Budapest. It was after the Fall. It was the strangest time of my life.

Then one day we woke up, yawned, shivered with cold, our skin covered in goose pimples, and discovered nothing had changed. We understood that there wasn't any such thing as "different." You are dragged down to the pit of hell, roasted a while, then, if one day some miraculous power should pull you out again, you blink a few times, you adjust to reality and go on precisely as before.

I was very busy, because the days were packed with nothing— whatever you needed to survive, you had to provide with your own bare hands. There was no ringing the chambermaid and asking for this, that, or the other, the way the powerful and wealthy used to ring for me, or indeed the way I myself had rung, impudently, out of a spirit of revenge, when the time came for me to be one of the rich. And, what's more, there wasn't even a place to live—in other words, no room, no maid, no bell, not even the electricity to make bells work. The taps did occasionally produce water, but that was not the general expectation. You'll never guess how exciting it was when we finally had water! There was no water on the upper floors, and water for washing had to be car- ried upstairs from the cellar in a bucket, right to the fourth floor: we used it for washing and cooking. We didn't know which was more important. Proper ladies—and I thought of myself as one by then— ladies who had raged and fumed because there were no French bath salts to be had in the wartime city-center drugstore, suddenly discovered that cleanliness was not quite as important as they had always assumed. They understood, for instance, that in order to wash, you needed water of some sort in a bucket, and that water was just the same suspicious- looking stuff in which people boiled potatoes. And since each and every bucket carried upstairs had to be carried up there personally, they sud- denly understood that water was a highly valuable commodity; so valu- able it was too important to waste on washing hands after dirty work. We wore lipstick, but we weren't washing our necks and other parts with such obsessive care as we had some weeks before. We survived, of course, and it occurred to me then that back in the days of the old French kings, nobody washed properly. Not even the king. Instead of washing, people doused themselves head to foot with perfumes of one sort or another. There were no deodorants then. I know that for certain, I read it in a book sometime. The great were still the great, the refined were still the refined, washing or no washing. It was just that they stank. So that's how we lived then. We were like the Bourbons: stinking but refined.

And still I hoped. My neck and my shoes were dirty, and though I had spent quite enough of my girlhood in service, it never occurred to me to become my own servant! I hated carrying that bucket of water up all those stairs. I'd pop over to girlfriends' who had kitchens with running water instead and use theirs. And there I dibbed and dabbed a bit and called it washing. Secretly, I enjoyed it. I suspect others enjoyed it too, particularly those who complained most about the lack of washing facilities. It was like being children again, rolling about in the dirt. It was fun. Having emerged from weeks of stewing in the pit of hell we enjoyed the mess, the filth; the way we could sleep in other people's kitchens; the way we didn't have to wash or dress to perfection.

Nothing happens in life without a reason. We suffered the siege as punishment for our sins, but our reward for all that suffering was the freedom, for a few weeks anyway, to stink without guilt, innocent as Adam and Eve in Paradise, who must also have stunk, since they never washed. It was good not having to eat regularly too. Everyone ate whatever was to hand, wherever they found themselves. For a couple of days I ate nothing but potato peelings. Another day I ate tinned crab, a side of pork fried in lard, with a cube of sugar from a smart café as sweet course. I didn't put on weight. There were days when I hardly ate anything, of course.

Then suddenly the shops were full of food and I immediately put on four kilos. I rediscovered the joys of digestion and began to think of the future. Now was the time to be chasing after passports. It was then I knew it was all hopeless.

Love, you say? You're such a nice boy. A proper angel. No, darling, I don't think love is a great help to anyone. Neither romantic love nor brotherly love. My artistic friend explained the confusion to me, how dictionaries mixed up the two kinds of love. He believed in neither. He believed in only two things: passion and pity. But they don't help, either, because both are only momentary feelings—now here, now gone.

What's that? It's not worth living in that case? You want me not to shrug like that? Look, darling, if you came where I come from . . . You don't understand me, because you are an artist. You still believe in something—in art, am I right? Yes, you're quite right, you are the best drummer in Europe. I hardly dare think there can be a better drummer than you in the whole world. Don't believe those shady saxophonists when they tell you about drummers in bands in America, drummers with the strength of four ordinary mortals, who drum Bach and Handel—they are only jealous of you and your talent and want to take you down a peg or two. I'm sure you are the only drummer anywhere worth listening to. Give me your hand, let me kiss those delicate fingers that scatter syncopation around the world the way Cleopatra scattered pearls. So! Wait a moment, let me dry my eyes. I am so sentimental. Looking at your hands always makes me want to cry.

So there he was, opposite me, on the bridge, all because suddenly we had a bridge again. Not many, just one bridge. Ah, but what a bridge! You weren't there when they built it, so you can't know how much it meant to us when we heard that Budapest, that great metropolis, had a bridge over the Danube once more! It was constructed at lightning speed, and by the time winter was over we were crossing the river on foot again! They used the remaining iron pillars of one of the bridges and patched together a bridge for emergencies. It was a slightly humped bridge, but it could carry trucks too. And the weight of those hundreds of thousands of people, that undulating wave of humanity snaking across in one direction or the other, from early morning when the bridge was opened right to the end of the day, standing in queues by the bridgehead on both shores.

You couldn't simply go and cross the bridge, of course. The queues wound through Pest and Buda like conveyor belts, the crowd moving evenly and slowly. We prepared for the crossing the way we prepared for weddings before the war. It was quite an honor crossing the bridge: it was something we could boast of. Later they built other bridges, strong bridges, made of iron, and pontoon bridges. A year later taxis were speeding both ways across them. But I remember the first bridge, the camel's hump, the queuing, our slow progress as we tramped over it, a hundred thousand of us with haversacks on our backs, our hearts weighed down with crimes and memories, crossing from one bank to another, on that first bridge. Later, when émigré Hungarians arrived from abroad, from America, and glided across the iron bridges in their splendid cars, I always felt a little sad and had a bitter taste in my mouth, sickened by the way these foreigners simply cruised over the river, turning up their noses and shrugging at our bridges; just using them, as if they meant nothing. They had come a long way, these people, they had only had a sniff of war, watching it from a distance as if it were a movie. Very nice, they said. Very sweet the way we live here and can drive our cars over these new bridges.

My heart ached when I listened to them. What do they know about it? I thought. I understood how they felt, the people who didn't live here, who weren't with us, who didn't know how a million others felt when they saw their lovely bridges blown into the air above the Danube, bridges that had been a hundred years in the building. And I knew what we felt on the day we could cross the river on foot again: breathless, like the Kuruc or the Labanc or the Turkish invaders so many centuries ago. Nobody can understand us if they've never lived with us! Why should I care how long the bridges are in America? Our bridge was made of rotting wood and scrap iron and I crossed it before most people did. To be precise, I was *among* the first, pulled along by the long queue of which I was one part, shuffling along with the rest, when I saw my husband on the other side, crossing from Pest toward the Buda bank.

I sprang from the queue and rushed over to him. I embraced his neck with both my arms. Everyone was shouting at me and eventually a policeman dragged me away because I was obstructing the human conveyor belt.

Wait, let me blow my nose. How sweet you are! You're not laughing at me: you are really listening. You are listening as intently as a child waiting for the end of a fairy tale.

But this was no fairy tale, my pet: there was neither true beginning nor true end. Life billowed around and within us then, those of us who lived in Budapest. Our lives had no firm boundary, no proper frame. It was as if something had washed away the boundaries. Everything just happened, unframed, without edges. Now, much later, I still don't know where I am, where things started or ended in my life.

It's enough to say that that is exactly how I felt when I ran from one side of the bridge to the other. It wasn't a calculated, conscious dash, since just a few moments before I had no idea whether the man with whom I had—but it was so long ago, it was before time began, in that period we call history—if the man who had been my husband was still alive. That time seemed an eternity away. People don't measure their lives with clocks or calendars, not personal time, the time that is genuinely theirs. No one knew whether other people had survived: their lovers, the people they had shared a house with. Mothers didn't know whether their children were alive or dead. Couples met by accident in the street. We seemed to be living in a time without history; in prehistoric time, before there were land registries, house numbers, directories. Everyone lived and lodged wherever they could find, wherever it occurred to them to live. And there was about this chaos—this Gypsy life—a peculiar domesticity. It might have been how people lived in the dim, distant past, when no one had a home and there were only wandering hordes and tribes, Gypsies with carts and unwashed children, journeying without destination. It wasn't a bad life. It was familiar somehow. Under all our accumulated garbage we seem to carry some memory of a different, less fixed time.

But that's not why I rushed over to him, not why I hugged him in front of thousands and thousands of people.

At that moment—please don't laugh—something broke in me. Believe me, I had been carrying on as normal. I put on my bra and survived the siege and what preceded it, with dignity: the Nazi monstrosities, the bombing, the terrors. Mind you, I wasn't entirely alone at that time. When the war turned deadly, desperately serious, I spent months with my artistic friend. I don't mean I lived with him; please don't misunderstand me. He might have been impotent for all I know. We never spoke about such things, but whenever a man and woman live together in the same apartment there is always some air of romance hanging about the place. There was no such air in those empty rooms. Nevertheless, it wouldn't have surprised me if he had rushed into my room one night and strangled me with his bare hands. I slept at his place sometimes because there were air-raid warnings every night and I couldn't always get home past the anti-aircraft posts. And now, much later, now that the man is no longer alive, I almost feel that I *have* slept with him, or with someone like him, someone who had decided to wean himself off the world, to give up everything people thought most important. It was like being on aversion therapy for him: he wanted to give up an exciting yet repellent obsession, one as addictive as drink, drugs, vanity . . . everything. My role in his life was to be his nurse—his dry nurse.

It's quite true that it was me who first sneaked into his apartment and then into his life. Just as there are cat burglars, you know, people who sneak into property, there are cat women who sneak into a man's life at an unguarded moment and, once there, make off with anything they find: memories, impressions, the lot. Later they grow bored of these things and sell them—sell everything they managed to stow away. Not that I ever sold anything I got from him, and I am only telling you this much because I want you to know everything about me before you leave me—or I leave you. He simply tolerated me being near him at any time, morning, afternoon, or night . . . The one rule was I was not to disturb him. I was forbidden to talk to him when he was reading. Often he just sat with a book and said nothing. Otherwise I could come and go as I pleased in the apartment, to do whatever I felt like. Bombs were falling all the time, and everyone lived for the moment, making no plans from one minute to the next.

It must have been a terrible time, you say? Wait, let me think about that. I think it was a time of discovery. Questions we never really consider, that we wave away with a gesture, became all too real. What kinds of things? Well, the fact that life is without meaning or purpose, for example—but much else too. We quickly got used to the fear: you can sweat fear out the way you do a fever. It was just that everything changed. The family was no longer the family; a job no longer counted for anything. Lovers made love in a hurry, like children gobbling their food, keen to grab as many sweets as they can, stuffing their cheeks with them when the adults aren't looking . . . then the children skip off to go play in the street, out in the chaos. Everything broke down: apartments, relationships. There were moments we could still believe our homes, our jobs, people at large had something to do with us, if only in a psychological way, but come the first bombing raid we suddenly discovered we had nothing at all to do with whatever was important before.

But it wasn't just the bombing raids. Everyone felt that beyond the air-raid sirens, the yellow cars rushing to and fro, the dispossessed, the armored patrol vehicles packed with booty, the soldiers making their way home from the front, the fugitives in covered peasant wagons, beyond the multitudes drifting around like Gypsies in caravans, something else was happening. There was no distinct war zone anymore: the war was happening in whatever remained of civilian life, in our kitchens, in our bedrooms, in our selves. A bomb had gone off in us, and everything that had previously held society together—even if it was no more than indifference or laziness—was blown away. Something blew up in me, too, when I saw my husband on that new humpbacked bridge over the Danube. It blew up like a bloody great bomb left at the side of the road by a Russkie or a Nazi.

It blew up the entire movie-style affair between us—a movie as dumb and trashy as those Hollywood productions where the managing director marries the stenographer. What I understood in that moment was that it was not each other we had been seeking in life, that the affair for him was about something else: the terrible guilt he felt under the skin, a guilt that had eaten its way into his flesh. He wanted to transfer to me the thing he couldn't lay to rest. What was it? Wealth? The fact that he wanted to know why there were rich and poor in the world? Everything the writers, the politicians, and the demagogues say on this subject is worse than useless. Forget the bald professors with their horn-rimmed glasses, forget the sweet-talking preachers and the hairy, bellowing revolutionaries. The truth is more terrifying than anything they tell you. The truth is that there is no justice on earth. Maybe that is what that man, my husband, was after: justice. Is that why he married me? If it was only my skin or flesh he wanted, he didn't have to marry me—he could have had that cheaper. Maybe he wanted to rebel against the world he grew up in, the way the sons of the rich rebel and become refined, faintly scented revolutionaries. Who knows why? Because they can't bear being who they are; because they are too lucky; because sport and perversity is not enough for them, and they must go and play on the barricades. Well, he could have gone for another form of rebellion, not the backbreaking torture of living with me. You and I, people who have risen from the depths, from the wetlands, or from Zala, don't understand such things, my dear. The one sure thing is that he was a gentleman. Not the way most of the titled nobility were. He was not like Sir This or Baron That, people who elbowed their way to a coat of arms. He was a decent sort of man, made of finer stuff than most bastards of his class.

He was the sort of man whose ancestors took land by conquest. They marched with axes across their shoulders, entered primeval forests in unknown territory, bellowed out anthems, and chopped down trees as well as the locals, while still singing. One of his ancestors was among the Protestants who migrated to America shortly after the initial voyage. He took nothing with him on the journey, just his prayer book and his axe. My husband was prouder of him than of anything else the family later achieved, such as the factory, the money, and a sackful of distinctions.

He was reliable because he was in command of his body and his nerves. He could even control money, which is harder. But the one thing he could never control was his sense of guilt. And what the guilty want is revenge. He was a Christian, but not in the way people tend to think of it now—it wasn't a business opportunity for him, not a certificate to flash at the Nazis so that he could get a rake-off, make a deal, and grab some of the spoils. He felt bad for being a Christian then. And yet, somewhere deep in his guts he was a Christian the way some people are doomed to be artists or alcoholics: he couldn't help it.

But he knew that thirst for revenge was a sin. All revenge is a sin, and there is no such thing as justified revenge. The only right a man has is to justice and to act justly. No one has the right to revenge. And because he was rich and Christian, and because he couldn't give up being either of these things, he was sinking under the weight of guilt. Why are you looking at me as if I were crazy?

It's him I'm talking about, my husband. The man who suddenly appeared on the newly constructed bridge walking toward me. And then, in front of thousands and thousands of people, I embraced him.

He stepped out of the queue but didn't move. He didn't try to push me away. Don't worry, he didn't bow to kiss my hand in front of that ragged, shivering crowd of beggars. He was too well brought up for that. He just stood and waited for the painful scene to be over. He was calm, his eyes closed, and I could see his face through my tears, the way women see the baby's face when the child is still inside them. You don't need eyes to see what is yours.

But then, as I was clinging to him for all I was worth, something happened. I smelled him. I smelled my husband and the smell struck me . . . Now listen carefully.

The moment I smelled him I started to tremble. My knees shook, I felt my stomach cramp, as if I were tortured by some peculiar illness. The point was that the man walking toward me on the bridge did not smell the way others did. I know that won't make any sense to you, but it meant something important then. What I mean is that he didn't have the corpse smell on him. Because even if, by some miracle, there happened to be a bar of soap or perfume in the cellar, the overpowering closeness, the lack of air, the stench of body functions, the blend of different foods and all those people with their chattering teeth and with the fear of death on them—all this had soaked into our very skin. Those who had never stunk before now stank in a different way from those who had. They covered themselves in cologne and patchouli: a different, artificial patchouli that smells far worse than the natural kind. It was positively sickening.

Not that my husband smelled of patchouli. I could smell him through my tears, with my eyes closed, and suddenly I started trembling.

Why? What was it he smelled of? He smelled of damp straw, if you want to know. Just as he had years ago, before we separated. As he did that first night when I lay in his bed and that sour, privileged, masculine smell made me retch. He was exactly as he had been—flesh, clothes, smell—exactly as before.

I let go of his neck and wiped my tears with the back of my hand. I felt dizzy. I took a compact from my bag, opened the little mirror, and applied some lipstick. Neither of us said a word. He stood and waited until I repaired my tearful, smeary makeup. I only dared look up at him once I had checked in the mirror that my face was fit to be seen.

I could hardly believe my eyes that he should be standing in front of me, on that improvised bridge, among queues that stretched into the far distance—some ten or twenty thousand people in the smoky, sooty town where there were few houses left unmarked by shell or bullet holes. There was hardly an unbroken window anywhere. There was no traffic, no policeman, no law, nothing: it was a place where people dressed like beggars even when there was no need to, deliberately looking wretched, ancient, and penniless, growing wild beards, stumbling about in rags to avoid trouble or to rouse others to pity. Even grand ladies carried sacks. Everyone had a backpack. We were like village brats, or travelers. And there was my husband, standing right in front me. It was the same man I hurt seven years ago. Nothing had changed. He was the man who when he understood that I was not his lover, not even his wife, but his enemy, came to me one afternoon, smiled, and quietly said:

"I think it might be best for us to separate."

He always started sentences that way when he wanted to say something very important: "I think" or "I imagine." He never spoke his mind directly, never hit you in the eye with it. When my father could take no more, he would exclaim: "Goddammit!" And then he would hit me. But my husband, whenever he couldn't bear something, courteously opened a little door each time, as if what he was saying were merely something to consider, a by-the-way thought, in the course of which the meaning, the damage in what he said, could slip by you. He learned this in England, in the school where he studied. Another favorite phrase of his was "I'm afraid." One evening, for example, he turned to me and said, "I'm afraid my mother is dying." She did in fact die, the old woman, at seven o'clock the same evening. She had turned quite blue by that time, and the doctor told my husband there was no hope. "I'm afraid" was a phrase that neutralized extremes of feeling and provided a kind of analgesic for the pain. Other people say, "My mother is dying." But he was always careful to speak politely, to say sad or unpleasant things without offense. That's the kind of people they are, and that's all there is to it.

He was being careful even now. Seven years after the war between us had finished, after the siege in the real war was over, there he was, at the bridgehead. He looked at me and said:

"I'm afraid we're in the way."

He said it quietly and gave me a smile. He didn't ask how I was, how I had survived the siege, or whether I needed anything. He just advised me that we might possibly be in the way. He pointed in the direction of a road near Mount Gellért where we might talk. Once we reached a place where there were no people, he stopped, looked round, and said:

"I think this might be the best place to sit."

He was right: it was the "best" place to sit. There was an intact pilot's seat in the wrecked Rata plane nearby, so there was just enough room for two people in the useless machine. I didn't say anything but obediently took my seat in the pilot's seat. He sat down beside me. But first he swept away the dirt with his hand. Then he took out a handkerchief and wiped his hands with it. We sat silently next to each other for a while, neither of us speaking. I remember the sun was shining. The place was very quiet, just wrecked planes, cars, and artillery.

Any ordinary person would imagine that a man and a woman might exchange a few words on meeting by the Danube, among the ruins of Budapest, after the siege. They might, for example, start by establishing the fact that both are still alive, don't you think? "I'm afraid" or "I think"—one could imagine that. But my husband's mind was elsewhere, so we just sat in front of the cave opposite the mineral springs and stared at each other.

I stared pretty hard, as you can imagine. I started trembling again. It was like being in a dream: dream and reality at once.

You know I'm not any kind of fool, darling. Nor am I a sentimental little tramp who turns on the tears whenever she feels on edge or when she has to say good-bye. The reason I was trembling was because the man sitting beside me, opposite the vast tomb that the whole city had become, was not a human being, but a ghost.

Some people only persist in dreams. Only dreams, dreams more effective than formaldehyde, can preserve apparitions like my husband as he seemed to me at that moment. Just imagine—his clothes were not ragged! I can't remember precisely what he was wearing, but I think it was the same charcoal-gray double-breasted suit I last saw him in, the one he wore when he said, "I think it might be best for us to separate." I couldn't be absolutely sure about the suit, because he had many others like it—two or three, single-breasted, double-breasted—but in any case the same cut, the same material, and by the very same tailor who made his father's suits.

Even on a morning like this he was wearing a clean shirt, a pale-cream lawn shirt, and a dark gray tie. His shoes were black and doublesoled. They looked brand-new, though I have no idea how he could have crossed that dusty bridge without a speck of dust sticking to his shoes. I was, of course, perfectly aware that the shoes were not new and that they only looked that way because they'd hardly been worn—after all, he had a dozen like them in his shoe cupboard. I had seen enough of his shoes on the hall seat when it was my job to clean those fine leather objects. Now there he was, wearing them.

They talk about something being "brand-new," fresh from the box the shop provides for you. Budapest was not so much a box as a mass grave out of which people were still climbing. It was the same mass grave he himself had emerged from. There was not a crease on the suit. His light-beige gabardine raincoat—"Made in England"—was casually draped across his arm, a very roomy coat, almost obscenely comfortable, as I remember. I was the one who unwrapped the package from London when it arrived. Much later, I was to pass the shop in London the coat had been bought from. It was there in the window among other things. He carried the coat in an almost careless fashion, thrown across his arm because it was a mild end-of-winter afternoon.

He wore no gloves, of course, because he only wore gloves in the very depths of winter when it was freezing. So I looked at his hands too. They were white and clean, his nails so unobtrusively manicured you'd think they'd never seen a pair of scissors. But that was him all over.

You know what was the strangest thing? When you put him up against that filthy, muddy, ragged crowd creeping over the bridge, his presence should have been practically incendiary. And yet he was almost invisible. I wouldn't have been surprised if someone from among the crowd came over, took him by the lapels, and shook and poked him, just to check that he was real. Imagine what would happen in the French Revolution, in those months of the Terror, when aristocrats were being hunted all over Paris the way children hunt sparrows with catapults, if an elderly nobleman appeared on the street in lilac frock coat and powdered wig, amiably waving at carts filled with fellow counts and earls on their way to the scaffold. There would be nothing to choose between him and my husband, each as spectacular as the other. He was mysteriously different from the toiling throng around him, as if he had emerged not from one of the many bombed-out houses but from an invisible theater, a piece of period drama for which he was appropriately fitted by the dresser. It was an old part in an old play, the kind that's never going to be put on now.

So this man appears on the smoking stage set of the city, a man who has not changed, who is untouched by siege or suffering. I worried for him. The mood was for revenge: you annoyed people at your peril, and once people were annoyed, there was nothing to stop them doing something. Guilt was at the bottom of it: it was guilt behind the fury and the desire for revenge, behind all those glowing eyes and lips spitting hatred. People spent whole days rushing around to grab what they could: a spoonful of lard, a handful of flour, one solitary gram of gold. Everyone kept a crafty eye on everyone else. No one was free of suspicion. Why? Because we were all criminals, all guilty one way or another? Because we had survived when others hadn't?

Now here was my husband calmly sitting beside me, as if he were the one innocent among us all. I couldn't understand it.

I closed my eyes. I had no idea what to do. Should I call a policeman to take him away? He hadn't done anything wrong. He hadn't taken part in any of the terrible things that had gone on, not then or before, all over the country. He hadn't killed any Jews, he hadn't gone after those who thought differently from him, he hadn't ransacked the apartments of people who had been dragged away to death or exile: he hadn't harmed anybody. Nobody could point a finger at him. He hadn't so much as stolen a crumb from anyone. I never heard anything bad about him, not even much later. He hadn't gone looting like the rest, far from it! In fact he was one of those who were robbed of almost everything. When I met him on the bridge at the Buda end, he was, for all purposes, a beggar like everyone else. Later I discovered there was nothing left of the family fortune, just a suitcase of clothes and his engineering diploma. That's all he took with him when he went to America, or so they say. For all I know he is working on some factory floor there. He had given me the family jewels long before, when we separated. You see how good it is that the jewelry survived. I know my jewels are the last thing on your mind, darling. You are just helping me to sell them out of the kindness of your dear heart. Don't look like that at me. You see, I have come over all tearful now. Wait till I dry my eyes.

What's that? Yes, it's getting on for dawn. The first greengrocers' trucks are out delivering. It's gone five o'clock. They're going toward the river, to the market.

Are you sure you're not cold? Let me cover you up. It's getting chilly.

What's that? No, I'm not cold. Not at all; in fact I feel a bit hot. Excuse me, darling, I'll just close the window.

As I was saying, I was looking at him, and what I saw gave me a cold shiver that ran through my knees right down to my toes. My hands were sweating, and it was all because this refined, familiar gentleman, my ex-husband, was smiling at me.

Please don't think it was a mocking or superior smile. It was just a smile, a polite smile of the kind people give when hearing a joke that is neither funny nor dirty . . . the kind someone well brought up smiles at all the same. He was pretty pale, no doubt about it. When you really looked, you could see he too had spent time in the cellar. But his pallor was the kind you have if you've been ill for a few weeks and then got out for the first time. He was pale about the eyes. His lips looked blood-less. Otherwise he was exactly as always, as he had been his whole life . . . let's say after ten in the morning, after shaving. Maybe even more so. But maybe I just got that impression because of everything around us, because he stood out from it the way an object in a museum stands out when they take it from its glass case and put it in a grimy working-class apartment. Imagine if that statue of Moses we were looking at yester-day in the dimly lit church were to be displayed in the home of some local mayor, between two cabinets. "My dear sir, this is not a master-piece like that statue of Moses." But he was simply being himself that moment, a museum object that had found its way onto the street. Smiling.

I'm very hot now! Just look how red my cheeks are—all the blood has rushed to my head. That's because I have never spoken to anyone about this. Maybe it has been preying on my mind without my knowing it. And now I get a hot flush as I am talking about it.

There was no need to wash this man's feet, my dear; he washed them by himself in the morning, in the cellar, you may be sure. He didn't need anyone to tell him that something had changed—he needed no sedative, no consolation. From start to finish he insisted that life had only one meaning, one point. It was courtesy. Good manners meant invulnerability. It was as if he had guts of marble. And this marble-inside, flesh-and-blood-outside figure, dressed in touch-me-not armor, would not come an inch closer to me. The recent earthquake that had shaken and shifted whole countries had no effect at all on his stony constitution. I felt he would sooner die than say a single word other than "I think" or "I'm afraid." Had he actually inquired how I was, or if I needed anything, I would have told him, and he would, I'm sure, have done anything to help: he'd immediately have taken off his coat or given me the wristwatch some Russian had absentmindedly forgotten to steal, and he'd have smiled just to show me he was no longer angry with me.

Now listen. I'm going to tell you something I've never told anyone. It is not true that people are invariably greedy and feral. Sometimes they are very willing to help each other. But doing people favors is nothing to do with goodness or empathy. The bald man was probably right when he said that people are sometimes good because there are too many obstacles to them being bad. The best we can say is that we are good simply because we're afraid of being bad. That's what the bald man said. I've never said it to anyone myself. Only to you now, my darling, my dearest love.

We couldn't sit at the cave entrance, opposite the natural springs, forever. After a while my husband coughed, cleared his throat, and said "he thought" it might be best if we stood up and, seeing it was nice weather, walked about the ruined villas of Mount Gellért for a while. And, yes, "he was afraid" that he would not have many more opportunities to talk to me in the near future. He thought we should use the time left to us. He didn't say it quite like that, but there was no need to, as I myself knew this would be our last conversation. And so we set off on our walk up Mount Gellért, along the steep roads, among ruins and dead animals. It was a sunny winter's day.

We strolled about for roughly an hour. I have no idea what he was thinking as I walked the slopes beside him for the last time. He spoke calmly, without apparent feeling. I asked him tactfully how he had got here and what had happened to him, and wasn't the world extraordinary and topsy-turvy? He replied very politely that everything was fine just as it was. It was all as it should be. What he meant was that he was utterly ruined, had nothing left, and was preparing to go abroad to make his living doing manual work. I stopped on one of the bends of the winding road and very carefully asked him—I did not dare look directly at him—what he thought might happen, how the world would turn out.

He stopped too, looked at me solemnly, and thought for a while. It seemed he took a deep breath before answering. He tipped his head to one side, gazed sadly, first at me, then at the bombed house in whose gateway we were standing, and said:

"I'm afraid there may be too many people in the world."

Having said this, it was as if he had answered any possible further questions. He set off for the bridge. I hurried to keep step with him, because I didn't understand what he meant. Quite enough people had died needless deaths at that time. Hadn't they always? Why should he be worried about there being too many people? But he didn't elaborate, just walked on like a man in a hurry, too busy to answer. I suspected he was joking or playing a trick on me. I remembered the two of them, my ex-husband and his bald friend, and how they used to play games where they pretended to be dull people saying the most obvious things. There are people who insist on calling a spade a spade and nothing else, people who when it's hot and everyone is dripping with perspiration, when the very dogs are dropping dead in the street, frown and point to the sky and pronounce in stern, magisterial tones: "It's hot!" And, having pronounced this, they look inordinately proud, the way everyone does when they have said something particularly obvious and stupid. That was a game they played. So now, having declared that there were too many people, I wondered if he was mocking me. He was right in the sense that the crowd on the bridge had the look of a natural disaster, that they looked like Colorado beetles in a potato field. The thought startled me and I changed the subject. "But really, what will you do?" I asked him.

I always used the impersonal *vous* form of "you" with him, *maga,* not *te.* He, on the other hand, addressed me familiarly, as *te.* I never dared address him that way. For other people he always used the more formal, impersonal manner, even for his first wife, his parents, and his friends.

He never liked the stupid, overfamiliar way people of the same class and same type went straight to *te* in the hope of demonstrating their mutuality, as if to prove they were members of the same important club. But he always addressed me as *te*. It wasn't anything we talked about; it was just the way things worked between us.

He took off his glasses, drew a clean handkerchief from his cigar pocket, and carefully cleaned the lenses. Once he had put them back, he looked over to the bridge, where the queue was growing ever longer. Quite calmly, he said, "I'm leaving, because I'm superfluous: it is me that is the one too many."

His gray eyes gazed steadily ahead. He didn't blink, not once.

There was no pride in his voice. He spoke in matter-of-fact tones, like a doctor diagnosing an illness. I didn't ask him anything else, because I knew he'd not say anything, not even under torture. We walked on toward the bridge. Once there, we bid each other a silent farewell. He carried on along the embankment toward Krisztinaváros. As for me, I took my place in the slow, winding queue and shuffled my way toward the steps leading onto the bridge. I saw him just once more, hatless, his raincoat over his arm, slowly but deliberately making his way, the way people do when they are absolutely certain where they are going— that's to say, to their own annihilation. I knew I'd never see him again. There is something about knowing such things that seems the first step to madness.

What did he mean? Maybe that a man is only alive as long as he has a role to play. Beyond that, he is no longer alive: he merely exists. You won't understand this, because you do have a role in the world: your role is to love me.

There! I've said it. Don't look at me so archly. It's getting toward dawn, you've just come back from the bar, and here I am, your Roman odalisque, fussing over you in a hotel. If anyone could hear our conversation, someone suspicious by nature, someone who could observe and listen to us, they'd think we were a pair of conspirators. They'd see a common woman who once found herself among the lords of the world, gossiping with her pretty lover about all she has seen there, betraying their secrets, and there you are, drinking it all in, because you want to know what tricks the rich get up to. It's a wicked world, he'd think. Don't go frowning and wrinkling that lovely brow. Go on, laugh. After all, we know the truth about each other. You're not just a pretty boy, you're an artist through and through, my one and only benefactor, the man I adore, who is helping me through what remains of the farce of my life. You help by selling the jewels my wicked husband left me. You help because you are kind and soft-hearted. And I am not really a common woman, nor ever was, not even when I took money from my husband the only way I knew, not because I needed the cash but because I needed justice. What are you grinning at? It's a secret between the two of us.

So yes, my husband was quite a peculiar man. I watched him leave and suddenly felt curious. I would love to have known what the man lived for, why he felt superfluous now, and why he was going away to be a house painter in Australia or an odd-job man in America. Wasn't the stuff he believed in so firmly, the role he was playing, just a ridiculous charade? I don't read the papers. I glance at the headlines when some bigwig gets murdered or a movie star is divorced; that's all I read, nothing else. All I know of politics is that no one trusts anyone, and everyone thinks he knows better than the next man. As I watched him walk away I saw a troop of Russian soldiers march past, rifles slung over their shoulders, bayonets fixed, big strapping lads who were in Hungary, whose presence meant everything would be different from now on, different from the time when my husband thought he had a role in the world.

I shuffled along in the queue, over the bridge, over the yellow, dirty, end-of-winter Danube. The river was high. There were planks, blasted remains of ships and corpses washed along the tide. No one paid any attention to the corpses; everyone looked straight ahead, carrying things in backpacks, bowed under the weight. It was as if all humanity had set out on a long, penitential march. So we wound over the bridge, hordes of us, each of us laden down by our own guilt. And, suddenly, I no longer felt myself to be important, no longer in a hurry to get to Király utca to trade my tattered paper money for nail-polish remover. Suddenly I saw no point in going anywhere at all. The meeting had upset me. Although I never loved the man, I was horrified by the idea that I didn't resent him, either, not really, not the way you are supposed to hate your enemy. The thought hit me hard: it was like losing something valuable. There comes a time, you know, when people realize it's not worth being angry. That is, let me tell you, a very sad moment.

It's almost dawn. The light suddenly becomes so hot, so effervescent! In Rome there seems to be no transition between night and dawn. Wait, let me raise the blinds. Look at those two orange trees outside the window. They've produced two oranges each, all four wrinkled and withered—the kind you only get in this town. Those two trees are like old people: the wrinkled oranges are the feelings they have struggled to produce.

Doesn't the light hurt your eyes? Myself, I like these Roman mornings, this sultriness. The light comes on so suddenly and so bright it's like a young woman throwing off her nightgown and going over to the window naked. There's nothing immodest about her then: she's simply naked.

What's that mocking laughter about? Am I being too poetical for you? Yes, I know I tend to talk in comparisons. I see you must be thinking I got this from the bald man. Versifiers and scribblers, you think. We women are always imitating the men that interest us.

No point in leafing through the album. You won't find anything. I don't have a picture of him.

I see the light is bothering you. I'll let the blinds down halfway. Is that better? The street is still deserted. Have you noticed how empty our little Via Liguria is even during the day? He lived here, you know. Who? Him—the bald man. Move over, I want to lie down. Pass me the small cushion. And the ashtray. You want to sleep? I'm not sleepy, either. Let's lie here quietly for a while. I like just lying still at daybreak, not moving at all but staring at the ceiling in this old house in Rome. When I wake up at three in the morning and you are still out at the bar, I lie like this for a long time.

What? Did the bald man stay in this very room? I don't know. Don't go on about it. Run down to the hotel desk and ask the porter if you want to know.

Yes, he might have stayed here.

So what! That I was following him? Mad, quite mad—what on earth are you thinking of? He'd been dead two months by the time I left home.

It's not true—you're talking rubbish. No, it was not his grave I was looking for in the Protestant cemetery. It was the grave of a poet, a poor English writer. The only part that's true is that the bald man once told me something about these famous graves. He himself is not buried there, though: his grave is in the cemetery on the outskirts, in a cheaper plot. In any case he wasn't Protestant like the English poet. No, he was not a Jew. What was he? I have no idea. All I know is that he wasn't religious.

I see from your look that you suspect something. You think I was secretly his lover after all and followed him here, to Rome? Nothing so sensational. There was nothing between us. Everything was very simple as far as he was concerned. God didn't make him an interesting, artistic figure like you, my darling. No, he was more like a clerk or a retired schoolteacher.

There was nothing glamorous about him at all, nor around him. No woman ever killed herself for him. His name never appeared in the papers; there was no juicy gossip for him to be involved with. A long time ago, I once heard, he did have some kind of reputation. But by the time the war had ended he was quite forgotten. He was dead as a doornail as far as society was concerned.

Believe me, there is nothing at all interesting I can tell you about him. I don't even have a photo of him. He didn't like being photographed. Sometimes he behaved as if he were a dangerous criminal in hiding, afraid that someone might find his fingerprint on a glass he drank from. He was like a thief living under an assumed name. Well, yes, he was interesting, perhaps, but only in that he fought tooth and nail against the idea of being thought interesting. He's not worth talking about.

Don't blackmail me. I can't stand it when you do that, begging and threatening at once. Do you want me to give him to you as well? Like the ring, and the U.S. dollars? Am I to give everything away? Do you want to leave me with nothing? Well, all right, I'll give you this, too. Once you leave me, of course, I'll be left utterly empty-handed. I'll have nothing at all of my own. Is that what you want?

Fine, I'll tell you. But don't imagine it means you've outsmarted me or that you're stronger than I am. It's not that you're stronger: it's just me being weak.

It's a hard thing to talk about. It's as if I wanted to talk about something that wasn't quite there. I can only talk about tangible things—I mean, what exists in the simpler kind of everyday life. But there are people who live not only in the everyday but in another reality, on some other plane. Such people might be able to tell you about what isn't there, and make it sound as interesting as a detective story. What this man told me was that everything was reality—not only tangible things you can actually grasp, but concepts too. If nothingness was a concept, he was interested in it. He'd hold nothingness in his hands, turn it about a bit, and look at it from every side, just as if it were an object. Don't blink at me like that; I can see you don't understand. I didn't understand, either, but then, somehow or other, I did start to see my way through to it. Being in his company, I saw how in his hands, and in his mind, even the idea of nothingness was developing a reality; that it was growing and filling up with meaning. It was a trick he had . . . Don't you bother with it, it's too airy-fairy for people like us.

His name? Well, it was a name people recognized once. To tell you the truth, I hadn't read any of his books before. When we first met I thought he was toying with me, as he did with everything and everybody. Then I got angry and sat down to read one of his books. Did I understand it? Yes, pretty well. He used simple words, the kind people actually use in conversation. He wrote about bread, and wine, about how people should eat, how they should walk, and what they should think about when walking. It was as if he were writing a textbook for simpletons who hadn't the least idea how to live a meaningful life. That seemed to be the subject of the book. But it was a sly book, because under all the apparent naturalness of those big simple, idiotic things, under the kind-teacher tone, there was something else, a kind of grimace of indifference. It was as if behind everything—behind the book, behind the fact that he was a man writing a book, behind his idea of the reader holding the book in his hand, a reader now charmed, now solemn, now sentimental, a reader struggling to understand the book's contents—there was a wicked adolescent watching and grinning with delight. That's what I felt as I was reading it. I understood it line by line, but not the thing as a whole. I didn't really get what he was after. I didn't understand why he was writing books when he believed in neither literature nor readers. No reader, however carefully he studied this book, could ever discover what he actually thought. The more I read of his book, the angrier I grew. In fact I didn't finish it, but threw it across the room.

Later, when I lived near him, I told him what I'd done. He heard me through with due seriousness, as if he were a priest or a tutor. He nodded. He pushed his glasses up to his forehead. And he agreed, utterly in sympathy:

"Disgraceful," he said, and made a gesture, as if he himself would have thrown it, and all his other books, across the room. "I quite agree— it was disgraceful, quite disgusting."

He gave a sad sigh, but he didn't explain what exactly was the disgrace. Literature at large? The fact that I hadn't understood his book? Or something that could not be written down? I didn't dare ask him what it was. Because he treated words the way druggists treat poison. When I asked him the meaning of a word, he would look at me full of suspicion, the way a chemist might look at a hysterical woman who walks in with her hair all over the place and asks for a sleeping potion. Or the way a grocer looks when a weepy servant asks him for lye. He thought words were poison, that they contained something bitterly poisonous. You could only take them in very weak doses.

What did we talk about, you ask? Wait a minute. I'll try to remember the kind of things he used to say. There isn't much. Hardly a cent's worth.

There was one occasion—during a bombing raid, when the entire population of the city was cowering in cellars, sweating and waiting for death—when he said humanity and the earth were of one fabric, and he quoted the fact that earth was thirty-five percent solid matter and sixty-five percent liquid. He had learned this from a Swiss book. He was very pleased with the fact. He talked about it as though it meant everything was going to be all right. Houses were collapsing around us, but he was not interested in bombed houses or in people cowering and sniveling in cellars. He started speaking about a German who lived a long time ago, a hundred years back or more—there's a small café here in Rome where you and I have been a few times, it's called the Greco, and that's where he used to sit, that German, a hundred or more years ago. No, don't bother racking your brains, I can't remember his name either. What the bald man told me was that the German believed that plants and animals and the entire earth were of one fabric . . . do you understand? He was reading so intensely, in such a fevered way, throughout the weeks of bombing, it was as if he had failed to do something very important, as if his whole life had been occupied by something else. He'd been remiss and now there was no time to learn all he wanted to learn—stuff like how the world works and so on. I'd sit quietly in a corner looking at him, making fun of him. But he took no notice of me, the way he took no notice of the bombs that were falling around us.

This man always addressed me formally. *Maga*. He was the only man of my husband's class, a gentleman, who never used *te,* not even in intimate circumstances. What's that? Then he can't have been a proper gentleman? That he was just a writer, not a gentleman? How perceptive you are! He might not have been a gentleman precisely because he always talked to me in the most respectful terms. When I was still a maid, my husband-to-be sent me over to him so he could have a look at me. It was his way of checking me over. I went obediently, like a lamb to slaughter. The way he sent me was exactly the way his family sent me to the dermatologist: to check that the new member of staff wasn't carrying any infectious disease. For my husband, the bald man was the equivalent of the dermatologist: in this case, though, it wasn't a matter of my skin but of what lay underneath. The writer accepted the request to examine me, but he was clearly not looking forward to it. He looked down on it in some way, on my confused husband's bright idea and the whole stupid notion of getting my soul attended to. He hemmed and hawed as he opened the door. He asked me to sit down but didn't ask very much, simply looked at me without meeting my eyes, as if he had a bad conscience. But suddenly his eyes lit up and I felt the man was looking at me as a person. There was real power in his gaze then. It's how the Commies conduct their interrogations, they say. There was no avoiding that gaze, no crafty way of ducking out of it into something more measured or pretending to be indifferent. He looked at me as though I belonged to him, as if he were free to touch me. He was like a doctor leaning over a frightened patient on the operating table, hygienically masked, scalpel in hand, so the patient sees nothing but that ruthless knife and those searching eyes that probe the patient's body, seeking the truth about the womb or the kidney. It was rare for him to have this look, nor did it last long. It seems he couldn't keep it up: his internal battery lacked the power. But that was how he looked at me then for that long moment. I was the embodiment of his friend's obsession; then he turned from me and the light in his eyes went out.

"Judit Áldozó, you may go," he said.

I went. I didn't see him again, not for another ten years. He was no longer my husband's regular companion.

I can't be certain, but I suspect he had something to do with my husband's first wife. When they separated, she went abroad. She lived here in Rome for a while. Then she returned to Pest and led a very quiet life. No one heard from her. She died a few months before war broke out, suddenly, of a thrombosis. She simply dropped dead. Later there was all kinds of gossip, as is normally the case now when someone dies young, someone who seems to have nothing wrong with them. Some said it was suicide. But no one knew why a wealthy young woman like her should have committed suicide. She had a lovely apartment, she traveled, she rarely ventured into society, her conduct was irreproachable. I asked around a little, as is fitting when one woman is associated with another woman's husband. But I couldn't get to the bottom of the gossip.

I do know something about the fear of sudden death. I am not a great believer in doctors; it's just that I scream and rush off to the surgery whenever there's something wrong with me—if I cut my little finger, for instance, or have a sore throat. Nevertheless I don't really believe in them, because there is something the sick know that a doctor never knows. I know that sudden death—that is to say, death without any warning, when someone is in full health—is not impossible. My peculiar friend, the writer and quack, knew something about this. Whenever I met him, you see, I'd feel quite strange myself sometimes. I felt I could die any moment, that it could be over there and then. I met him unexpectedly in Buda once, in a shelter, at about six in the evening. The shelter was a cave with many thousand people squeezed into it.

It was like being caught up in a plague. Everyone was preparing to die, sheltering in caves, shoving, and praying. The bald man recognized me and waved me over to sit on the little bench with him. So I sat down and listened to the distant, dull sound of explosions. It only slowly dawned on me that this was the man my husband had trusted to check me over. After a while he asked me to stand up and follow him.

The all clear had not been sounded yet, and the slopes of Buda were deserted. We walked through streets in deathly silence. It was like the city was a crypt. We passed the old café in the castle district—you know, that centuries-old *cukrászda* with the beautiful furniture. The air raid was still going on, but we went in.

It was all very ghostly: a rendezvous in the afterworld. The owners of the *cukrászda* had lived on the Castle Hill for generations—much like the saleslady who worked there—and like everyone else, they had rushed for the shelters. We were alone with all the mahogany furniture, the glass cases full of organdy-covered war-standard sweet pastries dusted with sugar, rancid cream tarts and dried meringues, and the bottles of vanilla liqueur on the glass shelves. There was no one in the shop, no one to greet us.

We sat down and waited. We still hadn't said a word. In the distance, on the far side of the Danube, anti-aircraft guns were booming while the American bombs dropped with a dull thud. A cloud of dark smoke was rising over the castle, because the planes had hit and ignited an oil reservoir on the far bank. But we took no notice of it.

Without asking or being asked, the bald man graciously set to playing the host. He filled two glasses with liqueur, took a plate, and put out one cream cake and a walnut slice. He was so comfortable moving around the old *cukrászda* he looked like a regular there. He offered me a sweet and I asked him whether he was familiar with the place and had he come here often.

"I?" He looked at me astonished, the liqueur glasses still in his hand. "By no means. Maybe thirty years ago, when I was a student. No," he added, looking round and shaking his head. "I can't remember exactly when I was last here."

We clinked glasses, nibbled the pastries, and chatted. When the all clear was sounded and the female owner, the serving lady, and an old woman emerged from the cellar, where they had rushed in terror, our conversation was in full flow.

It was a second start to our acquaintanceship.

The easy manner did not surprise me. Nothing about him ever surprised me when I was with him. It wouldn't have surprised me if he had stripped naked and started singing, the way religious maniacs do in the street. If, one day, he appeared with a beard, saying he had just come down from Mount Sinai, where he had been talking with God, it wouldn't have surprised me. It wouldn't have surprised me if he asked me to play a game of Bobo, then to learn Spanish or to master the art of knife throwing. Nothing would have surprised me.

So it didn't surprise me when he didn't introduce himself or ask me my name or inquire after my husband. There we were in that haunted *cukrászda* and he talked as if all that was superfluous, because people could get to the heart of things without them, as if nothing could be more tedious than explaining to each other who we were and what we were. There was no need to discuss a subject we were both familiar with, or to swap stories about the woman who had died. There was no need to remind ourselves that I was once a servant girl and that my husband-to-be sent me over to him—he, the keen surgeon of souls—so that he might check me out for social scrofula or leprosy. We talked as if we could talk for eternity, an eternity in which death was merely a brief interruption.

He didn't ask me how I was nowadays, where I lived, or who I lived with. He was more interested in asking whether I had tasted olives stuffed with pimiento.

What a crazy question! I looked him in the eye and continued looking, watching those gray-green, searching eyes of his, a worryingly serious pair of eyes. The way he looked at me in that quiet *cukrászda,* among the falling bombs, you'd have thought both our lives depended on the answer.

I thought about it, because I didn't want to lie to him. Yes, I answered, I had tasted them; naturally I had tasted them; I had eaten them in Soho once, in London, in the Italian quarter, in a small restaurant the Greek had taken me to. But I didn't mention the Greek. Why mention the Greek as well as the olives? I thought.

"Ah, that's good," he said, relieved.

In a slightly timid voice—I never dared speak to him as I really wanted to—I asked him why it should be particularly good news that I had eaten olives stuffed with pimiento.

He heard out the question in full seriousness.

"Because you can no longer get them," he briskly replied. "You can't get olives at all in Budapest now. You used to be able to buy them in the city center at a reputable delicatessen—" and he mentioned a name— "but it has never been our way here to stuff olives with pimientos. That's because when Napoleon came this way with his army, he only got as far as Győr, in the north."

He lit a cigarette and gave a nod as if there was nothing further to say on the subject. An old Viennese pendulum clock hung above our heads. I heard it tick. And there were still those distant explosions that sounded like a well-fed animal breaking wind. It was all very dreamlike. It wasn't a happy dream; nevertheless, I felt a curious calm, as I did later whenever I was with him. I can't explain it to you. I was never happy in his company—sometimes I hated him, and he often drove me to fury. But it was never dull being with him. I wasn't impatient or restless. It was as if I had taken off my shoes or bra in company, as if I could strip completely and divest myself of everything I had been taught. I was simply at peace with him. The most violent weeks of the war were to follow, but I was never so calm, so at peace with myself as in those weeks.

Sometimes I found myself thinking it was a pity I was not his lover. Not that I felt any particular desire for him or that I was desperate to creep into his bed. He had aged, and his teeth were yellow: there were bags under his eyes. I was half-hoping he was impotent and that that was why he did not look at me as a woman should be looked at. Or maybe he preferred boys and wasn't interested in women? That's what I hoped. All I could see was that he was unconcerned about me.

He would often clean his glasses with great care, the way a diamond cutter works at the rough stone. He was never careless in his clothes, but I couldn't for the life of me tell you what he wore. And yet I can remember all my husband's suits! I haven't retained a single thing about this man's external appearance, clothes and all.

And then he returned to the subject of olives, saying:

"It was always impossible getting genuine pimiento-filled olives in Budapest. Not even in peacetime, a long while ago. All you could get were those dry little olive buds without any filling. That's if you were lucky. Mind you, stuffed olives were pretty rare, even in Italy."

He raised his finger and pushed his glasses up to his brow.

"It's strange," he mused. "Soft, sourish, pimiento-filled olives were only obtainable in Paris, in the Ternes quarter, on the corner of the street named after Saint Ferdinand, from a grocer of Italian descent, near the end of the twenties."

Having said this, having finally brought to my attention every possible fact it was possible, at this stage of human evolution, to know regarding olives stuffed with pimientos, he gazed straight ahead with a look of utmost satisfaction and stroked his bald pate with one hand.

Well, he has definitely gone mad, I thought. I looked at him in astonishment. Here I was, sitting at a table on Castle Hill while the city was being bombed below us, in the company of a madman who was once a friend of my husband's. But it didn't feel bad. It never did when I was with him.

Gently, as if talking to a madman, I asked why he thought that olives, of the kind I had actually eaten some time in the past in a small Italian restaurant in that part of London known as Soho, were destined to play such an important part in my current and possibly future life. He listened to me carefully, his head slightly tipped to one side, and looked, as he always did when he was thinking, into the distance.

"Because that culture is over," he said in a friendly, patient manner. "Everything we considered to be culture is done for. The olive was just one small element of the many flavors that made up that culture. All these little sparks of flavor, these individual delights and wonders, worked together to produce the marvelous feast we call taste. Taste is an aspect of culture," he said, and raised his hand, like a conductor in a concert waving in some crescendo of destruction. "And it's all vanishing. It will vanish even if elements of it remain. They may still be selling olives stuffed with pimientos somewhere in the future, but the class that cultivated the taste for it and understood what it meant will have vanished. There will remain only the knowing *about* it, which is not the same thing. Culture is experience, I say," he intoned like a priest, his hand raised. "It is living experience, timeless as sunshine. To know *about* things is to know merely secondhand. It is like wearing secondhand clothes." He shrugged, then added courteously, "Which is why I am glad that you did at least have the opportunity of tasting olives." And as he finished the sentence, a shell burst nearby, like a precisely placed period, shaking the building.

"It's time to pay," he said, and stood up, as if the explosion had reminded him that it was all very well announcing the death of culture, but there were things to be done. He opened the door for me like a proper gentleman and we walked down the deserted Zerge Steps in silence. That is how our true relationship began.

We went straight to his place. On the way we crossed the beautiful bridge that within a few months would be mere wreckage in the water. Bundles of explosives were already dangling off it, the Germans having made meticulous preparations to blow it up. He gazed calmly, almost approvingly, at the neat arrangement.

"This too is doomed to destruction," he said as we crossed it, and pointed to the vast iron arches that suspended and counterbalanced the weight of the great bridge. "It will be blown to pieces. Do you want to know why? Well," he spoke quickly, as if answering himself in a complex debate, "because whenever people have given so much serious thought and applied so much expertise to preparing a plan, that plan will eventually be carried out. The Germans are brilliant at blowing things up," he said. "No one knows better how to blow things up than the Germans. So this suspension bridge, our Chain Bridge, will be destroyed as will, one after the other, the rest of the bridges, just the way they destroyed Warsaw and Stalingrad. They do these things to perfection." Having said this, he stopped in the middle of the bridge with his arm raised as if to declare the significance of the German capacity for destruction.

"But this is terrible," I cried out in despair. "All these beautiful bridges . . ."

"Terrible?" he inquired in a thin voice, his head tipped to one side as he looked at me. "Why terrible?" He was tall, a head, at least, taller than I am. Gulls were swooping between the arches of the great bridge. There were very few people to be seen. Dusk was a dangerous time to be out.

How strange he should ask me why I thought it terrible that all these marvelous bridges should be destroyed. He seemed to be surprised at my agitation.

"Why?!" I repeated angrily. "Wouldn't you regret the loss of such bridges? The loss of life? All those innocent lives?"

"Me?" he asked, still in that thin, surprised voice, as if I had accused him of not having given war and human suffering proper thought.

"But of course!" he declared, waving his hat. He was suddenly full of life and passion. "You think I don't care about bridges and people! For heaven's sake! Me?" he clicked his tongue, grimacing at the ridiculousness of the idea, its sheer stupidity. "Never—never, you understand." He turned to me, his face close to mine, staring into my eyes like a hypnotist. "I've thought of practically nothing else. There is nothing I've sorrowed over more than the destruction of bridges and humanity!"

He was finding it difficult to breathe. He looked hurt, as if he was holding back tears. He's an actor, I suddenly thought. A clown, a comedian! But I looked into his eyes and was shocked to see those gray-green eyes clouding over. I couldn't believe what I was seeing. There was no doubt about it, the man was crying. Tears were rolling down his face. Nor was he ashamed of his tears. He didn't care. His eyes seemed to have a will of their own.

"Poor bridge," he muttered, as if I weren't there. "Poor, lovely bridge! And poor people! Poor humanity!"

We stood perfectly still. Then he brushed away his tears, wiped his hands on his coat, and dried them, sniffling a little. He gazed at the bundles of explosives and shook his head, as at a scene of desperate neglect, as if the charges were a disorderly mass of rogue humanity, a bunch of useless adolescents that he, the writer, was helpless to address, having neither the words nor the power to bring them to their senses.

"Yes, all this will go," he said, and sighed. But I thought I detected a note of satisfaction in that sigh. Perhaps he felt everything was going to plan, that somebody had worked all this out on paper, done his sums and demonstrated how certain human instincts were bound to produce certain consequences. So, while he was full of tears and lamentation at the prospect, some part of him was pleased that his calculations had proved right.

"All right," he said simply. "Let's go home."

He tended to talk in the plural like that—"Let's," "Let us"—as if we had agreed on everything. And you know the strangest thing? I really did feel we had discussed and agreed on everything, talked things over at great length: everything important, that is, everything that mattered most to us both. What had we agreed? It might have been that I would become his lover some time in the future or that he might employ me as a servant. Without saying anything more we set off "home," the pair of us, over the doomed bridge. He walked fast, and I had to scurry after him not to be left behind. He didn't look at me on the way. For all I knew he had forgotten I was there, following him like a dog. Or like a member of his household staff who had accompanied her master on some errand. I kept a tight hold on the satchel in which I had stowed my lipstick, my powder, and my ration cards, the way I had guarded the little luggage I had once carried to Budapest when looking for a job. I was his servant, running after him.

And as we went along on our way I suddenly felt calm. By that time I had spent some years as a lady. I could blow my nose as delicately as I would at a garden party at Buckingham Palace, though I occasionally recalled that my father never used a handkerchief, because he simply didn't have one. He had no idea what a handkerchief was. He sneezed by pinching his nose between his fingers then wiping his fingers on his trouser leg. When I was a maid I blew my nose the way I learned from him. But now, jogging along beside this man I felt the kind of relief you feel at having finished some tiring, pointless task so you can finally rest. I knew that if we got to the statue of Széchenyi and I felt an urge to sneeze I was free to pinch my nose, then wipe my fingers on the skirt of my fine shantung-silk dress without him even noticing. Or if he did happen to glance at me that moment, he would feel no contempt and would not look down on me but simply observe how a woman in expensive clothes was blowing her nose like an ordinary peasant. He'd observe my habits the way he would the habits of some domesticated animal. And there was something reassuring about this.

We arrived at his apartment. I was as calm as if I were going home. When he opened the front door and let me into the dark, camphor-smelling hall, I felt at peace the way I did when I first left home and came to Budapest to find employment as maid-of-all-work for my future husband's parents. I was at peace because I knew that I had finally found somewhere to shelter myself from the wild, dangerous world outside.

And I stayed, already determined to spend the night. I fell asleep immediately. I woke at dawn feeling I was about to die.

It wasn't a heart attack, darling, or rather, it *was* that, but something else too. I felt no pain. I wasn't even afraid. A delicious calm spread through my whole body: a deathly silence. I felt my body had stopped functioning, that my heart was no longer beating, that its mechanism had run down. My heart had simply got bored and given up, I thought.

When I opened my eyes I saw him standing next to me, beside the couch. He was holding my wrist, touching my pulse.

But he didn't hold it the way doctors do. It was more the way a musician touches strings, or the way a sculptor taps at the stone, he was using all his fingers. His fingers were holding a conversation with my skin and blood, and through these, with my heart. He touched me as though he could see something in the darkness, like blind people who see with their hands, or the deaf who hear with their eyes.

He was still wearing the clothes he had worn in the street. He hadn't undressed. He didn't ask me anything. The hair that remained on his bald head was tousled round his brow and on his nape. The desk lamp was burning in the neighboring room. I understood that he had been sitting, reading, while I slept and suddenly woke to find myself dying. He stood beside me on the couch where I had made up a bed, and set about making himself busy. He brought a lemon, mixed some sugar in with the lemon juice, and made me drink the bittersweet mixture. Then he made coffee in a little red copper pot, a cup of Turkish coffee strong as poison. He took a medicine bottle and put twenty drops into a glass, diluted it with water and poured it down my throat.

It was well past midnight and the sirens were sounding again, but we didn't listen to their frantic howling. He only took shelter if he happened to be outside at the time and a policeman ushered him into one or another cellar. Otherwise he'd remain in his apartment and read. He liked reading at such times, he said, because finally the town was quiet. Indeed, there was an otherworldly silence . . . There were neither trams nor cars, just the thud of anti-aircraft guns and bombs. But that didn't disturb him.

He sat by the couch, occasionally feeling my pulse. I lay with my eyes closed. There was heavy bombing that night, but I had never felt as calm, as secure, as protected and hidden. Why? Maybe because I was aware of human care. That's not at all a common feeling with people, and it's no more common with doctors. This man was not a doctor, but he could help. Artists are the people who can really help you in times of trouble, the only people, it seems . . . Yes, you, my darling, you and all artists. He once happened to mention that a long time ago the artist, the priest, and the doctor were all one man. Anyone who knew anything was an artist. That is what I somehow felt, and that's why I was so much at peace—at peace and almost happy.

After a time I felt my heart beating regularly again. I could feel the whole mechanism working, the way I saw in the panopticum at Nyíregyháza when I was a girl. They had an image of a dying pope there, made of wax. A machine was working his heart. That was the way I felt when my heart started beating again.

I looked up at him, and I wanted him to say something, not having the strength to speak myself. But he already knew the danger was past.

"Have you ever had a sexually transmitted disease?" he asked in a friendly manner.

The question didn't scare me, didn't even offend me. It sounded perfectly natural, like everything he said. I made a gesture to say that I hadn't, knowing it was pointless telling him a lie as he would immediately see through it. Then he asked me how many cigarettes I smoked in a day. But, you know, I wasn't smoking back then, or at least not continually, the way I do nowadays in Rome. It's only here I started smoking recklessly, puffing away at that acrid American tobacco. Back then I only lit up after a meal now and then. I told him that too.

"What caused this?" I asked, putting my hand on my breast in the region of my heart. I felt very weak. "What was it? I have never felt anything like it before."

He gave me a careful look. "It is the shock of the body remembering," he said.

But he didn't say what it was the body was remembering. He carried on looking at me for a while, then stood up and, with slow faltering steps, as if limping, went into the other room and closed the door behind him. I was left alone.

. . .

There were times later when he would leave me alone like that, morning or evening, at any time, because after a while, without any formal arrangement, I moved in. He gave me a key without thinking twice about it, as if it were the most natural thing in the world. There was a woman who came to clean for him, sometimes even cook. But she didn't have to tidy after him. Everything was perfectly accommodating . . . even the apartment, those handsome, well-proportioned rooms with their old Viennese furniture. There was nothing particularly grand about the place: it was just three rooms on the fifth floor of a relatively new block. One of the rooms was filled with books.

When I first arrived he treated me as a guest. He would produce delicious tidbits out of some invisible pantry, such as tinned sea crab. While everyone else was living off beans he treated me to tinned pineapples. He even offered me vintage brandy. He never drank any himself, but he did store wine. He had a personal collection of the great wines of France, of Germany, of Burgundy, of the Rhine, and all the best Hungarian regions, the bottles covered in cobwebs. He collected rare wines the way other people did postage stamps or fine porcelain. And when he opened one of these bottles, he would examine it with rapt attention, tasting the wine like a pagan priest preparing for sacrifice. He would offer me a glass now and then—a little resentfully, I thought, as if he didn't think me quite worthy of the wine. He preferred to pour me brandy. Wine was not a woman's drink, he said.

He could surprise me with his opinions. He was generally a little fixed in his views, like an old person who no longer wants to argue about things.

I was also surprised at how tidy his personal things were. I mean his cupboards, his drawers, and the shelves where he kept his manuscripts and books. It wasn't the cleaning woman who was responsible for that, but he himself. He positively radiated order: he was quite obsessive about it. He wouldn't let ashes or cigarette butts pile up in the ashtray. Every half hour he would empty it into a bronze bucket that he himself would tip into the general waste in the evening. His writing desk was as neat as a draftsman's in an engineer's office. I never once saw him move furniture about, but whenever I got there it looked as if the cleaning woman had just left. The order was within him, in his person and in his life. But that was something I understood only later, and even now I don't know whether I really understood it. It was an artificial, not a living, order, if you know what I mean. It was precisely because the world outside was falling to pieces that he was so determined to maintain his own internal sense of order. It was a last line of defense against external chaos, a little personal revolt. As I said, I don't really understand it even now. I'm just telling you.

I slept that night with a proper, regular heart. He was right: the body was remembering something. But what? I didn't know then, but I can explain it now . . . He reminded me of my husband. I hadn't thought of him in a very long time, not having seen him for years, never having wanted to see him. I imagined I had forgotten him. But my skin, my organs, and indeed my heart had not forgotten. And when I entered the life of this bald man who had been my husband's close friend, my body instantly started remembering. Everything about him reminded me of my husband. There was something about the way this bald, silent figure had appeared out of nothing. He was like an ill-tempered, indifferent magician who is no longer interested in magic or tricks. It took me some time to understand why I was drawn to him, and what it was I remembered.

It was like a dream then, everything strangely dreamlike. People were being rounded up like dogs. Rounded up and murdered. Houses were collapsing. The churches were as crowded as the beaches had been.

Very few people remained in their homes, so there was nothing particularly odd about me going in and out of another person's apartment, but I knew I had to be careful and not make any mistakes or else he'd throw me out. Or he would disappear at the very worst moment of the war and leave me there alone. I knew that if I tried to seduce him or made myself too agreeable, he would simply open the door, and who knows where I'd finish up. I also knew there was nothing I could do to help him, simply because he didn't need anything. He was one of those unfortunates who can tolerate anything, any kind of deprivation or humiliation, who can put up with anything except the idea of being helped.

What's that? Was he a snob? Of course he was, among other things, a snob. He couldn't stand being helped because he was solitary and a snob. Later I understood that there was something under this snobbish manner of his. He was protecting something—not himself, no; he was trying to preserve a culture. It's not funny. I expect you're thinking of those olives. That's why you're laughing? We proles, we don't really get the idea of "culture," sweetheart. We think it's a matter of being able to quote things, of being fussy, of not spitting on the floor or belching when we're eating, that kind of thing. But that's not culture; it's not a matter of reading up and learning facts. It's not even a matter of learning how to behave. It's something else. It was this other idea of culture he was wanting to protect. He didn't want me to help him, because he no longer believed in people.

For a while I thought it was his work he wanted to protect. It's a lousy enough world to protect your work against. But when I got to know him, I was astonished to discover that he had completely stopped working.

So what did he do? you ask. He just read and walked. It might be hard for you to understand this, you being a born artist, a proper professional drummer. You can't imagine life without drumming. But he was a writer, a writer who no longer wanted to write because he no longer believed that writing could change human nature. It's not that he was a revolutionary: he didn't want to change the world in that way, because he didn't believe human nature could be changed by revolutions. One time he happened to mention that it wasn't worth changing society because people would be exactly the same after as before. It was something else he wanted. It was himself he wanted to change.

You don't get it—of course you don't get it. I myself didn't get it for a long time; I didn't believe him. I just trod carefully around him, happy that he was willing to tolerate me. The place was full of people leading secret lives, men and women, and Jews most of all. People hiding from the militia . . . Okay, okay, relax. I believe you, you had no idea what was going on in Budapest. You couldn't possibly know how people lived there, how they lived like insects, in silence. A lot of them slept in their wardrobes, the way moths do in the summer, with the smell of naphthalene all around them. It was the way I set up camp in his apartment too. I tried not to make any noise, to give no signs of life.

He paid no attention to me. Sometimes he sat up and, as if noticing I was there, he'd smile and ask me some commonplace question, politely, cheerfully, but always as though we had already spent years in conversation.

Once I arrived at seven in the evening. There was already an autumnal smell in the air, and the days were closing in. I entered and saw his bald head as he sat by the window in the half-light. He wasn't reading, just sitting there, his arms folded, staring out of the window. He heard my footsteps but didn't turn round.

"Do you know Chinese numbers?" he asked over his shoulder.

There were times I thought he was genuinely mad. But I had learned by then how to deal with that. The trick was to enter the conversation without any intervening talk, picking up exactly where he left off. He liked me to answer briefly in a word or two, just a yes or a no. So I obediently answered him. I said "no."

"I don't know, either," he calmly answered. "I don't understand the writing at all, because they use concepts, not letters. I don't have any idea about their numbers. I only know they don't use Arabic numerals. Nor the older Greek ones. So we may suppose"—this being one of his favorite expressions, and he would always raise his long forefinger at this point, like a teacher when explaining something to a particularly dense class—"that they have numbers unlike any other Western or Eastern ones. And that precisely," he declared, "is why they have no technology. Because technology begins with Arab numerals."

He looked tired sitting there, gazing out into the damp gray evening. The thought that Chinese numbers were not like the Arabic clearly bothered him. I simply stared and said nothing, because all I knew about the Chinese was that there were a lot of them, that their skins were yellow, and that they were constantly smiling. I'd read that in a picture magazine.

"So technology begins with Arabic numbers?" I asked nervously.

There was a great explosion that moment somewhere near the bottom of Castle Hill, the sound of an anti-aircraft gun being fired.

He looked over in that direction and, with a great deal of satisfaction, answered, "Yes," nodding as if delighted that his argument should be so vividly illustrated. "You heard that explosion? That's technology. It is one of the reasons we need Arabic numerals. It's much harder to multiply and divide with Greek or Roman numbers. Just consider how much time it would have taken for someone to work out how to write down two hundred and thirty-four thousand, three hundred and twelve in the Greek system. It is impossible, madam, quite impossible in Greek numerals."

He seemed satisfied with this. However uneducated I was, I understood his every word. It was just what the words added up to, the man as a whole, I didn't understand. You know—what he was. Who he really was. Was he a comedian? Was he mocking me? He looked excited, as though standing in front of a newfangled device, like someone holding a new kind of lock or a calculating machine. I didn't know how to get through to him. Should I give him a kiss? Slap him? He might kiss me back. But he might just put up with the kiss or slap and calmly make some kind of reply. He might say something like: did I know that with each step a giraffe takes it advances by fifteen feet? He did once say just that in the middle of conversation for no reason at all. He said giraffes were angels of the animal world out in the wild, because there was something angelic about their very being. Even their names suggested angels, their original name being "seraph."

We were walking through woods in the fall toward the end of the war. He was speaking loudly about giraffes, in ecstasies about how much vegetation they needed to consume in order to survive, so that they should be able to maintain those long necks and tiny heads, that great chest and those enormous hooves . . . it was as if he were reciting a poem, some incomprehensible hymn. He got quite carried away by his recitation, by the fact that he was alive and that such things as giraffes should exist in the world. I felt uneasy when he talked about giraffes or the Chinese like that. But in time I grew less afraid; it was as if I too could get drunk on his words. I closed my eyes and listened to his breaking voice . . . It wasn't what he was saying that affected me, but the strange, irrational loss of control—the way he was shy and jubilant at the same time. It was as if the world were one big festival and he the priest, bellowing like a dervish, chanting and proclaiming the meaning of the festival to the world at large . . . whether the festival was giraffes or Arabic numerals.

Do you know what else lay behind it? Lust.

Not as the world knows it or as people generally feel it. Lust as perhaps plants, huge ferns, scented lianas, or giraffes or seraphs know it. Maybe it is the kind of lust writers possess too. It took me some time to understand that he wasn't crazy, simply full of lust. It was the world that brought on his lust, the fabric of it; word and flesh, voices and stones, everything that exists is tangible and, at the same time, impossible to grasp in its meaning and essence. When he talked like that, he was as serious as people are in bed after an orgasm, when they lie there with their eyes closed. Yes, darling . . . Like that.

But it wasn't a dumb silence, not like he had nothing in his head. I mean, you too can listen beautifully when you're with the band, next to the bass sax, and you look round the bar so seriously, with that Greek-god profile of yours . . . But however majestic you look in your white dinner jacket, I can see on your face that you are simply listening, not thinking of something else. He listened like he had heard something about something else. And he could listen with great concentration. He could listen the way others shout. He was a sad man.

I never tired of listening to him. It felt pleasantly dizzy, like hearing music. But I did tire of his own listening. Because one had to listen with him and pay close attention to whatever it was he was not saying.

I could never guess what he was thinking of at such times. The times when he suddenly started speaking of giraffes or something like that and suddenly fell silent, I felt the true meaning of what he wanted to say was about to be revealed. But when he started listening he was simply far away from me.

It surprised me and frightened me a little. He was like the man in the fairy tale who has a cap made of fog and suddenly becomes invisible. He disappeared inside his listening. One moment he was there with me, muttering something in a cracked voice, about something I didn't understand, then he was gone, just like that, as if he were far away. He wasn't rude about it. I never once felt affronted because he stopped talking to me. Not at all! I felt he was paying me a compliment by being willing to share his silence with me.

You want to know what it was he was so good at keeping quiet about? So intensely, so logically? Oh, my dear, you do ask such difficult questions!

I didn't imagine, not for a moment, that I could pry into his silence.

But there were occasional signs that something was happening in him, and I began to understand. The time I met him he was setting out to strangle the writer in him. He had made thorough, systematic preparations for it. He was like a murderer preparing to commit a murder or a conspirator who would sooner take poison than betray his secret. Or, let's say, a missionary terrified in case he gave away some sacred formula to hostile savages. He would sooner die than do that.

I'll try to tell you how I slowly grew to understand him.

"Sin is the art form of the petit bourgeois," he once said in passing.

As usual, whenever he said something like this, he stroked his bald head the way a conjurer does when he produces doves from his top hat. Later he tried to explain his peculiar opinion. What he said was that sin, to the petit bourgeois—a pleb, in other words—was what vision and creation were to an artist. But an artist is after more than a plebeian. He wants to articulate some hidden message, then to say it, or paint it, or compose it in music: something that enriches life.

These things are beyond us, my dear.

He told me how bizarre ideas are realized in the mind of a sinner, how a sinner weighs up possibilities—a murderer, a general, a statesman, no matter which—and then, like an artist at the moment of inspiration, how he realizes his idea, quick as lightning, with breathtaking skill and ingenuity. How he commits the crime that is his dreadful masterpiece. There is a Russian writer—don't frown, darling, it ruins your magnificent marble brow, and his name doesn't matter in any case; I myself have forgotten it. I see how grumpy, how ill-tempered you become when I start talking about writers. You really don't like the type. But anyway, said my bald friend, there was a Russian writer who wrote a book about murder. And, so my friend went on, it is not impossible that this Russian might actually have wanted to commit a murder. But he didn't commit one, because he wasn't a pleb but a writer. He wrote about it instead.

He didn't want to write anymore. I never once saw him writing. I never even saw his handwriting. He did have a fountain pen, I did see that. It lay there on his writing desk next to the small portable typewriter. But he never opened the typewriter case, not once.

For a long time I didn't know what his problem was. I thought he had dried up, that he no longer had the energy either for sex or for writing. Instead, he was playing out some comic part, pretending to be hurt, putting on a dumb show because he no longer felt able to exercise his miraculous, unique gift, the gift only a "master," a vain, deluded, aging writer, possessed. The world would have to do without him. That's what I thought. I thought he'd realized he'd come to the end of his talent. No longer capable of making love to a woman, he'd set out to play the celibate, someone who has had more than enough of success in bed and was simply bored. The game was no longer worth the candle. Resentment had turned him into a hermit. But eventually I understood why he had stopped—what this long preparation was all about.

The man didn't want to write anymore because he was afraid that every word he committed to paper would fall into the hands of traitors and barbarians. He felt the new world would be one where everything an artist produced, whether in words, paint, or music, would be falsified, betrayed, sold down the river. Don't look so surprised. I can see you don't believe me. You think I am imagining it, making it all up! You couldn't possibly understand this, my darling, because you are a heart-and-soul, fully committed artist, an artist through and through. You can't imagine throwing away your drumsticks the way that man locked his manuscripts up in his drawer and let his pen gather dust. Am I right? I can't imagine it, either, because you are the sort of man who will go on practicing his art as long as he lives. Drum till you die. But this poor unfortunate was a different kind of artist, darling.

This poor unfortunate was afraid of becoming a collaborator, a kind of traitor, by writing anything at all, because he was convinced that in the days to come, everything writers ever wrote would be falsified. He feared his words would be misinterpreted. He was like a priest who is terrified that excerpts from his sermons should help sell mouthwash or provide a text for a political rant on some street corner. So he stopped writing.

What's that? You want to know what a writer is? A bum? Someone of less consequence than a mechanic or a lawyer? Yes, if that's the way you think, a writer is indeed a bum. And we don't need writers anymore . . . just as we don't need anyone without money or power? A waste of space, as my ex-husband put it?

Calm down, no need to shout. Yes, you're right, he was a bum. But what was he like close up? Not a lord or a minister of state. Nor a party secretary. Take money, for example; he was peculiar in that way. Believe it or not, he did have money. He was the kind of bum who secretly thought of everything, even money. Don't go thinking he was a crazy hermit, the kind that wears animal skins, lives on locusts he catches in the desert, and slurps water from tree bark the way bears do. He did have money, but he didn't deposit it in an account. No, he preferred to keep it in the left-hand pocket of his coat. When paying, he would draw out a wad and hand it over. It was a negligent sort of gesture since decent people keep their money in a bank account—the way you do ours, am I right, darling? When I saw him hand over money negligently, like that, I knew he was not a man you could cheat or steal from, because he would know precisely how much money he had, right down to the last dime.

But he had more than the worthless currency of our homeland. He had dollars, thirty ten-dollar notes. And French gold napoleons too. I remember he kept his gold in an old tin cigarette case that once contained Egyptian cigarettes. He had thirty-four gold napoleons. He counted them in front of me once, very anxiously. His spectacles were glittering at the end of his nose as he examined them and put the gold pieces to his nose to smell them. He put his teeth to each one and tried it in his hand. He gave each a thorough look and held it to the light. He was like a picture of one of those old money dealers, going about his business with ruthless, even malicious, efficiency.

But I never saw him earn a penny. When he was brought a bill he would study it with deep concern without saying anything, with great solemnity. Then he paid and added a handsome tip to the person bringing the bill. I do believe that, deep down, the truth was that he was miserly. One time, round about dawn, when he had drunk his wine, he started talking about how one had to respect money and gold because they had some magical property. He didn't explain what he meant by that. Knowing how much he respected money, it was surprising how extraordinarily grand his tips were. He threw tips around, not like the rich—I have known a number of rich men, my husband included, but never found one who handed out tips the way this bum of a writer did.

I believe the truth is that he was poor. But he was so proud he didn't think it worthwhile denying his poverty. Please don't imagine I could tell you what he was really like. I just observed him with a pained fascination. But never, not for one moment, did I myself imagine I knew what the man was like inside.

You asked me what a writer is. Good question. What is he, after all?

A big nobody! He has neither rank nor power. A fashionable black bandleader earns more than he does, a police officer has more power, the commander of a fire brigade has a higher rank. He knew all that. He warned me that society has no official way of recognizing a writer—that's the kind of nobody a writer is. Sometimes they put up statues of writers or throw them in jail. But really a writer means nothing in society. He is just a scribbler. You could address a writer as "Mr. Editor" or "Dear Genius." But he wasn't an editor, because he wasn't editing anything, and he couldn't be a genius, because geniuses had long hair and an imposing appearance, or so they say. He was bald, and by the time I met him he wasn't doing anything. Nobody addressed him as "Dear Writer," because it seemed to make no sense. Somebody was either a proper person or a writer. One couldn't be both. It's pretty complicated.

Sometimes I wondered—though I could never quite tell—whether he really believed what he said. Because whatever he happened to be saying, I felt the opposite was also true. And when he looked into my eyes, it was as if it were not me he was speaking to. For example, once—this was a long time ago and I haven't thought of it since, but it suddenly seems clear now—I was sitting in his room between two air raids with my back to the writing desk. I didn't think he was paying me any attention, because he was reading a dictionary at the time. I took my compact out of my handbag and started powdering my nose. Suddenly I heard him say, "Best be careful!"

I was startled and stared at him, openmouthed. He rose from the table and stood in front of me, his arms folded.

"What should I be careful of?"

He looked at me with his head to one side and gave a soft whistle.

"Best be careful, because you're beautiful!" he said in an accusing tone. But he spoke with concern, apparently seriously.

I laughed. "What should I be careful of? Russkies?"

He shrugged.

"Them? They just want to give you a hug. Then they'll be off. But there will come others . . . people who'll want to strip the very flesh off your face. Because you're beautiful."

He peered at me shortsightedly. He pushed his glasses up to the top of his nose. It was as if he had just noticed I wasn't plain, that I had a pretty face; as if he had never really looked at me the way people should look at a woman. So, finally, he was looking at me. But it was appraisingly, the way a hunter looks at a well-bred dog.

"Strip the flesh off me?" I laughed again, but my throat was dry. "Who? Sex maniacs?"

He spoke sternly, like a priest preaching.

"Tomorrow, everyone who is beautiful will come under suspicion. As will those with talent and those with character." His voice was hoarse. "Don't you understand? To be called beautiful will be an insult; talent will be called a provocation, and character an outrage. Because it's their turn now, and they will appear everywhere, from everywhere, emerging in their hundreds of millions and more. Everywhere. The ugly ones, the talentless, those without any character. And they'll throw vitriol in the face of beauty. They will tar and slander talent. They will stab through the heart anyone with character. They're here already . . . And there'll be more of them. Be careful!"

He sat back down at his desk and covered his face with both hands. He didn't say anything for a time. Then, perfectly charmingly, without any transition from one mood to another, he asked if he should put some coffee on.

That's what he was like.

But that's not all. He was aging, but sometimes it seemed as if, behind his hand, he was laughing vengefully at the process of aging. There are men, you know, who think old age is the time for revenge. Women at that age go mad, take hormones, put on more makeup, or take young lovers . . . But men when they age often go about smiling. And it is precisely this smiling kind of older man that is most dangerous as far as women are concerned: they are like a conquering army. At this stage of the great, boring duel between men and women—of which it is impossible to get bored—it is men who are the stronger, because they are no longer driven to fury by desire. They are no longer ruled by the body: they are in charge. And women can scent this the way a feral creature can scent a hunter. We can only rule over you men as long as we can hurt you. While we can carefully feed men with a few tidbits, a little give-and-take of power, then immediately deny them the merest taste of it and watch them shouting and screaming, writing letters, and uttering dire threats, we can relax, because we know the power is still ours. But when men are old it is they who have the power. Not for long, it's true. Being old is not the same as being ancient. Because the next stage is approaching, the time of dotage, when men become children and they need women again.

Go on, laugh. I'm only chattering on, being amusing, because the sky is almost light. See, you are so beautiful when you smile proudly, like that.

This man was sly and vengeful in his aging. Occasionally he'd remember he was getting old, and the thought would cheer him up, his eyes sparkling behind his glasses, and he'd look at me with delight and satisfaction. He was practically rubbing his hands together, happy because there I was in his room and he was aging and I could no longer hurt him. I would cheerfully have hit him then, torn the glasses from his nose, thrown them on the floor, and stamped on them. Why? Just so I should hear him cry out. So he would shake me by the arm or hit me, or . . . Well, yes. But there was nothing I could do, because he was aging. And I was afraid of him.

He was the only man I was ever afraid of. I had always believed I understood men. I thought they were eight parts vanity and two of something else. Don't grunt like that; I'm not talking about you—you are an exception. But I thought I knew them, knew how to talk their language. Because nine out of ten men thought that if I looked at them from under my brow as if looking up to them, I must be admiring their beauty or intelligence! I could lisp and simper with them, play pussycat, admiring their terrifying intellect, which I, a poor little nobody of a girl, an ignorant, innocent shrinking violet, couldn't properly grasp, of course, and certainly not understand. It was enough for me to worship at their wise, masculine feet, listening spellbound to their brilliant observations, especially since they were kind enough to permit me, silly woman that I am, to tell them how brilliant, how superior, they were at work, how one of them managed to put one over on those Turkish salesmen when he palmed them off with low-quality leather rather than top grade, or how another courted the powerful so faithfully that they eventually rewarded him with a Nobel Prize or a knighthood. That was the kind of thing they used to brag about. As I said, you are an exception. You don't speak, you just keep drumming. And when you don't speak, I know for certain that there is nothing you are trying to keep silent about. It's marvelous.

But the others are not like you, darling. The others are vain, vain in bed, in restaurants, while they are just walking along or putting on their morning coats to flatter the latest celebrity, or loudly summoning the waiter in a coffee house . . . everything about them declares vanity, as if vanity were the one true incurable human disease. Eight parts vanity, I said? Maybe nine. I was reading in the Sunday supplement of one of the papers that our planet is mostly water and that only a little of it is dry land. That's how it is with men; they're nothing but vanity supported by a few fixed ideas.

This one was vain in a different way. He was proud of having killed everything in him that might have been a product of vanity. He treated his body as if it were an employee. He ate little; his manners moderate and disciplined. When he drank wine, he shut himself away in his room as if he wanted to be alone with some perverse figure who suffered from an evil obsession. He didn't care whether I was in the apartment at all when he was drinking. He'd set me up with a bottle of French brandy, a few nice nibbles on a tray, and a box of Egyptian cigarettes, then retire to his room to drink. It was as if he didn't think highly enough of women to let one watch him drinking.

He drank rare wines and went about it seriously. He chose a bottle from his collection the way a pasha might choose one or another odalisque from his harem to spend the night with. When he filled his last glass, he would loudly declare, "To Hungary!" I thought he was joking at first, but he wasn't laughing when he raised his glass. He wasn't clowning. The last glass was always drained in honor of the country.

Was he patriotic? I don't know. He tended to be suspicious of patriotic talk. To him the country meant only the language. It wasn't by chance he was reading dictionaries at this time—nothing but dictionaries. He spent the night leafing through Spanish-Italian and French-German dictionaries. He did the same while drinking, or in the morning, as the air-raid warnings sounded, as if he hoped that in the middle of this terrible cacophony of destruction he might finally find a word that would serve as an answer. But most of the time it was Hungarian dictionaries and lexicons he read with a spellbound, adoring expression, as if he were in the grip of an ecstasy, enjoying a kind of mystical vision in church.

He would take the odd Hungarian word from the dictionary, stare at the ceiling, then pronounce the word, letting it flutter above him like a butterfly . . . yes, I remember, he once actually pronounced the word "butterfly," then watched it fluttering around him as though the word were the thing itself in the powdery golden sunlight, flitting this way and that, hovering, catching the sun on its lightly dusted wings, as he followed its angelic choreography, a Hungarian word doing its dance of the spirit, and suddenly he was happy and gentle because this was the greatest and loveliest experience left to him in life. In his heart, it seemed, he had already given up the bridges, the fields, the people. It was only the Hungarian language he believed in by then: that was his home.

One night when he was drinking he allowed me in. I sat down opposite him at the end of the big divan, lit a cigarette, and watched him. He paid no attention to me; he was mildly drunk. He walked up and down the room, shouting out individual words.

"Sword!" he cried.

He took a few faltering steps forward, then stopped as though he had tripped over something. He stared at the floor.

"Pearl!" he said to the carpet.

Then he gave a cry, put his hand to his brow as if it hurt.

"Swan!" he said.

He looked at me as though he were confused, as if he had only just noticed I was in the room with him. Believe it or not, I lowered my eyes and didn't look back at him. I was ashamed. I felt I was witnessing an immoral act, a lapse of taste, in which I was Peeping Tom, a voyeur, watching the sufferings of a sick man through a crack in the wall. It was like watching a shoe fetishist, someone who thinks the part more important than the whole. He recognized my presence through the fog of wine, and blinked once or twice in acknowledgment. He gave an embarrassed, guilty smile, as though he had been caught doing something faintly disgraceful. He spread out his arms by way of excuse, as if to plead he couldn't help it, the obsession being stronger than prudence or good manners.

"Cat's tail!" he stuttered. "Barberry!"

Then he sat down beside me on the divan, took my hand, and covered his eyes with his other hand. He sat there a long time without saying anything.

I didn't dare speak. But I understood that what I had just seen was part of the act of dying. He wasn't sacrificing his life thinking the world would submit itself to his mind. He was forced to concede that the mind was powerless. You won't understand this, my dearest, because you are an artist, a real, genuine artist, the kind that has little to do with the mind, because drumming requires no meaning. Don't get cross now! What you do is far more important. There, you see? But this man was a writer, and for a long time he believed in meaning. He believed the mind was a power, like any other power that is capable of changing the world: like light, like electricity, like magnetism. And he, being a human being, might control the world through his mind without the use of any other instrument—you know, like the hero of the very long Greek poem, the one they named a travel agency after not so long ago, remember? What was he called? Ah, yes, Ulysses. You wouldn't need instruments, you wouldn't need technology, you wouldn't need Arabic numerals. I think that's how he imagined it.

But then he had to learn that reason—the mind—is worthless, because the instincts are stronger. Fury is greater than reason. And once fury has instruments at its disposal, it whistles at reason. Fury and instrument launch their own wild dance.

So he no longer expected anything of words. He no longer believed that words put into rational order could help the world or humankind. Words, when they get twisted—as they have in our time, he said, meaning the everyday words spoken between us, person to person—are superfluous, useless gravestones. The truth, he felt, was that words, the human voice itself, had become one continuous boom. Voices change when loudspeakers start screaming and crackling.

He no longer believed in words, but he always liked them, tasted them, gulped them down. At night, when the whole city was dark, he could get drunk on a few words of Hungarian. He savored words the way you were savoring your Grand Napoleon the other day, when the South American dealer offered you smuggled hash. You drank the precious stuff with your eyes closed, with genuine appreciation, exactly the way he pronounced "Pearl!" or "Barberry!" Words were solid chunks of consumable matter to him, flesh and blood. And when he was in their grip, he'd spout nonsense like any drunk or madman. One time, I remember, he was grunting and shouting the words of some Asian language. I heard him and felt like running away. I thought I was witnessing some extraordinary Eastern rite, or had lost my way in this crazy world and was, for the first time, seeing an alien people, or what remained of them. I had blundered onto a strange man speaking strange words. The words came from far away, miles and miles away. It was the first time I had ever been aware of being specifically Hungarian. But that's what I am, God knows—all my ancestors Hungarians from the old Cumanian region. I even have a mole on my back—they call it a birthmark—that is often regarded as the signature of the tribe. It's called "the Mark of the Cumans." What? You want to see it again? Fine, later.

I remember my husband once telling about some famous Hungarian who was a count, then became prime minister. He was named after a river—Count Danube or Tisza, I forget which. This count fell in love with a woman my husband knew. He had heard from the woman that when this bearded count was prime minister, he would sometimes go to a special room at the Hotel Hungaria with a few friends and invite little Berkes, the Gypsy fiddler, to join them. Then they'd close the door and listen silently to the Gypsy playing. They drank little. Then, at dawn, this grave, stern nobleman, our prime minister, who wore a frock coat most of the time, would stand in the middle of the room and begin dancing to a slow tune while the rest solemnly gazed on. Strangely enough, nobody laughed at the idea of a man—a prime minister—dancing alone, at dawn, moving very slowly to Gypsy music. And this is what occurred to me that dawn, when I heard my friend shouting and waving his arms about in a room that contained only his books and me.

Oh, those books! So many books! I never counted them, because I knew he couldn't bear for me to be moving his books around. Only by squinting, out of the corner of my eye, could I size up the shelves. The room was filled floor to ceiling with them, the shelves bowing under the weight of the books, hanging at angles, sagging like a pregnant mare's belly. The city library has more books, of course, maybe a hundred thousand or even a million; not that I know why people need all those books. I've been perfectly happy with the Bible and a paperback novel, one with a lovely colored cover showing a count kneeling before a countess. I was given the novel by a magistrate in Nyíregyháza when I was just an apprentice maid; he fancied me and invited me into his office to give it to me. I have looked after these two books. The rest I just read as and when they came along. I mean, I read them when I was being a proper lady. Don't look at me like that! Believe me, I was obliged to read books, take baths, have my toenails polished, and say things like "Bartók liberated the soul of the people's music." But I grew pretty bored of that, because I knew something about the people myself, and a bit about music too. It wasn't anything I could say to ladies and gentlemen, of course.

All those books! After the siege, I sneaked in there again. He had already immigrated to Rome. I found only the shell of a bombed building, the books just damp pulp. The neighbors said the house had received several hits. The bombs had made a soup of the books. They were lying in piles and swamps in the middle of the room, which, it seemed, the owner had only just left. One neighbor, a dentist, told me that the writer hadn't bothered to save a single book. He didn't search among the wet piles . . . when he came up from the cellar, he just stood among the books and gazed at what was left of them, his arms folded. The neighbors waited beside him, curious, keen to see him pale-faced, bewailing his bad luck. But much to their surprise, he seemed to look on the wreckage with satisfaction. Isn't that strange? The dentist swore he was almost cheerful, nodding away as if something had worked out according to plan, as if some great fraud or slander had finally come to light. He seemed to have been expecting it. The writer stood in the midst of the havoc, among his damp and soggy books, stroking his bald head, murmuring, "At last!"

As the dentist recalled it, some people there felt affronted by this. But he didn't care whether they heard him or not. He simply shrugged and left. He spent some time wandering round town as many others did. But no one ever saw him near his old apartment again. It seemed he must have put a firm period to something the moment he stood among the piles of soaked books. The dentist suspected the writer was just playing the fool, putting on a show to prove he was not hurt by what he'd lost. Others wondered whether behind the sigh of relief there might not lie the realization of failure involving a secret political allegiance—the writer might have been a fascist, a Communist, or an anarchist, so that's why he said "At last!" But they couldn't be certain of anything. The books remained on the pile of rubbish in the bombed house and rotted away. It's interesting—people were stealing all kinds of things in Budapest at the time, anything from cracked bedpans to Persian carpets and dentures, whatever they could lay their hands on. But nobody stole books. It was as if books had been taboo. It was bad luck to touch them.

He disappeared soon after the Russians entered the city. Someone said he'd been seen on the back of a Russian truck on the way to Vienna. No doubt he paid with his hoarded gold napoleons or with dollars. They said they saw him with a few salvaged goods on top of a pile of raw leather, his head uncovered, his glasses on his nose, reading some book. Maybe it was a Hungarian dictionary. What do you think? I don't know. In any case he vanished from the city.

But we can't be too sure of that, either. There's something about this that doesn't fit into the picture as I remember him. I prefer to think he would have traveled by sleeper car, on the first sleeper that left the city. He would have put his gloves on when getting on the train, bought a few newspapers at the station, and when the train started he wouldn't have looked out, but drawn the curtains of the compartment so he shouldn't see the ruins of the bombed town. He hated mess.

That's how I imagine him. I prefer it like this. It's odd, really, now, when there's only one thing we can be sure of, and that is that he is dead . . . There is nothing else I know about him for certain.

In any case, he was, for me, the last representative of the old prewar world . . . that other world, the world of my husband, I mean the world of the gentry. Not that he had any truck with the gentry. After all, he wasn't rich, he had neither title nor rank . . . He belonged in a different way.

You know how the rich kept all kinds of tatty things "in storage"? He too kept something stored away. It was culture, or taste—call it what you will . . . it was that which he believed to be culture. Because, my one and only, it's important to recognize that culture is not what we proles imagine . . . It's not the splendid apartment, the books on the shelf, polite conversation, and colored toilet paper. There's something else, something the rulers don't pass on to the ruled, not even now, when everything is different from before, when the rich have understood that they can remain rich only so long as they shower us proles with all the trifles that only yesterday were the height of desirability . . . But there is something they won't be passing on. Because there's still a kind of conspiracy among the rulers, even now, though it's different from before . . . It's not gold, not libraries, not galleries, not fine clothes, not ready cash, not shares, not jewelry, not delicate manners they are hiding away, but something more difficult to take from them. Quite likely the writer would have regarded some of these so-called important things with contempt too. He said to me, one time, that he could live on apples, wine, potatoes, bacon, bread, black coffee, and cigarettes—nothing else. Nothing else was necessary in life. Add a change of clothes, a few items of underwear, plus the well-worn raincoat he always wore, winter and summer. He wasn't just saying this: listening to him, I knew it was the truth. Because, after a while, it wasn't only him who could be silent a long time. I quickly learned it from him. I learned he had to be listened to.

I think I listened pretty closely. I solved him like a crossword puzzle. Not with my brain, but with my lower body, the way we women feel and learn. I eventually came to the conclusion that nothing that was of importance to everyone else was of any importance to him. All he needed was bread, bacon, apples, and wine. Some dictionaries.

And, ultimately, a few tasty, luscious Hungarian words that melt in the mouth. He would leave everything that was important to others without a moment's hesitation.

All he loved by then was the sun, wine, and words, words without associations, just words in themselves. It was fall, the town was being bombed, civilians and soldiers both huddled in cellars—funny to think the soldiers were more afraid of the bombs than civilians were!—while he was sitting in the autumnal sunlight, having pushed an armchair over to the window. He had bags under his eyes. He was smiling, his mouth half-open, hungrily drinking in the late-fall sunlight in the deathly silence of war.

It seemed he was happy at last, but I knew he wouldn't live much longer, that this was a form of dying.

Because, however he rejected everything culture considered important, however he wrapped himself in his faded old raincoat, he still belonged to the world that was crumbling and vanishing around him. What was this world? The world of the rich and celebrated? My husband's world? No, the rich were just the dregs of something that would once have been regarded as culture. See—even as I pronounce the word

I am blushing as though I had said something improper. It's as if he or his spirit were here, listening to what I'm saying, sitting on the edge of the bed in the hotel in Rome, and when I pronounce the word "culture" he suddenly looked at me with that awful gaze of his, looking right into my guts, and asked, "What was that, madam? Culture? That's a big word! Do you know, madam"—and I can see him raising his forefinger as he looks at me seriously like a conscientious teacher—"do you have any idea what culture is? You paint your toenails red, I believe . . . And you like reading a decent book in the morning or before going to sleep . . . and you sometimes drift off pleasantly to music, am I right?" Because he liked talking like that, in a slightly mocking, old-fashioned way, like some character out of a nineteenth-century novel. "No, madam," I can hear him now. "That's not culture. Culture, madam, yes, culture, is a reflex!"

I can see him now as clear as if he were sitting here. Don't disturb me. I can practically hear his voice. The things he said.

So many people are talking about class war, saying that now we've got rid of the old rulers, we will run things our way—everything will be ours because we are the people. I'm not sure what that means, but I have a bad feeling that's not quite how it will work out. There'll be something the old lot will have kept that they won't be passing on. And it won't be anything you can take by force, either . . . Nor can you steal it by getting a grant and lazing about at a university . . . As I said, it isn't something I understand. But I feel there is something the bourgeois have hidden away from us. What is it? Just thinking of it fills my mouth with saliva. My whole body cramps and I curl up inside. The bald man said it was a reflex. What's a reflex, for God's sake?

Let go of my hand. It's just nerves: that's why I'm trembling. I'm fine now.

I never understood him straightaway when he said something, not that first moment, and yet I understood him, understood him as a person, so to speak. Some time later I asked a doctor what a reflex was. He told me reflex was when you tap someone's knee with a little rubber hammer and the knee kicks . . . that's reflex. But he meant a different kind of kicking, another sort of reaction.

Once he had vanished and I was looking for him in vain up and down the city, I felt that he himself was a sort of reflex, just as he was, raincoat and all. The man as whole, do you see? Not his writing. The thing you scratch out with your pen, that can't be so important; after all, there are so many books in the world, in shops and in libraries . . . Sometimes it seems there are so many books that all thought must have been squeezed out of them, all those words have left no room for thought, just words endlessly crowding and pressing on the page. No, whatever he wrote was certainly not that important. And he no longer thought about having written books—if anything, he was a little ashamed of it. When the subject came up in conversation, he'd give an embarrassed smile, as I remember once when, carefully but clumsily, I started talking about his books. It was as if I had reminded him of some youthful folly. I felt sorry for him then. There must have been some vast fury, desire, passion, or sadness raging in him. Mentioning his books was like sprinkling salt on a frog in the spirit of scientific inquiry, just to see how the electricity worked—you could practically see him jerking. His mouth twisted this way and that, and he wouldn't know where to look. It was dropping salt on a naked mind.

It's as if the great statues, the famous paintings, and the clever books were not things in themselves; as if he were a tiny living atom of everything that was being destroyed. He was being destroyed with the whole of which he was a part. Now it seems the statues and books will be around for a long time yet, even while the thing they call culture vanishes.

God only knows how this works.

I watched him and, as the bombs were falling, thought how stupid I'd been in my childhood—in the ditch, and later in the maid's room in that highly refined household, and then in London when the Greek taught me all kinds of airs and graces—when I thought the rich were cultured. Now I know that the rich just peck at culture, indulge in it a little, dipping in this or that dish of it, and chatter about it. That's something one learns very slowly and at great cost. Learns what? That culture is what happens when a person or a people overflow with some great joy! They say the Greeks were cultured because the whole nation rejoiced. Even the tinkers who made cheap little statuettes, and the traders in oil, and the military, the populace at large, and all the wise men who stood in the agora arguing about beauty or wisdom. Try to imagine a people that can experience joy. That joy is culture. But that generation vanished, and in their place came people who still spoke Greek, but couldn't feel or think as they did.

Do you fancy reading a book about the Greeks? Apparently there is a library here, where the pope lives . . . Don't look so insulted! The saxophonist told me he goes there in secret, to read. Of course, darling, he is just boasting when he says that. The truth is he really only reads detective stories. All the same, it is not impossible that there should be libraries here in Rome where they look after books and where we could find out how Greece came to an end. I mean, the thing people call culture. Because now, you see, there are only experts. But experts can't reproduce the joy that culture did. Is this boring you? Fine, I won't go on about it. I only want you to be cheerful and satisfied. I won't bother you with such foolish thoughts again.

You're looking askance at me. I can tell by your nose you don't believe me. You are thinking it is not Greek culture that interests me, and I simply want to know why this man died.

How sharp you are! Yes, I confess, I'd like to read a book that explained culture: what it is and how it can begin to fall apart one day. How it can come to pieces in the figure of a single man: the way his nervous system withers away, the nerves that contained so much life, that carried all the stuff people thought a long time ago, and which other people recall with longing, so that, for a moment or two, they feel they are better than the common run of animals. It seems to me that a man like that does not die alone—a great many things die with him. You don't believe me? I don't really know, myself, but I'd like to read such a book.

They say Rome was once a cultured city. Even those who couldn't read or write—the people in market stalls—even they were cultured. They might have been dirty, but they went to the public baths and, once there, argued there about what was wrong or right. Do you think the fool came here for that reason? Because he wanted to die here? Because he believed that everything that people once called culture, that gave them joy, was gone? That he came here, where everything was turning into one vast heap of rubbish but there were still a few monuments of culture remaining—that remained the way that you could still see feet sticking out from beneath the soil in Buda, in the Vérmező, after the siege: the yellow feet of the dead buried under twelve inches of soil? Is that why he came here? To this town, to this hotel? Because he wanted the smell of culture round him when he died?

Yes, he died in this room. I asked the desk clerk. Are you happy now, knowing that? There, I've given you this too. I don't have anything left. You've put the jewels in a safe place, haven't you? You are my guardian angel, darling.

Listen—believe me, when he died, it was in this bed, so the desk clerk told me. Yes, the very bed you are lying in, gorgeous. And I am sure he was thinking: "Now, at last!" And he will have smiled. These madmen, these peculiar people, always smile at the end.

Wait, let me cover you.

Are you asleep, darling?

Posillipo, 1949–Salerno, 1978

Epilogue

. . . Because I tell you, buddy, believe me I tell you how it really is. You just mind to keep a long way clear of people in the cement trade. What you staring at? Don't you know what that is? Don't you watch TV? You really are a novice. You have a lot to learn in our lovely big village, New York. I can see you're pretty new here, an economic migrant, or an illegal. Be glad if they let you stay. And keep your mouth shut. Because all kinds of trash is holed up here. But we two, we're from Zala, the pair of us, the old country, we Hungarians should stick together. Here's your *bludimari*. Drink up, brother.

As I say, be really careful that you don't go within a mile of the cement trade. Our street here, Forty-sixth, has enough safe rooms. But farther down, in Thirty-eighth, that's where the Family get together . . . you know, the Family. Avoid the place after midnight. And if you meet one or two of them, be careful to be on your best behavior. Because that's what they like, these padrones: full of good manners. How will you know a padrone? . . . Well, they dress smart to start with. They're highly refined people, silver hair, sideburns, everything just so. Suits and shoes all the best material cut to the best length. And they wear hats. They tip big. They draw of a wad of greenbacks from the pocket of their pants. They do it so, left-handed. They don't even look to see whether it's Washington or Lincoln on the front, they just throw it down. It's like Sunday in church, in the middle of mass, when the guy comes along with his green collection bag. You must have seen it in the movies—great film, right? But if a member of the Family calls you and invites you to attend an evening course, just be polite and say no thank you, not my line of work.

The padrones—they don't deal with cement—that's manual work. They do the brain work: they think. The manual work is left to the junior members of the Family, the ones still doing apprenticeships. It's casual work. The sucker goes home at night, not a worry in the world, doesn't suspect anything. Ten steps behind comes the casual worker, the apprentice. A car is waiting on the corner. The apprentice carries an iron crowbar under his coat. The bar has a hook on the end that's no bigger than your bent index finger. Once on the corner, the trick is to sink the sharp end of the crowbar into the sucker's skull . . . one quick move and it's done. No waiting, no argument. The guy collapses, just like that, then you grab him round the waist. You drag him into the car, take him down to the river where there's a box waiting. You tenderly deposit the happily departed in the box, fill up with liquid cement, nail the box down, and slide it into the water. The cops say there are dozens of them sitting at the bottom of the Hudson. It's like—you remember the story from the old country?—Attila's coffin. It's teamwork and it needs proper apprentices. But you take great care! Whatever the padrone says, you just keep saying, "No thank you, not my line of work." You stick to your job in the garage. You're a garage hand. We Zala folk must look out for each other.

It's not impossible, of course, that later you make it big yourself. Like, that's something else. But you have to know your stuff. Avoid the bars on Thirty-eighth, they're not for you. There's always work available, but have nothing to do with them. For example they might want a persuader. You know, the kind of guy who goes to the sucker and persuades him to pay twenty-five percent a week for the loan. Avoid them too, but be polite about it. Just tell them you can't take the *djob* because your accent is not up to full New York level. Accent is a big problem to them. These black guys wouldn't accept me in the band on account of my accent . . . me, who back home drummed for Tito when he visited Budapest. That was before '48, before the radio started howling on about Tito and his revisionist traitor dogs! The black guys said I drummed with an accent, my sticks were wrong. That's what I mean by accent—it's just jealousy and racism. That's my biggest regret. What else could I do, I got this job as a bartender. So now you know. Sit down and enjoy yourself, I'll pour you another.

Go on, stay, there is plenty of time. This hour of the day, after supper, there are few customers, at least till the theaters empty. We don't get cement trade here, anyway. Our customers are writers of one sort or another. It's not manual work like cement, but the pay's pretty hot. What's that? You'd like a go yourself? Go ahead, try. Who knows, you might strike it lucky, but it won't be easy. My experience, here in Manhattan, is that books are big-time.

You get to see a lot of life from behind a bar. After midnight, with the third martini down them, the one they put against expenses because it's part of the job, about midnight or so, among themselves, they talk pretty freely, these writers. I listen to them and think what big business it is here. It's not like over the Pond, in Rome, or in Budapest. My guardian angel, I called her "Sweetheart," whose photo I keep on the shelf—you see, I even got her a silver frame from Woolworth's—she told me she knew a writer back home who no longer wanted to write because he had grown sick of books. He really did feel sick and wanted to heave up each time he thought about it. The only things he still read were those crazy dictionaries. He must have been a weird creature, an oddment, like the Chinese deer at the Bronx Zoo.

The patrons here in New York are not that sort of writer. They don't actually write anything, but immediately sell what they haven't yet written. They earn a mint from books. They usually start arriving past eleven, when the nearby shows have finished. They soak up the drink, straight bourbons, every time. There's a regular, a little fat guy, who must be a real big-shot writer, because he even has a secretary and a lot of hangers-on with him, who are all ears when he talks. Whenever he says something they're all attention, like a congregation in church when the priest raises the host. I saw it with my own two eyes the time he thought of a title and the guy, his secretary, was straight on the line, selling it. He came back out of breath saying he had sold the title for two hundred thousand, a story his boss hadn't yet written and had only just thought of, one he'd maybe write, if the inspiration came. Everyone drank to the good news and when they left they left me twenty on the tray. That's because big-shot writers are always surrounded by pals. There's some really cute women in the gang too. If you really fancy writing I could introduce you to one of them.

I don't read books myself, that's not my thing. I'm happy enough to leaf through a good thriller, or the comics—you know, where the chick lies naked on the couch without a clue that her sexy days are over and her problems are just beginning. And her pimp leans over her, a knife in his hand, and there's a talk bubble that says, "There's nothing wrong with her, it's just a bit of blood on her neck." I like that kind of thing. Thrillers are good because the writers don't smuggle in clever stuff— the reader gets it straightaway, without the crap.

Go on, relax, have another—your *bludimari* is there, right by your hand. The *boss*? Don't worry about him. He's there behind that glass door, in the back room. Yes, the guy with the glasses . . . He's doing the accounts, not looking this way. Solid guy: a Mormon. No liquor, only warm water from a heavy-bottomed glass. And he won't smoke—he's above all that. He brought nothing from Utah, where his lot live, to New York, except his Bible and his Mormon ways, like having two wives. The second he picked up here, in Manhattan. Owns a chain of eight bars, two in Harlem. But our place here on the corner of Broadway is the smartest.

Because, you know, there are two theaters nearby. One where they sing and one where they just talk. Sometimes when they talk so much it gets to be a drag and the audience grow bored and walk out. I've not been in either so far, but one day I paid up a Franklin for the one that was all talk. Why shouldn't I be an angel, I thought—you have to support art. Don't know what angels are? People who finance a play. Investors. Drivers, hotel porters, headwaiters, they all want to be angels when there's a play starting on Broadway. But this one was no good, I wasted a hundred. There was a lot of talking on stage—too much. It's better when there's some nice upbeat music, a high-kicking chorus and singers, that kind of thing. I'm not investing in writers or literature again. A man's better off playing the numbers game. So you just wait and serve your turn in the garage.

You have to tighten your belt here, brother. It's a wised-up world we have here. You have to pay close attention, learn the ropes. This is my fifth year behind the bar. I am a proper mister now, a senior bartender. And I'm still learning. In this place, being close to Broadway and the theaters, what we get are chiefly highbrows. What are those? People with egg-shaped heads, their heads like duck eggs, all high forehead—and spots. There are some with big bushy beards too. They're all clever. You wouldn't believe how important they are. I listen to them from behind the bar and they stay till morning. They arrive about midnight when the others have gone, I mean those who come here for the atmosphere, candles behind red shades. Those who stay are all in the profession. They talk freely among themselves. I listen pretty hard, as you may imagine.

Because, you know, they're a powerful, dangerous pack . . . the devil knows how they do it, but in some ways they are even more powerful than the padrone. Everyone is afraid of them. They could even destroy the president if they didn't like him. Sometimes my jaw just drops when I hear them whispering together as to who's in line for their version of the cement, or who they're going to build up. Some of them come here from the night desk, guys who write social columns in papers. I hear them discussing who's screwing who and in what position. That's the free press for you; that's freedom, they're free to ruin those they don't like. Then they write books about it, print them in editions of a million. It's what they call culture, and it spreads. In every drugstore, in every subway station, in every supermarket, you find piles and piles of stuff like that. People like us can't get their kind of knowledge: we need higher education. It's an art, like drumming. The fact is, friend, I don't get lit-ter-a-ture, but back in my hometown, in Mátészalka, I served in the local barracks and we'd occasionally visit what *we* called a house of culture to see the girls. All I say is that the cathouse at Mátészalka was a moral institution compared to what I hear about lit-ter-a-ture here behind the bar. Back home we knew what we were paying for, and once we made a deal the head man there might say, "Give us another ten, soldier boy, and she'll take her top off too." As I said, I know nothing about books, but I do understand cathouses. When I was a kid I was a regular myself. All in all I can't say it was any worse than what they call culture now. These writers will strip for cash, exactly like the girls. I mean the lady writers, not just the men . . . They'll show you the lot, no knickers, from back, from front, whatever way you fancy it—if you pay. Culture meant something else to us in Zala. Papa bought the calendar once a year, and that was it. But my jaw just drops—I mean, just now I heard someone's getting half a million for writing the memoirs of the guy who throws the switch in San Francisco. Or he writes up the confessions of a girl that used to be a guy, or how a girl *became* a guy, and that gets to be culture. Culture's fancy work, brother—harder than drumming.

It's possible that what the regulars talk about here in the bar doesn't cover the whole field. There might be other kinds of writers in the neighborhood. I once overheard two guys who wandered in here talking in low voices about what this other kind of lit-ter-a-ture might be. The sort you don't see much of. The kind you hear about only once the writer has shuffled off to the morgue, having topped himself in his misery. These two guys, who wandered in here by accident, couldn't afford *bludimaris* but had to make do with beer. They were talking about books. They were puny little runts, scribblers of some sort, more like the guy Sweetheart was talking about in Rome. You didn't have to look hard— even a blind man could see these runts were not about to be guests at the usual party. Maybe they were the real thing . . . And maybe there are more of them, only you never get to see them because they don't hit the headlines, they're out there drowning their sorrows. I mean, that's what I understood as they muttered into their beer—that there were other kinds of writers. Guys who write poems, for example, who scribble in notebooks the way our great national poet Petőfi did. The devil knows. The only thing certain is that their kind don't tend to come here.

Ah, the drums. Well, that's sad, a real regret. It's not that it isn't a good *djob,* mixing cocktails in this bar. Like there's a salary and free meals. And tips. I could quietly carry on here till I retire. But I don't have it bad, anyway. I know a neat-looking Irish widow, a little second-hand, but friendly, if you get me? I have a car, an apartment, a TV. I even have an electric lawn mower out on the porch . . . no garden, but a mower's good for status. The widow and I went to Florida last winter, spent two weeks, living like lords on the Riviera. I got to admit, financially, it was a good deal leaving home. But it breaks my heart when I think of the music. The freedom is better here, but what's all that when

I can't be a musician? It's melancholy, you feel like an exile, like the patriot Kossuth felt in Turin.

It can't be helped. Artists don't forget, you know. Sometimes I remember how it was after the siege, sitting at my drums in the bar, putting my whole heart and soul into it, as God, and my talent, intended me to. That bar was in a house that'd been bombed out, but they got it in pretty good order. There was heating, atmosphere, Napoleon brandy, everything you need for a people's democracy. I had a solid reputation and the new bosses needed drummers. The gig would start about ten, but it was four in the morning by the time I got home. That was in '48 when the Commies took over culture. Business improved for a while. The new top guys came, throwing money about. Why not? They could do it. Everything belonged to the people, after all! Every so often some leftovers of the old order would stumble in, fancy dans who'd stowed away a few gold napoleons and now wanted to drink to forget. They were paying for their own funerals, telling sob stories about the past. But the boot was on the other foot in '48 when the new bosses came in. If they were seen to be nursing hangovers, it was for the people's sake.

Why did I leave when things were going so well for me? Long story, friend. I was like you, not cut out for finance. Then, one day, I discovered my place was in politics.

I tell you this in confidence, as brother to brother, you might as well know. After the liberation—I still get a sour taste in my mouth when I use that word—I stayed in Zala till '47, then moved to Budapest. I lived a quiet life there, no trouble to anyone. I like my privacy, see. So we'd been liberated, and the local count skipped it over the border. He wasn't altogether a bad guy, but he did happen to be a count.

Later, my old man—the one the Commies shoved into a collective on the rap that he was a kulak, just because he had four acres and a garden—my old man, he said the count was no good, but the way things turned out was no good, either. At least the count let you steal a little. But the new bosses, the guys in leather coats, who arrived in the village on a truck one day shortly after '45, politely invited everyone into the council house, strong-arming anyone who seemed a little reluctant, and persuaded them to throw everything they had into the common kitty, both their own and the land that had been divided up since, not to mention the animals—into the collective with them all! The new lot wouldn't let you steal, because they did the stealing themselves. Shut your face, they kept repeating as they kicked your head in, everything belongs to the people now.

One day the minister drove through town, a guy trained in Moscow. He was an educated man, in charge of collectivization. Because that was the delicate term they used: "collectivization." Well, this guy was good at it, because he'd spent the winter in Moscow and he saw at first hand how the numbers of kulaks had dropped to one million, because the comrades had collected their produce. But the old man and others explained that after collectivizing there wasn't enough left in the granary for the winter. He stayed sitting in his car while he told us we shouldn't complain and should understand that everything belonged to the people now. Then the minister went on to make a speech in parliament, demanding that any remaining craftsmen left in the village should also be collectivized, no matter whether it was the blacksmith, the carpenter, or the wheelwright, because they were all capitalists and exploiters, leeches who took money from the people. My old man was a smith too, shoeing horses and sharpening scythes all his life. It saddened him no end when he heard he wasn't really a blacksmith but a leech on the people. And then they took away his work permit.

I can't tell you the whole story, friend, not all at one go. It was a bad time. A friend of mine, who used to live in the village, had gone up to the capital just as the bright sun of freedom was dawning on us. One day he wrote me a letter. He used to play the flute so it broke your heart. That was the time they started "confiscating" corn from the count's granary. Chicks were mad for his flute playing. He wrote to say he now played sax in a people's democracy bar in Budapest, and that it might be an idea for me to come and join him because they needed a drummer. The old man swore a lot, the old girl cried. It was hard leaving them, but I felt the call of art. So I left.

Wait, the guests are arriving. Yes sir, Two scotch on the rocks, sir. You are served, sir.

Those two scotches are rogues, the pair of them. That one there, the one with the waxed mustache, is a faith healer, Christian style. He knows his business. The other one, the one with the sideburns, is an embalmer. If the faith cure doesn't work, you go on to the embalmer. He prepares the corpse the way the relatives want it. I could listen to them for hours when they talk about the next in line. Because there are various kinds of smile available. There's the saintly smile. There's the knowing smile. Then there's the at-peace-now smile. The saintly is the most expensive. The at-peace-now is cheaper. It's all done with paraffin, and there's a proper tariff. They come in at midnight after work and regularly sink three scotches. They're moderate, religious guys.

Back in Zala County where I used to live, washing corpses was done according to an old ritual. Here they do things differently . . . Pay them no attention, we can carry on our conversation. After midnight they're not interested in anyone that's still alive, it's just their way of saying *gut'abend*. They'll only be interested in you if you have paraffin to sell.

Where was I?

As I was saying, after '47 I felt I had hidden my talents away long enough and took the train to Pest. There were four of us in the band: the saxophonist, the accordionist, the pianist, and me on the drums. I'm not exaggerating when I say that was a great time for me. The new democracy was still settling down. It was all a bit heady. I don't even like to talk about leaving it: the thought's like a vise round my heart.

Because it so happened one morning I got an invitation from the AVO, the security police. I should be at their headquarters in Andrássy út at nine, though the street was called something else by then. Go here, go there, go up the stairs, go to that numbered room. I was sweating when I read the letter, but then I relaxed, because I realized they don't normally write letters to you, they just quietly come at dawn and ring. People, back then, were terrified of the doorbell. Bell-terror syndrome, we called it.

I gathered up all my papers: my certificate to show I was a qualified musician, and another to testify I was a faithful son of the people. Plus the local certificate to say my sympathies were on the good side in the war. I'd got these papers together in plenty of time. There were guys I worked with who could vouch for my sympathies, who themselves were on the good side. I had a clutch of other papers too, but those were from before, complete with stamps and photographs . . . I didn't think this was the occasion for them. I flushed those papers straight down the john. I had an old revolver, a six-shooter, one of my brothers left behind when he went to "pursue his studies" in the West in '45. I'd long ago buried that at the end of the yard. I thought it best it should rest there, because if the AVO did a search and found it, I'd be heading for the bone yard. So I put everything in as good an order as I could, then, one morning, set off in the direction of the Opera, to security HQ.

I passed the Opera and read on the posters that they were doing a piece called *Lawherring* or something that night, complete with orchestra. Well, brother, I thought, you'll never get to see *Lawherring* if the AVO break you. It was a sad thought, because despite being a proper musician I'd never been to the opera. There wasn't anything of that kind back in Zala—no one ever sang from a score. But there was nothing I could do about it, I just trudged on toward dreaded old number 60. It was with a heavy heart because no one ever said it was a breeze being invited to number 60. I'd never been there before myself, but I'd heard that the fascists used to call it the House of Loyalty. Well, kiddo, I said to myself, you might be walking into history right here. I had no idea what was waiting for me. Will they be thinking I'm clean, or has someone grassed me up? I was trying to work it all out. If I got six months, I'd manage fine. I swore to myself I wouldn't panic and that I would watch every word I said, because nothing could be worse than dropping the wrong word at the wrong moment with these guys—it would be a bad mistake.

I had the feeling I was at the turning point of my life. A guy in a flat army cap was at the gate to check my summons, and he sent me upstairs. Another uniform told me to sit on a bench in the corridor. So I sat down meek as a lamb and looked around me, with a degree of curiosity, not so much as I thought would be noticed.

There was a lot to see. There'd been an early-morning change of shift—you could see it was an all-night job for the comrades. Everyone wore uniforms of the kind our soldiers did a few years back—say, three years before. The leather belt was the same, only the armband was different, that and the braid. The faces were familiar too, guys from really poor backgrounds . . . I thought I'd seen one or two of them before. But my stomach was all cramped up: it was like I was sleeping after a really heavy meal followed by a glass or two more than was strictly necessary. I gazed openmouthed, as it was the first time I'd seen something like this close-to, with my own eyes. What it told me was that that famous thing highbrows call "history"—well, things don't really change: in fact they're always exactly the same. I sat on the low bench taking it all in, glancing up and down the corridor, watching busy comrades going about exactly the same tasks as their brothers had done three years earlier.

The comrades' job was to escort whoever was next in line to the right interrogation room. Some of them needed escorting because they couldn't walk. It seemed they must have got a bad pain in their feet overnight in the middle of some official conversation. So they needed support, which the guards offered by grabbing them under the arms. There were a few who went on their own feet, but not many. It was, believe me, deadly quiet along the corridor, but sometimes you could hear noises, like the sound of a scream in the middle of a polite exchange of ideas. Even so, screams behind closed doors were better than silence, because silence might suggest that the conversation was pretty well over—that some poor guy had run out of debating points.

It was half an hour before they called me in, and it was another hour before I came out. They didn't escort me; they didn't need to support me under the arms. I went on my own two feet, head held high. An hour earlier I had no idea what was in store for me. I was a different man coming out an hour later. Believe it or not, I'd been given a job.

I walked home slowly as if I'd drunk a little too much last night and was having to tread very carefully in the morning. One deliberate step, then another deliberate step. I went straight to my pad on Klauzál tér, the square where I'd been living six months. It was a joint tenancy, because in my situation, I couldn't afford a pad alone. The guy I shared the bed with did day shifts from early in the morning, going out to Rákos on the shuttle service. The bed was empty and I lay down with my clothes on. I felt like the life had been kicked out of me. I stayed there till dark.

It all came back in pieces. It was like when you take a pill to make you sick up what you don't need. When they invited me into the room I imagined I'd find some huge, barrel-chested goon there just itching to beat me to a pulp. But that's not how it turned out. It was not some crude hulk but a guy with withered legs, quite old, with horn-rimmed glasses. He wore no uniform, just plain clothes, and he spoke quietly and politely, smiling all the way through. He offered me a chair and a cigarette, just as they do in thrillers, like a detective before a grilling. I saw my cadre papers lying on the desk in front of him, and noticed how he'd leaf through them now and then. But it wasn't a close examination—he was just picking up a point here and there with his finger. It seemed he'd already read and mastered it all. He softly asked me to tell him, if I didn't mind, what I was doing in '44.

I had to think quickly. Keep your cool, I thought, let him see you're no chicken. I took the papers I'd prepared from my pocket—they were all officially stamped with the proper stamps. All I said was that I'd never been disloyal to my nation.

He seemed to be happy with that answer, nodding, as if he expected no less of me. Then, still gently, in a thin little voice, he asked me if I knew anyone in Budapest who had served in the Arrow Cross, the fascist militia.

What?! I gasped. Me? Know militia? What kind of militia? Like a police force? Like the Wild West?

He saw I was no fool and started reassuring me. Fine, he said, fine, he won't ask me any more about that, since he could tell I was sensitive about the militia. But he'd still like to know if I knew anyone in this beautiful cathedral city of ours who might have escorted people of a different religion down to the Danube at dawn in the winter at the end of '44. Women, children, old people?

He looked at me so hard it was like being stabbed in the eye with an old lady's knitting needle.

Well, I really sweated then. I took a gulp and told him straight that I was in Zala at the time and I didn't even know where exactly the Danube was then. And, I added, quietly and modestly, yes, I'd heard that there were regrettable excesses in Pest at the time.

When he heard this he opened his mouth and watched me the way a shortsighted hen looks for grain. He said nothing for a while, just blinked a few times. Then he cheered up. He looked so cheerful he was like the virgin whose tits have just been tickled.

"You're a wise man, Ede," he nodded. He gave a sigh and added, by way of acknowledgment, " 'Regrettable excesses' is good. You have a way with words, Ede."

I confessed that Ede was just my professional name, that I was Lajos at home. He waved that aside as if to say it didn't matter. "Ede or Lajos, you are a man respected among your peers," he said. I could tell he was sincere. I felt the guy was respecting me. He clicked his tongue and rubbed his palms together; then he threw away his cigarette and spoke in a changed voice. He was still gentle, but his horn-rimmed eyes never left mine. It was no longer knitting needles but proper needles squeezed under your nails.

He lifted up my cadre papers, waved them about, and said he was no fool, either. Did I believe him when he said he was no fool? Of course I believed him, I said. In that case I should think over very carefully what he was about to say. The bar where I was a drummer was a classy place, he said. Lots of people go there, mostly decent democratic people, but not just them—others too. The People's Republic needed citizens who were loyal to the people, because the place was crawling with enemy agents. He lit a cigarette at this point but didn't offer me one. He carried on staring right through me. There was no shining a desk lamp in the eyes, the way they have in the books when they grill a guy. There was nothing, just a desk and a man. And there were iron bars on the windows in case the visitor should feel nervous and take a fancy to leaping through the window for a stroll in the sunshine. And on the other side of the door there was always that strange shuffling. And the smack of boots on the stones below. And, occasionally, a word of encouragement when some visitor was too slow in answering. That's all.

Then he started speaking to me like he was the smart kid in a school full of idiots. He had the spiel off by heart. What he said was that music, night, and drink loosened tongues. So while I am drumming I should listen hard. He was very patient in explaining this. But, fact is, it was like a lesson learned at school. He told me what to look out for. He was wise to how people behaved in bars. I was to keep my eyes on any relics of the old world, the world of the gentry—guys who still had cigarettes and appetite enough to console themselves with drink. Then I was to look out for the new sort, the sort who aren't Commies but just pretend: pigs desperate to stick their snouts in the trough, people who waste no time sticking on all the right badges. He taught me patiently, almost lovingly, the way teachers in kindergartens teach the kiddies. He went on to say there was a whole new society out there, and it included all sorts of people. Honest, sons-of-the-soil rulerists, smart city-avenue turbanists,* highbrow writers the lot of them, "progressive" horn-rimmed-glasses types with pipes in their mouths, the sort who sit on the fence cheering on old-style proper Communists, encouraging them to finish their dirty work for them, to do away with the old world and get the new one ready . . . And when they do get rid of the old world, the rulerists, the turbanists, and the horn-rimmed-glassesists are all there, waving them a cheery "do-si-donya" and "well done," adding, "now fuck off back to the Urals." Then they get off the fence, and politely, cleverly, take over anything of value that still remains in this pretty little country, and stow it away in their ample pockets. But in order for them to do that, the old-style Commies have to fuck off back to the Soviet Union first, those that are still alive, anyway—that is, after Uncle Joe had finished buggering the comrades about, maybe because they weren't the best of buddies, not the way they should have been—not, at least, how the boss pictured it—or simply because, like the fools they are, they wormed their way into the affections of the Father of the People, and took jobs that did for them later. Or they were Trotskyists. Or Spanish Civil Warists. And while the old guard are still feeling the backs of their necks just to make sure their heads are still there, they, the rulerists, the turbanists and the rest, all the "progressives," start putting it about that there is a different, neater, better way of being a Communist. But the Party begs to differ on that matter—I noted the glint in his eye as he said this—because these educated wise guys who want to set about teaching the masses scientific Marxism don't have a clue that the masses despise them and don't believe a word they say. You have to have rotted five years down the mines with them, a long way underground, before they believe you. Then you have to have worked your way out of the mines and spent the next five years at a bench with a vise screwed into it, snips and hacksaw in your hand, cutting sheets of metal. If, after all that, you do start talking about Marxism and Leninism, they might just listen to you. But people who sit on the fence and shout encouragement to the masses, telling them to struggle on because the time will come when

*This is a joke impossible to translate directly. Ede / Lajos is mispronouncing the names of the two leading, opposing schools of Hungarian writing in the twentieth century: he says *népis* instead of *népies* (popular ruralist) and *turbánus* (or turbanists) instead of *urbánus* (urbanist, cosmopolitan).

they, the progressives, will teach them the finer points of Marxism—
well, they'd get a few dirty looks, I promise you, he said. You want to
look out for this type, he said, because that's the sort of people you find
in bars now. You could tell from the way he said it what he thought of
those who were desperate to dip their snouts in the trough without ever
having worked down a mine or in a labor camp . . . he despised them as
much as he did the gentry. He had it all off pat, the way you learn things
in school.

My heart beat fast, faster than I ever beat with my drumsticks,
because I could see that when he picked out someone he'd make sure
they couldn't wriggle out of it, or escape . . . though he might enjoy
watching them try. I was looking for the emergency exit, but all I saw
were walls and bars on the window. Once he paused for breath I quietly
asked him to tell me straight what he wanted me to do.

He took a sniff, then told me never again to call at number 60, never
even to come near. Once a week I was to ring a number. When someone
answered, I was simply to say, "I'm Ede, greetings to the old man." The
voice would then say he'd be delighted to meet me, but where and
when? The best place would be City Park, on a bench. Or, in winter,
near the marshalling yard at Lágymányos, where there are lots of nice
little places that serve liquor. You can spend hours there chatting away
in private, in a cozy tit-to-tit. He listed the kind of people to watch at
the bar, in the order of importance. If I see someone going into the toilet and then, shortly, another guest walking in after them, I have to
hurry after them to check if one of them has left a secret note or some
cash. I am to leave the cash there and immediately ring the number he
gave me, he said, and they would take care of the rest as an emergency,
a matter of priority. The People's Republic looked after its own, he said,
and rubbed his finger and thumb together in the old "money" sign. As a
drummer you can pretty well see and hear everything that's going on in
the bar.

Then he coughed, as if to say now he was coming to the succulent
plump heart of the matter. The comrades. I had to watch even the comrades, he said, lowering his voice. Because not every comrade was genuine, a true, up-to-his-elbows, worker of the state—there were some
who just pretended to be comrades. If I saw the liquor had loosened
their tongues, that they were leaning together, whispering quietly, and,

say, this was toward dawn and I could see they were getting too cozy, all on the same wavelength . . . I was to find out and report their names.

He went on like this for an hour, then he summed up. He said I was to make sure I worked hard. If I did, my papers would end up filed away in the records and I'd have a nice, peaceful life, having helped lay down the foundations of happiness in the people's democracy. He picked up my own file and waved it about. Then he leaned back in his chair, took his glasses off, and started wiping the lenses. A shiver ran right through me as our eyes met. My legs were stone cold from my knees down to the tip of my toes. What it came down to was that he wanted me—a drummer—to sing for the AVO, to sing like a fucking canary. He folded his arms and calmly gazed at me.

I mumbled something about needing time. Naturally, he said, polite as ever. You have till noon tomorrow. He gave me a nice friendly good-bye smile, all teeth, like the handsome guy on those old Lysoform ads used to. I went back to my pad, no longer thinking how nice it would be to go hear *Lawherring* at the Opera. I lay on my bed till the late afternoon. I ate nothing. I drank nothing. My throat was dry and I felt like shit.

It was getting on to dusk by the time I managed to sit up. I put on my tuxedo. It was time to go to work. But then, as I was putting my black tie on, something stirred in my stomach. Or was it my head? I don't know even now. All I knew was that I was in a hole. These guys had picked me, a drummer, to sing for them. I was to be like those waiters in the hotels, like those chambermaids in the embassies, like those smart chicks with sharp ears who work in offices. I didn't need to be told what they wanted me to do. I chewed it over a long time. I didn't need to sign up for day courses or attend a night class. I knew the score without all that. It was clearer than daylight that those they had once fingered were theirs for keeps. I was stone cold sober and shivering. It was evening before I set off to work.

It was a real nice evening, just like spring. Some of the band was already hanging around the bar. Two were old buddies, family, and I trusted them. The sax guy from Zala who brought me up to the capital, he was a brother. The pianist reckoned himself a highbrow. He was a quiet guy who was only in the band because he needed the cash; I didn't think it was him that shopped me. The accordionist had been doing jazz for years, sometimes he'd be called home at dawn . . . it might have been love interest, but it might have been an AVO pimp. I wasn't sure about him. I just felt a great sadness thinking the glory days, my pure music days, were over. There is no greater sadness for an artist than the sense that the savor's gone out of his art, that it's time to give up everything he has ever learned. Don't go thinking I'm crazy or that I'm pulling some tragic act. Everyone in the business knew I was the best drummer in Hungary . . . I tell it how it is, no false modesty. Sweetheart told me as much. She knew what she was talking about. She'd worked for rich Jews in London, a refined bunch, who taught her a lot.

That night it was late before the place started buzzing. It was midnight when the first big payers appeared. All three were secretaries of state. They wore striped pants and fancy ties. There were many shortages in the country at the time but there was no lack of secretaries of state, not so anyone complained, anyway. They'd go around in huddles, like field mice after rain. These were fine, handsome examples of the type. They'd brought female company with them, and it's likely the chicks too were state workers because, I tell you, friend, they carried plenty of flesh on them. They weren't about to go on diets. The waiters hurried over to show them to a table near the band and they settled down there. They gave us a nice genial smile. They were in a good mood and you could see from their clothes they were new in the job, that they'd been something else before. I recognized one of them since I'd seen him in the bar before, selling rugs on the installment plan. Best not ask where he found the rugs. A lot of people were collecting rugs from bombed houses at the time.

Two regulars arrived with them, the poet Lajos Borsai and the war correspondent Joe Lepsény. They were in every night, holding forth in the bar. The poet made his living after midnight by wearing his patriotic heart on his sleeve and blubbing about his terrible life. He worked out which new customers were worth milking, then made his way over to their table. If they were already a little over the limit he'd pull his mother's photograph from his pocket and his voice would fill with emotion as he showed it around. He had two mothers . . . one, a dignified woman, with her hair wreathed round her brow the way Queen Elizabeth had it when praying at the coffin of our great national hero Ferenc Deák. The other was a tiny, humble-looking little old lady dressed in peasant costume, complete with head scarf. He'd size up the guests before deciding which mother to produce. This time he sat down with Baron Báróec-sedi, who had arrived with his latest bride, a muscle-bound retired police sergeant. His taste ran to that kind of thing. The baron was a regular too. The poet began in a broken voice:

"This time of the year the yellow clover is just coming into bloom in my little village back home . . ."

But the baron wasn't in the mood. He glared at the poet. Báróecsedi was a pretty fat guy, and a little on the jealous side. He blinked suspiciously at his bride, the retired policeman. They looked at each other with pouting lips, like the lovers in that famous picture, the one Sweetheart once showed me in the museum in Rome, *Cupid and Psyche*.

"Look, Mr. Borsai," he growled. "I'd be grateful if you left these Christian agricultural matters out of it. I am a nervous old Jew with a bad stomach. I am not impressed by the fact that the yellow clover is in bloom. If it's in bloom, let it bloom," he added angrily.

The poet was offended and went to sit with the secretaries of state. "Cigars for the press!" he cried.

The waiters rushed to bring the cigar tray and the poet picked up a fistful of Hungarian Symphony cigars from a tin box, stuffing them into his pocket. One of the secretaries of state, the muscular one, who had been given a medal of some sort, waved the headwaiter over and told him he should add it to the bill as official state expenses. Joe Lepsény, the war correspondent, seemed reluctant and refused, despite the others encouraging him to fill his pockets too.

"No thanks," he sniffed. "Tomorrow morning I'm due at the supreme council of the Ministry of Economics."

Full of respect, one secretary of state asked him whether there was an important decision about to be taken.

"No idea," the war correspondent replied disdainfully. "But they have American cigars."

They looked at him with envy because it was rumored that Joe had been nominated to the State Committee for the Administration of Forfeited Estates. It was one of the most prized positions in the People's Republic. The sax player said he started drooling every time he thought of what would happen if a Forfeited Estate and Joe Lepsény were left alone in a room together. You know, the estates . . . rare paintings, antique furniture, all the stuff the gentry left behind when they hit the westbound trail in fear of the Russkies arriving. The sax player was in seventh heaven thinking of this, his solos sounding more melancholy than ever. Everyone looked respectfully at Joe Lepsény, who remained a war correspondent even though there was no war anymore. He wore riding boots, a windbreaker, and a deer hunter's hat with a chamois tail stuck in the band, as well as a red-flag badge in his buttonhole. Later, after the revolution, he turned up in the West. He claimed to be an aristocrat from Budapest, but someone ruined the story by saying he was nothing of the sort but a laundry worker from one of the city slums. That wasn't generally known in the bar back then. In any case this was not time to start playing at comrades, because the place was really coming alive.

It was gone midnight and there were no tables left by the time the president of the Emergency Committee arrived with his *disooze* friend and a sidekick—everyone knew the sidekick was head screw at the town prison—so they had to produce an extra table from somewhere and make a place for it near the band. There was a great deal of running about, because it was a real honor for the bar to have such a famous man be a customer. I have to admit he was quite a guy. No one had heard of him a year ago; then he surfaced like that monster at Loch Ness in Scotland that's been in all the papers. The saxophonist blew a brief fanfare to celebrate the great man's arrival, his cheeks puffed out like apples, while I added a discreet and respectful drumroll.

Then they turned on the purple light because wherever the *disooze* went you had to have proper mood lighting. The proprietress, a famous lard-bucket of a woman, who carried on as before supplying nonprofessional women to her select clients, didn't know where to put herself in all the excitement. She personally filled the celebrity guest's glass with bourbon. Everyone watched, deeply impressed. The secretaries of state looked on in awe because the president of the supreme council outranked ministers. He was master of life and death, since politicals who'd been condemned to death turned to him with their last appeal for mercy. If he'd had a bad day he rejected the appeals and they were got ready for the drop. No one ever asked him what he did and why. The proprietress whispered in the pianist's ear that she had had her finger on the pulse of the market for thirty years, that she knew every unlisted telephone number in town, knew where exclusive goods might be offered to big spenders, but that she had never seen such glittering company in the bar all together at any one time.

Báróecsedi bowed from his seat to greet the president, who responded with an indulgent wave. The president was a big-time trophy Communist, a high-class medal shining in his buttonhole, but it was the baron and his bride, the waxed-mustached police sergeant, those all-but-extinct creatures, remnants of the old world, that he greeted most warmly—more warmly than he did the secretaries of state or Joe Lepsény, that upstanding, badge-wearing Party notable. I watched it all and remembered what I'd been taught in the morning: that real Commies, the true, dyed-in-the-wool, long-in-the-tooth sort, felt a deep-seated, jaw-clenching hatred for those who had only lately adopted republican colors. They loathed them more spectacularly than they did the old guard of *boujis* and barons. I watched everything like a hawk, since from that time on, every moment I spent there, I was, for all purposes, in my office. I was at work.

The president looked like something out of a fashion magazine, like an English lord dressed for the club, a lord, what's more, bought brand-new from the shop. Suit, shoes, everything—it was all made to measure. He smiled graciously at everyone, like a proper emperor who knows he has absolute power and can afford to be charming, generous, and condescending. The *disooze* he'd arrived with had been his night-and-day companion for a while—she was a fine, fat piece of trophy flesh herself, famed for attending every show trial at which the president showed some guy the way to the gallows, because such things amused her. She was a dyke. She sang in a hoarse whisper and specialized in torch songs. The boss turned the lights down low so it was purple everywhere, like patchouli. We waited awestruck to see what the celebrity guest would order.

The big-time guest must have had a hard day, because he closed his eyes as he drank and seemed to be lost in thought. Then he whispered something to the *disooze,* who obediently took her place at the mike, and in a cigarette-stained voice, straight from the heart, she crooned a heartbreaking ballad.

"*You're the one light in my darkness!*"

I only had to touch the drums very gently, tapping them with my fingertips. The saxophonist marked time, carefully watching the head screw as if he thought some plot was being hatched. The screw was constant companion to the president, just in case the great man had a brain wave that needed immediate acting on. Here in the bar he was the one who could give concrete form to the president's thoughts and carry ideas through. The tear-jerking ballad being over, the secretaries of state clapped their hands raw. Báróecsedi spread his arms to show how transported he was, that no dyke could sing more beautifully than this dyke had just done. He knew what he was talking about: he was in the business himself. The president stood up, kissed the artiste's hand, and led her back to the table. The head screw also leapt up and busily set to polishing the chair the lady was about to sit on with the sleeve of his jacket. The poet covered his eyes, as though such heavenly raptures were too much for him. He really got off on it.

I put the sticks down. The president ordered Champagne for the band. With all the low lighting everyone was in the mood. It was like an angel had flown through the place.

It's true, friend. As long as I live I'll be tasting the last glass of bubbly I drank that night in the bar. I was sitting close to the president and I saw the head screw looking at his watch. He stood up, leant over the table.

"With all due respect, comrade, I have to go. There's work to be done at dawn," he said quietly, and with one hand he demonstrated what kind of work that would be. The president looked serious. He nodded and said aloud, "I know."

"At six," the head screw whispered, "Double act."

"Then you must go, Ferenc," said the president. "After that, go home—and get a good snooze in."

The guy gave a broad smile.

"Yessir, comrade!" he said, and clicked his heels.

They shook hands. After the screw had marched out military fashion, a short silence settled on the bar. The *disooze* was crooning fine prose into the president's ear. Those sitting further off couldn't hear what the screw had said, but you could see from their expressions they got the general idea. The saxophonist folded his arms as though he were engaged in some spiritual exercise. The pianist leaned over the keys, wiping his glasses like there was nothing he could do about anything. The accordionist lit a butt to show that he was through with art for now, that he was on his break. We avoided each other's eyes, but we all knew what "six o'clock" and "double act" and "snooze" meant. It wasn't just those, like us, who had heard the words who understood. Others did too, all those who saw the way he said good-bye.

The president had had enough of smooching. He tapped the fleshy upper part of the *disooze* and gestured to Comrade Waiter that the serious partying was about to begin and the band should strike up. He winked at us too, in a lordly way, to get us playing again. That's the time the stink started.

At first I thought someone had left the john door open. Or one guest had been caught short, and whoops—too late! I looked around but didn't see anything suspicious. Discreetly, carefully, and because she was close to me, I tried to sniff the *disooze*. The patchouli was thick on her like gas on a marsh. But the stink rose above it. I was astonished that the others couldn't smell it as I did. It was as if they hadn't noticed anything.

The sax player took up the tune. We played our hearts out. We swung, but the stink was still there, in fact growing stronger. It was like there was a crack in some pipe in the sewers. It was everywhere, mixed in with cigarette smoke, the smell of fine food, and the high odor of expensive wine. It wasn't like lime or dishwater or fertilizer. And I couldn't tell where it was coming from: not from the corridors outside or from under the floor. I took a sly sniff of my own hand in case something had stuck to it. But there was nothing special there. All I knew was that never in my life had I smelled anything so foul.

I drummed away, dutifully. But then I started feeling sick. I looked around me. There, in the dim light, was high society chattering, sipping, and grinding away like nobody's business. They were our customers, our guests. They sat in their places quite happily without reacting to the smell. It was just like it used to be in the old days . . . they showed nothing—there was no panic, no twisting and turning—it was like they hadn't noticed they were up to their ears in hell. The stench hurt my nose. But I carried on, looking on in astonishment, everyone in the bar behaving like the gentry, people calmly carrying on while everything was seething around them, like everything was just as it should be. I remembered what Sweetheart told me, how middle classes never show what they're feeling, but continue polite, not moving a muscle, however much things stink and fester. It was just like that here. They could afford to be like that, because they were in charge now. You really would have taken them for gentry. It was just that there was this terrible smell everywhere. My stomach was heaving. In a break I stood up and quietly went to the john. No one paid any attention to me.

But the stench followed me. I stood in the john staring into the bowl. My head was a mess because all I understood was that something was over, done for, and that I couldn't go back in there and drum, not ever again. It wasn't my head talking—it was my stomach. I had a coat hanging in the cloakroom, one that used to belong to my dad, that I kept for cold mornings. I hung the tux up on the hook, pulled on the coat, slipped my black tie into the pocket, and whispered to the attendant that I had a bad stomach and needed some air. It was coming on for dawn. I went straight to the station and sat in the waiting room. I figured that since my AVO appointment was for noon they wouldn't start looking for me before then. There was an express bound for Győr. That's what I was waiting for.

I couldn't tell you, not if you twisted my arm, what I was thinking while waiting for the train. I could spin you some story about patriotic feeling or this or that other thing, but I wasn't feeling patriotic or nostalgic. Because the thing hit me like a blow to the gut in the middle of an AVO exchange of ideas. I thought of Papa and I thought of Mama, but they were like images on a screen at a movie, there one minute, gone the next. People I met here in America would later tell me how they were all broken up with regret when they set out. One guy said he folded a piece of Hungarian soil in his handkerchief. Another had stitched photographs into the lining of his coat. But I took nothing with me, just the black tie that I had to wear for work in the bar. I didn't brood over it. All I thought was I had to get out as fast as possible. Győr was the city I had to head for, because I'd heard it was nearest the border. The guy who told me gave me an address he'd got from someone who'd done the trip himself. I figured the tobacco I had with me was enough to last me the journey. I had a little pouch of it on my back. I had a thousand in cash, all in one-hundred bills, and a bit of change. I'd never used a bank in my life, thinking it was safer to keep my money under my shirt.

The stench seemed to be lifting now. I felt hungry. I grabbed some ham from the buffet and sank a glass of cheap wine. All I understood of everything that had happened to me was that nothing that had ever happened before mattered anymore. I had to go. But where? . . . Out into that dark bastard of a world where I couldn't understand what people were saying. I didn't speak too many languages then. All I knew was *davay* and *zhena*. I didn't think that would be enough out there. But then, as I was chewing my way through the ham sandwich, in the middle of eating, I started feeling really hungry . . . hungry to be away. A hunger for any place, however far. I didn't care if it poured, if I suffered sunstroke, the thing was to go.

We arrived in Győr at ten. I called in at a hardware store and bought a tin mug with a handle, the kind they store lard in when making salami. It used to be a regular joke that I was the kind of guy who goes to the village to buy lard. In Győr I picked up the contact I'd been given. There were two others waiting to cross, two Commies. At two in the morning we set off on a cart, then left it somewhere a few miles before the border, got off, and walked. Soon we were lying flat on the ground. There were observation towers, guards, and sweeping lights. There was an eclipse of the moon that night. The rain was dripping down, the dogs were barking. But our guide, an old Swabian, lay in the mud and was pretty relaxed about it, muttering how there was nothing to fear, the wind would blow our scent away. We were in some kind of meadow, muddy patches and sparse grass. We lay there for about an hour or so. We had to wait until they changed the guard. The Swabian said it was easier moving about then.

We didn't say much, and even then only in whispers. One of the Commies was cursing quietly, because he was an old-time socialist and now here he was having to leave his beautiful homeland, slithering along on his belly in the mud. It's true, we were crawling along on our bellies, flat out, the way corpses are carried downriver to Mohács.

It was then I bit the grass.

I remember it clear as day now. I'd never eaten grass before. There I was, flat on my belly in the mud of the motherland, when suddenly I found myself eating grass. I'd bitten into the mud. I could taste the clay. I don't know what was up with me, the devil alone knows . . . I'd no idea. All the same there I was, chewing the grass and the mud like an animal with rabies or like someone who'd drunk too much strong coffee so it drove him mad. I bit the grass, the way they say someone bites the dust in battle, like they've crossed over and joined the other heroes in heaven. What caused it? Being pushed around so long in the morning? Who knows. And now I'd taken a bite of home soil. That's when I realized what I was doing.

It didn't last long, and I soon came to my senses. But I was in shock. The grass and the earth together tasted more bitter than the Champagne the president had lavished on us in the bar.

Here was the border of my lovely little country, it was night, it was muddy, and the stars were out. I was an animal. But not only an animal. I was a man, and for the first time in my life I was conscious.

As you yourself know, then and before, there was a great deal said about our national soil. Others were chewing on that soil long before I was, and I don't mean literally. They were bringing up "our national soil" at the national assembly, scattering it round in parliament, and shoveling it in handfuls from soapboxes. There was a stream of comrades coming to the village to explain to the people that the land was ours now. Before, it was four acres for Papa, and four thousand acres for the count. And all the vast spread of land everywhere in the country, all that soil, was ours . . . I heard it when I was a kid in diapers and have carried on hearing it ever since. The moment I first drew my boots on, they told me, "That's national soil, comrade—the land is yours." But now I realized I'd never really understood when they said, "The land is yours." What was the soil? The land? The country? The nation? All I remember is that there were always shortages, always the sheer slog. When the count skipped it shortly after they carved up his estate, what was left to me of his land . . . when dad was spitting out his broken teeth in the village hall because they put his name on the kulak list and he didn't want to sign his acres away to join the collective . . . what did the land mean then? The soil? The country? My head was spinning. It was like waking from a mixed-up dream.

I lay there on my belly on the land, on my country's land, like a freshly washed corpse, the thoughts in my head whizzing round and round like a carousel. There was a song we used to sing when I was a kid at the village school. *"If Earth is our Lord's Easter bonnet / We're the sprig of flowers on it . . ."* The words came back to me. But however I tried I couldn't pick up the smell of flowers. Maybe because the meadow we were crawling across was partly marsh . . . The wet mud, the marshy feel of it, brought back a lot of memories. I was sorry to lose my drumsticks. I'd left them in the bar. They were good sticks, made of hazelwood. You couldn't get the like in Rome. I don't need them in New York, because they won't let me play. I can't practice my art. Lying there in the mud, I was wondering what else I'd left behind . . . What, after all, did it mean to have a country, a homeland? This country in particular?

Life is hard, friend. I remembered what I'd been there. First it was "Yes, Your Worship" and "Dirty prole." Then I discovered I was the nation, the people, and that everything was mine now. But the fact is nothing was ever mine. This hadn't occurred to me before. Not that I'd ever ranted on about my homeland this and my country that. I didn't think anyone owed me a living. But now, there on the border, it all came back, all mixed up. It seemed to me there were different notions of my country. They explained to me that it used to belong to the gentry. But now there was a different country that belonged to the people. But what did I have, me as myself? What was my country? And if I did have one, what had happened to it? Suddenly it had slipped from under me and, frankly, I didn't know whether it really existed anymore, and if it did exist, where it was. It must have existed somewhere, because I could smell it right here, in the mud where I lay. Much later Sweetheart told me—it was late at night—that when she was a girl she slept in a ditch, and dormice and squirrels used to scamper over her. The smell of that ditch must have been something like the smell of the marshy meadow I was lying in. It was the smell of mud she must have breathed in when she first found herself in the ditch, the ditch that was her home, her soil, her motherland. It was what I could smell as I was leaving it behind. But it was different from the smell that I wanted to escape in the bar. It wasn't a choking smell like that, but something more familiar, like our own smell. Because that's me, that's how I smell. It's an earth smell, and that earth smell had followed me all the way to the border. It was as if that was all that remained of home for me.

Now that everything was changing I knew just one thing, that once I was over the field there wouldn't be that foul smell in my nose, the stench I first noticed in the bar. The stench that remained in my nose and had soaked through my skin. It was like sleeping with a whore and still smelling of her in the morning so you have to scrub and scrub to smell clean again. All I knew is that I didn't feel like playing the drums for any of them. I wouldn't sing like a canary for them. I'd sooner be stretched out in the mud, on the border.

It was dawn when the searchlights went out. The Swabian, who'd started out digging wells, had become a gamekeeper, then, finally, a kind of one-man business smuggling undesirables, gold coins, in fact anything that could be moved, across the border, now gave the signal. We went on all fours, like dogs, scurrying like that out of the country. I left the country covered in mud—in every sense. The rest was routine. I'd coughed up five hundred as a deposit, and now that it was over I gave him another thousand as agreed. The Austrian cop who came across us was already bored, because, day and night, there were countless numbers of us crawling out of the woodwork, people screwed by the people's democracy. But in the end it was all quite simple. They put us in a camp first, but I didn't stay long. After eight weeks I got the visa from Rome. My brother sent it, the one who'd left me with the revolver. I got the work permit because dagos respect artists and there was a constant need for drummers there. By fall I was drumming in a bar.

Wait, a lady customer. Welcome, my fair lady. Just a martini dry, as usual? You are served, lady.

Take a good look at her without her noticing, because you rarely see anyone like her. They say five years ago she was well known on Broadway. She played in the theater next door, big place, where they don't sing, just talk. She was a hit like you wouldn't dream of. She'd run up and down the stage in a black wig because she was supposed to be bananas and raved in English at her husband that he should liquidate the houseguest who happened to be an English king. She rushed around here and there with a knife in her hand and she was supposed to be, it said on the program, Lady Makebed or some such thing. So then she got the call from Hollywood because they told her she'd make a stash there, she'd be Miss Frankenstein. But they had ideas . . . first they took out her teeth, then they started reshaping her private parts, and that was all okay, but then they wanted to monkey with her face, and the plastic surgeon was a fraction out in his measurements, so she got fixed with this permanent half-smile, there, as you can see . . . She can't do anything about it, it's like she was greeting you with a smile, her mouth half-open. There weren't going to be any parts for her with a mouth like that, but they got her a return ticket and sent her back to New York. Here they told her she couldn't speak the parts with a half-open mouth, she was all wrong for them. Ever since then she's been coming to this bar. She's sold the fur. After the third martini she gets sentimental and starts weeping. But her mouth is so fixed she still looks as though she's laughing. She parties and weeps like our happy forefathers, the Hungarians of old. Don't look at her or she'll be over immediately in case you don't mind paying. I've put a dozen martinis in the book for her, all on credit, but I'm not going to say anything. We artists got to stick together when we're broke. Another for you? What you looking at?

The photo? It was the one in the passport, I've just had it enlarged. Where could she go without a passport? To join the angels, friend. You don't need passports or photographs there. No jewelry, either. Take a good look at her. That's what she was like. But not just like that. By the time I met her she was like a flower at the end of the season.

I don't like talking about her. She's been gone ten years. Soon after that I too said "Ciao, Roma" and crossed the Big Pond. They say what's gone is gone, why fret about it? Yes, but heaven knows it's not always like that. Some things don't disappear quite so easy . . . because this picture isn't the only reminder I have of her. I remember more . . . her voice, for a start. And some of what she told me. She wasn't like the usual kind of woman I met. The rest have vanished without a trace. But I remember this one.

Because, as you probably know, with artists like me, chicks more or less just pass each other the house key. There were all kinds, I needn't list them all. There were cute little thin girls. There were big ones. There were showgirls with boobs out to here, but also women with class, women with a position in life . . . women with taste who sensed their time was almost over, who'd grown wild and started firing on all cylinders . . . but, let me be clear, all of them wanted just one thing, which was that I should love and adore them, and only them, forever.

This one was different. She wasn't a bag of nerves. She told me straight from the start, no beating about the bush, that the only thing she wanted of me was that I should let her adore me. She wasn't insisting on full-blown romance with hearts and flowers. Cigarettes were all she needed—that is, apart from adoring me and making a fuss of me.

At first I thought she had fallen for the artist in me. I'm not one to boast, I'm simply recognizing the fact that there's something irresistible about me . . . especially now that I've had the bottom set of my teeth fixed. What you laughing at? It's just as I said. They don't come to me because I look good. I'm not like those snotty kids with one-track minds who hang around in bars . . . It's the artist in me, that I still am, though they can't know my true quality . . . The Irish widow I'm currently fixed with will tell you the same. It's the artist that's the draw, that knocks them out.

It took me time to find out what her trouble really was. Because there'd been someone, someone who was and wasn't there . . . Her husband? No, he'd vanished from her life, she wasn't interested in him. It was someone else, another one who left the country. So then she followed him from Budapest. But she missed him—the guy had popped it before the kid arrived in Rome. The useless bastard had died on her, he wasn't going to wait for her. He's dust now in the Roman cemetery, like Sweetheart. At least they're together now. When she discovered her knight-at-arms hadn't waited for her, she got real depressed. She was so lonely in Rome, she was like a virgin widow mourning for a guy who'd died before they could get married.

We met in a café in Rome. A Hungarian paper was sticking out of my pocket. It caught her eyes. Because back then I'd buy a Hungarian newspaper or some such thing when I was feeling a bit nostalgic. Then we got together. I don't want to make it seem smoother than it was. She was a bit cool at first, but she soon came to. Neither of us were doing anything in the evening so I invited her to the bar. Next day I moved in with her at the hotel, and it became our love nest. Fall was real nice in Rome that year, nice weather. The good life didn't last that long, but long enough for me to discover the truth. One evening when we were down to our last penny she told me everything.

Was it the truth? Can't be sure of that—I mean, you never know with women. But I felt she was kind of emptying herself out, holding nothing back. She was no shy violet, not a giggly little girlie given to blushing. For once in her life she wanted to tell someone the truth, or whatever she thought was the truth. It might have been all fantasy, as it always is when a woman is really hard pressed. She started with her husband, who was still alive somewhere but was no longer her husband. And she finished with this bald guy, the one she followed to Rome . . .

she followed him like someone with a real itch. Because by that time she could no longer stick the people's democracy.

So I heard her through, right till dawn. It was kind of exciting, a bit criminal, talking through the night. She spilled the beans on what life with the gentry was like.

I was prepared to take it with a pinch of salt, if you know what I mean. But she convinced me, because, well, the kid was like me, she'd worked her way up into high society, starting lower than even I did, me, a boy from Zala! She came from the underclass. Literally. She pushed her way out of the mud the way a zombie does in a graveyard. She spent her childhood in a ditch in the wetlands along with the rest of her family. Her dad was an occasional farmhand, but then Sweetheart went to work as a maid for the gentry. For some time she was just a scullery maid, a nobody with bad shoes, someone to wash the toilet out after Their Lordships had used it. But eventually one of the crazy *boujis* started getting the hots for her, and it turned out to be the master's son. She made him wait for it until he married her. Pretty soon she became Her Ladyship.

Then, one night, she told me what it was like living in this oh-so-refined, well-mannered house once the world was stood on its head. The old order was going right down the drain. I liked hearing about that. I was sure she was telling the truth. But it was like a fairy tale too, like something from another world, a world I wouldn't have minded taking a peek in, what they call "the rich man's playground." But I only got to first base. The ladies I went with never invited me into their parlors or to their social affairs.

This particular story stuck in her mind. Because at that time, and even now, there's a lot said about the end of the class war because it's over now that we proles are winning. The upper classes are just ticking over, playing extra time before the game is up.

But when there's no one to talk to in the bar, I sit and think. Did I, a prole, really come out on the winning side? My boss there in the back room is a nicer guy than the bailiff was back in Zala. I've got a car, an Irish widow, a TV, an icebox—I've even got a credit card. In other worlds I'm a dude, a proper *dzhentleman*. And it's all on the plan. If I ever got curious about culture, I could afford to buy a book. But I hold back, because I had a hard time of it and I've learned to be modest. I don't need a book to tell me the class war is not being fought out in the streets now. But a prole remains a prole and the cream remains the cream, it's just that we avoid each other in different ways now. A long time ago, the devil knows how, it came about that the poor guy had to sweat to produce everything the rich guy needed. Today, though, the rich guy has to rack his brains to see how he can get me, the poor guy, to buy everything some middle guy produces. He wants to force-feed me, to cram me like a fattened goose. He needs to fatten me up, because the only way the middle guy can remain the middle guy and the rich guy the rich guy is if I buy whatever the middle guy tries to palm off on me. The middle guy's job is to hand me all kinds of crap on credit. It's a mad world, friend, and its rules are pretty hard to figure out. Take my car! It's parked there on the corner. It's brand-new. Whenever I get in it and turn the key, I remember what it was like when I was a kid—a car! my God!—I ran around barefoot and was dazzled any time a trap with a couple of horses trotted past me, a trap with the driver up front with shiny metal buttons on his vest, a ribbon hanging off his top hat, cracking his whip like a cop handing out a beating. Two horses! That was the dude back then. But now it's like my cart has a hundred and fifty horses pulling it along—that's horsepower for you! And sometimes when I draw up alongside a bus I think I'm the hundred-and-fifty-first, because I could get home easier by subway or the bus. Some Saturdays, the widow and I and a few pals get in the car and drive out to the sea, where we eat a burger, but we don't get out, because why should we? Then we go home. But I need the car, because it's status. Same with the tape recorder. I've recorded everything from singing "Yankee Doodle" through to reciting Our Father so the world can keep my voice for posterity . . . but now it just sits in a corner gathering dust and I can't think what else to do with it. I don't even have to multiply and divide, I let the gizmo do that for me. There's a computer guy who comes in here who sold me one those pocket calculators. You just press the buttons and up come the numbers. That makes me as smart as Edison, right? And there's that other machine where you don't have to write out everything, you just photocopy your Dear John letter and hand it to the mailman. And there's the shaver—I mean, it scrapes the monkey off you. And the toothbrush—electricity again—see the ones I've just had done, I could pass for a bishop. On credit. And . . . I lose track. I've got a newfangled camera where you just push a button and it spits out your picture, just like that. You can have endless fun with your girlfriend this way and be confident your fun won't pass through someone's developer, you can keep your screwing in the house the way my mother used to keep soup. And this is all mine, me, a prole! My mama, who all her life washed the underpants in a tub, wouldn't believe her eyes if she were here. I'd buy her one of those pants washers—and dryers too. Electric! Because all this is mine now, it belongs to the working-class boy! Not to mention the world—the whole wide world is mine, because . . . see here, the bellboy, a snotty-nosed kid, has just taken his bride on a flight to Africa, to Kenya, on credit, on installments . . . I could do it myself . . . And should I want to really indulge myself, I could pay for sex with as many people as I like. I could join a club. It's like the stud farm back in Zala, when they lead the bull in. I could join and become a member. Certainly opens your eyes! Quite a life, eh? But look around, use your own eyes. When I first arrived in this enormous gut of a country, I didn't have a nickel. And today? Take a good look at me, look me up and down—believe it or not, I swear to God I am in debt to the tune of eight thousand greenback dollars! Go out and do it yourself, sucker! And don't leave your mouth hanging open, I can see you don't believe me. Ask anyone in the neighborhood, they'll all tell you. Just hang round awhile and you too can have a lawn mower and an electric cooker with a red light to fry your burgers in a proper scientific manner. And everything is there on tap, because your middle-class middleman is waiting there, his tongue hanging out, just dying to make a lord out of your bottom-line prole. You too will get consumer fever, the way I did, the way a sheep gets fleas.

Okay, slide me that glass. There . . . you know, every so often, despite being a prole, I sometimes feel this big emptiness in me. It's like the way His Ex-Lordship suddenly feels homesick. The worst thing is the way they won't leave you in peace. There's advertisements everywhere—buy this, order that. I'll order up a one-way ticket to heaven next, just so I get some peace. When I was in Rome I heard how back in the old days, when the Caesars were around, the top Roman guys used to tickle their throats with a peacock feather so they could heave up in order to make room for the next delicious thing. That's what those advertisements are: peacock feathers. They get you all excited, and I don't mean just me, but the dog and the cat besides, since they can see what great things the dogs and cats on TV fill their bellies with. That's the class war today! We've won, buddy! It's just that I have to touch my head to check it's still there, and to see if I can stuff any more into it.

When Sweetheart was cleaning out the john back home, being rich meant something different. She spent a whole night telling me about it.

I can't remember everything she said. We talked like we were trying to spin out a never-ending good-bye. But some of those things come to mind now and then. It was like it wasn't her speaking at all those times, not Sweetheart at all, the girl who'd made her way up from the very bottom—I mean, she never went to school, not like Her Ladyship, the one she served. And Sweetheart could really talk, talk like a tape recorder, like recorded speech. Her mind was like a narrow strip of sound tape: it preserved every little thing, every bit of background noise. Every syllable stuck to it the way a fly does to flypaper. You say it: it stays there. Maybe all women have a spool of tape inside them like that. And maybe, once in their lives, they find just the right set of equipment, one that catches their voices just so, and then they say everything they've been saying to themselves, inside themselves, all those years . . . It's quite a fashion item now, the recorder, and women soon catch on to fashion. Sweetheart quickly extracted the important information from the stuff the gentry used to chat about in their own secret language, the kind of language only the invited and members of the family spoke. It's like the way only Gypsies understand Romany, the horse dealers and the guys in caravans. The gentry had their own self-made language too. It's like not saying what you really think but doing a kind of dance around it while smiling sweetly all the time. The times people like us curse, they keep quiet. And they eat different stuff. And they get rid of it differently too, not like us proles. But Sweetheart saw all this and was a quick learner. By the time she met me, she could have been a professor at some institution where they teach civilization to the spiritually deprived. From the moment she started scrubbing out the john she learned everything from the gentry, things she could never have dreamt of in the ditch. Believe it or not, it turned out that later she had not only jewels, not only furs, but her own nail-polish remover. What's up? You don't believe me? I tell it as it is. Mind you, she herself spoke about it in an embarrassed kind of way, as if the deal weren't quite straight.

She paid attention to everything; she was like a sparrow that pecks up grains in horseshit. That was till she met the bald guy, some kind of writer, who was highbrow, like the big shots here in the bar, but in a different way. He was the sort of writer who didn't want to write anymore. And some of the things he said got under Sweetheart's skin—they excited her. She told me in a shaky voice that she had never slept with him, that they only had soul-to-soul chats, that's all. It might have been so, I guess, otherwise she wouldn't have followed him to Rome. The clown must have given her some ideas that made her feel a little giddy. He rambled on about how there was something that couldn't simply be demanded at the barricades or extorted by threatening to bomb people. It was something really extra, like the shivers you get when you're at it in bed. And when it comes to things like that, a prole like me begins to suspect that it's pointless having every bargain going, that there's no real happiness to be got till he's wrestled some special magic from the old master's fist.

It was something like that, she was saying. Sweetheart couldn't really understand it herself, but I saw how it excited her. And now, much later, I myself am scratching my head trying to work out what it is that bugs us all. The stuff the bourgeois have that still remains to get. It's hard to get, of course, because the bastards have taken good care to hide it. My insides itch when I think of it. There was a time when only the upper classes allowed themselves to suffer from nerves. But nowadays I see how nervous a guy in jeans gets when someone different from him comes and sits next to him on the subway. Or at the movies. Anywhere. He gets nervous, makes sure he has no body contact, and gives his neighbor—so different from himself—sidelong glances. He suspects that he is not as important as that other guy, the one next to him, the one with the pressed clothes and spectacles. It's not the guy's manner that gets to him—I mean, I learned that a long time ago, and I'm as well-mannered and as correct in my behavior as the newly elected chairman of the local council. It's something else, the devil knows what, whoever invented it.

Sweetheart quickly learned everything you need for good manners. But the bald guy said something to her that wouldn't let her be. Right down to when it seemed it wasn't her speaking. It was someone else speaking through her, the way someone plays an instrument, a violin or a piano. The music is what comes out. When this idiot half-ass scribbler disappeared from her life, from our lovely Budapest, she couldn't just let him go, so she followed him . . . Eventually she confessed that he'd died there in Rome, among the statues, in the very hotel, in the very bed in the very room where we were sleeping, that's when we weren't making hay. That's women for you. Take it from me, buddy, listen to experience. They'll follow whoever they've really set their eyes on, providing they haven't already slept with them. They get all screwed up and twisted with frustration. They are set on the idea that the guy they want should become a part of them. They visit the cemetery and get upset when they see someone else's flowers on the grave of the poor faithless departed. All because a second-rate poet tells them there's something better in the world than grub and booze. What is it? They call it "culture." And the clown goes on to say this culture thing is all a kind of reflex.

Have you any idea what that is? Neither of us really got it: not her, not me. Afterwards I couldn't help looking it up in the dictionary . . . I actually took a walk down to the library and looked up "reflex." I thought about it, I turned it over and over in my mind till I was quite sick of it, but ended no wiser. It was compulsive, like when someone's constantly touching their nose to check it's still there . . . The dictionary said there was the learned kind and the inherited kind . . . you ever heard of such a thing?

But that's the shit with culture, you need it for status too now. I can't see why people sweat tears over it, because it's not like it's a secret anymore. It's all there in the big encyclopedias. You just take the book from the shelf and there you are, you got culture. So what is it? Oh yes, it's a reflex too. Look, I'm a simple guy, as you know. A modest man. So I'm telling you straight, I am genuinely cultured. Just look at me! I know I don't play the drums anymore, but I still got reflexes . . . Sometimes, when I'm at home with my Irish widow—she's religious—I take out the drums and I drum like I see on TV, like that black preacher when he's whipping up his flock. The widow grows dreamy then, leans her head on my shoulder, and her breath comes short until she too gets the reflex. Nobody could say of me I don't have a reflex . . . So am I still a prole? Is there something left for me to take from the gentry that I haven't yet taken? Something they don't want to give me? . . . You and I saw the Commies up close, didn't we? They can do their song and dance about what it will be like when everything belongs to the masses, the people. The union guys here have worked it out that they get a better deal here with Count Rockefeller and Prince Ford than they'd get from the fruits of their socialist labor. The pay's better. We know by now that it's all talk and big words. Is it possible, then, that the class war is still not over? Is there anything the bourgeois has tucked away from us? And should a prole lose his hair over that?

Wait a moment, I see the lady is crying. I can't bear to look at her when her eyes are full of tears but her mouth is grinning. I must look after the embalmer too . . . look how enviously he's looking at her, because she's got that holy smile without the use of paraffin.

Look, this is what she looked like the moment before she got on the plane without a return ticket. Go on, have a good look. I look at it sometimes myself.

One evening there was someone else who was looking at her. Year ago, about midnight, when the place was almost empty, these two customers came in. The play in the theater next door had just failed, because it was all talk, all philosophy. They arrived about midnight, they sat here where you're now sitting. They sat opposite the shelves where we keep the goods. And they looked at the photographs.

They were quiet drinkers. Refined types. You could see they were classy guys with proper reflexes. But you could also see they were drawing their pensions. It's the kind of thing you immediately notice. Three-eighty a month, plus sickness benefit. One had snow-white hair like Father Christmas. The other had sideburns, like he'd still fancy a good time, but could no longer afford it, all he could afford being a bit of extra hair on the side of his head. I wasn't really listening to them, but they were speaking a different version of English from the rest . . . they spoke like they hadn't grown up with English but learned it. But they'd learned it not here in the U.S.A. but in England. Both wore glasses and well-traveled suits. I noticed that Santa's sleeves were longer than they should be, because they weren't made to measure for him, he'd bought the jacket cheap, off the peg at a thrift store—I guessed he hadn't paid more than two Lincolns for them. All the same, they were nice guys, by which I mean they had no money.

But they went through their *bludimeris* like there was no tomorrow. They chatted away quietly. I half-heard them discussing the fact that in a country as wealthy as America very few people were happy. I pricked up my ears then, because I myself had formed that impression. That's hard to see when you're new here, and from over the water, but once you get used to it and become a regular Joe, like me, well, you get to thinking about it too, and soon there I am stroking my chin as if I'd forgotten to shave. Because, no good denying it, here where people have everything they need for the good life, it's as if happiness—I mean real, joyful, ear-to-ear-grinning happiness—simply escaped them. Over at Macy's nearby you can really buy anything you need in this world. You can even get a lighter that never needs new fuel. It comes in a case. But you can't buy happiness, not even in the drugs department.

That's what the two customers were saying. Actually it was the one with the sideburns doing all the talking, Santa just nodded. And as they grew ever more absorbed in their philosophizing it was suddenly like hearing Sweetheart's voice. That last night she was saying something about how culture and happiness were the same thing . . . or maybe that's what her scribbler hero said. I didn't understand it then, I don't really understand it even now, but when the two old guys started talking I remembered her words. I listened in discreetly.

They didn't spend a long time on the subject. The one with the sideburns happened to mention, sort of casually, that there was a lot of amusement in this great country, but pure joy, the joy that comes straight from the heart, was rare. When I think back to that now, it seems the joy is going out of Europe, but here, in New York, it's as if it hadn't caught on in the first place. The devil knows why! But he couldn't have understood it, either—the highbrow, I mean; he must have been an educated man—because he pulled a face and said the best thing would be if the government put up people's pensions, then they'd have something to be happy about. On that they agreed. Then he paid and left. Santa remained, ordered one more, and lit a butt. When I offered him a light, he pointed at the photograph with his thumb and asked me in Hungarian, but casually, as if getting in on a conversation that had been going some time, "Were you there when she died?"

I leaned on the counter with both hands. I thought I was going to collapse. I looked at him hard. I recognized him. It was her husband.

I tell you, I'm not ashamed of it . . . My heart beat in my chest like someone was drumming in there. But then I took a deep breath and simply told him I wasn't there. At dawn, when I returned from the bar, her face was still warm, but she didn't say anything.

He nodded graciously, as if it was what he expected. He asked me questions in a low voice and smiled now and then. He asked if money was short and whether the jewels saw her through to the end. I assured him she hadn't a care in the world, because I was there looking after her. He noted this, and nodded like a priest at confessional who listens through to everything, then offers you three Our Fathers. He would like to know, he said, but always polite and friendly-like, if she had a decent funeral, with everything necessary. I answered him obediently, but all the time I was clenching my fist. But he carried on in exactly the same voice.

I never discovered, not then, not later, how he found me, how he knew I was working there. How did he come by the details, the hotel, the jewels? . . . I'd never seen him in the bar before. Later I went to the Hungarian quarter on the right bank and asked people, but no one had heard of him. But he knew all there was to know about me, even the fact that my performing name was Ede. I knew that because he asked, again perfectly friendly, "And are you happy, Ede?"

Like an old acquaintance. No, not like that . . . Like a boss meeting an employee, as if he were still in the chair and me under it. I answered politely. But as I told you, I was clenching my fists all the time. Because it was dawning on me that someone had grassed me up. You know, the way he spoke so quietly. He was so polite, so natural. As if I weren't even worth screaming at. He could have called me names, what would I have cared? He spoke to me like we weren't on opposite sides. That's why I felt so angry, that's why my fists were clenched. Because if he screamed at me, shouting "I know everything, now talk!"—well, we would have been equals. If he said, "Look here, Ede, I'm long retired, but I'm still the doctor and you the patient," well, I'd have answered him as best I could. If he had said, "I played the fool with that woman, but that was a long time ago and it doesn't matter anymore—tell me how she died," I'd have muttered something like "Sorry, nothing I could do, that's how it was." If he hits me, fine, I hit him back. We may roll around on the deck a little while the boss rings the cops and they take both of us away; that would have been fine too, it would have been gentlemanly. But this quiet chat in the crazy enormous world, here in the bar . . . it made the blood rush to my head. Because such quiet words counted as offense in our situation. I felt my fingers itching and my gorge rising.

He took a Lincoln from his pocket. I could see his hand was trembling. I started closing up the till. He didn't say anything; he didn't hurry me. He leaned on the counter and winked, as if he had had one more than was befitting a gentlemen of his standing. And he started smiling, a saintly kind of smile.

I looked him over carefully out of the side of my eye. You could see he was at the end of the road. Old clothes, a shirt he'd clearly been wearing for days, and those glassy eyes behind the glasses. It didn't need careful examination to see that this man, who had to be addressed as "Doctor"—that's what I remember—who after the siege on the Danube embankment had left her standing there, as if she weren't the woman he'd gone crazy over, but someone who once worked for him that he had no more use for—this man was now strictly lower-class. And he still thinks he's superior? I could feel the gorge rising in my throat and had to keep swallowing. I was all worked up inside like I'd never been. If this big shot left the bar now without confessing that the game was up and that it was me who had come out on top . . . You understand? I was afraid there'd be trouble. He gave me the Lincoln.

"It's for three," he said. He took his glasses off and polished them. He stared straight ahead in that shortsighted way. The bill said three-sixty. I handed back one-forty. He waved me away.

"Keep it, Ede. It's yours."

This was it. The flashpoint! But he wasn't looking at me, he was trying to stand up. That wasn't too easy for him, and he had to clutch at the counter. I looked at the one-forty in my palm and wondered whether to throw it in his face. But I couldn't speak. Eventually, after a good deal of trouble, he managed to straighten up.

"You parked far away, Doctor?" I asked.

He shook his head and gave a smoker's cough.

"I don't have a car. I'll use the subway."

I answered him as firmly as I could.

"Mine's parked nearby. It's new. I'll drive you home."

"No," he hiccupped. "The subway is fine. Takes me right home."

"Now you listen to me, buddy!" I bellowed at him. "I'll drive you home in my new car! Me, the stinking prole."

I came out from behind the counter and took a step toward him. If he refuses, I thought, I'll knock his teeth out. Because, in the end, you just have to.

It was like the cat got his tongue. He squinted up at me.

"Okay," he said, and nodded. "Take me home, you stinking prole."

I put my arms around him and helped him through the door, the comradely way only men know, the kind of men who've slept with the same woman. Now that's real democracy for you.

He got out at One Hundredth, just before the Arab quarter. He disappeared, like concrete in the river. I never saw him again.

Here come the writers. You'd best clear off—quick, that way, to the left. There might be a labor-camp vet from the old country among them . . . No harm in being careful. Call in again at the end of the week. And mind to steer well clear of the cement trade.

Welcome, gentlemen. You are served, sir!

A NOTE ABOUT THE AUTHOR

Sándor Márai was born in Kassa, in the Austro-Hungarian Empire, in 1900, and died in San Diego, California, in 1989. He rose to fame as one of the leading literary novelists in Hungary in the 1930s. Profoundly antifascist, he survived the war, but persecution by the Communists drove him from the country in 1948, first to Italy, then to the United States. His novel *Embers* was published for the first time in English in 2001.

A NOTE ABOUT THE TRANSLATOR

George Szirtes is the prize-winning author of thirteen books of poetry and several translations from Hungarian, including Sándor Márai's *Casanova in Bolzano* and *The Rebels*. He lives in the United Kingdom.

A NOTE ON THE TYPE

The text of this book was set in Bembo, a facsimile of a typeface cut by Francesco Griffo for Aldus Manutius, the celebrated Venetian printer, in 1495. The face was named for Pietro Cardinal Bembo, the author of the small treatise entitled *De Aetna* in which it first appeared. Through the research of Stanley Morison, it is now generally acknowledged that all oldstyle type designs up to the time of William Caslon can be traced to the Bembo cut.

The present-day version of Bembo was introduced by the Monotype Corporation of London in 1929. Sturdy, well balanced, and finely proportioned, Bembo is a face of rare beauty and great legibility in all of its sizes.

Composed by Creative Graphics,
Allentown, Pennsylvania
Printed and bound by Berryville Graphics,
Berryville, Virginia
Designed by Virginia Tan